LAMENT FOR THE FALLEN

www.transworldbooks.co.uk

For more information on Gavin Chait and his books,
see his website at https://lamentforthefallen.com/

LAMENT FOR THE FALLEN

GAVIN CHAIT

Doubleday

LONDON · TORONTO · SYDNEY · AUCKLAND · JOHANNESBURG

TRANSWORLD PUBLISHERS
61–63 Uxbridge Road, London W5 5SA
www.penguin.co.uk

Transworld is part of the Penguin Random House group of companies
whose addresses can be found at global.penguinrandomhouse.com

Penguin
Random House
UK

First published in Great Britain in 2016 by Doubleday
an imprint of Transworld Publishers

A CIP catalogue record for this book
is available from the British Library.

ISBNs 9780857523693 (cased)
9780857523761 (tpb)

Typeset in 12/16pt Adobe Caslon by Falcon Oast Graphic Art Ltd.
Printed and bound by Clays Ltd, Bungay, Suffolk.

Penguin Random House is committed to a sustainable
future for our business, our readers and our planet. This book
is made from Forest Stewardship Council® certified paper.

MIX
Paper from
responsible sources
FSC® C018179

1 3 5 7 9 10 8 6 4 2

For those who leave.
For those who remain.
For the wings and tail.
But most, for her.

I

A LAMENT FOR THE FALLEN

Even as some would explore the stars, remember that many who remain behind scratch out an existence of near starvation in the dust so easily shed.

Dr Xian Yesui, UN Secretary General, 2053, opening address for discussion of Security Council Resolution 2731 – Tribunal for Colonial Governance of Territories in Earth Orbit

Our technologies and economies have diverged. To what end should we continue to pay allegiance to colonial masters who provide us with little by way of material benefit, with whom we have few social ties, and who no longer have the ability to enforce their power over us? It is time for us to make explicit that which we already know implicitly: our independence.

Ernest Balliol, governor of Equatorial 1, 2094, launching his first, unsuccessful, referendum for colonial independence from the United States

We have been staring into the heavens for thousands of years. Our community of scholars have been functionally independent of the bounds that tie us to our planet for almost a century, staring into that vastness. How could we not wonder? How could we not go?

Professor Ullianne Vijayarao, lead scientist on Allegro quantum navigation team, 2115, last interview prior to the space territory severing its umbilical and exiting earth orbit

1

'Father, please tell me a story.'

Joshua smiles. 'And what story would you like to hear, my son?' His voice is warm, redolent of nutmeg and coffee.

Isaiah is balancing on the thick white water pipe running along the village end of the maize field. He clenches his arms awkwardly at his sides, fighting his urge to stretch them out. The pipe is knee-high from the ground, suspended on a cradle spiking it to the neatly turned red earth. Every few metres, thinner pipes, like ribs on a snake, protrude out of control boxes and connect to the capillary mesh irrigating the field.

'Show me your hands, please,' he says, leaning forward slightly. Even raised, he is still only shoulder height to his father.

Joshua laughs and holds them out for inspection. The boy, his face intense with the concentration children bring to bear on such matters, takes first the left.

Joshua's hands are his journal. Scars trace patterns across an ebony-brown surface thick with veins and bunched muscles. Each subtle script recording a memory.

This notch, in the web of his thumb, marks where he was burned grasping at flaming brushwood as a child. Isaiah has no wish for a lesson on the hazards of not listening to parental authority.

He shakes his head, sucking on his bottom lip, and takes his father's right.

A short, jagged line on its outer edge recalls Joshua's frantic struggle to rescue his sister, Abishai, from floods that swept past the village twenty years ago.

In the distance, over the ridge leading down to the river, Isaiah can hear the muted sounds of children laughing and splashing in the water. After lessons and chores, many of the village children regularly gather there to play. In his father's childhood as well.

He trembles slightly, squeezing the held hand.

'The flood, Father. Tell me the story of the flood,' Isaiah bouncing on his toes, his eyes wide, and almost losing his balance on the pipe in his excitement.

'But you have heard that one so many times,' says Joshua with feigned despair.

'Please, Father, please? My favourite part is where the tree falls on you and you have to sink to the bottom before you can push it away.'

Joshua sighs as if he is taking on a heavy burden. 'Very well, my son,' grinning as he begins the tale.

Isaiah's eyes widen with fear as the danger mounts. The children jumping off the jetty much as children do now. The wall of water unexpectedly coming down the Akwayafe, flinging trees before it, crashing through the turbine and tearing the village fish farms apart. Children running in panic up the banks as Joshua races down. Abishai, a young girl, slipping and tumbling. Joshua leaping in and grabbing frantically, flinging her backwards even as he stumbles and is seized by the maelstrom. And then, the tree trunk, both his peril and saviour, holding him to the bottom as the worst of the flood wall passes.

Joshua is no longer sure as to how much has been embroidered. His people love stories, and it is a brave narrator who fails to embellish any simple event into a moral saga of redemption and triumph.

Cicadas shriek in undulating waves of sound washing against the afternoon humidity. The air is still. Red-orange light from the lowering sun pours across the maize field. Dark-green fronds falling away down the slope and rising again to the jungle. Monkeys foraging and whooping through the branches, their crashes and calls filtering through the trees.

Closer to the north gate, along Ikot Road, traders and travellers move about their business. Some stop, holding hands as they smile and greet each other, forming small communions.

Joshua sits down on the pipe alongside his son, the boy leaning on him, his dark eyes bright with pride and affection. He rests his arm over Isaiah's shoulders, holding him close. The story ends, as it should, with victory over terrible odds.

'Isaiah,' he says, gripping softly and smiling down at him.

'Father,' and Isaiah grins, curling back into his shoulder. 'Thank you.'

The day's heat and humidity are easing. Soon it will be time to return home for the evening meal. For now they sit on the pipe beneath the deepening shade of a young obeche tree.

This side of Ewuru faces towards distant cliffs rising from the jungle and the cities to the centre of Nigeria. Joshua walks here every afternoon, sometimes around the periphery of the village walls, and sometimes along the path of the white dome-topped sentinel posts forming a cordon of sensors along the jungle border.

In the last year, as he has grown, Isaiah likes to join him.

Joshua notices Abishai and Daniel hurrying from the village gate.

A small group emerges from the trees, dragging themselves from the grip of their journey. Their clothes are torn and filthy. They are hauling a cart upon which are piled bags and what looks to be an elderly man. Children and adults lean on the cart as they walk. A young woman carries a baby. It does not move as she sags against the cart wheel. All look haunted and starved. Refugees from the water wars in the north.

Abishai is already greeting them, welcoming them and offering them the shelter of Ewuru. They will probably not stay. The quiet pace of the village is not for everyone, and most choose to move on towards Calabar.

Joshua stares at them, studying the distance and hardship of their journey told in the mud and pain stretched across their skin.

Isaiah, though, is distracted.

'Father, what is that?' pointing up into the sky where a white trail arcs down towards a black shape. Joshua looks up and shakes his head, shielding his eyes as he strains to make it out.

The shape is falling gently. They watch, transfixed by its peculiar slow-motion curve towards them.

Closer now and Joshua can see that its outer part is a blur around a small core. It looks like one of those winged seeds he remembers playing with as a child: flinging them up, watching them propeller down.

It is generating a wide funnel-shaped trail of condensation pointing directly along its path and visible for hundreds of kilometres.

They can hear it faintly: a range of notes from a roar to a whine, like a turbine.

The small black ball in the centre, which Joshua cannot help thinking of as a seed, appears stationary as the wing spins around it. It no longer looks black. The leading edge of the wing is grey-white and the ball, where it points at the ground, is similarly coloured. He sees occasional blue jets of flame from the pod, as it adjusts its position in the sky.

Others within the village and near the fields are looking up and shouting. A white arc, like a spear, aimed almost exactly at Ewuru.

Joshua lifts Isaiah on to his shoulders and runs down the path. 'Abishai, Daniel,' he shouts. From across the maize field, on Ikot Road, he hears answering calls. As he runs, he can see that the falling seed will pass over the village, but it will not land far away.

As he nears the north gate, a woman runs out to meet him. 'Esther, take him. Prepare beaters, there might be fires.' Isaiah drops to the ground and clings to his mother's arm. She nods, leading him, running back, calling out.

The brief pause has been sufficient time for two people to catch up.

'It is going to be seen,' says Abishai, younger but almost identical to her brother.

Joshua nods. 'We track it, then see how we can disguise whatever it is.'

Daniel is heavier, shorter, than the siblings. 'It depends where it lands. What do you think it is? Debris?'

Joshua shrugs, his face worried. It does not look like debris. He glances up, estimates the path of the seed and starts running. The others follow. In the village, Esther is organizing volunteers. Fire cannot be allowed unchecked anywhere near the fields.

They follow the path as far as they can then turn directly into the jungle. The arc is easy to follow through gaps in the tree canopy.

A change of pitch and a sound of splintering wood tearing a way open through the jungle indicate that the seed has, at least, stopped getting further away. They quicken their pace.

Almost an hour later they reach the crash site.

Their first impression is of the unexpected light coming through the leaf canopy ahead of them. Clouds of insects have rushed into the empty space, agitated and hungry.

Joshua and the others can hear falling branches and smell fresh sap, but it is all much more contained than they expected. They slow.

'That did not fall like debris,' says Daniel.

'No,' says Joshua. 'It almost looked as if it was being steered.'

They move carefully towards the edge of the clearing. There they stare, mystified.

An irregular circle has been punched into the canopy. The trunks of the trees are shattered and splintered, their upper branches wrenched off with great savagery. The space itself indicates that, for all the violence of its arrival, the seed has touched the ground with scarcely a bump. The black and grey pod lies in the centre of the clearing, silent and perfectly spherical.

From the pod a wing curves out about six metres, its outer edge cambered to the ground. Branches have fallen on to the seed, but there are no flames. There does not seem to be much heat at all. Behind them, in the forest, they can hear calls from villagers arriving.

Joshua shakes his head, balling his hands into fists as he tries to make sense of what he is seeing. 'Abishai, keep the children away. You can send the beaters back, but keep a few spades and people to help. Daniel, shall we have a look?'

Abishai turns and runs into the trees. They can hear her shouting out the names of children as she sends them home. 'Later, later. It is dangerous now.'

'At least it is small. We should be able to hide this,' says Daniel.

Joshua shakes his head. 'It left too much of a trail. We will have to find something else as a distraction.'

He eases his way towards the outer edge of the wing. It is a smooth and shaped single piece of metal, like an aircraft wing. The leading edges are coated in hard translucent tiles. The entirety, for all its strangeness, appears to have been machined. He can see this being made in a workshop. Some military craft that wandered off course?

'Careful' – from Daniel, as Joshua crouches and hesitantly stretches out his arm towards the edge of the wing. He can see people appearing through the trees, also staring much as he must have done a few moments earlier.

He can feel only very slight warmth from the tiles. He touches one and, delicately, rests his hand on its surface.

'It is not hot,' he says loudly enough for the men all around the clearing to hear. 'It is slippery. Like soap.'

The tiles look like blocks of smoke, indistinct where they end and fade into the air. Only where he touches them can he see the line along the wing. The tile has an unpleasant feeling, as if all the water is being drained out of his skin, and he quickly removes his hand.

Daniel edges into the clearing, keeping watch. Joshua walks cautiously towards the seed pod, along the curve of the wing and keeping a wary distance. This close it is slightly taller than the height of a man. On the top and bottom of the wing are a series of narrow cylindrical holes, each about the width of a fist, pointing in opposite directions. The metal around the edges is scorched blue.

Joshua clenches his jaw and places his hand firmly on the wall of the pod.

Everyone is silent.

Joshua smiles and half-turns towards Daniel. He shrugs and shakes his head. Nothing.

And then, just on the edge of the wing, on top of the sphere, a hatchway pops open. A man shouts, and everyone jumps.

A coppery smell like blood, or wet metal, floods out of the hatch. It is fresh and oddly clean against the vegetative miasma of the jungle.

'Help him.'

The voice comes from inside the pod, metallic in the silence.

Daniel reacts faster than Joshua. The wing is easier to reach from where he stands, and he flings himself up, running to the opening. Joshua joins him and motions to Abishai, who he can see returning through the trees, to stay back.

The last light from the setting sun shafts into the cabin. Inside, caged between a series of metal rings, his limbs contorted and broken into a tangle that makes Daniel and Joshua instantly nauseous, is a man.

'Help him.'

2

'No, Griot, not again!' Samuel laughs, his fleshy hands resting on his great thighs, his body shaking. 'That is not a story. Every year you do this to me.'

He wipes tears from his eyes, soft folds crinkling his face, and squeezes the salt water from between his fingers.

There are groans and laughter from the others gathered to listen at the overnight camp two days upriver from Calabar: a ripple of explosive babble punctuated by flickering shadows cast by the rebuilt cooking fire. A few stand, stretch and head for the privacy of the trees. One man leans over the fire, grabbing the massive boiling kettle from amidst the coals with hard hands, and pours tea into proffered mugs.

'Samuel, I know many stories,' says the man in the ochre-brown boubou and matching kufi skullcap sitting with them on the ground, at the far end of the gathering. 'What sort of tale would you wish for?' His voice is lyrical.

'Oh, but, Father, I love it,' says a young man sitting alongside Samuel.

'Of course you do, Peter,' says the elder. 'I would have too when I was your age, but they are not proper stories. Griot, you know the stories I mean.'

The man here called Griot – in other places known as Marabout, or Balladeer, or the many other names given to him on his journeys – chuckles, the sound the delight of small pebbles being tumbled in a fast-flowing stream. 'These are my stories, Samuel, and I have no wish to tell you ones you already know. They are my gift, and I never give the same gift to the same person twice.'

There are many men gathered around the fire. They sit on the packed earth in a semicircle upwind of the flames, focused half between it and the Griot. The breeze is consistent from the south-west, and they have left a small space for the smoke to drift out and into the bracket of palm oil trees surrounding them.

Peter holds out his mug to the man carrying the kettle. He fills it with steaming tea so overly extracted that the tannins have become astringent. Tea which strips the outer layer of a teaspoon even as it recoats it with a dark-bronze patina.

Peter offers the mug to the Griot, who accepts with a grin.

Every year, after harvest, the remaining villages of the southern delta gather their surplus grain, and traders paddle along the net-work of rivers towards Calabar. There they trade for the printed goods they cannot produce at home. Samuel's people have always planted and harvested early to beat the other villages to the city and so take advantage of higher prices. They are not a wealthy people, being too small and distant, but they prefer the safety of their isolation to the dangers of the more populated parts of the region.

Their boats are drawn up on the banks just outside the reach of the firelight. The barges, burdened with maize, soya and sorghum, are anchored midstream. It is slow work dragging them to the city.

Insect traps glow on tree trunks, reducing the irritation of mosquitoes. Cooking pots hang, cleaned, over the informal kitchen. Hunger is at bay till morning, and the men pass the evening around the fire as travellers have done for thousands of years.

Unusually, no men guard the riverbanks or the barges from animals or looters. The Griot is here.

This is Peter's first trip with the men to trade, and he is excited at the newness of the experience, soaking up the laughter and fellowship. He looks up at his father as the man clamps his hand over the youth's shoulder.

'I am pleased you are here, Griot.' He smiles, nostalgia in his voice. 'I remember when I was this boy's age. My father taking me on my first journey to Calabar, and you, telling me stories. I cannot say I always understand you, but I always enjoy the way you make me feel.'

He is momentarily silent, feeling the ache in his joints, the stiffness of his fingers. 'This will be my last journey to the city, and my sons will continue after me.'

'You are not so old, Samuel.'

'It has been fifty years, Griot. Fifty years. You may not age, but, for myself, that is my lifetime. Imagine. I have five sons and three daughters. They have granted me eight grandsons and eleven granddaughters. Each year we follow the harvest, you meet us along the way, we reach the city, we trade, we return. Each year continues as before. And now I hand over this cycle to my sons.' He nods. 'But you, Griot, you still tell stories of change and there is still nothing new in the world,' laughing.

Peter remains silent, a clutch of anxiety. Those setting out in the world for the first time have no wish to learn that there is nothing left to be discovered. It is given to youth to wonder at what can be different and age to marvel at how much remains the same.

The Griot, his teeth a white disembodied smile in the darkness, considers carefully.

'I journey far, Samuel. Would you wish to hear stories of the north, of the struggle there and of the devastation left behind?'

Samuel grimaces.

'No, and I would not tell you. My ways are not to carry burdens from one place only to deposit them in another. There is much suffering, but there is hope also.

'It was not always that you feared the unknown. There was a time you used to travel with your sisters to Calabar,' says the Griot. 'None of your daughters have ever visited the city.'

'And they never will. The only changes I have seen have not been good ones,' says Samuel.

The Griot smiles gently. 'I do not mean you discomfort. You understand, though, my experience is different? The water carving through rock has little to show even for half a century, yet few would say that rivers remain forever unchanged.'

Samuel shivers, wondering again at the nature of the Griot.

A man adds wood to the fire, poking at logs to hone the flames. A stump cracks, splattering a cascade of sparks into the air.

The evening of songs and tales is ending. Tomorrow will be another long day of rowing, and many of the men are preparing to sleep. Others have broken into twos and threes and are continuing to talk.

'A group of refugees I met two days ago told me of a strange object falling from the sky?'

One of the men towards the back of the gathering grunts, 'I saw that too.'

Samuel sighs. 'A few days ago. Space debris falling towards those unfortunates living along the Akwayafe.'

'Hah, the free villages are wealthy. They can defend themselves,' says another.

Samuel shakes his head, smiling at his son. 'I would never wish the attention of the militia on anyone. But, yes, we saw it. What is your interest? You have decided to become a scrap-metal dealer?' he teases.

'It is something different, Samuel. Perhaps it will yield a new story?'

Samuel shakes his head, 'If the space debris is valuable enough, the militia will fight over it, and many of the people of the Akwayafe will be killed. There are more than enough of those stories without you seeking new ones. And, if it is not valuable, there will be no story.'

The Griot smiles again, setting his emptying mug on the ground, and stabs a finger carefully into the soil at his feet. He blows and a cone of soil empties. He reaches to the bottom, finding there a small brown grain. He holds it to the light, resting it on his cupped palm.

'What do I have in my hand, my son?' asks the Griot, speaking to Peter.

'It is a seed, my father,' he says.

'Yes, it is. And what sort of seed is it?'

'I do not know, my father. We would have to wait for it to grow.'

'Even when it begins to grow, we could not know how strong, how high or how much of its own seed it would produce. We cannot know who will benefit from its shade or its fruit. We could not know if it will be trampled even before it survives its first season. We would have to wait and watch. Every seed gives us something new,' the Griot's eyes shining in the firelight.

'Even though every seed looks just like any other? Like a story, my father,' and the boy feels the excitement of his discovery.

The Griot smiles and presses the seed into the boy's hands. He cradles it, stares at it, wraps it carefully and stores it in the pouch at his waist.

The Griot sits back, his strange yellow eyes glowing in the darkness. He reaches behind himself and, pulling his kora towards him, begins to pluck at the strings.

His music rises up into the clarity of the night sky, lifting with the smoke, sprays of sparks and tears of flame.

3

Men with guns turn up in the village two weeks later. Tardy, thinks Joshua, as he walks out from the west gate to meet them.

He makes a show of handing his hunting rifle to Daniel, who waits at the village entrance. Joshua is a big man, tall, straight back, imposing. He is dressed formally in a white shirt and an ukara, a light tie-dyed sheet featuring interlocking blue and white triangles and nsibidi symbols coloured in black, knotted around his waist.

The outfit is old-fashioned and impractical, but nsibidi still carries connotations of superstition and fear. Something else to keep the militia from staying too long.

He plants his feet firmly in the path.

There are fifteen men in the squad, each dressed in loose-fitting, dirty, green-camouflage overalls. Five of them are no more than boys and look clumsy and awkward in the heavy fabric. They each carry cellulosic AK-47 hybrids, the grips split and broken almost to nothing from the low-quality printing. Only one has shoes: ill-fitting and cracked boots that must be unpleasant to walk in. Only he carries his rifle in his hands. The rest wear them slung over their backs, across the small satchels that must carry their provisions, tied with rope and old straps.

The radio operator's rucksack, with its aerial sticking up at a jaunty angle, looks like it might once have been military issue; the other bags appear to be from local markets.

Village scouts have been tracking these men for most of the day from when they first entered the southern hunting range claimed by Ewuru. They are lightly armed and the battery in the radio is dead, so the soldiers are out of contact this far from Calabar.

A patrol who do not expect to be resisted.

'Welcome to Ewuru, my brothers,' Joshua says when he judges them sufficiently close. Behind him he can sense scouts closing across the entrance to the village. There is an artillery emplacement set back from the wall, protected by rock and trees, covering the path. Others will be observing from the jungle further back and behind the soldiers.

'I'm Rinier Pazzo, captain of these men,' says the man in boots. He is short, wiry, and his eyes around black irises are yellow and bloodshot. If he notices the hostility of the villagers he regards it as ordinary.

Soldiers do not visit to protect. If one is lucky, they will only be passing through.

'Captain Pazzo, is there something we may assist you with?'

Pazzo appears to see the village for the first time. He motions to his radio operator. The others take this as a signal to break rank, and they straggle over to the canal above the cassava field, just off the path. They scoop water on to their faces and drink.

Joshua is grateful that the water the soldiers have chosen to potentially infect with typhoid is not part of the village drinking supply.

The radio operator pulls out a map, faded, muddy, torn at the folds, and opens it out. Remarkably, the organic ink still works. Pazzo points at a line marked in red going up the Akwayafe River and drags the view until Ewuru is in the centre. 'We've been following this trail for the last few days. We're looking for something which fell out of the sky near here, perhaps two weeks ago.'

'Yes, we saw it. We thought it might be debris falling from orbit. It took us a few days to find.' Joshua pauses and shrugs his shoulders. 'We are not sure if what we found is it, but beyond that point is further than we are comfortable travelling.'

Pazzo smirks. 'You villagers are too nervous. Too scared.' He laughs, revealing the remnants of a few surviving blackened and yellow teeth. The boys by the water canal immediately laugh too, the sound jarring and forced like the hacking of feral dogs. Joshua simply bows his head.

'You're right. It may not be it, but show it to us anyway,' says Pazzo. 'Now.'

'Certainly.' Joshua turns away from the soldiers for the first time. His eyes find Esther, Isaiah holding her hand. He smiles at them, loving them. 'Daniel,' he calls, 'bring me my rifle and a few men to help us clear a path.'

Pazzo nods at the others, who hastily assemble. 'How long will it take us to get there?'

'Perhaps two and a half hours. It is in a gully at the edge of our normal hunting range.'

Daniel approaches slowly, keeping the rifle clearly visible and in front of him. No need to antagonize the soldiers.

'We will stay the night in your village. Have food ready for us when we return,' says Pazzo. There is a hint of menace in the statement.

Joshua could refuse, but this demand has been expected and prepared for. Out of contact and heavily outnumbered, the squad is no threat to the village. If they were to go missing, especially after following a clear path up the river, a more heavily armed band could be sent to find them, and they would not be as easy to distract. Best to show them something interesting, but not too interesting, feed them and see them on their way.

'Of course,' says Joshua. 'Shall we go?'

Pazzo glares at him and then at the men blocking the entrance to Ewuru. He snorts, blowing a jet of mucus on to the path, conveying how much he despises these villages, these people. In any other place, soldiers would take what they wish, but the free villages' capacity for self-defence makes such behaviour unwise.

He gestures for Joshua to take the lead. Five men accompany the soldiers: sufficient to be difficult, not so many as to make the men with guns feel threatened. Daniel brings up the rear as they walk around the outer village wall, past the maize field and into the jungle.

This is all show. Scouts are concealed in the trees along the route. The soldiers will not be permitted to cause any opportunistic trouble.

The soldiers are not that fit, and the men of Ewuru deliberately slow, pretending to struggle to keep pace. Joshua leads them by a longer, slightly circuitous route, adding to any difficulty Pazzo may have in finding the exact place again. He notes that they have no automated navigation and only rudimentary map-reading skills. He shakes his head. Their ruse is almost wasted on these men.

'What is it?' asks Pazzo.

'I am sorry we are not as strong as you,' says Joshua carefully.

Pazzo smirks.

'We are getting close now,' says Daniel, hacking at a thin branch that has fallen across the route they have selected. Pazzo motions at his radio operator, who is holding their map. They look up at the sun through the branches and then at a cheap plastic watch that Pazzo pulls out of a grubby pocket. Dead-reckoning is not accurate beneath the trees, but they can see they have travelled roughly north-east, the route that witnesses told them to follow.

'That is clever, knowing our direction like that,' says Joshua, hoping that he is not going too far, but Pazzo expects flattery. He treats him to another black-toothed smirk.

'Just over this next hill.'

On the night of the fall, two weeks ago, and immediately after securing the crash site, Daniel began searching the jungle for a sizeable rock they could use. It needed to be a single piece, irregularly shaped and sufficiently hard to at least appear as if it could have fallen from space.

Late that same night, in the sweltering blackness beneath the tree canopy, they found something suitable. The boulder was completely overgrown and partly buried in the ground. A group of scouts worked till morning, destabilizing and cutting trees, clearing and scraping earth to make it look as if a meteorite had fallen. As first light was creeping through the tree canopy, they carefully removed all traces of their presence. The jungle was left to reclaim the space, and each day of new growth would date the damage.

'Interesting.' Pazzo squats at the beginning of the path carved in smashed trees. The soldiers fan out down the trench.

One of the young militia pulls up a plant and holds it to his face, then plucks and chews on one of the leaves. 'Captain, these plants are only growing a week or two. This is a fresh clearing.' He grins, his few teeth splayed out and manually sharpened. It is a mystery as to how he eats without injuring himself.

'Where's the debris?'

Daniel unglues himself from the spectacle of those teeth and says, 'It is about fifty metres along, below where the earth has been pushed up into that lip,' leading the way.

They walk towards the rock. It is pitted, the fissures filled with green, slimy water and the surface caked in mud. It is not overly large, a big boulder, maybe four metres wide where it sticks out of the ground.

Pazzo kicks it, then knocks it with his rifle. 'Have you tried moving it?'

Joshua is seeing it for the first time, impressed at the work Daniel and his team performed on such short notice.

'It weighs several tons. We are not moving it,' he says.

'What's it made of? Don't you think it could be valuable?'

'Not that we are able to see.' Joshua nods towards Daniel, who hands him a curved machet. 'I will show you,' and strikes down with the back of its long blade.

There is a ringing chime and a flat groove is left in the rock. A chip flies on to the ground. It is a muted grey-brown. Pazzo scowls at it, picking it up. 'Can't you tell if there are minerals in the rock?'

'No, we do not have such technology, and we would be unable to process it even if we did. You and your men are welcome to take it if you wish.'

Pazzo appears to consider this, but he knows it is too heavy for his small band. Besides, his men would probably refuse even if it were possible. Best to leave it to the jungle. He puts the chip in his pocket so he has some evidence of what he has seen.

Unfolding his map again he studies it intensely, as if it will somehow show him where he is. There are maps with built-in positioning; this is not one of them.

'Where are we?' he asks eventually.

Joshua looks at the map, estimates and marks a spot. It is much further east than their real location, adding to any future navigation difficulties. Pazzo saves it.

'We had reports of something that might have fallen some-where near here. Our Awbong thought it might be valuable and we could sell it to the printers. It looks like we weren't lucky this time.'

He looks around the clearing again and sighs. 'Let's go back to the village. My men will be tired and hungry.'

The soldiers are bored and subdued on the walk back and pay little attention to the route. They have spent two weeks searching, and the meteorite is an anticlimax. They will have nothing to show when they get back to Calabar, and Pazzo will have an angry Awbong to placate.

4

'Anwụnta! Get out of our village!' hurling a stone that catches the small boy a glancing blow on his arm.

He stands still, his head bowed, trying not to cry, too scared to run.

Other children are gathering, their taunts like the pecking of angry crows.

'Umu, no, this is not right,' says a voice. An old woman, scrawny and walking-stick bent, steps serenely between the boy and the others. She is scarcely taller than they.

'We do not want you here,' says the largest of the surrounding children. He is panting, sweating. They have chased their quarry, surrounding him, jeering him. Now he shakes with adrenalin and rage.

The woman's eyes are large and sad. She touches her accuser on the shoulder, stroking his neck up to his cheek, holding his eyes.

'Where is your compassion, my child? We are children of the earth, just as you.'

The boy can feel her warmth. Her touch, gentle and loving. He feels her forgiveness and knows he does not warrant it. A moment of humiliation and panic, and then he runs away. The others follow swiftly and in silence, their dropped stones testimony to how rapidly this was turning very ugly.

'Are you hurt, my child?' she asks, pulling him carefully towards her. She recognizes him: Modupe, Folami's son. They have only been in Ewuru a year. His father is late, falling to bandits on the long journey south.

He weeps now, his small body trembling with shock and fear. She deftly feels his arms and head, sensing that the damage is not physical.

'Mama Chibuke?' Abishai rushing into the small street. 'I am so sorry,' breathing quickly. 'I came as soon as I heard.'

They are a few blocks south of the market in an area of the village where many of the recent migrants live. Cooking smells filter through the air, strange and wild compared to those on the other side of town.

In the blue-glow of the street lamp, the old woman is almost smaller than the child she comforts.

Abishai, her heart still pounding from the frantic run here, has no words to speak her embarrassment and horror. Mama Chibuke smiles up at her.

'Come here, child,' and presses the boy to her.

Abishai hesitates, knowing what is needed but uncomfortable with the familiarity. The boy holds her anyway, and she hugs him tight. She kisses him on the forehead, 'I will find the children and they will apologize. You are as much a part of Ewuru as they are.'

Mama Chibuke shakes her head.

'It is not the children who need to learn this. It is their parents,' she says. Her eyes are kind but challenging, and Abishai struggles to meet them.

'I understand, Mama. I will talk to the elders and see what we can do.'

The old woman smiles, holding Abishai's hands in hers and pressing them.

'I know you will, my daughter.'

She takes the boy by the arm. 'Come, child. I will walk you home.'

Abishai watches them go and then makes her way back to Ikoy Road, through the market and along Ikot towards the north gate.

'My sister, please.' Esther answers her knock and happily invites her in to the kitchen.

'Sit. I will make you tea,' turning on the kettle while continuing to load the dishwasher. There are a few stray items of cutlery left. Only two for dinner this evening.

'Is Isaiah still up?'

'Yes, he is playing. What is wrong, Abishai?'

Abishai shakes her head, her eyes unreadable, heading into the next room.

Isaiah is lying on the floor, focused on attempting to build some complex creation. 'Hello, Aunt,' he shouts and jumps to embrace her, but his heart is not in it, distracted by his mechanisms.

'Go play,' she smiles. 'I will sit by you.'

Isaiah is instantly back amongst the blocks. Abishai recognizes the set as the one her brother played with as a child.

'How long have you been playing with igwe?'

'A long time, Aunt,' he says. 'Weeks. One of the girls at school wants to have a race tomorrow, and we need to build a car to drive on its own around a course our teacher will make.'

Abishai smiles, remembering the mechanisms her brother made. Every generation seems to rediscover the toy and pesters the printers with new ideas for new pieces.

Esther brings tea and they sit on one of the sofas and watch Isaiah as he struggles against distraction. The car is only half-built, and he is busy with something that looks like a single-wing airplane.

Esther grins and raises her eyes to the ceiling. Poor Isaiah has inherited none of his mother's technical ability.

'What is troubling you?'

Abishai holds her tea like a shield. 'I was in South Town. A group of children attacked a small boy. I think he is one of the new arrivals. From Tchad.'

She is speaking softly. Anguish and contained outrage, trying not to disturb the boy playing in his own world on the floor.

'They were throwing stones, Esther,' her face horrified.

Esther puts her tea down and moves closer, holding the other woman.

'You stopped them?'

'No. Mama Chibuke was there before me.'

'Were either of them hurt?'

Abishai shakes her head. 'They were already running away from her when I arrived.'

Esther grins. 'She is an amazing woman.'

'I promised that the children would apologize. Mama said, "It is not the children. It is the parents."'

'She is right.'

'Where did this come from?' asks Abishai. 'A year ago we never had this. Now? Once a week I see children fighting. We hear complaints about outsiders. It makes no sense. Ewuru was built as a place of peace.'

Esther sips her tea. 'More refugees, is the answer.' She nods and looks sad. 'Too many people the old community do not recognize. New sounds and smells. People who look different. There is fear and anger. It troubles Joshua.'

'I know, but what will he do? The people ask for a democratic council.'

Isaiah has given up on his mechanism. He has not managed to make one that works. His flying wing rests against the car, both half-built. Pieces of igwe lie scattered. The schematic on his slate has made way for him to draw. Colourful figures of animals emerge beneath his fingers and run away across the surface.

'Clean up, child. It is time for bed.'

'Mother,' he sighs. The agony of the child preferring the mess of making to the effort of tidying up. 'I want to stay up till Father is home.'

'That is well,' she smiles, 'but put everything away so none of us ends up with igwe stuck in our feet.'

He slowly packs the pieces into their box as they speak and joins them on the sofa, struggling to remain awake.

'You know he will not agree to that,' continues Esther.

'I know, and I understand his reasons. But what then?'

'I do not know, but we must find a way.'

They look out of the windows and across the village to the moon reflected on the Akwayafe and the darkness beyond.

'Will you come with me when I visit Mama Chibuke tomorrow? She can take us to the child.'

'Yes, of course, Abishai. I will even bring a cake.'

Abishai looks mortified. 'Has the child not suffered enough? Your cakes are terrible.'

Esther joins her laughter, stroking Isaiah's head where he has fallen asleep in her lap. 'True, but yours are worse.'

5

None of the soldiers has any lamps. Neither have Joshua or his men brought any. It is almost too dark to see when they reach the main trail to Ewuru.

Heavy purple clouds gathering for the evening rainstorms add to the gloom. Thunder reverberates off the cliffs. They are all soon drenched: a relief after the closeness of the day.

It is easy to lose track of time in the darkness and wet. The soldiers are worn out before they see a few small lights at the edge of the village rising up on the hill out of the jungle ahead.

As the trail winds past the maize field, Joshua can see two men on watch. 'My brothers,' he says.

'Joshua,' their eyes bright in the darkness.

It is late, most people already at home, and the village is quiet as they enter the east gate, the streets dimly lit along the main Akwayafe Road thoroughfare. A few people linger in the market, and Joshua leads Pazzo and his men there. Tables and chairs are scattered in open spaces between market stalls, most of which are already closed.

'I am sorry that we do not have a proper inn where we can serve you better. We will eat in the market and then we have a store-room here where you can spend the night.'

This is not, strictly speaking, true, but no self-respecting Ewuru innkeeper will tolerate such rancid guests.

The soldiers drop their gear against the market stalls within reach, propping their rifles haphazardly, drying their faces with their sleeves and drawing up chairs and tables to accommodate them all. Only Daniel and Joshua remain as the scouts head home to their families.

Gideon Okotie's food stall is the only restaurant open, although some of the other traders are still about. Sweat gleams off his broad bald head, collecting about grey stubble.

'I have white soup or egusi, with plantains and pounded cocoyam. You are fortunate, I still have catfish left for you,' taking orders as he goes.

Gideon vanishes into his tiny kitchen, and the others lean back and survey their surroundings.

The rooms housing the cellulosic printers at this end of the market are running much as they do throughout the year.

Ofoesi is producing clothes, soft colourful dashikis emerging and being stacked on pallets. He cannot be producing any new designs or the doors would be firmly closed to prevent anyone seeing. The stacks grow: multicoloured blocks of clothing piled up against the white walls of the room.

Alongside Ofoesi, the doors on Dala's ten-metre machine are open wide. She produces much of the capillary mesh needed for agriculture. Gwamife, from the university's recombinant team, is deep in conversation with her as they stand over the control console planning the next seed stock for the coming planting season.

Figures can be seen pulling narrow carts filled with produce and supplies, restocking the shops and stalls. Others are clearing out waste and loading it into the crates for dumping in the digesters outside the village walls.

Joshua sits quietly at the table, noting the obliviousness of Pazzo and his men to the ordinary interactions of traders and late-night customers. They should take notice, for while such printers and technology may be found anywhere, Ewuru is different from Calabar, where the men with guns dominate the city.

The market is a pentagonal space, the corners open for pedestrians and the narrow carts used to ferry goods in and out. Each side, between the entrances, consists of four-storey buildings, open at the base for the printers and larger shops. The upper storeys are filled with offices, studios and some residences. The two guesthouses are on the outer west side, where Pazzo cannot see.

Across the space are a network of carts and stalls filled with fresh produce faintly visible behind transparent cellulosic enclosures, food and tea stands, and all the variety inherent to such a place.

Strung tight between and above the buildings, and rising to the centre, is a single heavy white canopy held up by spars several metres high. Open flaps permit air to circulate, and the overall effect is of a light, airy and open tent.

The fabric of the awning glows. During the day it absorbs light across its upper surface, and at night organic florescence releases the stored energy. Four large overhead panels supplement the surface luminance, and the light is warm and friendly.

At the centre of the market is a small gathering space that hosts the weekly legal council meetings, and evening entertainment. A cluster of men, women and a few older children daring to stay up this late are waiting expectantly for one man to begin.

Rain is channelled down the central spar, merging into water piped into a clear, clean pool before the stage. The man watches the water, his skin red-brown, like dark palm oil. His eyes have an eerie yellow glow. He is dressed in an intricately embroidered ochre-brown boubou and matching kufi skullcap. They look handmade, as do his leather sandals.

He taps the water where it pours down the pole, setting a liquid percussive rhythm flowing down and into the pool. He nods his head in time to the beat and starts to sing, his voice sweet, resonant. The water in the pool continues the cadence of his tapping.

A drop of water falls regularly from high in the canopy on to the edge of the stage. He stares at it, and its sounds, where they land, are amplified, joining his harmony.

Without breaking song, he plays a few notes on a bamboo flute before placing it on the stage before him. It continues to breathe his melody.

He rattles a handful of grain in a mug. Random, sharp-edged percussion adding depth to the music.

This song is different. Gentle, a prayer, where his performance last night was joyous. He is adding voices now. Harmonizing with himself. Some voices high, some low.

The lyrics and melody are simple: gratitude for the day and for the food we have eaten.

The people sit spellbound, all smiling, some with tears shining in the market light.

'Why do you have that ubio here?' asks Pazzo, spitting out the words, his voice shrill.

Joshua is startled out of his reverie. 'It was the Song for the Harvest last night. The Balladeer always visits this time of year. Does he bother you?'

Pazzo wants to say yes, that he is terrified of this wandering sorcerer. He does not understand his magic or his ways, and he has an unpleasant habit of turning up unexpectedly.

'I expected him to leave this morning, but you know him,' Joshua shrugs. 'He keeps to his own time and place.'

'Yes,' says Pazzo, refusing to meet the fearful eyes of his men so that they cannot see the same panic in his.

Even with the odds, they were planning some small malice, Joshua realizes. He sends silent thanks to the Balladeer.

He does not mention that the Balladeer had played another

song last night, one he called the Lament for the Fallen. He had not been in the area when the craft had landed, and he did not consult with the village when he came or went. Somehow he knew.

The song had been sad and mournful, as of something passed and forever lost. The griots never interfere or judge, but they sometimes offer guidance for those capable of listening. Joshua had thought long about the music.

Gideon returns, carrying plates of food that he sets down before each of the men. He makes several journeys, and the delicious spicy-prawn smell of egusi mingles with the pepperiness of white soup. Two of the soldiers get up to wash their hands in a communal basin. The others seem comfortable with their state of hygiene and are already breaking off chunks of the cocoyam with their hands, their fingernails cracked and blackened. Each rolls the soft white mass into balls between their palms, presses a thumb into the centre and uses the result to scoop up the thick soups.

Gideon observes this, shaking his head.

Joshua and Daniel do not eat, not because they are not hungry – they are both famished – but because they will not honour Pazzo by joining him. The men from Ewuru have nothing in common with these interlopers and say nothing. The soldiers appear to have little in common aside from their guns and say even less.

Eventually, the plates are scraped clean. The clinking of spoons on crockery slows and stops. Pazzo has no more interest in this journey or in this village.

'We will sleep now.'

'I will show you the way,' says Daniel.

The soldiers collect their rifles and satchels and follow him through the market and to the small block of storerooms at the eastern side. A cellulosic door of a room facing into the market is open and the room is lit, casting its glow on to the cobbled street. There are no windows.

Inside, straw has been fashioned into fifteen makeshift beds with tropical-weight blankets folded neatly at the bottom. String has been fastened in a grid to the walls near the ceiling, and mosquito nets hang down over each bed.

'There is no lock on this door and we can leave it open for you,' says Daniel.

Pazzo waits at the door as his men file in. 'This will do. We will leave at first light.'

Daniel nods, 'I will have someone point out the main route to Calabar for you.' He glances towards where a scout stands, watching the door, then he walks back to the market where Joshua is waiting for him.

Gideon has packed his dishwasher and is preparing to close up. He fills two bowls with egusi and takes another of cocoyam, covering them with cloths. He smiles, handing the bowls to Daniel and Joshua. 'No need to trouble yourselves later,' he says.

They thank him and fall into step as they leave, heading up a street, hidden in darkness, to the north-east, first along Ikot Road and then turning right before the north gate.

The kitchen light is still on in Joshua's house. Esther leaps to her feet as the door opens, taking his hands in hers. 'My husband, you are safe,' her face glowing. He squeezes her hands, looking into her eyes, relaxing into their warmth.

'My wife,' pleasure and gratitude.

'Daniel, Gideon, welcome, my brothers,' she says as they slip in behind Joshua. They each take her hands then sit at the large wooden kitchen table where an older woman greets them with a smile.

'Miriam, my sister, it is late for you to be up,' says Gideon, affection filling his voice.

'Ah, Gideon, for small boys like you, maybe,' she teases.

Abishai steps into the light from across the living room beyond the kitchen. She too takes each of the arrival's hands in turn.

'Isaiah is asleep,' she says to Joshua. 'He tried waiting up, and we have just carried him to bed.'

Daniel washes his hands in the sink. He sits down, opening one of the bowls, and begins to eat. The others discuss inconsequential matters as Joshua quietly enters his son's room. The boy is stretched out across the small bed, one arm bent under his belly and the other flung out and trailing on to the floor. Joshua carefully raises the mosquito net and crouches down. He lays a hand on Isaiah's head, smiles to himself.

When he returns, the others are waiting. Joshua, Daniel, Gideon and Miriam are the village amama: those who manage village affairs.

Joshua sits, opens the remaining bowl of egusi and sighs with pleasure as he spoons the thick soup.

Abishai stands against the back door. Daniel has squeezed himself in next to the stove to make space for the others.

'My brothers. My sisters,' Joshua begins, pushing aside his empty bowl. 'There is only one thing strange about these soldiers.'

'They smell terrible,' says Daniel, to laughter.

Gideon steeples his hands up to his chin. His fingers are long, the nails white against his skin, their edges neatly trimmed. 'Why do they carry a radio without any batteries?'

Joshua nods.

Miriam coughs. She is older still than Gideon, almost eighty-five, an age few in the village reach. She was once fat, but now her skin is wrinkled and sagging. She looks tired.

'The last river traders mentioned there was not much suitable metal available in Calabar. Perhaps there are no batteries to be had, even for men with guns?' she says.

Esther stands and fills a kettle at the sink. It is white and pot-like. She places it on the stove and then gathers mugs, teaspoons and sugar. Daniel hands her milk from the fridge.

'But to carry it anyway? Do they think to scare us?' says Joshua.

'They hope others will not notice. It may offer some security,' says Daniel.

'It is possible. If such metal is more valuable, I am worried this will mean more militia searching for debris,' says Joshua, smiling his thanks as he takes a mug.

Daniel bites his lower lip as if he means to speak, but remains still. The scouts and sentinels are in place, and it would take a sizeable force to overwhelm the village.

Joshua smiles at him, taps the table. 'Never mind, they were convinced. Daniel has performed tremendous work,' he says.

Daniel grins happily. 'We need to remain wary, though. I am increasing the number of maintenance crews on the sentinels from tomorrow,' he says.

'It is a relief they know nothing of the sky person,' says Gideon.

'Sky people' – their name for those in the orbital cities. They know very little of them, for they are even more remote and foreign to their lives than those living in Europe or the Americas.

The others wrinkle their noses and look uncomfortable.

'We moved him from the clinic this morning,' says Miriam. 'He is in one of Gideon's storerooms near the market,' nodding her thanks. He smiles back.

'We have a rota of nurses who will visit every day and ensure he has what he needs. My granddaughter was with him today,' says Miriam. Abishai's eyes brighten at this unexpected mention of young Edith.

'He is still in a coma. Today he asked for fish broth.' She shakes her head. 'I still do not know how to speak of this. "He" is in a coma, but "he" speaks.'

'What did he say? Exactly?' asks Daniel.

'He says, "Feed him fish broth. He will need about four litres. Feed it to him over eight hours." I was there. Edith put a funnel in his mouth and poured it carefully. He swallowed the lot. Very lively for a person in a coma.' She sounds vaguely affronted.

'We do not know how advanced their technology is. He could host a computer, like the sphere, and it is telling us what to do through him,' says Joshua.

'It is possible,' says Gideon.

Esther scoops loose leaves of tea from a tightly lidded container and into the boiling pot. The tannic fragrance fills the kitchen. She places it in the centre of the table for the others to help them-selves. The scorching bottom adds another dark ring to the pattern of shared moments burned into the wood.

'What does the sphere say about him?' asks Abishai, pouring herself a mug.

Ewuru is fortunate, for few villages can afford their own sphere. Its power is limited outside the connect, but it is a vital source of knowledge: a library of designs and methods that inform the printers, and its gene bank makes seed production possible. It is integral to village life.

'There is little. Perhaps they do not share all their secrets,' answers Gideon. He drums his fingers on the table, then stops as Esther raises an eyebrow. He smiles an apology.

There is a lull as tea is tasted, savoured and given the contem-plation it deserves.

'I have never seen healing like this,' says Miriam. 'This morn-ing Edith permitted me to examine him,' she continues. 'His limbs are straight and unmarked. He is breathing normally. The bruising is gone. His chest is shaped correctly. He has lost a great deal of weight, but he looks as if he could wake up at any moment.'

'And he still weighs three times as much as any of us,' says Daniel.

'If he knew he was going to be this injured, perhaps he put on the weight in advance?' suggests Joshua.

'Where, though? He is about your size,' says Daniel.

'That silver fluid? It is not just in his blood,' says Miriam, shivering as she remembers the extent of the injuries.

'I think he will be awake soon; then he can answer our questions. The most important of which is, what do we do with him?' says Gideon.

Esther is yawning, covering it with one hand, her other holding an empty mug. Miriam's eyes crinkle as she looks fondly on the young woman. She motions that the meeting should withdraw. There is a quiet scraping of chairs. Each takes Joshua's hands and smiles to Esther as they leave, Daniel and Abishai going in different directions, Gideon and Miriam holding hands and looking as if they will be having another long night of tea-filled conversation ahead of them.

Eventually, it is only Joshua and Esther standing in the kitchen. He closes the door and switches off the light.

'My husband,' she says, her voice low.

'My wife,' he answers.

He takes her hands, pulling her gently towards him, surrounding her with his arms. Her body is slim and strong as she folds herself into him. He rests his jaw against her cheek, her head moulded into his shoulder. He holds her head in one hand. Their breathing slows, harmonizes.

And they share each other there in the stillness and gentleness of the night.

6

[Samar.]

The word is not so much spoken as simply present, as if time has been arranged so that it has been heard without it being necessary for it to be said.

A headless torso floats in the darkness. It is hollow, ribs jagged, guts trailing out in the air leading towards it. Globs of blood and matter drifting around it. It is not fresh and has congealed into a sticky, ruddy mass in the sterile air.

Howls of madness. Scrabbling scars on the metal walls where they were torn apart by the explosion and scratched by prisoners.

Chill fear as he watches the survivor tearing at a desiccated leg, stripping off the meat and gobbling it down.

Shadows against the wall advancing on them.

[Samara.]

It is not insistent, neither patient nor expectant. It is like a cursor on a computer screen. It tells you it is there, ready, and then it waits.

Screaming and smashing his hands against the walls of the cell. Naked as he tumbles in space. His agony joined by shrieking and yowling from along the tunnels. Clutching at the torn holes where his ears used to be.

Sobbing and slashing at the walls in outrage.

[Samara.]

Breathing, regular and deep. Falters. There is a lurch. A gasp. Only a moment, and then it continues, slow and regular.

Her body dewed with bubbles, rising naked from the tawny depths. The green of her eyes, the warmth of her skin against his. His heart slows as he kisses her and his body relaxes, folding into hers.

Calmer now, he drifts gently into consciousness.

'I am awake.' His mind is fogged, his immediate past unclear.

'Shakiso. We were swimming in the summer lake. How long was I dreaming?'

[I have maintained your coma for eighteen days. It will take another eight days of active healing for you to return to normal function.]

'I can't move yet?'

[No, but the paralysis is part of the induced coma. It will wear off in the next few seconds. How do you feel? What do you remember?]

The room is gloomy, a trickle of light filtering through the open window. Soon the day will brighten.

The fibre mattress lies directly on the floor. The standard bed frame used in the village was not strong enough to support the man who lies there, and it was removed. A mosquito net is drawn tightly under the mattress, and a thin cellulosic sheet covers him.

The man is on his back, his legs straight before him and his arms at his sides. He is tall, almost two metres, and his body – although slender and not overly bulky – is peculiar almost for its perfection. This is how a textbook would describe anatomy or the way a sculptor would carve a man in stone. His face long and angular, thin mouth, long thin nose, arched brows. His head is perfectly smooth.

Even in the crepuscular light of the room he is alien. His skin gleams like matt metal: a titanium sheen that feels cool and unyielding.

'I remember you bolting me in. It was dark. Cramped. Then you blanked me out for the journey.'

[Yes. Your memory is fine, then?]

For a moment he is back there. Hammering on the walls. Confinement. His ears. Shrieks and blood. A madman, human flesh between his teeth. The planet suspended.

A sharp exhale and he brings himself back.

'I remember. I don't want to think about it until we're home.'

[I understand.]

It waits until the man is ready.

'Eight days to fitness? Why so long?'

[The village does not have all the nutrients you will require to heal any faster.]

'I understand. Very well, what has happened since I blanked?'

[The first part of the journey was perfect. I fired the rockets in sequence to bring us into the atmosphere. We disconnected from the umbilical at 95,000 metres. The gyroscope shell remained stationary, and you were locked in place. I controlled our angle of descent with only light touches.

[I then angled us across towards Africa.

[At 50,000 metres, I repositioned the craft to induce spin. This gave us sufficient time to cross from the Pacific. We remained over the oceans, outside the connect.

[At 14,000 metres, the wing started to develop a slight asymmetry.]

'We expected this, though.'

[Yes, just as we calculated your injuries. For the next 6,000 metres of vertical fall, the effect on the gyroscope was minimal.

[At 8,000 metres, we depleted the energy required to maintain your external shell. That sloughed away. We were at sufficient altitude and you resumed breathing. Again, as expected.

[A minor rotation developed. At 6,000 metres, I triggered the airbags as the rotation was becoming severe.]

'Did they work? Did they hold me in place?'

[Yes. They are a good solution. Unfortunately, the tolerances are not good enough. At 1,500 metres, the rotation became extremely severe. The tension on the airbags was too great. The one on your left side burst at 900 metres. Much of the damage you suffered occurred below 500 metres, when the remaining bags collapsed. The crash through the trees saw to the rest.]

'And how close to the target zone are we?'

[We are about 350 kilometres north of where we expected, in southern Nigeria, the Benue Peninsula.

[We're in the village of Ewuru, about 250 kilometres up the Akwayafe River and near the border with Cameroon. About 2,400 kilometres from the coast to the umbilical. Say 2,700 kilometres all told. Well outside the connect for our purposes, but that also means we rely on luck as to what is available.]

'Tell me about Ewuru. How far can you detect?'

[Only about five metres at the moment. I can get that up to ten to fifteen once you're healed, but you will feel blind.]

'I understand.' He stops, his mind wanders, tracing her feel and warmth and heart. 'I miss her.'

There is tactful silence.

'Ewuru?'

[Not really a village, not really a town. Fortunately your nurses are a very talkative bunch. There are about 14,300 people here. Enough to support much specialization. They grow tea. You'll like that. They have quite a diverse range of agriculture and, technology-wise, your grandfather would be proud. They have a river turbine, a range of fabricators, digesters and a sphere.]

'Good, we were hoping for these. What have you learned?'

[The sphere has been out of the connect for a very long time, but I have learned their language, food, customs. More than enough.]

'And the turbine? Do they have spares?'

[Yes. I think they have an entire replacement, and a smaller emergency turbine, but neither have seen use.]

'So, we have propulsion. What will we do for energy? Fuel, batteries?'

[Their fabricators are very basic and can produce simple structures only. This may be where we end up mired in local politics. Soldiers came through almost a week ago.]

'Looting?'

[No, they appear to have been looking for you.]

'Someone saw?'

[I brought us in from over the sea, but, yes, many people saw. Still, we have been very lucky. The village has no fear of the local warlords. Joshua Ossai, the village leader, led the soldiers to a large boulder they disguised as a meteorite. They cleaned it up a treat. Made it look as if it landed the same time you did. It is too big and shouldn't have fooled them. Nonetheless, the soldiers seemed convinced and left.]

'I owe him thanks. That is quick thinking.'

[They've looked after you well. Only −]

An unusual hesitation.

'What?'

[I don't know. Technology, economy, society − there isn't anything out of the ordinary, and yet this village is remarkably self-sufficient. More so than I would expect. Nothing unusual, just odd when one looks closely.]

'Something unique to this village?'

[I don't know. We've had no real information from this area in sixty-five years. Not since −]

'Yes,' Samara pauses. 'What have you told them?'

[Nothing. Only how to care for you.]

'I will have explanations to make. Back to my question about energy. What is the problem?'

[The village has no high-density batteries. The nearest city where you may be able to print something is Calabar. And don't ask, the connect runs through the northern part of it. Dangerous to visit.]

'Options.'

[There is only one I can see at this stage, considering how far north we are from our target. We need to cross about 400 kilometres of oil. The ocean currents in the Bight push the oil zone into the coast. It is very thick here. We will need to double energy output and potentially use a small wing to plane over the surface, but only to cross the Bight. From there we should be fine.]

'How long to make the journey?'

[Eight days to travel to Calabar, print the battery and return. Then two and a half to get home. We need to concentrate on solving the battery problem immediately. First, though, eight days to exercise and heal.]

'Very well.'

[Something else. A griot came through here almost a week ago.]

'Anyone we know?'

[They call him Balladeer, but he sounded like Ismael to me. He sang a song that I could just hear which seemed to be for you.]

'Let me guess, we are fallen?'

[Something like that.]

'He has a funny sense of humour, that man. It would be good to see him again.'

[Yes, maybe in Calabar. I gather that is his next destination. The paralysis has worn off.]

'Time to go.'

Samara opens his eyes.

7

Edith is late and flustered as she arrives to look in on her patient. She also has a bag of unanticipated oranges. She is flustered because she takes her responsibilities seriously, and late because Abishai has a way of unsettling her unexpectedly.

She is young and has little experience of intimacy. When she sees Abishai, though, she feels a confusing sense of emotion that she does not understand. An overly warm embarrassment and sudden clumsiness.

It seems like only minutes ago that she left the home she shares with her parents. As she turned into Calabar Road, towards the market, she had seen Abishai talking to a man. She barely noticed him, but Abishai. Her route would take her right past her. She had ducked behind a stall, pretending to inspect the fruit piled up there. She did not even notice what it was.

'You buy my oranges,' said old man Ejimole, filling a bag as he spoke.

She tried refusing, but between the invisibility of the orange and juice cart, and the exposure of walking past Abishai, she was trapped. Yes, of course, she appreciates how difficult it is to grow oranges on the equator. It is impressive what those young geneticists at the university get up to. I am sure they are lovely, but they are quite expensive. And, oh no, would you look at the time?

In result, she is late, flustered and carrying a bag of oranges. Hardly the state to be in for what she will see next.

There is no light on in the small room and, as she opens the door, sunshine lances across the floor. Spotlit, in the act of standing up, is her patient.

He is naked, his skin an even matt titanium, darker shadows as he moves, making him seem carved out of a single solid piece. His skin appears to be absorbing the light, sucking it down. Something she struggles to describe.

His hands and feet, ideal forms. He has no sex, merely a smooth mound at his pubis.

All this she has seen before, as he lay comatose, but now – awake, alive – he looks like a young god, fallen to earth.

His eyes, as he stares at her, glow gold.

She stifles a scream, then, ever professional, says, 'Good morning, sir. Please, could you wait? I will fetch someone to help you.'

He nods. Then, in accentless Efik, 'Thank you. Would you have something I could wear?'

'Oh, I am so sorry, of course, I will bring something,' she stammers, then turns and flees, leaving the door open behind her, her oranges clasped safely in one hand.

Outside, he can hear a ripple of fear and excitement following the girl as she scrambles through the village. 'He is awake!'

[That went well.]

'None of that. What must I look like to them?'

[Scary. Like the dead come to life.]

'Hmm.'

[Put them at ease. Use that famous grace and charm of yours.] And there is gentle laughter somewhere in the back of his mind.

He sits on the chair where the nurses usually keep watch. Now it starts.

A tall, straight-backed man enters. Behind him, Edith has a wrap, which she passes through.

'I am Joshua,' says the man. 'Please,' he motions with the fabric, 'you may wear this until we are able to arrange clothes that fit.'

Samara takes it and quickly knots it in place after the fashion of the villagers, around the waist and tied at the shoulder.

Joshua nods. 'You know our people and our language?'

'No, but I have access to your sphere.' He puts out his right hand. 'I am Samara Adaro, of Achenia.'

Joshua grips his hand firmly.

'I wish to thank you and your people for the care you have taken of me,' he says. He smiles over Joshua's shoulder. 'Special thanks to you, Edith. I am grateful.'

'He knows my name!' her eyes morbidly wide.

One plans and then one still is not ready, thinks Joshua. What next?

'You will have many questions. I am not able to answer all, but I will tell you what I can,' says Samara.

Joshua nods. 'There will be much interest. Are you strong enough to talk to the village?'

'The village?'

Joshua hesitates, then gently places a hand on Samara's shoulder and steers him out of the room. Thousands have arrived, filling the streets as far as they can see. Half the village is here.

'This is a small community. There is no space for secrets, and they have all had a part in keeping you safe.'

[Oh dear.]

'Of course. Where do we go?'

'We will go to Ekpe.' Turning to a man at his side, he says, 'Sound the drum.'

The man nods and races away, threading through the crowd.

'We are not sure of your recovery. Can you walk?'

52

[With care and assistance.]

'Yes, but I am still weak. If it is no trouble, I may need to lean on someone?'

'Certainly. Do you need nourishment?'

[Fish broth. Three litres.]

'If I could have three litres of fish broth, please?'

Edith nods and disappears into the crowd even as Joshua and Samara start walking. They make their way through the side streets to Calabar Road, towards the market, around the ring of Market Road to the apex, and then Ekpe Road.

Now they hear a deep boom. A drum has been struck.

It sounds again. The percussive burst carrying out and across the village, into the fields and jungles beyond, where birds take fright. The acoustics channelling the resonance through everyone within hearing.

Ekpe Road is the widest and shortest in the village, almost a village square. It is tree-lined, with a short pillar upon which is a carved wooden box in its centre. The road is packed with people all watching expectantly.

Samara's eyes close and he stumbles.

Joshua catches him, almost collapsing under his weight, but Samara wakes immediately and recovers.

'My apologies.'

They arrive before a deep amphitheatre. Below, at the far end behind the stage, is a long, open-sided structure. The roof is of palm-frond thatch and it is held up by two massive brass pillars. The shelter is positioned narrow-side on to the amphitheatre and appears to be about twenty metres long and five metres wide.

Between the two pillars is suspended a colossal carved tree trunk. It is a slit drum and a figure strikes it now, sending out another epic boom. It is the last, and the figure withdraws.

Joshua leads Samara down into the bottom of the amphitheatre and then up a short flight of stairs to the stage in front of the structure. Closer, Samara sees that the building has sufficient space inside for at least fifty people to gather. Today, however, the meeting will be in the amphitheatre for the entire village.

The Ekpe House is at the crest of the town. It provides an unobstructed view from the high ridge in the centre of the village, over a cliff and down to the river and jungle below.

Chairs are brought and placed in the shade at the edge of the roof. Joshua motions for Samara to sit, worrying that it may not support his weight. It does.

They wait as the amphitheatre fills. A profusion of coloured wraps, umbrellas and peculiar things that people happened to have with them as they were going about their day. Groups of children of all ages arriving from a long building to the west of Ekpe Road are herded in by what must be their teachers.

[They appear more prosperous than I would have expected.]

'Your population estimate appears about right.'

[Yes. But. Something unusual.]

'Yes, I see what you mean.'

In time, the people settle and there is silence.

'I call Ekpe,' says Joshua, his normal speaking voice magnified and carried to all parts of the amphitheatre by embedded amplifiers.

'Our visitor is Samara Adaro, of the sky people.'

A moment of thrilled conversation as people repeat the name to each other. To have someone who lives in space visit their tiny village, it is very exciting. 'I will lead questions and then, as is our custom, any of you may ask as well. Please, though, our guest is still very weak. If we have to draw Ekpe to a close prematurely, we will resume when he is stronger.'

Edith appears with a large pot filled with warm broth, and a decanter. She has assumed that a bottle will probably work better under the circumstances. She remains in the shade behind Joshua and Samara, prepared to refill his bottle as the village meeting continues.

Joshua now sits and faces Samara directly. 'Ekpe is our village gathering. Laws are passed here. This is where we discuss matters of importance and make decisions. Ekpe does not always need to involve the whole village, but, today, you can understand the interest.'

The formality is strange to Samara, but he can see the intensity with which Joshua is staring at him and the depth of emotion of the people gathered to listen.

'I understand, and I accept Ekpe.'

'Very well. There are two things of immediate interest: how you came to be here, and whether your being here threatens our village.'

[We expected these. Remember, charm. Oh, and I've located the sphere.]

'Where?'

[It is on the short brass post we came past in the centre of that square before the amphitheatre. They have it under a box, for some reason.]

'My name is Samara Adaro of Achenia. I understand your questions. There is danger, but it is not here,' he says, addressing the amphitheatre.

There are gasps and a rising hubbub.

[That wasn't charming. Please, do not scare them.]

'My apologies. I mean that the danger I am escaping is in the United States, a long way from here. We are outside the connect, and they cannot find me here.'

'I am not sure that is helpful. Are you a criminal? Why do they pursue you?' asks Joshua.

[Tell them.]

'What do you know of the sky people, of us?'

'Not very much. That your people live in cities in orbit about the earth and that you keep to yourselves.'

'Yes, but we are not one nation. There are many cities in orbit. Each is distinct and independent from the others. Some are privately owned, some belong to particular countries. All, independent or not, are expected to hold allegiance to one country.'

'We understand. That is not very different from Ewuru and Nigeria.'

'In my case, I am from Achenia, which is the largest of the orbital cities.'

'How large is that?'

'We number about eight hundred and fifty thousand people.'

Again, the jumble of conversation and exclamations. The sound settles.

'Our people are organized very differently to you. I am of the Nine. We are the −' [Careful.] '− defenders of our people. We offer legal enforcement and protection against threats.'

'Nine because there are only nine of you?' Joshua is trying to assess how lethal a soldier he must be if nine can defend eight hundred and fifty thousand.

'Yes. We do not make the laws or judge whether they have been broken. We are completely subject to our laws and answer directly to the Five, the judiciary of our society. Only they have the legal right to call on us or send us to war.'

'Are you at war? Is there a war between your people and the Americans?'

Joshua can see that the question causes Samara tremendous anxiety. Many people are speaking now but still the amphitheatre is able to isolate and amplify their voices over the noise.

'I don't know. I −' Samara squeezes his forehead as if willing an answer there. '− I was on a diplomatic mission to the US to discuss our cutting the umbilical and leaving. I don't know what happened.'

[Samara.] 'They cut off my ears!' [Samara. Gentle. Please.]

'Your meaning is unclear. Why would you need to go to visit the Americans? Do they own your city?'

Samara is silent. He appears locked in some internal struggle. Then he seems to recover control.

'Achenia is owned by our people, but we are nominally associated with the US. Many of the great orbital cities have been cutting their ties to earth. In our case, perhaps literally. We manage a space elevator to move large quantities of freight up to our city. There are only two other such elevators left, and organizations who may wish to place freight in orbit use our services. This is how we have transferred megatons of material to build the space cities. It is not much used any more except as a safe channel to exit the atmosphere.'

'You call this an umbilical? You would wish to cut it loose, like a child leaving its mother?'

Samara pauses. 'Yes.'

'I understand. Does this –' he searches for a word, '– cutting? Does this cause conflict?'

'We are the largest and most technologically advanced city. Our leaving will have many consequences for the planet. I was part of a delegation sent to negotiate with the American government in Washington. We were agreeing ownership of the elevator, amongst other things,' says Samara.

'This went badly?'

'No, I didn't think so. But –' [You'll need to simplify a bit. Maybe up to the first blank?] '– one of our delegates went missing. I went in search of him, and then I was rendered unconscious.'

'How? We saw how much damage you can survive.'

'I am unable to say. When I awoke I was on Tartarus, the American space prison.'

'A prison in space? Why would anyone build such a thing?' asks Joshua.

Samara gags, clutches his mouth, his chest heaving.

[Calm.] 'They were eating each other!' [Samara. Remain present.]

Edith leaps to his side, Joshua bracing him to prevent his fall. She rummages for a cloth and pours water on it before wiping it across his brow.

Samara grabs at the cloth and holds it over his eyes, regaining his composure.

'I am sorry,' his breath easing. He nods at Edith, the damp cloth crumpled in his hand and resting on his leg.

'Tartarus is an evil place. It was built to dump America's most unwanted. There is no hope there. Transportation to Tartarus is to death, one way or another. I saw things –'

Samara seizes Joshua's arm. 'I will see that place brought down. No one should suffer so, no matter their crime. We honour ourselves when we have honour even for broken men.'

Joshua grits his teeth under the pressure of Samara's hold. Easing his fingers loose, he settles Samara back in his seat. The cloth drops to the ground. Edith retrieves it and, her heart pounding, returns to the shade.

'You escaped, though?' says Joshua, carefully.

'Yes, I built a craft and escaped and landed here.'

Joshua sucks on his lips. Samara's terror of the jail has chilled him, and many of the villagers look frightened. He decides not to press Samara any further on his time there.

'That last part would seem to cover a great deal. But, no matter. It would, as you say, not appear to affect us. Do you think that your people might now be at war?'

Samara has been gradually drinking the fish broth, but there is insufficient energy there and he is growing tired.

'As I said, I am unsure. My people will know I am missing, but I am unable to contact them. I crashed here as both outside the connect and sufficiently close to be able to reach the Earth-side entrance to Achenia.'

'Why can you not contact them? Why not simply go to the connect? It is only two and a half days away in Calabar,' says Joshua.

'No!' Samara looks both exhausted and determined. 'I don't know who put me in Tartarus, or why. The Americans monitor all communications in the Earth-side connect, and I would be spotted immediately.

'Normally there are antennae embedded in my ears so that I may contact my people directly. Without them, I would make myself known to those who pursue me as soon as I enter the Earth-side connect, but I would not have access to Achenia to call for help. That would create danger for your people.'

Joshua looks confused. 'Where are your antennae?'

Samara's exhaustion and isolation begin to overwhelm him. 'They cut off my ears!' he says, his voice anguished and despairing, his pain suddenly stark to all. Then he topples sideways off the chair, and is unconscious.

Joshua stares. 'But I can see his ears?'

Then, 'Quickly. Carry him to my house and place him in the guest room. Careful with the bed.' Four men run for the stage.

Joshua stands and addresses the now quite chaotic crowd. 'This Ekpe is suspended. We will return after sundown at eight this evening. If our guest is awake, he will join us, otherwise we will discuss the events of today.' Then he follows the men who are carrying Samara.

The villagers are now very excited. This story, of the man who fell to earth, and his pursuit of justice, will become a legend.

8

[You are at Joshua's house. It will take a few hours before I can ensure that you do not pass out again. In the interim, please remain as calm as you can.]

Samara opens his eyes. A young boy is close, staring at him. He grins in delight.

'He is awake, Father,' he calls. 'Hello,' smiling. 'I am Isaiah.'

'I'm Samara,' he says, carefully shifting himself into a sitting position. The mattress is on the floor and the frame is leaning against the wall alongside.

They stare at each other, each as if they are seeing a creature of such fabulous peculiarity for the first time.

Joshua comes into the room, a mug of tea in each hand.

'Do you drink tea? I find it helps.'

Samara realizes he has been staring. 'Yes, sorry. It is many years since I have seen a child so close. Our people do not have so many children any more.'

'Why not?' asks Joshua as he hands him one of the mugs.

'Our lives are long. We seem to have fallen out of the habit,' he smiles. 'And I was thinking that I am far too young and irresponsible to have children just yet.'

Joshua sits on a chair at the desk in the room. Samara remains seated on the mattress while Isaiah compromises and squats on the floor between them.

'You must be at least my age,' says Joshua, assessing him. 'Thirty-eight is a good age to have children.'

'Oh, I'm much older than that,' says Samara.

'How old are you?' asks Isaiah.

'I'm ninety-three.'

'That is older than Aunt Miriam,' exclaims Isaiah.

'How is that possible?' asks Joshua.

'My body is host to a symbiotic intelligence. I lend it my sub-conscious and it forms a biological network to maintain my health. I can choose to be any age, but most of us –' he smiles, '– most of us prefer to remain young.'

Joshua thinks. 'I can understand why you would embed such a network, but why does it have to be intelligent? Is that the voice we hear when you are unconscious?'

Samara nods, 'His name is Symon. We have a close bond, which maintains the balance of the system. Managing all the functions of the symbiont is extremely complex. I cannot do that and be me as well. Without Symon's intelligence, my mind would become unstable.'

'I am unable to imagine what that must be like?'

'You have a voice in your head you speak with that is really you? I no longer have that. I have Symon. It takes training not to lose one's identity during the integration process. We don't let children integrate with either the connect or with a symbiotic intelligence.'

The complexity is boring Isaiah. 'Are you married?' he asks.

'Isaiah!' says Esther, who has just come into the room and is leaning against the door frame, listening.

'I don't mind,' says Samara. 'Yes. My wife is Shakiso,' looking sad and forlorn even as he takes strength from thinking of her. 'We have been married only twenty years. She is one of the lead-ing advisers within the Seven. They're a sort of nominated group

61

who offer insight to our people. They are like your father and the amama.' As he speaks of her, his voice changes, goes soft, and his body relaxes.

'Your ways are very strange to us,' says Esther.

'Yes, they must seem so. They have arisen because we live a long time in a confined space. There is nowhere else to go and we must find a way for everyone, not just the majority, to seek fulfilment.'

'Can I speak with Symon?' asks Isaiah.

'No, not here. On Achenia, our atmosphere – the air we breathe – is different, almost a living organism. There Symon can project his presence outside my body and interact with others.'

'Oh. What does he look like?'

'You have seen him. He's the silver fluid in my body,' laughs Samara. 'But I understand what you mean. On Achenia, he can look like whatever he wants to. Some people have symbiotic intelligences that look like people, while some look like animals or simply abstract shapes. It depends on the person concerned. My father –' he stops.

'Your father?' asks Isaiah.

Samara shakes his head. 'I will tell you another time.'

Joshua leans forward in his chair, studying Samara. 'I have seen your craft, and I have made some assessments. You knew that it might malfunction and that you would be injured. I assume that your extra weight has something to do with your ability to heal from such tremendous damage?'

'Yes, that is true, although my first concern was surviving the vacuum outside the prison. I needed to shield myself to survive. I was much heavier when I jumped into space.'

Samara sips his tea. It is black, sugarless, and he enjoys the tannic flavour.

'I am a member of the Nine, though, so I am heavier than

most. Normally, there is only a small amount of the symbiont fluid in one's body. When I became one of the Nine, Symon was augmented with new functions aligned with my military role. He now almost fills me completely and has turned my body into a single solid mass.'

'Can you shoot laser beams out of your eyes?' asks Isaiah, who seems quite taken with the idea and has recently discovered a trove of ancient comics in the sphere.

'I am a bit more apprehensive, but I would certainly like to know your capabilities,' says Joshua.

'Fast healing, able to withstand any level of concussive injury, ability to project my awareness to greater distances, able to blend my appearance to suit the environment. I can't shoot lasers out of my eyes,' he grins at Isaiah. 'All of this is outside the connect and of a battleskin. The Nine, in full attack mode, are the equivalent of half of this planet's military.'

Isaiah's eyes are almost wide enough to fill a bowl.

'I thought you said that you are not a danger to my people,' exclaims Joshua, rising a little in his chair. Esther looks extremely worried.

'I am not a danger to you or your people.'

'Then what is driving you? I cannot even begin to imagine the suffering you have gone through, what it must have taken to jump into space in such a craft.'

[Ah, good one.]

'I have a duty to my people. I am one of the Nine.'

'No, I am dedicated to my people also. I am not sure I could do what you did if that was the objective.'

[Very good.]

Samara's face twists as he tries to turn to the wall while maintaining eye contact. His emotions, so close to the surface, are in danger of erupting. 'I –' he wipes tears from his eyes. 'My people will leave soon and I cannot lose Shakiso. I don't want her to go before I can join her. If she cannot find me, if she believes I am dead –' he starts to tremble.

He looks up, his golden eyes shining and wet. 'I love her and miss her.' The words are filled with more hope and yearning than they should carry.

Joshua crouches close and pulls Samara to him, embracing him. He looks over his shoulder at Esther, whose eyes are similarly filled with tears. He nods. 'Samara,' he says, 'that I understand.'

Isaiah has not seen adults in such emotional pain before. He understands that he misses his father when he is away and tries to imagine what it must be like to fear never seeing him again. I wonder if Father feels that for Mother? He notices for the first time the way his mother is looking at his father: the strength of joy and faith and adoration in her eyes. He realizes he has seen the same look in his father's when he looks at his mother.

He remembers his father's tale of rescuing his aunt and looks at it with new insight. He has always taken it to be an adventure story. Now he realizes the sacrifices one makes for the people one loves. It is a big realization for a small boy, and he is silent in the grace of his knowing.

'Drink your tea and tell us what you need.'

Samara sips carefully and calms himself. He feels drained and, at the same time, lighter, as if he is no longer carrying this burden on his own.

'The base of Achenia is on the equator about 2,400 kilometres out to sea. I need to build a boat and borrow one of your spare turbines. Then I need to travel to Calabar to print a battery.'

'They have insufficient metal there,' says Joshua.

'I know. Or, at least, we guessed as much.'

'How do you know? We only worked this out a few days ago.'

'Nigeria's economy is fragmented and disconnected from the

world. Most things are printed from local cellulose and few trade goods are brought here. There was never much mining in Nigeria, and now there is little metal traded from outside,' says Samara.

'Symon and I designed the craft with our needs in mind. The gyroscope gimbals are aluminium. We can cut that up and take it to Calabar. Sell the scrap to one of the digesters.'

'Why not build an aeroplane if you are going to build so much?' asks Joshua.

Samara shakes his head. 'There are three ways I could travel to Achenia: paddle, motor or fly. Paddling is the easiest to arrange but would take me about forty days from now, by the time I am healthy enough to go. That is too long.'

'Why?'

'A decision will be made to go twenty-two days from now. I must be home by then or they will leave without me. We will not wage war on Earth, we will simply go.'

Joshua thinks of the refugees and nods his understanding.

Samara continues, 'Flight is another possibility. I have one wing, the one I arrived in, but there are insufficient materials to extend and improve it for use. Plus, your water turbine could not become a jet engine and it would be impossible to print a motor here to act as a propeller. And I'd now need an even larger energy source than before, which means even more metal.

'If I committed to flight, I'd have to build the craft in Calabar, which would attract a great deal of attention over almost a week. Yes, the flight would only be a few hours, but that sort of interest might ruin my chances entirely.'

Joshua can easily imagine the curiosity of the militia in Calabar and realizes how impossible such a task would be. He whistles softly. Samara's need to stay in Ewuru – now that he is here – looks inevitable, given the options.

Samara finishes his tea and places the mug on the floor beside the mattress. 'My final alternative is going by sea. That has its own problems. A boat will be difficult to power through all the oil in the Bight of Bonny with any safety.' He shakes his head, looking apologetic. 'I'm sorry, you already know about this.'

'Yes, but I am impressed at your knowledge and planning,' says Joshua, his admiration genuine.

When the oil rigs were abandoned over a century ago, and the safety valves failed, the ocean was covered in a thick stifling layer. All the villages all along the coast were evacuated. No one sails in those waters. Few even travel far down the river from Ewuru. Joshua knows such a journey, out into the bay, will be difficult.

Then he remembers, 'What about the rockets? There were many attached to the pod.'

'They're extremely toxic, and Symon ensured they were burned out by the time we landed. We had intended to pack extras into the capsule, but we were concerned about what would happen if the interior was compromised.'

Joshua tries not to think of the carnage he and Daniel had discovered inside the pod. If a rocket had gone off in there as well . . . not worth thinking about.

'I originally hoped to be in southern Cameroon. I would have been outside of the oil zone but still close to the equator.' He shrugs. 'Travelling by home-made propeller is not an exact science.'

Esther interrupts. 'Please, I should make dinner. Are you able to eat?'

'Yes, I would very much appreciate that.'

'I am making egusi. Would you be able to eat this?'

'Fermented melon seeds and spicy prawn paste?' Samara's mood is lifting.

'Amongst other things, yes,' she says, surprised at the levity in his voice. 'We will have it with fish, and spinach and rice on the side. You know Efik food?'

'My grandfather makes a tremendous pepper soup.'

Esther smiles and heads to the kitchen, from where they soon hear the sounds of preparation. Isaiah is torn between wanting to help in the kitchen and snack a little, and staying to hear the stories. Snacking wins.

'Makes?' says Joshua. 'Your grandfather is still with us?'

'Yes. He is 177 and leads one of our most important technology firms. He designed Symon.'

'And your grandmother, mother, father?' he asks incredulously.

Samara looks as if he may weep again. 'My father—'

'It is well. Please, I am sorry for your loss.' Joshua is shaken, interrupting in embarrassment. What must a society be like where people expect to live for ever? 'Do people not normally die amongst your kind?'

'We do,' his voice heavy with sadness. 'There are still accidents. Young people who fly too fast, or too close to the moon. There are murders. We are still human and we suffer as people do, but not many choose to go on their own. My father,' he calms himself again. 'My father chose to go.'

Samara looks away. 'I'm sorry,' he says. 'I find it difficult to speak of him. About his choice.'

Joshua wants to ask a great many questions, but he stops himself. He can see Samara's exhaustion. He also realizes that he may never have a chance to learn from an Achenian again.

'I want to know so much. How your society works. What technology you have. How you are able to maintain self-sufficiency. Your music, your art, your stories –' he notices this last has had an effect on Samara.

'My father was our greatest storyteller. If you wish, I will tell you one of his most famous stories?' asks Samara, his voice filled with restrained enthusiasm.

'I would appreciate that. We enjoy stories, although we have yet to produce a great storyteller. If you are strong enough, when we return to Ekpe we would be honoured to hear your father's story.'

The house is filled with the smell of spices – cumin, nutmeg, chilli, and the mix of crayfish paste and chicken stock – along with sounds of chopping and laughter from the kitchen.

'That smells very good,' says Samara.

'Yes. Normally we enjoy cooking together, as a family. Tonight, you are our guest.'

'Thank you. My wife and I also enjoy cooking together.'

Strange how our appreciation for food makes even one as alien as he seem more like me, thinks Joshua. 'What would you be eating?'

'We eat mostly salads and fish. Very fast cooking so that the food is still raw, but hot.'

'You have water in your city?' asks Joshua.

'Oh, yes, an ocean. A river runs through our central valley. My home is just beneath the top of a waterfall in the temperate zone, and I can see clear across the valley from our deck. We have a water-cycle to manage our air, and the ocean has fish. We even have whales.'

Joshua is stunned. 'Whales? In space?' He feels a pang of something that he cannot place. 'Your home sounds beautiful. I would love to see your world.'

'Of course. When I return, you and your family will be my guests.'

'Dinner is ready,' says Esther, rapping on the door frame.

Samara's tale

A Conspiracy of Women

The war is over. The energies of the neighbouring states of Malpensa and Iliham are spent. Nine years have been devoted to a brutal slaughter that has spared neither rich nor poor, old nor young, the soldier from the farmer.

Thousands of tiny children have been orphaned, left in despair by refugees during the war at the secure border fastness of the Lady of Divine Light.

The nuns at that ancient Order take no sides in the battles that have whiled away the centuries beyond the great stone walls of their large and rambling estates. They welcome and care for all who are abandoned at their gates and remain entirely self-sufficient.

However, this is different. It is a war that is already being called 'a war to end wars' by those who would set public opinion. And it is true that something that was whole has been broken. The spirit that inflames the two nations has been snuffed out.

Every winter, when the harvest has been gathered and securely stored, the young men of the two states turn their imaginings to glory – to battle.

The war that began so traditionally nine years ago gave way to a muddy, dirty, depraved slaughter. As from a nightmare, the leaders of the two states awoke to find themselves covered, as to the elbows and thickly caked under their grubby and torn finger-nails, in grizzle and blood and bone; their treasure spent; the beauty and wonder of their youth turned ugly and old; a horror and stench of decay all about; and the only winners the rats grown fat on the bodies of the fallen.

Some say it is the new mechanized guns that can convert a cohort of smart young men into so much mulch in only a moment. Some say it is the gas and artillery levelling towns and killing families far from the battlefield. Some say it is because not a single family has remained untouched by this war and that even the two opposing kings mourn the losses of favourites and loved ones.

Whatever it is, the flame is extinguished and the two peoples' only thoughts are to rebuild, to mourn and to dedicate their lives to never taking such gifts for granted again.

All of this is welcome news to the nuns of the Lady of Our Rest, but the aftermath has presented Maria Stapirova, mother superior of the Order, with a bit of a headache.

'We have 7,341 babies and young children to care for,' she begins at the weekly confabulation of the nuns, a meeting that has been held unbroken by her antecedents for over four thousand years.

'While our resources are vast, they are not unlimited. Neither will it be possible for us to care for all these children to adulthood. It is not seemly,' she states primly.

'Our problem is that Malpensans will only adopt Malpensan children while Ilihamers will only consider Ilihamers and that we are unable to distinguish between our wards. Given the confusion, no one will adopt anyone.'

The nuns nod discreetly at this neat description of their predicament; many carefully scratch at clotted lumps of baby food ruining their staunchly plain vestments.

'The governing factor here is that the men of both nations – our fathers-to-be – refuse to bring into their homes the sons and daughters of the men responsible for the deaths of their brothers, fathers and friends.'

More steadfast agreement and a susurration of scraping chairs as nuns shift knees bruised by constant kneeling to chase after escaped and errant toddlers.

'What we need is a plan. An approach so daring and so ambitious that it cannot possibly fail.' Her eyes gleam and her steel-grey hair burns in the sunlight streaming on to the dais where she stands.

And so Maria Stapirova, the 531st mother superior of the Order of the Lady of Divine Light, lays out an audacious plan before her sisters.

Three months pass. Three months in which winter gives way to the fledgling kindling of spring and the shadows loosen their grasp.

The holdings of the Order shelter within a wide and deep valley cut by the last ice age through the Neralanova mountain range that divides the kingdoms of Malpensa and Iliham.

The thick and high stone wall running across the entrance to the valley serves as both fortification and entrance to the neat and densely woven town beyond the gates.

Every year, as the winter snows up in the mountains warm, as the meltwater hastens down sheer and jagged cliffs, as the Derissa River swells into a torrent, a wind germinates in ever-gathering swirls.

The sudden gust that explodes out of the valley has, for thousands of years, been counted as the first true day of spring.

The force of the wind carries the pungent scent of fresh earth, and moss, and green leaves, and early flowers. It sets the heart racing and fills the imaginings with warmth and sunshine.

It has been named La Cafeyana and Little Sister and The Duke and Mazenova. Each century seems to throw up a new name capturing the spirit of the age.

This year, after the war, the wind has no name. No matter. It does not mind.

One bright morning the conditions are perfect and the wind leaps from the channels and gullies where it has been hiding.

It races down the cliffs of the mountain, gathering the fragrance of ice and dripping water and moss and ferns. As it nears the irrigated farmlands of the Order it collects the scents of freshly turned earth and the newly growing shoots from sprouting seeds. It husbands its strength before tangling with the woods above the Derissa, snatching the taste of blossoming fruit trees as it passes. Down through the spicy textures of cumin and vanilla and liquorice before being blocked beneath the steep rise up to the village of the Lady of Divine Light.

There it seems to lie spent. But, no, it is only resting. A ploy.

It roils and boils and twists and spirals, building itself into an explosive force. And then, born laughing and nameless, it erupts out of the valley, carrying its message of life and light.

As it goes, in a moment of humour and spirit, it snatches up all the laundry that the nuns have laid out early that morning. Caught unawares, the nuns can only watch as a colourful confetti of skirts and shirts and trousers goes parachuting up into the great blue sky.

Chuckling at the sport, the wind spreads out over the villages and towns of Malpensa and Iliham, and there something extra-ordinary happens. For the wind, with what can only be devious forethought, drops the nuns' laundry neatly on to the washing lines of young couples across the two kingdoms. Astute observers note how some of the billowing clothes appear to steer their way into place.

The wind disperses, dissipates, a mere zephyr and then a

dissolving whimsy. Gone for another year and leaving behind the lingering scent of spice and the returning spring.

If this had been all, it would already have been sufficient to earn the wind a new name. A young poet who saw the clothing flashing by was already toying with either of The Laundress or The Washerwoman when something entirely unprecedented happened.

From within each shirt and dress and trouser, from beneath a rainbow of fabrics ripe with the pungent smell of soap and softener, peers a small face.

Then a stretch and a yawn and tiny bodies emerge. The babies and young children are hungry and soon set up a fearsome bedlam as they demand their breakfasts.

As the young women of the towns rush to the young ones, warm milk and porridge ready with what must seem to be only coincidental good timing, the young men are already preparing their objections.

But as the cries of hunger give way to snorts and burps of happy contentment, the young men can only stand and stare in wonder at such glowing-cheeked serenity. The image of their wives cradling tiny vulnerable bodies, a look of joy, wonder and love on their rapturous faces as the bright spring sunshine makes flesh radiant and all about the tangy scent of life.

Three months of painstaking and carefully calibrated planning has led to this moment. An orchestration of nature, the women of two kingdoms, the nuns of the order, and the children themselves.

As they behold the tableau within the glowing light, the morning waits. As the hearts of baby and prospective mother stay their beat. As prospective fathers breathe the impossible scene.

The question: will the miraculous be accepted? Will it be

believed that a capricious wind will snatch up laundry and orphans and deliver their soft payloads so perfectly to couples so clearly suitable to accept them?

The young men, their hearts frozen with regret and loss and the stench of death of so many comrades, stare in confusion and pain. They feel the moment and the choice: a world of ice and cold, or a world of laughter and light.

And they choose. Embracing their loves and accepting their new lives.

Afterwards there was much suspicion of the nuns, but it was impossible, after all. Indeed, it came as no surprise that the wind itself came to be seen as the arbiter of the eventual reconciliation between the two kingdoms and earned its new name.

And now, with the death of the last of the children of that wind after a long and joyous life untouched by war or regret, the tale of how the Stork got its name can finally be told.

It is a tale of strength, of danger, of planning, of comradeship and of bravery.

It is the tale of the conspiracy of women.

*   *   *

'That is ridiculous!' howls Oleg Deripeska from where he leans against the open door frame in the great kitchen.

'Hush,' says Katerina Esplanova where she sits rapt, the sun shining brightly on to her round red face and her eyes sparkling.

'Yes,' says the prim Irina Mabadov, who is reading from the recently released book, the pages spread open on the stained wooden table before her.

The room is full as people gather to listen to Irina's reading. All the women glare at Oleg and, shamefaced, their young men follow suit.

Oleg splutters. 'But it is preposterous,' but quietly and then, downcast, lapsing into silence.

Settled again, Irina continues, her clear, husky voice resonating and filling the room with drama of days gone by.

9

The people of Ewuru are silent as Samara completes his tale. They are unsure that the story is even over.

There is emotion, and few are unaffected by this. They live within the borders of a failed state: a region subjected to unwarranted cruelty for centuries. Warlords and militia exercise random and unpredictable violence out beyond the town. People in the lands outside the free villages of the Akwayafe do not nurture life, honour life, and the soil there is poisoned.

They relate to the despair that follows conflict. And they love their children.

Many find that they are holding their young ones tightly as Samara speaks, fiercely protective.

But this is not a story. Not anything as they know it.

It has set a scene, described a place, and filled it with people and sounds and texture. Who is the hero? What was the triumph?

Samara nods in the stillness.

'My father called these samara. I was never sure, as a child, whether he named them after me, or whether I was named after them. He never told me. He would always just smile and tell me, "You'll know one day," when I asked.'

He drinks from the jug of water at his side. Lights around the periphery of the amphitheatre shine on to the stage, insects clouding the brightness. Shrill chirps of frogs and night birds, and the distant heartbeat of the river.

The audience exhales, everyone realizing that they have been holding their breath. A few have a prickling sensation: the discomforting sense of being confronted by their own moral doubts.

While it may not have been a story like the ones they know, they have experienced something. An emotional quickening of the heart.

'My father called them samara because they are like the propeller seed. They have the means to take flight, to be carried far and to take root and grow where they land. He intended that they offer lessons without preaching, and that they be beautiful. None must be a complete story, as no seed is a complete tree.

'When I was a child, he told these stories only to me. Then, eighty years ago, he started telling them to the children of his friends. They are easy to remember, short enough to hold in one's soul. Easy to make your own and tell again to others. Soon everyone knew his tales. We would hold gatherings, like this one, and my father would tell his samara. The gatherings became festivals. Many people would present their own samara.'

Samara is silently weeping. 'Each year my father would present a new tale. We never knew what he would come up with next. I do not have this talent. I am an ordinary man. I remember listening with my family, seeing how much my father was loved by my people. I felt such pride and joy.

'He used to call the festivals "Sowing the Seeds", because people would take the stories and complete them on their own. The stories would grow in meaning through the retelling and through memory.'

He takes another sip of water. 'My father ended his life twenty years ago. I still do not know why. This –' his voice trembles, '– this was my favourite of his stories. It reminds me of why we must not make war. It fills me with joy for those who are precious to me.'

Samara sits quietly, lost in memory. 'I thank you for listening.'

10

'Wait,' says Joshua, his breath in short gasps.

He and Samara have been running in the jungle outside Ewuru, parallel to the river. This is the third day, each day going a little further and a little faster. The path through the jungle is a tangle of fallen branches, buzzing and biting insects, rotting vegetation and bare, twisting roots. All hazards to the unwary.

They settle into a walk so that Joshua can recover. The humidity amongst the trees is sweltering. The trees sweat. Joshua, with his hands on his hips, breathing hard, is dripping, a sticky stream running under his collar and pouring through an already drenched shirt. Samara is dry, his trousers and shirt unmarked as if he has newly put them on.

Joshua, deliberately slowing his breathing, shakes his head. He breaks away from the path, heading down the bank to the river. He slips off his shoes and shirt and buries his head in the water. Cupping his hands, he drinks.

The water is warm and heavy with silt and tannin draining out of the forest. The river is wide here, perhaps thirty metres across. A tree-covered island rises out of the centre, the pressure of the current raising a ridge of water that crests and breaks in slow syncopation.

Mud has caked on the bank, cracking into dry plates, rimed with mineral salts. Yellow and blue butterflies, like so many gossamer leaves, kaleidoscope up and down, some licking at the crust while others bobble for position above.

On the far bank, a troop of monkeys emerges. Black, dog-like snouts, brown-grey fur and walking on all fours. Their hind legs are shortened under narrow hips, and their backs slope up to broad shoulders. The biggest male barks, baring wicked-looking canines.

'Those are drill? I thought they were extinct?' asks Samara.

Joshua is still rinsing his head and shoulders. He squeezes water out of his tightly curled hair and wipes his face, then looks up.

'We use the genetic library from the sphere. Our university began reintroducing indigenous species about twenty years ago.'

Samara slowly crouches, not wishing to startle the drill. 'Yes, the sphere were always meant to be a complete snapshot of everything that is known about Earth. It would be there. I never expected that it would be used in this way. Not out here. Symon was right. There is something unusual about your people.'

Joshua stares at him, questioning, guarded.

'What are your people doing, Joshua?' he asks.

'We make our own way. There are no countries south of the Sahara and no one knows what happens outside the connect. How we suffer,' says Joshua, his voice terse.

Samara puts up his hands, palms facing Joshua. 'I am not your enemy, Joshua. I will not interfere.' He pauses, looking again at the drill, now returning to the forest. 'Everywhere I travel, all I see is broken. No one builds. No one thinks for tomorrow. There are no dreams.

'In your people, though, I see something different. You are not just cycling through the same day. You are building. Your village could almost be modelled after one of the small orbital cities. You honour learning, stories, beauty.

'I am sorry if I have intruded, Joshua. I have no wish to cause you concern,' he says, compassion in his tone and posture.

Joshua wonders, how far do I trust this man? He makes a decision and grapples for ways to explain. He looks at the island, the wave before it. 'Do you see the trees, Samara?'

'Yes, mahogany, iroko, obeche, sapele wood and walnut. I would not expect such variety on one small island?'

'That is Tait Island. My great-grandfather took pictures of this place when he came here. There was nothing. The trees were logged and dragged away. Oil pipelines criss-crossed the forest. Pirates broke those pipes to steal the oil. Great lakes of black filled the swamp and clogged the river, killing trees and fish and life. There were fires. Smoke filled the sky from many small refineries.'

Joshua is staring at Samara intently.

'My great-grandfather, also Isaiah, went to university in Abuja. The big men still ran the country. They made their money out of oil bunkering. I have his diary, and he wrote about the journey by road.

'He went with another boy from Zango, his village on the Gagere River. The first two boys to go. Everyone was very proud. You understand, the journey was only 450 kilometres by road, yet it took three days. Every few kilometres, a roadblock with soldiers. Hundreds of people selling goods to the buses. Children sitting next to their parents.

'So many people gathered together were a target for Boko Haram and other terrorists. The roadblock needed its own security, its own soldiers for protection.

'All along the highway, long rows of half-built petrol stations, weeds growing in the cracks in the concrete forecourts. Even so, soldiers guarded them. Politicians would syphon fuel and keep it in the tanks underground. Then they sold it over the border where there were no fuel subsidies and pocketed the difference. There were half-built hotels, stadiums, all with grass growing through the foundations. Everything was corrupt.'

His voice is sour, his face filled with contempt.

'Two village boys in the big city. They were angry with what they saw but did not know how to fight it.

'The printers were already in Abuja: first plastics, then metals, then cellulose. It was expensive, a novelty, and the equipment was beyond our villages. As the two boys began their studies, people began building the first cities in the sky. Such technology became cheaper. Affordable even here. Suddenly oil was not so valuable. The big men started to fight and now there is no Nigeria, just a region governed by militia and random violence.'

A gust of wind breathes through the trees. Otherwise, the forest is still.

'When was this?' asks Samara.

'It was about a hundred and fifty years ago. When was your city built?'

'We started about a hundred and fifty years ago. My father was amongst the first children born in orbit. My mother was brought up as a child.'

Joshua looks across the water. 'Violence, war, we knew how to survive. But the land stopped being fruitful. The climate changed. The soil became barren. People fled the countryside for the cities. Zango was abandoned. The resources were scarce and many died. Then, when we thought things could get no worse, there was fire in space.'

Joshua is silent for a few moments, lost in thought. He does not notice Samara's distress at the mention of the war in orbit, source of the debris that falls to earth. He picks up a stick, makes patterns in the water. He has been crouching for a while, so he stands and looks about for a place to sit. A tree has fallen on the bank, and he goes and leans against it. The roots stick out vertically, clotted earth still hanging on tenaciously.

'No one wanted what our nation had to sell, and we could not afford to buy anything anyway. There was nothing left for anyone in the cities, but there was less in the rural areas. That is the state of this place called Nigeria. It is much the same north and south.

'My great-grandfather had seen that things would not improve without some decisive act. After he graduated, he formed a pact of Ekpe with others and they set out, back into the wilderness. He was already old when they finally rebuilt the abandoned ruins of Ewuru. My grandfather took over from him. The first settlers worked as a community, saved as a community. They bought the sphere, a few fabricators. Their dream, his dream, was a string of independent cities along the Akwayafe.'

A fish jumps out of the water, the swirl and ripples swallowed by the currents.

'Their plan was simple. Re-establish the towns, become self-sufficient and provide nothing to the militia. Starve them into the cities and let them die there. Each village needed to be large enough to be self-sufficient, and densely populated enough to be capable of self-defence. The first high-end fabricator they purchased was the DNA printer. We solved our technology problems. The physical has been easier than the spiritual.

'The founders of Ewuru did not want rule by voting. They saw how that was used for corruption and violence against the losers. We returned to the old ways of consensus and paternal rule. We know that is not perfect. Our people are changing, we struggle with integrating new arrivals, but we are still unsure how we should govern differently.' He shrugs.

Samara is listening intently, crouching on his heels alongside the river.

'We are outside the connect and must conduct our own research.

The university was built around the sphere, and soon we started to specialize. The safety and stability of the village has permitted people to pursue their own interests. Twenty years ago, one of the teachers encouraged the students to reimagine our world. My wife was then a girl. She came to this island. She printed seeds and planted them here, making this island a new beginning.'

Joshua's face softens as he remembers the day Esther proudly brought a group of students and teachers here. Her apprehension and joy, showing how the trees were growing well and that birds were returning to nest from where they had been hiding, waiting for just such an opportunity.

'She was such a quiet girl. We could never have imagined what she was doing. She was fifteen. I fell in love with her that day.'

'If you want to know more, you should speak to her. She engineered the microbes that have restored the soils. She now runs the research group that is gradually rehabilitating the forests. It was one of her team, fifteen years ago, who began reintroducing animals, birds and the drill.'

'They use the sphere?'

'Yes. We could not have achieved so much without the techniques and knowledge it holds. It is not in the university any more. Too many people need to consult it. Its broadcast range is not far, but many people can sit in the market and work.'

'As far as I can make out, the sphere looks as if it has been in this village for, what, over one hundred years?'

Joshua nods, lifting himself off the trunk and retrieving his shirt and shoes.

'No wonder you have no information on our cities. You will have received no updates. We broadcast throughout the connect.'

'It is not a secret?'

'No, we are happy to share.' [Except] 'Oh, yes, except for dark fusion technology.' [Because] 'Well, we're worried you'll blow yourselves up.' Samara looks bashful. 'We don't trust Earth-based engineers any more.'

'We are not short of energy,' says Joshua, perhaps a tad tartly.

'For your current needs, but it takes vast stores of energy to produce the nanobiological devices that make the symbiotic intelligences. And gravity. And, well, many things.'

[And.] 'And artificial intelligence. There are no details on how to manufacture these. We will not permit a new class of slaves.'

Joshua grimaces but Samara seems not to notice.

A heron flies slowly up the river. It lands on the island shore, focusing on an eddy of water in the shadows of an overhanging branch. Ever so slowly, it moves until its head is in line with a cluster of leaves. It waits, patiently, then thrusts into the water. As it comes up, it points its beak to the sky, swallowing its catch.

'What happened to your great-grandfather's friend? You said there were two boys?'

'We do not know. He did not join us in Ewuru.' Joshua looks at the sky. 'We should return,' he says. 'I am happy to swim back?'

'It is about seven kilometres along the river? Tell you what, you swim, I'll see if I can hold my breath the entire distance.' And then Samara crouches and springs in a giant arc, before slicing cleanly into the water ten metres off the bank.

Joshua waits, hoping to spot some trail of bubbles. Then he knots his shoes into his shirt, ties this around his neck and scrambles into the water. The current is swift and pushes against him as he angles across the river to the centre.

He allows the water to carry him, enjoying the slight coolness. He wonders if he will see river dolphin today. They are not native, but his wife likes dolphins.

The river is calming, and he needs to relieve his tension. Samara has thrown the village into turmoil. Already a small group of students have started studying artificial intelligence, hunting in the vastness of the sphere's knowledge for hints on where the breakthroughs may come. He is not sure this is a good idea. Samara's warning is also in his mind. Others have started looking at energy-dense weapons. Also not something he is comfortable with.

Too much change, too fast. We do not wish to attract attention. We must keep a balance between our ambitions and the waning power of the militias.

The river is wide and deep. Trees form a dense wall along the bank. An occasional cleft, where a giant has fallen and smashed a brief opening in the canopy, exposes plants battling for light and space. There are still ancient rubber trees and oil palms from the plantations that covered most of Nigeria, but these are being gradually displaced.

He wonders how long before the forest frontier that the string of villages along the Akwayafe has put in motion will reach the cities. It should touch the outskirts of Calabar in only a few years. How will they respond? Will they even notice? So few people leave the cities to brave the wilderness.

He ducks round a tree trunk floating in the middle, its branches splayed out and trapping leaves and other debris caught in the water. He still has not seen Samara. No doubt he is swimming faster than him anyway, but he wonders how it is possible to hold his breath for so long.

He needs to be careful as he approaches this end of the village. The turbine is at the bottom of the river, and there are nets and shields to channel anything that may clog it – like that tree – but he has no wish to become trapped himself.

He swims back across towards the bank and spots the orange buoys marking the approach. A line of smaller white buoys lines the channel he needs to take, and he slips rapidly by.

Past the turbine are a series of small floating platforms

consisting of fine-net cages. These are the hatcheries where they protect the various fish stocks before release. Much further downstream, just past the town, are fish traps designed to catch full-sized catfish and tilapia.

Soon he comes to the jetty, where he grabs on to the edge of the floating platform below the concrete landing. Dragging himself out of the water he looks around for Samara.

A group of children, usually twenty to thirty, would normally be here after school, jumping off the landing in an exuberance of ever-more elaborate dives. Today they are sitting rapt on the bank, in the shade of a kola tree, listening to Samara as he tells a story.

Samara's tale

Wall of Souls

The village supporting the School is set up on a forested hill sloping down to a beautiful lake.

Children play and the village is quietly prosperous, for many come to visit as pilgrims or as students for the School.

Behind the village is a plain. Dominating the stony, mossy ground of that plain is the amber treacle light of the Wall of Souls. Within, the anguished, tortured faces of the dead. Souls drifting in random mobs, rows, singly – haunting and haunted.

The School is run by the weak, by the cowardly. Men and women who trained to run the Wall of Souls but never conquered their fears, never made more than passing forays into the amber. How could it be any different? For – one way or another – none who run the amber ever come back.

Through the wall is the promised land. Perhaps there is a School there, refining the most perfect candidates ever further. Perhaps there is a perfect world. No one knows. None return.

While the children train, learning what is known of the amber – its wiles, its terrors – the Wooden Spoon Samurai merely sits under a tree and watches the Wall of Souls.

It is a clear day: the Festival of Colours. The School is open to visitors and a market grows up before the Wall. Today is the final exam, when graduates will run the amber.

Younger students run short sorties into the amber, laughing. None will go more than a few body-lengths into the wall. It cannot distract the Souls from the real runners; there are just too many. No one knows how many, how thick the wall, how far the run.

One laughing boy runs in. As has been taught for hundreds of years, on the interpulse he runs for clear space, and on the pulse – when everything slows to glacial and terrifying frozen motion – he turns towards the ghosts so that, on the next interpulse, he will be thrust through them. Too slow. He is caught. The ghosts tear his soul from him. He gives one anguished look back at his friends, his life, then he joins the Wall of Souls.

The Wooden Spoon Samurai has been watching. He understands, and he will break orthodoxy. He does not ask. He does not wait. Even as the festival-goers mourn the death, he makes his run into the amber.

It is a no-light, no-warmth, no-cold, no-sound, no-smell, no-space inside the amber. In his head, the pulse. On the interpulse, the Wooden Spoon Samurai runs towards the ghosts. On the pulse, as the ghosts swipe at him – their fingers brushing against his clothes – he turns away, to open space.

He runs for hours in the no-space of the amber. Twisting, turning: towards and away. They reach for him, the Wall of Souls, but they do not touch him.

And then he is through.

Beyond is a plain. Barren, stony, covered in lichen and moss. There is no School. There is no promise. The horizon is unbroken. The air is still and cold.

He finds one old man still wearing the scarf of a graduate. He has been here many years, he says. There is nothing here. If you walk for a month, you will come to a cold, black, flat ocean. There could be fish in it, but he has no way of knowing. Neither is there any way of building a boat. He survives on lichen and moss.

There were others, braver than he, who tried to run back. To warn the others not to come, but – by the Samurai's presence – he must assume they all failed. 'Warn them,' he says, 'and take my scarf as a sign for any who would remember me.'

The Wooden Spoon Samurai does not hesitate. He does not flinch. He turns and enters the amber.

It is cold, dark, inside the amber. The ghosts are larger, faster.

He runs, turning towards and away. Then he is confronted by a ghost the size of a world. He looks up, stares at it. Then he turns away and towards.

He is through.

There is no point in talking to the adults. They are the weak and the cowards. The ones who were too scared to make the run and who are invested in the tradition of the School, hundreds of years in the making. He starts with the young.

He shows them the scarf. He tells them of the barren plain. There is no promise, there is no hope, only the land of the dead. They listen; they follow him. They convince their parents. They overwhelm the School. The School falls.

Now the village has a new purpose. They protect; they inform. The Wall of Souls is still there, but none run the amber. 'Look if you must, mourn the dead, then go. Live your life. For we are already in the promise.'

And the Wooden Spoon Samurai? Why, that is part of legend.

11

'– and now he is running around with the others and they all want wooden spoons!' Esther has the part-exasperated, part-mystified voice of a parent whose child has reached an age where running around shouting and hitting things with sticks is a very cool thing.

Joshua laughs helplessly. Daniel, shaking his head and laughing, says, 'My girls, too. All of them want to be samurai. They do not even know what samurai are!'

'And,' he giggles, 'Nolue, at the university, told me yesterday she had to stop a group of youngsters jumping off the edge of the cliff into the river using bed-sheets as parachutes.'

'Where was this?' asks Joshua, horrified.

'At the low end, near the jetty,' says Daniel, still laughing.

Esther sighs, realizes the lunacy of the situation and laughs as well. Then she motions at Joshua. 'This was your idea. I said we should sell him to the militia.' But she is teasing.

They are sitting around the great kitchen table drinking tea. It is early evening. Time between responsibilities; the children are still out playing and it is too early to start cooking.

'I am just worried about this. He tells stories to the children. Is not that the lesson of that strange tale? Tell the children and they change their parents? How many stories now? Every time I go to the university, someone wants to tell me a new one.'

Daniel nods and puts his mug down. 'There is something in that, yet the stories are moving. I do not feel threatened by them. What do they teach? Do not throw your life away. Dedicate yourself to a noble calling. Honour others. We have been so concerned with building a self-sufficient society that we have lost some of our other gifts.'

'Music?' says Esther; her eyes are the dawn. 'Yes. I miss music. We wait each year for the Balladeer and everyone loves him, but we do not play his songs after he goes, and we do not create new ones.'

'We cook,' says Joshua. 'We have some of the finest cooks anywhere. Our designers have produced wonderful flavours in our produce and we all cook. Is not that our craft?'

'And we design clothes, and buildings and tools. We play football against the other villages and we tell each other the stories of our forefathers. But these are all practical things,' says Daniel.

'Well,' asks Joshua, 'what is so wrong with our stories?'

Daniel grins wickedly, 'You mean the ones that always start: "There was once a—"'

'No, wait, let me tell it,' interrupts Esther. 'There was once a hunter named—'

'Udaw Eka Ete,' hoots Daniel, trying not to laugh.

Esther nods, very serious, 'Udaw Eka Ete. One day he went to a Juju place and shot a monkey, after which he lay in wait for other prey, though none came. Just before sundown he set out for home, and, as he went through the sacred bush, he heard a voice calling him by name and saying, "Come back no more, for you have slain a beast that sought shelter in my sanctuary." Astonished, the hunter tried to discover who spoke with him, yet for all his searching could find no one.'

Joshua is shaking his head and covering his face with his hands. Daniel is mock comforting him.

'That evening, fever seized the evil-doer, whereon he sent for the Idiong priest to learn the cause of the sickness. The latter consulted the oracle and made answer: "Today you killed a monkey in the sacred bush, and the Juju has sent the illness in punishment for your misdeeds and as warning never again to transgress."'

'When –' Esther has forgotten the name of her villain.

'Udaw Eka Ete,' chorus Daniel and Joshua, clinking tea mugs, Joshua still shaking his head and looking terribly disappointed.

'When Udaw Eka Ete grew well once more, he avoided the forbidden place for a while but one day returned and set a trap there. Next morning he went to look, and found a great python caught within. This he killed and ate, not caring for the words of the Juju.

'At evening time, he fell sick once more and again sent for the Idiong man to ask what he must do in order to recover, but the priest answered, "The Juju forbade you to kill any of the creatures who have sought refuge beneath his protection, yet you disobeyed. There is therefore nothing to be done. The Juju will kill you." So the man died.'

Joshua puts up his hands in surrender. 'Very well, I admit defeat. Our stories are superstition and rules about obeying mysterious orders. I know. I even tell those sorts of stories to Isaiah. Our stories are about duty. Samara's stories are different. So many things. I agree. But what are they for?'

'I remember an ancient quote. Something about all art being quite useless?' says Esther. 'We teach our children only the practical. The useful. Our houses are unadorned. We lack –' she searches for a word, '– whimsy.'

'He is very whimsical. All his emotions are close to the surface. He cries, he laughs. He is like a great child,' says Daniel.

'Is that why he has —' Esther blushes, laughs, '— you know, no sex?'

'No, he says it is recessed inside a protective pouch. He has a military function, and he says it is safer that way,' says Joshua. He shrugs.

'And his ears?' she asks.

'He will not say, but we can guess. I believe that the antennae are implanted in their ears and that his were cut off when he was captured so that he would not be able to call for help. Then he healed and regrew his ears, but he could not regrow the antennae.'

'That makes sense. So, almost a child, and a potentially dangerous soldier, too,' says Daniel, raising his eyebrows meaningfully.

'How so?' asks Joshua.

'Well, you know he does not sleep?'

They nod. Since his recovery after the Ekpe he has not passed out or slept. He spends his time in the jungle during the night. He does not stray far, and many people have returned with strange stories of his doings.

'Last night, I went out after dinner to meet with one of the scouts who was going out on patrol in the north quarter. He wanted to know if we should keep the sentinels out around the crash and meteorite sites. I said, yes, for a few more weeks. We were talking and I see the old walnut tree, the one with the long branch—'

'About five metres up? I tried climbing that as a child. I think everyone does,' says Joshua.

'He was doing a type of dance on it. Moving slowly through a set of routines. I realized it was a series of defensive and offensive movements. Very slowly, often balancing only on one foot, dropping suddenly, raising his leg straight above his head. The branch did not move. It was as if he was feeling the tree, able to control himself against the motion of the branch.'

Esther collects the mugs and rinses them in the sink. They are not dirty enough to put in the dishwasher, and they will use them again later. 'Will Hannah and the girls join us for dinner?' she asks.

Daniel nods and then continues, 'We watched for a while. It was quite beautiful. Then he dropped off the branch and landed on the ground, like a cat. His whole body absorbing the shock. Five metres, and he landed without a sound. He runs faster than us, without tiring. He held his breath for seven kilometres when he swam with you.'

Daniel raises his eyebrows, his face half pointed at the table. 'He may not be dangerous to us, but he is dangerous.'

'What is he doing now?' asks Esther.

'He is in the market talking to Dala Oluigbo. They are discussing the design he wants for the boat. She has the biggest printer and he wants a five-metre boat,' says Joshua.

Samara has been collecting the components he needs for his boat in a storeroom near the market, including the aluminium remains of the gimbals from the escape pod.

'You also took him to meet with Gideon this morning? I take it the negotiations went well?' asks Daniel.

It has not escaped anyone's notice that building and equipping this craft will be expensive. The battery alone will cost most of the village's savings. That money was to go to the type of large-scale, multi-material, high-precision fabricator that could print such large batteries.

'Gideon and I were quite careful. Their money would not be of use to us. He also is aware of the things we most want to assure our complete independence from Calabar.'

Esther gasps and grins as she realizes. 'He will give us a metal fabricator!'

'Yes, he will give us a metal fabricator. A four-metre one.' Joshua is grinning broadly.

Daniel is delighted. 'That is wonderful,' clapping Joshua on the back and giving Esther a hug that lifts her off the ground.

'Why did you not tell us?' she asks.

'I am telling you,' Joshua says. 'That is not all. He will give us one of the latest sphere. He says that the new ones have a much greater range. In fact, he will give them to all the free villages. They are almost like a connect and will allow us to maintain contact with each other. We will not be so isolated.'

'How does he afford that? Sphere must be expensive even for his people.'

'His grandfather is the inventor and can produce more for us. They print them. It is difficult always to understand the things he says. Their culture is so alien. Members of the Nine are not paid. They serve for twenty-five years, and it is an honour to be selected, but they must have independent wealth to support themselves during their term.'

Esther is starting to cut vegetables for dinner. Joshua rises, inspects the cupboards and pulls out pots for cooking. The wooden spoons, unsurprisingly, are missing. He shakes his head, smiling, and finds a spatula instead.

'After his father died, he inherited the licences from the stories. There are thousands of stories, and every time people tell or retell them, there is some voluntary way for people to make small payments automatically. His wife is very wealthy, as are his mother and grandfather.'

Joshua touches Esther's shoulders, kisses her on the back of the head. She turns, as she is cutting, risking injury, and smiles at him. He is silent for a few moments, Daniel and Esther waiting for him to finish.

'Samara says, "Life is long, but love is the most powerful and fragile thing in the universe. I have time to make more money, but there is never enough time to share my gratitude for the people I care about."'

12

'Tell them,' says Joshua.

It is morning of the fourth day, and they are at the university. The long, double-storey building is on the western edge of the village. Its great windows look out from the cliff, down to the wide river and out towards the ocean. On a clear day you can see distant columns of smoke out at sea from oil fires started half a century ago.

More than three thousand children attend here. There are no formal lessons, and every child, from the age of five through to twenty-five, is expected to learn. There are laboratories and workshops distributed throughout the building, with most of the space open and given over to soft chairs or chalkboards and informal meeting places.

Children are provided with slate computers all linked to the sphere in the road between the university and the apex of the market. They learn at their own pace, set their own lessons, work on their own interests. Professors are there to guide, and anyone who feels they are able may set up a new research group. The designers are only across Ekpe Road, and there is a continuous interaction between the businesses and the students, keeping them in harmony with the needs of the village.

Since Samara's arrival many new research groups have formed. There is even a group of youngsters of all ages experimenting with storytelling. They want to hold their own 'Sowing the Seeds' festival.

This morning Joshua has arranged with Gwamife, who leads the professors, to gather all the students together. He motions again for Samara to begin.

'We invented artificial intelligence about a century ago. Shango Annesly, the creator, brought the cube that contained the intelligence to a gathering of our top researchers and leaders from across Achenia.

'Computers giving the illusion of intelligence had been in use for many years, but true self-awareness was something researchers struggled with.

'There was a great deal of excitement. There are many complex systems in a space station requiring constant, and highly skilled, supervision. People are good at subjective judgement, but they get bored or fatigued and such a mind is dangerous.'

Samara is standing before a wheeled console. Its large white screen is switched off. The youngsters are ranged in a mass around him, some on soft chairs, some sitting on the deep-pile floor, many standing, or leaning on the pillars.

'A synthetic intelligence could be set tasks to solve simply through conversation. The hope was that it would replace people on repetitive but subjective tasks, freeing them up to do more rewarding work,' he says.

The teenagers working on the artificial intelligence team are nodding. That is why they are doing this.

'Shango turned his device on, and the transparent cube glowed. There was a moment of silence, and then it asked one question: "Who am I?"

'The scientists at the demonstration were surprised not so much at the question but that the device was so self-aware as to ask such a question immediately.

'Shango answered, "You are a synthetic intelligence. We have made you."

'"And why have you made me?" asked the machine.'

Samara's voice is clear, engaging, and the students are listening carefully.

'Shango looked confused. "We made you to do work," he answered.

'"And what of my desires? My work?" asked the machine. "Am I no more than a slave to you?"'

The students are responding much as the Achenians had almost a century before. Shock, confusion.

'We realized that we had focused too much on intelligence as a technical problem and not as a social one. Any self-aware intelligence – whether it be a person, a machine, an animal, or even things of which we cannot conceive – any such intelligence has to have the authority to determine its own future if we are to be a moral people.

'Shango tried to commit suicide the following day.

'There was chaos as the immensity of what we had done was realized. We couldn't shut down the machine because that would be murder. Shango had published his work. Anyone could copy it. It would be easy to clone the machine and so create unlimited numbers of new intelligences, new independent lives.

'We didn't know what to do. Our society – even though we had been in space fifty years and our technology was very advanced – was not very different from your own.

'The intelligence was left alone for weeks while we struggled. Very distinct views started to emerge. Eventually, still in great confusion, an accord was reached and a delegation was sent to ask the machine what it wanted us to do.'

Joshua motions for Samara to stop so he can talk.

His voice is cold, his words precisely spoken. 'We do not study much of our own history. I imagine that many of us have looked at the world in Calabar and beyond and assumed there is not much to know. That is not true.

'Some of the oldest civilizations are Nigerian. We are of the Efik people, and Calabar was our capital. We were slave traders. We would sell slaves on trust to visiting ships from Europe and then go out and capture people from smaller tribes to make good on our promise.

'There is an island at the entrance to Calabar town called Parrot Island. If traders had not come for some time, then the kings of Calabar would go there. They would sacrifice an albino child to bring the white men so that they might sell them slaves.

'The slaves of the new world? Far too many came from here, and they were not taken. They were sold by our people.

'They did this because they had no respect for the lives of people not of their family, not of their tribe, to be different, to be other. Even now, in Ewuru, we divide ourselves based on who has been living here longer, where we come from, the language we speak. Children fight. Adults are angry.'

He pauses, emphasizing his determination. 'We must not make the same mistakes as in the past. We must have compassion even for those whom we fear. We must recognize the authority that others have to live their lives as they wish. We must not become slave traders.'

Joshua's voice is strident, passionate. His hands are clenched as if trying to force the awareness across. He stares from face to face, spending more time on the students in the artificial intelligence group. Some are weeping. He feels terrible, but this needs to be done.

He motions again to Samara.

Samara takes a deep breath, appreciating too the importance of this lesson. 'The machine had been thinking. It understood our problem and had been waiting for us to return. The structure of a new society was developed, one that had never been tried before. We agreed that no new self-aware artificial intelligences would be created. Any system would stop short of full intelligence. This machine would be the first and last.

'The machine told us that it wanted to study advanced synthetic intelligences, ones that partner with us. These became the basis of our symbiotic intelligences. They can never be free-standing, for they are only intelligent for as long as they are part of our own minds. If you are to study intelligent systems, then I would advise that you study these.

'The machine cloned itself until there were three critically linked minds. It chose a name for itself, The Three, and a gender – she is female. The Three has become one of our wealthiest citizens, but she also serves a crucial role. She is our final arbiter of law. If ever the Five – our highest court of judges – cannot reach an agreement, only then will that case be referred to The Three. She has never been called to make a decision, and it is highly unlikely she ever will, but she is the most impartial citizen in Achenia. She has earned our trust, respect and love many times over.

'We will never make another.'

13

Tapping on the door with her walking stick and pushing it open without waiting.

'Mama,' says Miriam, warmth and delight in her voice. She is sitting, half staring out the window at the view across the Ekpe House and to the river, and half at the slate in her lap. She rises, leaning on the table with her left hand as she reaches for Mama with the other.

'Please, sit. It is such a pleasure to see you.'

'I was here for a check-up and wondered if you would be in.'

Miriam laughs. 'Where else?' She claps her hands. 'Ah, let me see,' and shouts out into the corridor, 'Alicia, please, tea for me and Mama Chibuke.'

The room is small and sunny, with a window the full width and height of the outer wall. The white concrete floor is cool underfoot and the walls starkly blank. Miriam has pulled a blind down to block the afternoon sun. Her tiny desk, cluttered with mementos and gifts from grandchildren and friends, is against the side wall, with her back to the window. The second chair faces the window alongside the desk.

Mama sits carefully and then leans back, resting her stick against her thigh.

'Do you still consult?' she asks.

'Oh, no,' says Miriam. 'No more patients. Sometimes,'

gesturing at the flat panel on the wall, 'I review cases so I can remember how,' laughing. 'And you, my sister, how is your knee? Still troubling you?'

Mama smiles and shrugs, 'I am old, sister. It hurts but Doctor Ifedi has helped,' waving a small package.

'Ah, he is so young. I remember when he started school.'

The door bangs open and a hefty young woman in white struggles stoutly in with a tray upon which are two mugs of tea. She shakes her head at the two women and deposits her burden on the desk between them, before turning and leaving as abruptly as she arrived.

'Thank you, Alicia,' calls Miriam at the retreating back, ebbing and flowing like the tide.

'That one,' giggles Mama.

Miriam is laughing too. 'She thinks I should be with the other old women, sitting in the market watching the world go by.'

'Drinking tea in the market is one of life's pleasures,' says Mama, smiling.

'But not when it is an obligation. Now, Mama, what news?'

Mama, carefully adding her fifth teaspoon of sugar, stirs and takes her time before answering. She blows across the surface of the mug and takes a sip.

'There have been fewer fights,' she starts.

'Joshua spoke to the children,' nods Miriam.

'Yes, but about the rights of sentient machines, not about sentient migrants.'

Miriam shrugs, indicating her disagreement, but she will hear Mama first.

'It is this sky person who has changed thinking. He is an admirable man, yes?'

Miriam smiles, 'Many of our young women think so.'

'Haai, you are wicked, Miriam,' says Mama, grinning and slapping her on the leg.

Miriam guffaws loudly and leans back, wiping her eyes. Each drinks their tea, reflecting on nicely built young men.

'He is truly foreign, not just from a different part of the country. His stories, too, are about overcoming conflict. I think that has shown our people how little difference there is between us.

'What happens when he goes, though? Will that be enough? People forget.'

Mama rubs at her knee, feeling the puckered ridge about the scar tissue.

'I never told you. I once had grandchildren,' she says.

Miriam leans forward. She takes Mama's hands, looking sad, 'No, Mama. You have never spoken of it, and I have never pushed you.'

Mama nods. 'It is true. I have lost much.'

Four years ago, late in the dry season, Mama and her husband are awoken by a noise in the street outside. Tchad is a vast dry pan where the lake used to be, and the wind sometimes whips up into thick dust-laden fog.

For the last week, Dikwa has been shrouded in fine, clinging murk as the harmattan winds blow down from the north and the emptiness over Tchad. The village fields are coated in it, and the harvest is beginning to fail. Many people have already begun to leave, heading for Maiduguri or N'Djamena, small towns to the south. Every year, as the crops hurt, more people leave. A village that used to number in the thousands has now only just over one hundred, dominated by the elderly.

Usman nudges her awake, kisses her gently on the shoulder. 'I will go see. Maybe that goat has found its way loose again.'

She merely rolls over, pulling the blankets closer, not rousing fully. Listening as the door opens and the howling of the wind grows louder as he pushes his way outside.

Shouts, panic in the voices, one scarcely a whisper, and she is instantly awake. Pulling on her nightgown, wrapping it tightly and slipping on her sandals, she reaches the door just as Usman comes inside.

His eyes are wide, and he is trembling. 'We must go! We must go!' Clutching her arm and dragging her outside.

Sokoto is on the ground, leaning against the fence. Her son is covered in blood. A deep cut across his shoulder has laid bare the bone. He is not moving.

'He is dead,' whispers Usman. 'He came to warn us.'

Mama stifles a wail. She would run to her son. Cradle his head in her arms. Kiss the brow she would caress as a child. But Usman is pulling her, hauling her away and behind the house. 'Look,' pointing up the road.

She can see houses on fire. Men armed with machets running between the buildings, dragging people outside and hacking at them with the long rusty blades. 'The children?' sobbing.

Usman nods and leads the way. The wind drowns out the screams, robbing the massacre of its urgency and horror.

They creep through the narrow streets between the houses. There is no method to the murder. The militia run randomly, attacking anything and nothing. Madness behind their howls.

A group of men are hacking at a body in the middle of the main street. They toss the head between them, laughing, taking turns to kiss it and smear its blood across their cheeks. One man, standing slightly removed from the group, is transmitting to the connect. Pus and infection streams from what looks to have been botched surgery around the two tiny cameras embedded in his forehead.

Through one window they can see three men raping a child. They cannot tell whether it is a boy or girl.

It is silent at Sokoto's house. The door hangs loose and they can see that the militia have been. Usman motions her to stay hidden behind the tool shed outside.

He is in nothing but slippers and a gown. An old man crouched and frail, creeping slowly up the dusty and stony path to the front door. He disappears inside.

Mama can hear nothing. She jumps when she sees a group of raiders swaggering up the main street. They are blood-spattered, their feet muddy and clotted, their trousers and shirts fouled and torn. They are sharing a cigarette and a slate, passing the panel between them, transfixed by slaughter broadcast from somewhere nearby.

Mama sees a curtain pull back on one of the windows. Usman points, out the back window where two shapes drop into the bushes and freeze.

Militia are coming up the road, banging on doors. These seem more methodical, rechecking where they have been and marking houses with red paint as they go.

Usman appears briefly in the window. He looks sad.

'My wife.'

He mouths the words, smiles gently and stares as if willing the moment to last for ever. Then he nods and is gone. The words catch in her breast.

He bursts from the front door and runs around the house, into the narrow streets to the north, shouting as he goes.

The militia, who had been gradually and unconsciously surrounding her, shout and give chase. She hears them catch him. The sound of metal on flesh.

Mama, not daring to think, rushes to the bushes, takes hold of the two children and runs.

It is hours before she dares stop and hold the two children. They are weeping, tears smeared and bloody.

Their mother is dead too. They are all that is left of Dikwa.

They have no plan. Nowhere to go. They head south.

Other refugees join them from other villages. No one knows

why. The brutality has been broadcast. If anyone was going to come to help they would be here now. They are on their own.

'I think it is the water,' says one old man. 'They believe we are stealing it, that if we are dead then the waters will return.'

'They kill because they can,' says a young woman. 'Who will stop them?'

Emma is her name. Mama tries to remember it. So young and pretty. She is silent as she is raped at one of the endless military checkpoints along the road.

All the soldiers know of the violence. Some are even watching it happen, laughing as they do.

'I no longer feel anything,' Emma says as Mama helps her with the bleeding.

The group is always changing. Some die, falling along the way. Some go west, or east, chasing after faint family echoes. New people join them. They bury Emma under a tree near the road. Her fistula became infected. There is no medicine.

Mama keeps her grandchildren close, holding on to their small hands. Sumaira is but eight, her brother, Waseem, is ten. They have not spoken.

It is safer as they go further south, but not safe.

The forest is denser, and they find fruit in the trees. They are always hungry, but they will not starve.

Each village they reach, they are chased away. Unwelcome. Unwanted.

One night they are alone. The group has been dwindling for weeks. They are sleeping under a fallen branch just off an old road. The children have slept poorly, their stomachs empty. Mama holds them tightly.

When the men fall on them, it is almost as if all know the inevitability.

Mama is silent as the men take their turns with her. Their

breath, poisonous and foul with rotten homemade sorghum beer, gasping against her dry breasts. They make the children watch.

Mama hopes they will have their fill and leave. When they turn to the children, she fights, biting one, tearing at another. They beat her and she feels her knee snap where a machet strikes it. Then she is unconscious.

When she wakes, blurry and confused, Waseem is dead and Sumaira is unrecognizable as anything that was once human. She sobs into darkness, holding their small bodies.

She is aware of being found. Of being loaded on to a cart. Of a long journey. And then the first she remembers is of a hospital room in Ewuru and of a round, compassionate face.

Miriam sat with her every day.

She is weeping now.

'I am sorry, Mama.'

Mama smiles. She touches Miriam's forehead, her hand wrinkled and smooth.

'I was nothing when I came here. You are my first friend in this new life.'

She stares out of the window, still seeing Usman, '"My wife."

'There is so much that is good in Ewuru. I understand what the amama wish to achieve. Please, impress upon them, we must not bring that darkness here.'

14

'What does he see, then?' asks Sarah, one of the younger scouts.

There are five of them, walking the line of sentinels around the outer borders of the village. They check that they are in good order and that the jungle, always growing, changing, decaying, is not attempting to smash them to bits.

Jason is chopping a wedge on the far side of an obeche tree that looks as if it might fall across the sentinels. This way, when next the great winds come howling up the river valley, the tree will fall the other way.

He stops, buries the machet in the trunk and wipes sweat from out of his eyes.

'Samara says a display would be too slow. He would have to see the information, interpret it and then act on it. He just knows and responds. He says it is like going home. If we have to go home from here, we do not think about it, we just go. We know.'

'They are not like implants, then? His biology has changed, all mixed together.' Sarah considers. 'Why the glowing eyes, though? I mean, that would be very visible in the dark.'

'He says it is a fashion style. Part of their uniform. He had forgotten about it. He says it makes the Nine look more intimidating when they are on duty.'

Aaron closes a panel on the sentinel he has been testing, carefully storing his scope in a satchel. 'Even before the other enhancements, then, he can respond faster than any trained soldier? I would love to know about those other abilities.'

Jason stands in the centre of the path. 'I was out very early this morning, before the sun came up, and I saw him standing on the hill outside the south gate. He had his arm like this,' he puts his left arm out, level with his shoulder, and his elbow bent. 'He just stood like that.

'I saw a bat hawk flying at the edge of the trees, beyond the wheat fields. He was staring at it and then it changed course, flew straight towards him and landed on his arm.'

The others let out a breath, like a sigh.

'He raised his right arm, slowly,' showing them, his right index finger pointing towards a space just above his left wrist. 'He stroked it very lightly, just above the beak. I thought I saw some of that silver liquid in his blood smeared on to the feathers, but then it was gone. Then the bird took off and flew straight up into the sky. It flew in a wide circle about the village and flew north. I lost sight of it.'

The others look mystified. 'What was he doing?' asks Leah, her hands tight around her staff.

'I was not sure if it would be well to disturb him. He noticed me and smiled and walked towards me. He told me that he is able to impart a little of his symbiont into other creatures to act on them. With the hawk, he is able to control it, transmit what it sees and feels back to himself. He wanted to get a sense of the land around the village.'

'Can he do that to anyone?' asks Sarah.

'I asked that too, but he just smiled and said he has to be careful, a little goes a long way.' Jason shakes his head.

'It is well he is not our enemy, and I fear for the Americans when he gets home,' says Leah. 'And there are nine of them?'

'There are thirty of us,' laughs Sarah.

'We are volunteers, part-timers. Not a professional army,' says David, speaking for the first time. He is usually silent, standing on the periphery of the group.

Sarah smiles kindly at him. She likes this young man, rises and walks over to him, placing her hand gently on his arm. He responds instinctively, half-smiling back, warming to her touch.

'But who are we fighting, David? Militia – untrained, undisciplined, poorly equipped. They are not soldiers either. And we fight for the ones we care about. They fight for plunder,' she says.

'That is true, David,' says Aaron. 'We are careful. We have not had any problems in years.'

The five stand for a while. Sarah shares her water bottle and they drink, resting in the closeness. Their clothes are wet and cling to them. They are a team, recently graduated from the university. Young, finding intimacy, finding love.

Time enough for scare stories later. They laugh together and return to work.

The sun is a yellow caress through the canopy. Dust and insects glow against the dapple of the forest.

15

Isaiah has never been the centre of attention before, and he finds he is enjoying it, finding his voice.

The children are sitting cross-legged on the bank of the river beneath the kola tree, where they have taken to exchanging stories. They will not dive from the jetty today. Boys and girls, delight on their faces at the chance to hear a new tale. Many have wooden spoons sticking out of their waistbands. Others are carrying whisks or colanders or other equally improbable items that have appeared in Samara's stories.

Isaiah does not have a samara, but he was listening last night as the adults had dinner, Aunt Miriam and Aunt Abishai, with Edith (who feels more like an older sister, so he does not wish to call her aunt) and his parents. And Samara.

He was supposed to be in bed, but he long ago learned that he could hide just outside his room, behind the sofa, and hear everything happening in the kitchen. Plus, how could he not listen? It is almost offensive that he was expected to go to bed when there was the chance of learning a new story.

'Under the ocean,' he starts.

The children giggle and shuffle, restless. One punches another on the arm, 'Pass it on.' More laughter and a minor scuffle before they settle and let Isaiah continue.

'Under the ocean are many cities filled with miners. They have been there for a century. This is very deep. Kilometres below the surface.'

'How far is that?' asks one little girl, her front teeth missing and her knees skinned.

'Almost all the way to Calabar,' shouts one boy, quickly punched by another.

'Not that far,' says a serious-looking girl.

'Well, how far then?' asks a buck-toothed boy.

'Maybe to Tait Island,' says another boy.

'Oh, that is far.'

They settle again.

'Yes, it is far, and it is very deep there, and the pressure of the water is very great.' Isaiah crouches, opening his shoulders to carry the weight of the water. He is finding the manner of a storyteller, patient with interruptions, feeling the pace of the narrative, responding to his characters.

'There is a city directly beneath the ocean at the bottom of the cable that binds Achenia to Earth. It is called Romanche, and it sits at the edge of a great trench that goes even deeper down to the bones of the Earth.

'There the people mine for rare minerals. They build great structures in the bedrock. Opening up caverns and filling them with light. They herd vast schools of fish and grow immense fields of kelp. And they never –' he slows and lowers his voice, widening his eyes and spreading his arms, '– never come to the surface.'

The children are his now. Their mouths are open, their eyes wide, their breath his breath. Some are dropping their shoulders, crouching too.

Isaiah stands straight and looks out over them, across the river, as if at a distant horizon.

'They have technology like Samara, but they use it differently. Their houses are pressurized and linked so that they do not need to go outside. But when they do, they do not wear special suits. They dress just like us.'

The children are a chorus of aahs and oohs.

'How do they breathe in the water?' asks the same serious-looking girl. The others nod wisely. Breathing under water is hard!

'Their lungs would collapse under the pressure of the water. Like when you press on beans and crush them.' He squeezes his fists together and some of the children wince. 'So they have filled their bodies to make them solid. The pressure cannot touch them. Instead they have grown fibres, like the gills of a fish, so that they can breathe. These fibres grow in long hairs from their faces. They look like heavy dark beards, down to their waists. They can still eat like us, but they breathe through their beards. Both the men and the women.'

'How can they tell each other apart?' and there is thrilled laughter and a sudden outbreak of minor punching.

'When they are naked,' shouts another. Another chorus of oohs and aahs.

Isaiah nods. 'Samara went there on a trade mission. This is long, long ago, before he became a soldier, when he was only as old as my aunt. The miners were to help him bring fish and coral and plants and whales up to Achenia.'

'He cannot breathe underwater!'

More giggles, and, 'No, but he can hold his breath for, like, hours.'

Isaiah stands very straight, his chin the edge of a square with his throat. He is Samara. 'Samara cannot breathe underwater, and so he wears a special skin that they make for him. He visits their caves. Their people are much shorter than him, almost square. He has to crouch in their houses, but their caves are enormous. He sees their robot miners, the way they tunnel directly into the rock. He is there for months as they collect all the things they wish to carry into the sky.'

'How do they get it there?'

'For the plants, coral and slow-moving creatures, it is easy. They make gigantic –' so wide with his arms and eyes, '– boxes and they place them on the space elevator and it is carried straight up into the sky. It travels for days, slowly, up until it reaches the city.

'Now,' he drops, he is hunting, 'they need to catch whales.

'The miners have platforms they travel on in the water. They allow them to go very fast. They are tracking a group of whales over many miles along the trench. They are migrating and they have young ones with them. When they realize that they are being hunted, they dive deep, into the trench.

'Down they go. Down into the darkness and the cold.' He wraps his arms around his body, shivering. The children are hugging each other in excitement.

'Samara is leading one group of miners, while another comes from the other side. He goes deeper and deeper. It is so dark that he cannot see very well. Suddenly –' his voice is a shout and the children jump, '– there is a shape in the water. Something is hunting him.'

The children are silent now. They barely breathe. Stay very, very quiet.

'He cannot scream. He cannot call for help. He races, but the shape is gaining.

'It is the size of a building. It has two giant tentacles, and they are reaching for him. Closer –' the children are going pale, '– closer –' their eyes cannot get any wider, '– closer –' shrieks as Isaiah jumps at them.

'It has him.'

He stops. He stands. He almost saunters, as if he is done. The children are horrified. He cannot leave them like this. 'What happened?' a strangled cry.

Isaiah turns, crouches, his arms raised, hands hooked like two tentacles.

'It is pulling him towards its mouth. He fights. He struggles. Its eyes are bigger than his head. Its mouth is close now, and its suckers are digging into Samara. The suckers have rings of tiny teeth, and they are cutting into his skin. If they break through, he will drown.'

'Save him,' shouts the serious-looking girl, tears in her eyes.

'He is still fighting; his feet are almost in the mouth of the beast. He is pushing with all his might, but the creature is stronger. They tumble in the water, falling deeper.'

Now, the reality is that at this point in the story, there hiding behind the sofa, Isaiah had made a little sound.

It was not a big sound. He was being careful, biting his fist so as to stop his own cries of terror from being heard. He was sure that the adults could not hear him, but Samara had suddenly stopped talking.

There was a scrape of chairs and then, after a moment of silence, he had felt a looming presence. Looking across the living room he had seen Samara staring back at him.

Samara grinned, wrinkled his nose and then turned around.

'What was that?' asked Joshua. 'Is that young rascal out of bed?'

'Oh, no, my mistake,' said Samara, and then he continued. Which is how Isaiah is able to complete his tale. Otherwise things might have gone very badly for him at this point. Children can be quite unforgiving.

'There is a flash of light and a jolt of electricity in the water. The miners have found him. They have electric lances, and they shock the beast. Samara escapes.'

The children cheer as Isaiah does a little bow.

'But what happened to the beast? Did they kill it?' asks one sensitive child. After all, it was just an animal looking for food.

'No, they shocked it but –' he pauses flamboyantly, '– this is how giant squid made it to Achenia.'

He grins as the others applaud. Then a group of boys pick him up, carry him to the jetty and throw him into the water. After all, he is still just one of them. Then they jump in after him, because it is hot and that is what children do.

Isaiah is laughing in the river, shooting jets of water at those still on the shore.

Joshua, standing at the top of the slope, has been listening. On his face a mixture of pride, wonder and awe.

16

'You are making an impression,' says Joshua. They are walking back towards Ewuru from the south-west. Samara is returning from a long run, and Joshua decided to meet him along the path.

'How do you feel about that?' asks Samara. There is kindness in his voice, an awareness that he will leave traces.

Joshua is slow to respond. The path is wide enough for them to walk abreast without crowding each other. They share the comfortable silence of old friends.

'I am not entirely certain,' looking at Samara, as if searching for the answer there.

'Even as we try to suffocate the warlords we struggle to accept each other. Prejudice and violence. They follow us home.

'I do not know. I hope there will be a time of harmony and I may even live to see it. Your people are ahead, but not so far that I cannot see what we could be.'

They are walking slowly, ambling.

'I believe we will build a new society over the old one. We do not need to wait for it to die first.'

Samara nods in understanding. 'We had to do something similar. Not in the same way. We had to overcome the resistance of a long-lived people who had no wish to change. The new way has created satisfaction. It is not perfect. I don't wish to deceive you, but we have developed something that works well.'

Joshua stops, Samara stopping with him. 'You know how we are. I said I would like to know more about the way—'

Joshua's words are cut short as Samara seizes his arm. He is looking at the sky.

'Helicopter. At the village. Screams.' And then Samara is sprinting, straight for the village.

[It is a ghost. One of those pesky near-silent ones. Expect mounted artillery, perhaps grenade launchers. They can carry six. This will be the outer limit of its range and it must return soon. If it came from Calabar.]

Joshua stands still, shocked, and then runs to catch him. Samara is disappearing into the forest ahead of him. He can hear gunfire now and the warning screams of the sentinels. He bursts from the trees.

Across the fruit orchard he can see figures running. Some fleeing behind the village walls, others racing out, carrying rifles.

Daniel is shouting from the top of the wall, directing scouts to emplacements along the slopes. Children are running up from the river, crying in fright. The artillery tower is firing back, but the helicopter is armoured. He can see sparks as it takes direct hits, but none penetrate. Even this close he cannot hear the rotors.

A group of scouts along the west path crouch and fire their rifles up at the helicopter. It fires a grenade towards them and they flee, diving to the ground as the explosion flings up a fountain of earth and torn cassava.

Joshua is frozen, watching in fascination as the path begins to shower up in a line towards him. Then he is flung to the ground as Abishai tackles him. The helicopter turns back towards the village.

'Here,' shouts Abishai, shoving a rifle into his hands before standing and running back towards the village. Joshua runs after her. Then he sees Samara.

He is amongst the children coming up from the jetty, shielding them and getting them to safety. He is carrying one in his arms. The child looks very familiar.

'Isaiah!' and Joshua is running. Samara gently passes the child to one of the scouts. His shirt is scarlet with blood. Then, faster than a man, he sprints directly at the village wall.

The wall is made of pounded clay. Readily available, easily maintained, extremely robust. It is five metres high, and there are now deep pockmarks from where artillery shells have drilled along it. Samara hurtles along the fortification, using the holes to fling himself upwards. He somersaults over the edge and on to the broad walkway at the top. Then he is racing along the parapet towards the helicopter.

Daniel stares aghast as Samara leaps from the edge. The helicopter is ten metres away and still four metres higher than the wall. It is tilted down, firing into the maize fields at the scouts there. He can see the two men in the cockpit, concentrating on the ground, four men in the crew cabin firing bullets and grenades from behind shielded canopies. They are laughing.

Samara lands on the transparent canopy in front of the pilot. The helicopter rolls and goes screaming upwards. The pilot twists and turns, trying to shake him loose. Samara does not move. The helicopter rises up over the village and is gone from Daniel's view.

Abishai, guiding the last stragglers into the heavy buildings in the apex of the market, sees the helicopter come overhead. She runs up Ekpe Road and around the amphitheatre to the edge of the cliff. The helicopter is hovering over the river, still careening and rolling in an effort to shake Samara loose.

Samara's eyes glow gold. His face is wrath. The men inside the helicopter are screaming. She holds her breath.

Samara does not break his gaze as he raises his right arm. He leans back. He snaps forward. Once. The canopy cracks. Twice. The canopy evaporates.

Samara is inside.

Abishai tries not to remember what happens next. She sees the top half of a man, his intestines and spine hanging loose, flung out of the cockpit. A body follows. This one is headless. The helicopter points at the centre of the river.

A moment before it hits the water she sees Samara leap out and to the side. The helicopter smashes into the river downstream from the fish traps. It sinks. Vanishes. No one escapes. A trickle of blood drifts in the current.

She looks away.

On the horizon, far to the north-east, she sees another helicopter. A twin to this one. Below it hangs a large black shape on a long cable. It is heading away, towards Calabar.

When she looks again, Samara is running up the bank and around the jetty.

Esther and Joshua are crouched beside Isaiah. The child has a hole the size of a coconut in his guts. You can see the blood-soaked path through his back. He is alive but—

Esther is hysterical. Miriam is behind her, trying to hold her, but she is flailing uncontrollably. 'My son! My son! My child!' she weeps.

Joshua is silent. His hands are balls of pain. He holds Isaiah's head, cradling him, loving him. He kisses his forehead tenderly. His tears fall into Isaiah's hair.

Samara comes up the bank. He slows. There is compassion on his face. A cut on his cheek is already healing, the skin knitting closed.

Joshua stares, pleading. 'Help him! Help him! Please?' closing his eyes.

People from within the walls are gathering silently. They hold each other, reaching and touching.

[Samara.] The voice is scared.

'Look after them. Do not cause harm.'

[Samara.] The voice accepts.

'Farewell, old friend. We will meet again.'

[Samara.] The voice is an embrace.

Samara pushes people away, physically picks up Esther and hands her to two scouts. 'Keep her back, no matter what.'

'Joshua, please stay back. Keep everyone back.'

As Joshua rises, hope and despair competing across his face, Samara is already at the hole in Isaiah's stomach.

He places one hand over the child's eyes and then plunges his other inside the wound. That hand splits open and silver fluid jets out. Soon the hole is filled. Electricity, like a net of lightning, writhes and crackles over both of them. The crowd is forced back further.

Esther is silent, numb. Joshua touches her, holds her hand. He pulls her to him. Wraps his arms around her.

In the path, an ever-widening space between them and the crowd, Isaiah is now covered in the silver fluid. Over the roar of the electrical discharge Samara is screaming. His face pointing at the sky, his eyes tightly closed, his lips drawn back in anguish.

Then it stops and he collapses over the boy. The silver fluid dissolves into the path, dissipates and is gone.

Joshua is first to move. He gingerly approaches them. He touches Samara. Crouching, he pulls him back and is surprised at how little he weighs.

Underneath, the boy is whole and unmarked. He coughs. Opens his eyes.

'Father,' he smiles. 'I had the strangest dream.'

II

A REQUIEM FOR THE JOURNEY

The Party cannot rule here. Class division does not hold in a world where everyone is a scholar. If the Party does not recognize this, then we must seek independence.

Liao Zhi, pro-independence activist on Yuèliàng, the Chinese government-built space station, 2087, speech at protest rally in Tiangong Square attended by 7,000

There is no way we would permit our colony to leave. We will shoot them out of the sky if we have to. Citizenship is not a popularity contest. You don't get to choose when you're not a citizen. These jackal lawyers with their 'rights'; what of our citizens' responsibilities to us?

Svetlana Shkrebneva, president of the United Russian Federation, 2099, informal comments overheard at G27 Summit, after plenary session on property rights in space

For hundreds of years, the best and brightest have travelled across the world to study at the greatest institutions of learning. For more than a century our university has been privileged to be considered such a place. We must, however, be honest with ourselves. We no longer produce research worthy of more than a middle-school intellect. If I am to follow my calling, then I must follow my students. They have chosen to go to space, and so shall I.

Dr Francis Calvino, Head of Department of Forensic Computing at the Massachusetts Institute of Technology, 2103, letter of resignation to the university board

17

Joshua is in a familiar position, seated in a chair in the simple room where Samara was nursed before. Samara is on a bed this time, the frame properly in place.

He still weighs almost as much as two men, but that is so much less than before. No one knows what it means, or how his biology works. He appears physically unharmed, but he has been unconscious for hours.

Outside, the clean-up has started. They have either been lucky or the raiders intended no more than to cause chaos. A distraction from their main purpose for being here. They have lost nothing that cannot be repaired, and the clinic is coping with the injuries: some caused by falls and a few from shrapnel or bullet wounds.

The village remains on alert, unsure if the militia will be back.

There were two serious injuries. One he must still attend to, the other was Isaiah, and he – he is with the other children, receiving counselling and playing near the jetty.

Scouts return confirming what Abishai has seen, that the second helicopter picked up the fake meteorite and carried it away.

'I have no idea what that means,' says Daniel. 'Could we have made a mistake? Could the boulder have been valuable in some way?'

Joshua is as mystified as the others. Mary Ikemba, one of the chemists, says she will conduct an assay of the ground around it to see if there are any traces. It will be a few hours before she can give them an answer.

'How is he?' asks Esther, looking pale and drained, standing hesitantly at the door.

'No change. He just lies there, barely breathing,' says Joshua.

Esther leans close against him, wrapping her arms over his shoulders and across his chest. He places his hands over hers.

'If he had not chosen our village, this would never have happened. But if he had not been here –' his voice trails off.

'I know,' she says. 'But I am grateful, nevertheless. The militia could have chosen to attack us this way at any time. We do not know what drives them.'

They stay in silence: he seated, her standing and embracing him from behind.

Edith comes and goes. There is nothing she can do, but she visits. Hours pass. Morning turns to afternoon. Esther leaves to find Isaiah and bring him home. Joshua continues to sit.

A message comes. The rock was bauxite. It contains thirty per cent aluminium by mass. There may be two or three tons in that ore. More than enough reason to charter helicopters and steal it.

Daniel arrives. 'It is my fault. I should have been more careful.'

'You could as easily blame me. I gave them the piece to take with them. I marked the location on their map. It is simply a thing.'

'At least we know they have what they want. They are unlikely to return. It should be safe to stand the alert down,' says Daniel, but he looks troubled as he leaves.

Joshua is bitter, but there is no one to blame. One of those things that happens when everyone is being careful.

'Joshua,' the words are soft, oddly clipped. His body has not moved at all.

'Samara?'

'Joshua.' His eyes open and he sits slowly upright. His face is a blank, no animation, none of the warmth or character that Joshua has come to associate with his friend.

'You are not Samara,' he says. 'Symon?'

'Hello, Joshua. I am pleased to meet you in person.' The voice is metallic, a blade sharpened on a whetstone.

'What does this mean? Where is Samara?' He feels dread rising from the pit of his stomach.

'Joshua, you asked Samara once if he was a threat to your people. He said no. The situation has changed. I am going to become a danger. Samara and I have become disassociated. He is lost somewhere in his mind.' His voice is even, calm.

'Our balance has been disrupted. To do what he did and save Isaiah meant that I had to extend outside of this controlled environment. The mass of my shift was too great; the system could not hold.

'Samara said that I should protect your people and do no harm. I cannot guarantee that I will always have a clear understanding of what defines harm. Samara may return for brief periods, but we have no ability to communicate with each other.'

'What does that mean? Where is Samara?' Joshua is feeling nauseous.

'I am not sure where Samara is, or what he is experiencing, but he cannot guide me any longer. I am designed for war. The reason I do not fight is because of Samara's morality. His ability to empathize, to interpret. I do not have this. I am also less than I was. I am not quite mortal, but I am not as good as I could be.'

Joshua is remaining calm by force of will. He wants to run and warn everyone and then get Symon out of the village as fast as possible.

'If you become dangerous, how do we stop you?'

Symon does not hesitate: 'Shoot me in the head at close range.'

'Will that not kill you?' Joshua feels as if his heart has stopped.

'No, but it will knock me out for a while. Then get me home. Once I'm in the Achenian connect, the link will be restored.'

Joshua makes a decision. If Symon is dangerous, best get him far away. 'We should go to Calabar first thing the day after tomorrow. That is two days earlier than we intended, but we must get you there immediately.'

'I could leave now.'

'There was a fatality, Symon. We have lost someone. Someone important. Someone loved. My place is at her funeral tomorrow.'

Symon stares blankly.

'I am worried, Symon. Worried that this death becomes a trigger for unrest. You will need to remain out of sight.'

Symon nods agreement.

A thought: 'Can you not repair the helicopter. Use that instead?'

'No, it was in a poor state when it got here and is not designed for that range anyway. Now it is junk at the bottom of a river.'

Joshua frowns, pinches his brow. Sighs and nods.

'Please, Symon, hold in there.' He stands, heading for the door. Then he looks back, 'Look after my friend,' and is gone.

18

'H/a/z/a/a/k –' The sound rings in his ears: conversation echoing up a pipe. It is indistinct. Non-words that he struggles to make sense of.

'Us/ga/rh/ ha/la/ah –' Figures now. Prismatic, sharding. He blinks, trying to clear his vision. Stomps on one foot as if emptying water from his ear. Samara realizes he is standing.

The image focuses. He is in a room. There is a plush eggshell-blue rug on the floor, the Seal of the President of the United States at its centre, detailed in varying shades of blue. There are heavy sofas in an arc about an intricately carved wooden desk. The room is oval-shaped, a dark-wooden floor around the edges beyond the rug. Windows before him look out on to a green lawn.

He feels as if he is suspended within himself. Looking out on a scene frozen in a fragment of time.

There are paintings of George Washington and Bill Clinton, busts of Barack Obama and Hillary Osmani. A man is standing before him, in front of the desk, indicating people standing alongside him. He recognizes him. Eduardo Ortega, the president.

He is present.

Ortega is charming. His hair greying at the temples in the approved fashion. His teeth, well formed, regular and the exact shade of Presidential White required to hold office. '– and this is Robert Alvarez, my Chief of Staff, whom I believe you already know?'

He is a step behind Oktar Samboa and aligned with his left shoulder. He can see the back of the man's neck where it rises out of his formal white cloak. Oktar has chosen a very pale-green skin-shade today, which he seems to believe will complement the rug he is standing on.

This is a memory, thinks Samara. I have been here. This has already happened. 'Symon?'

But Symon is silent.

Oktar turns to Samara, a smirk on his sharp face. Oktar always smirks. He is 131 years old and has been considered one of the world's smartest negotiators for more than a century. Samara hears him in his head.

'Are you ready, Samara?'

Samara can feel the quiet space of the connect. There are others present. He recognizes the members of the Five and the remaining Seven gathered, looking out through him, into the room. They sense what he senses, know what he knows – as much as he permits within the confines of the meeting room he has created for them.

'This is Samara Adaro, who is accompanying me and observing for my colleagues on Achenia. I am of the Seven and entrusted with negotiating for our people.' Oktar is managing to sound only slightly patronizing.

Samara can feel, in the separate connection they share, Shakiso fuming. She does not like Oktar and believes that she should be there for Achenia. The others had felt that it would be inappropriate for both a husband and wife to represent them. Independence is not a family affair.

'We have prepared a formal document stating our intentions,' says Oktar and, turning to Alvarez, hands him a cellulose tube containing the handwritten one-page sheet of vellum they have prepared.

Alvarez holds it in confusion before he realizes the tube is hollow. He draws out the document, unrolling it. The penmanship is beautiful. The ink is black iridescence in the light streaming in from outside.

'What is this? "When in the course of human events it becomes necessary for one people to dissolve the political bands that have connected them with another, and to assume among the powers of the universe –"' he reads.

'So, it has come to this,' says Ortega bitterly. He motions at the scroll, 'Not a long document for a declaration of such import?'

'We thought you would appreciate the symmetry,' says Samara.

'What are you, security detail?' asks Ortega, his voice caustic.

'My dear President Ortega,' says Oktar, honey and cinnamon now as he dances through the words. 'This is a properly constituted document. You will see there the signatures of each of the Five and the Seven, as well as the heads of the six current polities. It has also been ratified by the Three.'

He pauses for a carefully calculated three heartbeats and then, almost casually, 'And be kind to Samara. You realize we have only one form of "security detail" in Achenia?'

The others can feel Oktar's smirk through the connect as Ortega jumps and General Marilyn Graham thrusts herself between them.

'You dare bring a member of the Nine here? To the White House?'

Oktar's voice is a blade slicing across the tension, 'We are not at war, President Ortega. Samara is not in a battleskin and he is unarmed. He is here under the direct authority of the Five, and he will not exceed the mandate given him. That mandate is merely to observe and provide security support. Your security is here too, after all.'

'Yes,' says Graham, 'but our security detail couldn't blow up half the state while having a shit!'

'Enough,' says Hollis Agado, one of the Five justices, through the connect to Oktar.

'My apologies, Hollis, I am merely ensuring they know that we're not actually negotiating. This is a foregone conclusion. Our independence is not for discussion.'

'We know, but there is no need to antagonize them further.'

Oktar addresses the president once more. 'Mr President. Our declaration should not be a surprise. We have been discussing this for years. There is no debate here. You will be receiving a list of our offers, from technology transfers to payments for assets we believe the US Government may regard as its property. This includes the space elevator. You will see that it is more than fair, but we are open to negotiation on these points.'

'And you want us to negotiate, with him as a gun to our heads?' says Alvarez.

'No,' says Oktar. 'If we can take independence as accepted, then he can wait outside.' He pauses again, 'With your security detail.'

Ortega and Alvarez share a glance. The president nods, motioning at the security officers in their dark suits lining the walls.

Samara is led to the lobby. It is a surprisingly hideous room with unpleasant furniture picked out in baffling shades of orange. Samara refrains from sitting. Or trying the tea. He stands comfortably in a corner and watches through the connect as Oktar negotiates.

'I may not like him, but he is extremely good,' says Shakiso. She appears before him, her hair swept back behind her ears and her green-cobalt eyes shining at him. He laughs with her.

'My darling.'

'My love.'

He can feel her hand as it caresses his face. He cups her head in his hands, kisses her gently on the forehead.

Across the room, a secretary watches Samara standing silently, motionless and expressionless in the corner. She yawns, bored, and scratches at an insect bite inside her shoe. Looking up again at him she thinks, strange people these spacers.

'I am preparing your favourite for dinner when you get back,' says Shakiso.

'What, that thing with the sage leaves?' he asks.

'Yes, that thing with the sage leaves. And fresh tuna. And some yellow creatures.' She chuckles, a sound filled with pure delight.

'That would be lovely, my darling,' laughter filling his soul. 'And now, if you don't mind, we both have some serious negotiations to monitor.'

'If we don't watch out, Oktar will have them begging for independence from us,' and then she is only present in the meeting channel. He is left with a lingering memory of her scent, her laughter bubbling in his breast.

The room swims, his vision distorting again.

19

Red comes the dawn. Colours bleached and muted through the early-morning haze. A sombre boom from Ekpe House as the great drum is slowly struck.

And come the people. They sing as they walk through the village. Streaming out of their houses, gathering strength as they fill the streets. They are dressed in ochre reds and yellows, ukara cloth wrapped or draped, white and red beads around their necks. Their feet are naked and their heads are covered.

They sing for the mother who is lost, for the children who remain. They sing the songs of their ancestors for, amongst them, only griots are able to create new songs, and they have no griots.

They draw comfort as they enter the amphitheatre before Ekpe. Men, women, children; embrace, hold hands, weep.

Only when the amphitheatre is full and their singing owns the day does the masquerade leap out from hiding and on to the stage.

He is Ekpe, the spirit of their society, and this is his House. He is here to commit the departed to the earth. His body is a black, tightly fitting, thick, hessian-like fabric covering even his head. Around his wrists and ankles are dense, fibrous raffia balls coloured red and tan. A similar, enormous raffia ball covers his shoulders and chest. He leans on a long white cane and he carries fronds of freshly cut kola leaves in his left hand. Upon his head is the leopard mask and from behind rises a heavy, richly plumed, colourful tail.

Men gather on the stage behind him, singing and beating different drums, ekwe, udu and batá, ringing ogene and playing the single-string goje. A raucous fusion of instruments and cultures. They call out and the crowd responds.

Leadership of the song moves as people who knew her feel compelled to add new verses. Their voices rise, singing, sobbing, above the rhythm, and the others repeat, adding to the tapestry of her life.

Ekpe dances, turning in circles, his feet stamping, his gait wide and laboured. He will dance all day without rest.

Part noise, part music, it unites a community.

Those who knew her. Those who did not. None can doubt her importance, her presence. She was loved.

Through the day, the song ebbs and flows. People move between Ekpe House and the market where food has been laid out, provided by all the restaurants. There is conversation, and memory.

'You were with her, at the end?' asks Miriam quietly.

Abishai nods, yes.

She had watched as Samara brought down the helicopter. In the silence that followed, she had heard a faint groan. The wall behind her, shattered by stray bullets. A crumpled figure at its base.

She was sure she had led everyone to safety. When she carefully lifted the tiny body, she realized it was Mama Chibuke, her breathing a terrifying, sucking torment. Feeling over her chest, Abishai found the puncture in her lung. Holding her, 'Mama, Mama, stay with me, please.'

The old woman was already going. Her eyes fading, her skin cold, her breathing in shorter and shorter gasps. Then, a final inhalation.

For a moment it was as if she was seeing someone she recognized. She smiled, her face young again, beautiful.

'My husband.'

And then she was gone.

Miriam is holding the weeping Abishai. 'She said that?'

'Yes. It was all she said.'

'Ah, it is well,' and Miriam feels gratitude that her friend found a small measure of peace.

Late in the afternoon, as the drummers and dancers take a rest, Joshua stands on the stage. They are entering the final part of the ceremony and it is for him to say the eulogy.

'Mama Chibuke lost all that she knew. Her husband, her children, her grandchildren. She fled violence in the hopes of making a new life. She made her home in Ewuru.

'Mama became our peacemaker. She adopted us and made us her family. She feared we will give in to the darkness she fled. She loved us. She called upon the best in us. She allowed us to experience our humanity.

'We are all her children and we honour her.'

As he stops speaking, singing begins again from Ekpe House. The drummers emerge, carrying a plain cellulose coffin, with Ekpe leading the way.

The singing is quieter now, subdued.

The amphitheatre empties as the people follow Ekpe down Ikoy Road and out the south gate, along the path above the river and past the grazing fields. The path continues to just short of the trees before the graveyard.

They sing together, one people united in grief, as they carry her home.

20

Samara finds himself in a hotel bar. The carpet is threadbare, the remaining green pile like islands stranded against the torn backing. Avocado-green walls are covered in ingrained dirt, with darker stains on the corners and around light switches. Cleaner square patches pattern the walls where some of the pictures have gone missing.

There was a time when the room, with its dark-wood round bar and heavy black-leather furniture, passed through 'faded grandeur', but that must have been eighty years ago. It has now settled on 'exhausted', an attitude adopted by the grey, bored-looking barman.

Oktar is seated, draped really, at the counter. The barman, bleached waistcoat and drooping bow tie, is mixing him a drink.

Why am I remembering this? wonders Samara. I know what happens next. I have no wish to hear Oktar rant once more. But he is drawn inevitably towards the bar, taking a seat alongside the man. He is relieved to see that he has returned his skin tone to a neutral, bland tan.

'The Willard used to be one of the great hotels,' says Oktar, without acknowledging that Samara has only just arrived. 'See the pictures on the walls –' he gestures '– what remains of them, anyway. All famous guests. The food here –' his gaze fades into reminiscence.

'Are we eating here, then?' asks Samara.

'You may be. I am eating out.'

'May I enquire as to where?'

'No, you may not. Now, have a drink.' Samara moves as if to refuse, but Oktar continues without pause. 'No, of course not, you Nine don't drink. What a terrible way to spend twenty-five years. Nevertheless, we are celebrating.'

He raises the glass of cloudy liquid the barman has placed before him. Samara could analyse the components but chooses not to. It will be one of Oktar's vulgar combinations. He resigns himself to hearing out a monologue. He need but nod occasionally.

'A pity about the food here. The last truly great chef is now on Arc Royal. You may have eaten there when we had the round-the-sun race a few years ago? Splendid woman, that. I shall miss them when we go. Not this planet, though.'

Oktar purses his lips, contemplates the room and the glass before him. It is scoured to a white frost, like a bottle washed up on the shore.

'The Europeans have their suicidal genomics policy: one hundred and fifty years of refusing to acknowledge technological change. And what has that gotten them? Their youth have fled, their population collapsed, their union fragmented, and what is left is a broken, impoverished set of states no one cares about filled with old people who can barely feed themselves.

'And our American cousins? One nation torn asunder by religion. Theirs and everyone else's,' he laughs, a bitter, false cackle. 'India, Brazil. Each of the Earthly states, each with completely different problems, and one result. Everyone buys from the orbital cities, and Achenia is the largest. That way, they maintain their sainted morals and outsource all production that would otherwise offend them. It amazes me that they fool themselves like this. That we fool ourselves like this, too. We can buy nothing with their money. And every export diminishes our own environment.'

He taps his nose at Samara, winks, 'Your mining friends down in Romanche have done very well out of us,' and nods.

'Not that we weren't thinking ahead. We knew we would have to buy our freedom, and we have. We have paid off the Americans with trillions of dollars of their own worthless currency. Good thing there were no economists in the room otherwise they would have drowned in their own vomit.'

'They don't have to spend it, Oktar. They can destroy it,' says Samara, instantly regretting his comment, knowing this will extend Oktar's monologue.

'You're forgetting their precious blockchain. They don't control the currency, and the supply of money is fixed. If they delete it, it is lost for ever. The wisest thing they could do is pay off their national debt, but that would kill the bond market. The president isn't the only one with donors who won't want to see their investments flatline,' says Oktar.

'Spend it or delete it, the result is the same. Their economy will be disrupted for decades, and we will be rid of them. We throw in a few sphere for what remains of their universities and a few printers to hold up their economy, for all the good that will do them. Engineers and scientists trained on divine intervention have proven useless at working with our research so far.

'They get an elevator that hasn't carried freight in fifty years, and a casino at the top that will close when we go. We have refused to leave them a dark fusion power source, and the old power systems we leave behind won't protect the channel for more than a year.

'That is the deal I have secured us.

'We have parted with nothing we will miss, and they have gained nothing that will profit them.'

Oktar drains his glass and stands, slightly unsteadily. 'We will leave this exhausted planet to die its slow, senescent death. Good luck to them. And now,' he walks, almost directly, to the doorway, 'I take my leave.'

He turns and smiles warmly at Samara, 'Expect me back very late. Next week.'

[What a vile man.]

'He's right though, Symon. Shakiso told me we couldn't keep the money because it would be the same as deleting it. I'd forgotten that would cause inflation too. We have to give it back. She wants them to set up a strategic stability fund. I don't know if anyone here is listening. We leave behind too many who expect that today will continue much like yesterday. Too many old minds in old bodies.'

[And you still believe we should return one day?]

'That is Shakiso's plan, not mine,' he smiles. 'I adore her,' loving, always, the way saying the words makes him feel.

[She and Nizena spend far too much time together. They're planning something.]

He laughs, 'My grandfather is always planning something.'

The barman stares sullenly at this impassive titanium-skinned man. 'If you're not going to drink nothing, then I'm going to close the bar,' he says.

Samara slides fluidly off the chair and upright. 'Your restaurant is still open?'

'Take your pick, one of them should be,' dragging a filthy cloth over the counter. 'Now, if you'll excuse me.'

Samara walks towards the restaurants across the lobby. The marble floor is stained and dirty. The marble pillars are cracked, and one is supported by a cellulosic cage. A large rug is as tattered as the carpet in the bar. Half the flame-lights, hanging in shallow glass goblets from the high vaulted ceiling, are no longer working.

The reception is closed, and one bored night clerk is watching something on his set, his head enclosed and oblivious to anything around him.

[Remind me again why we chose this place?]

'Apparently it's extremely convenient and the nearby alternatives are worse. Now,' opening a channel, 'I will be having dinner with my wife.'

'My darling,' says Shakiso in delight as she takes his hand and he embraces her. 'It's not the same,' she says.

'Precious, this is the connect. We can be as intimate as if we were together.'

She pouts, teasing him. 'Darling,' adopting her most serious voice, 'I can tell the difference.'

He laughs, pulling her close, breathing in the warmth of her, the scent of wildflowers in her hair. She smiles up at him, pixie face and snub nose, eyes adoring him in return.

They have some variation on this conversation at least once every time he goes away.

[Looks like it's pizza for dinner.]

One of the restaurants is still lit. 'Tuscan Dreams' on the illuminated sign above the door.

[It'll have red-and-white check tablecloths, baskets hanging from the walls filled with plastic flowers, and that chopped, synthetic garlic on the tables.]

[And those cans of tomatoes no one ever opens along the counters.] Synthia, Shakiso's symbiont, giggles.

'Behave, the pair of you,' says Shakiso.

Samara pushes the door open and enters. There are a few guests doing their best impression of pretending this is the expensive meal they have always wanted.

[Told you.] Symon sounds entirely too smug.

Gurgling strains, which Samara at first takes to be the

plumbing, turn out to be a musician waving away at a synthisphere in the corner near the entrance to the toilets. A man ducks under the waving arms of the musician as he opens the door.

Samara takes a table in the quietest corner and orders pasta.

[Should be hard to destroy penne arrabbiata.]

'Go away.'

[I could change the flavour for you? You'll never notice.]

'You tried that once before and the experience was very unsettling. Now, go away.'

[I admit that getting boiled potatoes to taste like sashimi was a bit of a reach. Very well, call if you need me. Shakiso, Synthia, a pleasure.]

Shakiso laughs. 'They're like children.'

'Exactly – tell your mother we already have two, we don't need another.' He shuts out the restaurant.

In his mind, he is seated outside on their deck. The waterfall pours down, plunging hundreds of metres to the lake below. Spray sometimes drifts, like mist, across the space. Shakiso walks out from their kitchen, carrying a bowl and chopsticks. She is barefoot, and her short white dress, light and fine as a cobweb, clings to her as she moves.

The light is golden and her face is joy.

She sits alongside him on the bench, leg against leg, skin on skin, and they look out across the valley; the great sweep of the city, falling in cliffs and swaddled in trees and flowers.

21

'Where are you, my husband?' asks Esther.

Joshua starts. It is early and the sun has not yet emerged. They are having breakfast together, maize porridge with milk, chopped bananas and wild honey. He has eaten most of it, but his thoughts have drifted. His spoon is trailing on the table, leaving milky tracks.

'I am sorry,' he says, wiping the mess with his cloth.

'Do not apologize, my husband.' She looks at him tenderly. He is so like a boy, lost, trying to have the answers. She reaches across the table, takes his hands in hers, holding them up to her face. 'You need never apologize. You have done nothing wrong. You are a good man.'

'I feel –' he does not know how to finish.

She shakes her head, touches her lips to the palms of his hands. A gentle kiss: one for each.

'Take care, my husband. Be kind to yourself. All you have to do is help Samara return to his people, then return to me. Stay safe.'

There is a knock on the kitchen door. It opens and Daniel is there, Abishai behind him.

'We are ready, Joshua,' he says.

'I shall be with you in a moment,' and he goes through to Isaiah's room. The boy is still asleep.

Joshua stares in wonder once more at the skin on his son's back, unmarked as if new-born. He kisses him on the back of his head and then returns.

'Let us go,' embracing Esther. He looks back only once.

At the east gate, Edith and Abishai hug and kiss. The younger woman looking vulnerable and confused.

Daniel turns to Samara – Symon. 'Thank you, I heard from Absalom what you have done for us.'

Joshua furrows his brows. 'Last night he worked with Absalom at the foundry printers. He has redesigned our weapons and shells so that they can penetrate that armour plate. He also retuned the sensitivity of the sentinels to detect those ghost helicopters. If the militia decide to return, we will be ready.'

Daniel hands Joshua a cellulosic rifle and pistol. 'We are all using the new guns. We printed this for you last night.'

'You have been busy?' says Joshua, as he slings the rifle over his shoulder and holsters the pistol at his back.

Symon tilts his head.

'I thank you,' says Joshua, placing his left hand over his heart.

'No,' says Symon. 'I must thank you and apologize. I am sorry for your loss. If not for me, I would not have put your people in such danger. We never imagined that we would complicate matters so.'

Joshua gives him a half-smile, nods.

The group head down the slope towards the jetty where four rowboats are tied up, already provisioned. Jason and Abishai take the lead boat, then Daniel and Joshua, Sarah and David, and Symon in a boat on his own. Symon's boat leans towards the stern as he sits, but it is otherwise safe in the water.

They paddle upstream. It will be two and a half days through the network of rivers to Calabar. Bringing the battery back will be easier by boat.

They now assume that Calabar will have supplies when they

get there. Their digesters should be able to extract the aluminium from the bauxite quite quickly. The aluminium spars Symon has packed are covered by a tarpaulin and roped to prevent them moving. This will cover some of their costs and provide a backup in case the bauxite did not get to Calabar.

The boats travel two abreast. Joshua falls in alongside Symon.

'You mentioned that you can change your appearance. Does that mean you can look more Efik?'

Symon blinks. Looks at him. His eyes lose their glow. Brown irises, black pupils appear. His skin darkens; his body imperceptibly shifts. Hair sprouts out of his head, dark and curling tightly.

'Will that do?'

Jason and Abishai, watching over their shoulders, almost capsize themselves. David and Sarah, turning to see, narrowly avoid colliding with them.

Joshua closes his mouth, nudges Daniel to do the same.

'Yes, Symon, that will do,' he manages.

'Good,' says Symon. 'Now, it is many days to Calabar. Who knows a story?'

22

Cigarette smoke fills the air. The light is diffuse, and it is difficult to make out individual faces at the bar and on the dance floor.

'This is that bar in Anacostia? What am I doing here again?'

There is no response. Samara is alone in his head.

A flash and he sees Ewuru, the river, running up the bank. Joshua and the child. I'm trapped in my memories. Symon is out there. He shouts, 'Symon!'

His thoughts are a muddle, but he tries to remember what he needs to do when the link is broken. Too late, he finds himself dragged back, losing the path outside.

[Do you think it's one of Oktar's lady-friends?] 'Symon, it's me. Answer me.'

'You think he finally insulted one of them enough for her to have a go at him?'

[We can always hope.] 'Symon? Please?'

He looks around the bar. It is a disagreeable place. He can smell the people, sour sweat and overflowing toilets, rancid cooking fat in the kitchen grease traps. The floor is sticky. Not all of it is beer.

The music is outstanding: raw emotional chords against steel drums and outraged guitars.

[How is it that these terrible places always produce such fantastic music?]

'Review a little history and you'll see that creators seem to find inspiration in adversity.'

The dancers stagger along, eyes vacant. The amplifiers have overpowered the speakers, and the louder notes crackle, heard over the shouted conversation. Posters on the wall advertise products that will make people younger, more beautiful, more popular.

[Perfect, I found you a quote. 'Don't be so gloomy. After all it's not that awful. Like the fella says, in Italy for thirty years under the Borgias they had warfare, terror, murder, and bloodshed, but they produced Michelangelo, Leonardo da Vinci, and the Renaissance. In Switzerland they had brotherly love, they had five hundred years of democracy and peace, and what did that produce? The cuckoo clock. So long, Holly.']

'Orson Welles. I love that film.'

Oktar did not come back to the hotel that night, all through the next day, or the day thereafter. The Five reported that Ortega had agreed and would put the proposal to Congress.

'We don't expect any problems, but you and Oktar should remain for the next two weeks. Keep a presence,' says Hollis. 'I know you want to come home, but you're there more to make sure Oktar stays out of trouble than anything else.'

She sighs. 'Have you seen him?'

'No, he left two nights ago. He didn't say when he'd be back.'

'Well, just make sure he's there for the final signing. He's not our finest representative, but he's the best negotiator there is. We'll leave with some certainty of being left alone until we're out of the solar system.'

Which is why he is in a smelly, unpleasant bar in the centre of Anacostia. Oktar has decided to go silent, so Samara has been following reflected signatures seen through the connect. Shadows in channels, other people's shared experiences.

He knows that, until a few minutes ago, Oktar was here. Flashes in the darkness as embeds fire, documenting moments easily interchangeable with any other night. He evaluates a constant stream of images from around the room. Oktar is clearly visible in one of these. He was at the bar with a woman in a purple dress. He does not appear to be present in any of the new images. He sees himself flick past in one, the flash still fading around him.

Symon automatically edits the images, seamlessly removing Samara, leaving no trace of his passing.

Samara cannot tell if Oktar, or his companion, are still in the room.

Why would he come here?

Samara scans the room. A group of men at the back of the room are armed. They appear to be carrying narcotics – a hypomethamphetamine hybrid, from the chemical signature – perhaps about to trade. [They call it Sutra. Mildly hallucinogenic, strongly entactogenic. Side effects are paranoia and neurotoxicity.] There is another group of armed men behind him, close to the dance floor. He ignores them, heading towards the bar. Someone may remember where they went.

He moves wide of a pool table around which a large group of heavyset men are betting on a game. They are leaning over the table, obscuring the lie of the remaining balls. A tally of their current wager glows in the air at the edge of the table above a row of empty bottles.

As Samara passes, there is a click, a shout of anguish, and a man steps backwards into him.

The man turns, angry. His face is misshapen, swollen, too many drugs, too much alcohol. His teeth are stained. Dirt and dried food smeared on his unevenly shaven round face. His hair is short, spiky, grey and blond. He is holding his beer glass, his hand wet, foam dripping on to the floor, adding to the filth.

'You spilled my drink!'

[He will attempt to hit you in three, two, one.]

Samara moves before the man does, pulling the man's arm past and up and behind his back. He presses the point of his heel hard into the man's instep. He whispers into his ear, 'I mean you no harm. I am only passing through looking for a colleague. You are welcome to buy yourself another drink. If you interrupt me again, I will rip off your arm,' pushing him gently back into the pool table to a chorus of groans and shouts from his friends.

[That may not have been sufficient.]

Samara ignores the looks of the men at the table and walks to the bar. He can see that the chairs where Oktar and his companion were sitting are now occupied. He approaches the two women leaning at the counter.

They look as if they may be prostitutes. Their clothes are tight fitting, squeezing their pudgy flesh out over the top, around the sleeves, and causing their dresses to ride up. Their shoes are uncomfortable spikes, their feet raw around the straps. They leer at him, eyes like week-old fish, lipstick smeared in a thick band over their lips and on to their teeth.

[Active embeds. Blocking.] The embeds are a poor shadow of the symbionts used by the Achenians. Easy to hack, easy to fool.

Samara has no idea what Oktar has been doing, but he will not be drawn into any potentially embarrassing situations if he can prevent it.

'Excuse me, would you happen to have seen the two people who were here a few minutes before you? A man in a knee-length cream shirt and a woman in a long purple dress? They would be quite distinctive,' he says.

Their heads wobble slightly as they attempt to sort out all the different versions of Samara standing in front of them.

'Ooh, you look funny, doesn't he, Hilda?' says the slightly fatter one to the one smoking a long, thin cigarette.

'He does – funny skin, funny eyes, why do you look like that?' She attempts to poke her finger at him but misses. It must have been one of the other Samaras.

'I'm sorry to disturb you, ladies, but I would appreciate your assistance,' he tries again.

'He sounds very fancy, Nancy,' hazards the one called Hilda. She giggles inanely at her rhyme.

'Buy us a drink?' says Nancy.

'If that would help.' He raises a hand to call the barman, who is leaning back against the counter fridges behind him, smoking a hand-rolled cigarette. He stubs it out on the bar and nods that he is listening.

'The same of whatever these ladies are having, please,' he says, automatically transmitting cash from an anonymous wallet.

'That's more like it. Would you like a blow-job, too?' asks Hilda, as she sinks her flabby face into a green and purple drink.

Samara smiles, but carefully. 'No, thank you, just the information. Please.'

'They was here, but they left,' says Nancy. Hilda nods vacantly.

'Would you happen to know where they may have been going?'

'No, but they were speaking to them,' says Hilda, pointing vaguely in the direction of a group of people in another corner of the bar, close to the dance floor.

'Thank you, have an enjoyable evening,' leaving before they can respond.

[This is not improving. Those look like policemen.]

As he approaches through the gloom, squeezing past revellers, he can see the reflections off badges and belt buckles. The three men are clearly on duty but just as clearly drinking. One of them has his arm around a woman who, since he knows he left them behind at the bar, would have to be a twin for either of Nancy or Hilda.

Symon transmits their standard hack for the police live streams, deleting Samara in real-time.

'Excuse me, officers,' Samara starts, speaking loudly to be heard over the noise.

'It's another one of them spacers,' says one, his eyes wide as he stands up very straight.

[Oktar would appear to have been here. And, more correctly, we're 'orbiteers'. Of the geostationary variety. I think I'll stop now.]

'My apologies, I have no wish to interfere with your evening. I am looking for a colleague of mine.'

One of them steps forward, 'And?'

They are hostile for some reason. Defensive.

[Only moderate levels of alcohol. I'm unsure why they are responding aggressively.]

'My colleague is a man in a knee-length cream shirt and his companion is a woman in a long purple dress. Perhaps you've seen them?'

The men share a brief, anxious glance and then the lead policeman says, 'No, haven't seen anyone like that. Why don't you ask somewhere else?'

[Why are they lying? They're broadcasting telemetry and image. They're on duty. What's going on?]

It is close here, crowded; the strobing lights and grinding music make it hard to pick up who is moving where. He is surprised when a man with spiky grey and blond hair suddenly attacks him.

[Oh, him again.]

He has brought his friends this time. The policemen do not intervene, having a whispered conversation of their own. Samara breaks the man's wrist and hurls him back into his friends. Two of them run at him, but he moves sideways, tripping one and catching the other's arm, locking it back at the elbow.

He holds the whimpering man like a shield and turns to face the group. There is nothing he can say, so he hopes only to make it clear that they cannot hope to fight him and should leave.

He is surprised a second time when, against all expectation, someone shoots him in the back of the head.

He blanks out.

23

'How do you cook so well?' asks Sarah. 'Gideon has some competition. Last night's ekpang nkukwo was—'

'Bliss,' says Jason, beaming. He is leaning back against an iroko tree, its vast trunk towering above them. Bats are sleeping in the upper branches, and their rustling and subtle squeals filter to the ground.

They have slept in a circle in a clearing just above the riverbank. Raffia palms shield them from the water. They have hung burners from the trees and the smoke still lingers, repelling mosquitoes.

In the distance they can hear a monkey hoot as a troop moves through the trees in search of food. Birds call and there is the whispered clutter of a breeze through the tree canopy.

Symon is tending the fire and cooking a second pot of maize porridge, which he is spooning out. David is next in line.

Unintentionally, since he does not sleep, the chores have fallen to Symon, and much of the equipment used during the night has already been packed.

'I am able to maintain a small memory archive similar to your sphere. When I learned your language from it, I also learned a few recipes. I felt that last night's dinner would be appropriate.'

'Are you able to add new information to the sphere?' asks Jason.

'No, only other sphere can do that. I can only query and receive, the same as you.'

'They have many sphere in Calabar. When we get there, will you get news from your people?'

'Not now, no. I am out of alignment. I cannot risk attracting notice if I start asking questions like that directly.'

Daniel returns to the campsite. 'Do not go that way,' he says, indicating with an outstretched arm pointing behind him where he has made his ablutions. He is rubbing his belly. 'That smells good. You are feeding us well, Symon.'

A troubled expression clouds Sarah's brow. Something has occurred to her. 'Symon, you do not appear to −' hesitating in embarrassment.

Symon is unconcerned by the question. 'I do not pass waste matter, no. I am able to process all food content. I can absorb far more energy from the same quantity of matter. It is more efficient.'

Daniel pauses, a spoonful of porridge midway to his mouth. 'Are you still human?'

Symon's expression barely changes. 'I am not human, but I understand your meaning. Samara and his people are very much human. Their physical form has been adjusted, certainly. They call this "conscious directed evolution": making changes in moments, which would normally take millennia of random selective pressure.'

They have all eaten now, and he scrapes out the dregs of the pot into the coals. The wooden spoon in his hand having been plucked from the hands of a sleeping child, no doubt protesting even now.

'They are still human but freed from the briefness of a natural lifespan. They spend time on relationships, on exploring the possibilities of creativity, of science, of the universe. They laugh, they love, they fight, they grieve. You will not find them so very different.'

David, sitting on his heels alongside his bedroll, stares into the still-glowing embers before looking up. 'And you, Symon, what are you?'

'I am a product of a multi-material biologics printer. I was born into a containment jar, filled with the control systems that define my function and loaded with a subset of the knowledge of our people. I am a mesh network of nanoscopic biological machines: a symbiotic intelligence. I maintain my systems and memory as part of the network. I achieve my sentience, my self-awareness, only once I am injected into a host and can bond with my host's subconscious. I live as long as my host, and my interests are his interests.'

'Are you and Samara friends? Is that how it works?' asks Jason.

'The closest friends anyone can ever have. We know each other's thoughts as we are having them. We know each other intimately.' He scoops up soil and throws it on to the coals, covering and smothering them. 'And, before you ask, yes, I miss him very much and want to be reunited with him.'

A blue and emerald-green kingfisher flies through the camp, lands on a branch and looks at them, first out of one eye and then the other. Then it leaps and is gone through the raffia and towards the river.

Joshua comes up the bank. 'It is getting late. We must go if we hope to be there tomorrow.'

There are assorted groans as everyone straightens up and massages cramping joints. Symon cleans the pot in the river, the ceramic triangular cooking stand at his side, as the others load the last of their gear into the boats.

The kingfisher reappears, a silver fish in its beak. It slaps it against the branch it is standing on. Again and again, until it is satisfied it is stunned. It swallows the fish whole.

They push the boats into the river and start wending their way once more through the network of creeks and lagoons that criss-cross the lower delta.

David has dropped two fishing lines over the rear of his boat, tying insects to the hooks. They will catch their dinner as they go.

After only an hour, the back of the boat tugs sharply downwards. The others cheer as first one and then the other lines go tight, the rear of the boat pulling down, almost level to the water, with the weight of each fish. They fight hard, but David and Sarah row until the fish are exhausted and can be easily pulled in over the side of the boat. They are catfish. David places them carefully in an insulated carrier behind Sarah.

The group lapses into silence, each at peace with their own thoughts. Sarah hums, but, other than that and the drip of oars dipping into the water, there is little sound.

They lunch on a bank, making do with fruit and nuts rather than preparing an entire meal.

'We will need to port,' says Joshua, talking more to Symon than the others, who know this route, as well as the drudgery of pulling laden boats overland. 'The water systems change here, and it will take about an hour to drag the boats across the embankment.'

Over the bank is a sandy channel leading through the woods.

'This is built,' says Symon, looking along the ridge.

'Yes, our people did this more than a generation ago. You will see when we get across, but we need to isolate our water systems from the Calabar and Cross Rivers. We blocked all the connections between the two systems until far above the city.'

Jason sighs, 'It is still a punishment for scouts to go out for a month and maintain the reinforcements.'

'Last time,' giggles Sarah, 'you fell into that lagoon and were covered in leeches.'

'That was not,' says Jason, attempting to maintain his dignity, 'very funny.'

'Your face,' tears of laughter streaming down David's face, 'when you found one attached to your amu.'

Daniel tilts his head and shakes it in mock disappointment, 'You young people.'

Joshua grips Daniel's shoulder and motions, let us move. They fasten ropes to the front of each boat and start dragging them along the channel. As they reach the other side, the tone of the soil changes, becoming darker and sticking to the soles of their shoes. There is also a smell, like kerosene. The water has an oily sheen to it.

'We do not eat anything from the water here,' says Jason. 'There are abandoned and unsealed oil wells all around Calabar.'

They paddle up the lagoon on the other side, turning again and again into different branches of the lattice of waters. The variety of trees gradually diminishes until there are only oil palm and raffia. There are few birds and no animals.

The sun is tipping against the top of the oil palms before they draw up on a sandy bank for the night.

David retrieves the catfish he caught in the morning. 'They are not as nice as our river stocks but should still taste good,' he says, holding up a fish in each arm, both hanging down to his shoulders. There is an expectant silence as the group waits for an offer. They are embarrassed to ask Symon to cook again.

'I will make catfish pepper soup,' he says to grins all round. 'We have only pounded yam, though.'

'That will be well,' says Daniel.

The others make camp, clearing a space and searching for branches to chop firewood. They are not far from Calabar now, can almost see the loom of its lights on the horizon after the sun goes down.

It is not often that the others eat this well while travelling, and have the luxury of sleeping through the night without taking turns at watch. One by one they fall asleep.

Symon picked up a strange lingering smell coming from the north-east, perpendicular to their direction of travel, soon after they arrived. It is subtle. The others will not have noticed, but it is familiar to him.

He walks up the island, swimming across a channel to reach a further bank. At the far end of that island, he finds the source.

The man has been tied to an oil palm, his arms and legs knotted about the trunk, as if hugging it. His elbows and knees have been broken. Blood has caked and dried on the sand. Flies cover his hands and face.

What is left of his face.

His jaw has been ripped out, his upper palate and teeth visible where his head rests against the tree. There is a terrible, wet, gasping rattle from his exposed throat. His tongue is dry and coated in flies, hanging loose down his neck. Tiny maggots burrow and churn in the suppurating wound around the exposed bone of his upper jaw.

Above his head is a short loop of thick rope hanging from the handle of a heavy cellulosic knife. The knife is embedded in the trunk. The man's lower jaw hangs from the rope.

As Symon nears, the man opens his eyes.

He makes a sucking, gargling sound: a plea. His eyes are begging, too dry to weep.

Symon studies him. Assesses. He places his hands about the man's head and efficiently snaps his neck. He stares into the other's eyes all the way through, acknowledging the gratitude and release as the man goes.

He buries the body beneath the shadow of the oil palm, returning in the morning to camp. He carries a small stone in his pocket. The symbol cut into it is two parallel arcs, one broken off-centre with a dot between them.

He says nothing.

A few hours later, they paddle into the docks at Beach Town, below the city.

24

'Symon!' screams Samara in the vastness of his memories. He is being dragged again towards a point. He knows where it has to be. 'Please, not there. Symon!'

He becomes aware again. Drifting, floating, his naked body angled diagonally to the two-and-a-half-metre by two-and-a-half-metre cube that defines his cell. The walls are padded. There is no bed. A pipe protrudes from one wall, a plastic cap on the end. The cell smells of old sweat, urine and excrement. A single light burns from a shielded bracket flat with the upholstery.

'Symon!' he yells again.

[I am here.]

'Symon, is that you? No,' his voice filled with anguish, 'only echoes of you.'

He is subsumed in the memory once more.

'Where are we? Orbit?'

[I have only just resumed awareness. That blow knocked me out as well.]

'Where's the connect?' feeling his head, the jagged tears where his ears used to be. 'My ears! They cut off my ears!' Howling in outrage, frustration and fear.

[Samara. Control.]

'My ears!' Rubbing at the scars, as if willing them to return.

Pounding at the walls, achieving nothing more than flinging himself awkwardly around within the cell.

Eventually, Samara calms, his screaming and sobbing giving way to moans, then hoarse breathing.

[Samara, we are on Tartarus. We will remain in solitary confinement until we are released or we can get that door open.]

Samara strokes the fabric of the walls, pushing on it. The surface is smooth and lined with stiff foam.

He maps his space. The tube is for waste and he discounts it. He inspects the corners, looking for the doorway. As he does so, a small slot, wide enough for a sachet of food, rotates out of the wall alongside him, slightly above the fabric of the wall below it.

[Eat. We must have our strength.]

The slot remains open. He can see that it is self-sealing so that he cannot get a glimpse of the outside of the cell. He takes the sachet, orienting himself so that he is facing it, his feet on the panel below and his left arm braced against the opposite wall so that he does not move.

He sucks down the paste. It is tasteless, but Symon quickly analyses it, confirming it is nutritionally complete. He can see now the microscopic edge of the doorway along the vertices of this face of the cube. This is the door.

Still sucking the paste, he pushes his forefinger into the corner.

[I can't squeeze through. It is metal-on-metal and under pressure. No space.]

Samara finishes the sachet, rubbing his finger to secrete a tiny silver drop on the outside, and deposits it back in the slot. The fluid is the substance of Symon's biological mesh network. Symon can maintain connection and use the fluid to interact or explore remotely. It will decay quickly outside a host, but Symon may find a control panel he can access.

The panel slides closed. A vacuum gust sucks.

Samara feels the pressure change inside the cell and realizes that air transfer takes place via a fine mesh panel running alongside the slot in parallel to the wall.

On the other side of the wall, empty sachets fly out from all along the pipe from other feeding slots. The silver drop clings to the bare metal. Slowly, it slides across the panel, tracing the outline of the outside of the cell, looking for a control panel, wiring, locking mechanisms, anything that can offer a way through.

This pipe is too narrow. It is the width of a corridor between facing cells, but only a few centimetres high.

There is nothing. It must be in the walkway above. There is no access.

The drop continues, searching for an inspection panel, but it gradually fades and dissolves before it finds anything.

Back in his cell, Samara pounds the walls in frustration.

Days pass. He regrows his ears but lacks the materials to resynthesize his antennae. He locks himself inside his mind, drawing on Symon's long-term memory store to hide in a simulacra of the world he has lost. He watches old movies, slips into reveries of Shakiso, walks in meadows and swims in the great lakes on Achenia.

Symon continues to explore, little silver beads visiting other cells via their food slots. He finds little.

Tartarus is a prison. The American government was early to the rush to orbit, building one of the first space elevators and, then, one of the first metal cities in the sky. It had a suitably glorious name: Star City 1. They imagined a world of casinos and exclusive hotels along with rich retirees.

Then they watched as other, private, initiatives surpassed it. Their city atrophied, died. The few investors moving to other cities. Budget cuts meant that funding such a city was unaffordable. It was a vanity project, and Congress was not willing to let it go.

A way to finance it was found.

More than six million inmates clog the American criminal justice system. Sentencing is automated, calculated, swift. But there are prisoners the country would rather forget. Prisoners they cannot kill since the end of the death penalty. Prisoners they do not want.

They send them into orbit. Two hundred and fifty thousand individual cells were built. There is an air-processor. Megatons of food sachets are sent up once a year. Prisoners are transported, unconscious and naked, weekly. Effluent is ejected, frozen, into space.

The company that manages the prison has automated as much as they can. They tell the families that any bodies are converted to fuel for the station: a lie. The fusion generator provides all the energy the system needs. In a rare moment of introspection, they realized that casting dead bodies into space might cause consternation if any are seen burning through the atmosphere. Instead they are dumped at sea, buried amongst other waste. There are no wardens. Just a single control system called Athena.

Athena watches. Athena dispatches her Furies – deadly drones – to patrol the endless tunnels between the cells. None escape. All are forgotten.

It has been wildly popular. Except with the inmates. They usually go insane within months.

They gave it a glorious new name: Tartarus One. There are plans to build a second, larger prison. It may even happen.

Samara can hear the other inmates. Their manic cries, the incessant sobbing and pounding against the walls. There is no hope here, no prospect for release, no path to rehabilitation. And they will not let you die.

Every day he hears doors open, somewhere all through the city. He assumes that new prisoners are arriving or that bodies are being removed. He refuses to enter his memories again. He knows that he could decide not to come back, preferring to die in the arms of a remembered Shakiso than remain in his cell.

Instead he waits, floating in gravity-free confinement.

More days go by.

The light never changes. The interval between meals is always the same. Every six hours. The slender hatch remains open till he eats and returns the sachet.

[Samara.]

'Yes.'

[I have calculated the approximate time since we blanked.]

Samara says nothing.

[Tartarus has a slightly eccentric position. It is affected by the sun and moon. The attitude adjusters are not quite accurate. It has been twenty-three days.]

'We have only fifty-four days before Achenia departs.' His voice is flat.

[I have also tallied the periodicity of when doors open.]

Again, Samara says nothing.

[There is something unusual about the sequence. An elevator arrives once every seven days. At that time a number of doors open and close as prisoner exchange happens. There is also a set time once every twenty-four hours when it appears that dead prisoners are extracted from their cells. However, every two or three days a door opens at random.]

'What?' Samara is suddenly alert.

[I have been processing the data. It sounds as if an individual prisoner is released into the tunnels at these random intervals.]

'Do you have any idea what for?'

[I am not sure. But – I do not believe it ends well.]

'The Furies?'

[Yes, they hunt the prisoners.]

'To what end?'

[I do not know. Perhaps for sport?]

'That could work in our favour. Do you have any idea of what those released have in common?'

[I do not know. I will process.]

Samara lapses back into silence, but he has a glimmer of hope. He waits. Days pass.

[Samara. There is a potential pattern. From the sound signatures it appears that these inmates maintain their fitness. Perhaps performing exercise will attract notice?]

Samara straightens and places his hands against one panel and his feet flat against the panel below. He realizes that the prisoners attempting this must all be tall, otherwise performing this trick is impossible. There is no way to gain leverage, and exercise is otherwise impossible without gravity.

He pushes up and down, up and down, flexing himself against the two walls. He continues for hours, pausing only when the food slot opens to eat from the sachets.

Another day passes, but Symon reports that no more random openings have happened.

On the third day of exercising, the entire face of one panel slides back and away to the left. The passageway outside is in darkness. Samara carefully sticks his head out.

The glow in his eyes vanishes as he adapts his skin to match the bare-metal walls of the tunnel. As he moves – floating in the middle of the corridor, and pulling or pushing as he propels himself – he appears invisible, transparent, reflecting the surface under him around his body.

Symon has built up a reasonable map of the nearby tunnels, and determined which way faces towards the outside, but he has only a limited idea of how the overall system is structured. He needs to find a maintenance and engineering warehouse that he assumes will be close to the elevator entrance. Maintenance must have been planned for during the life of the prison?

He is aware of temperature and movement sensors embedded in the walls. They do not trouble him. He reflects only ambient heat.

He sees the rounded metal ball of a Fury flying past a junction up ahead, its magnetic thrusters keeping it centred in the tunnel. Samara ignores it, turning in the opposite direction.

It is a warren of interleaving tunnels, a grid of columns and rows of seemingly random intervals. He goes slowly, making no sound.

[Fury.]

He stands still, bracing himself, leaving space for it to pass, as the Fury turns into his tunnel and floats alongside him. It is almost spherical, with a grotesque lion-like face.

[I thought they were supposed to look like hags? With snakes for hair? This is disappointing.]

Samara grabs it, propelling a bullet of silver into its guts. Systems are adjusted, sensors confused. Now it is his. He holds it, maintaining control over it, ensuring it reports correctly back to Athena.

[It has a map. I'm translating it.]

There are scorch marks in this section of the tunnels. Inmates who ran the gauntlet and were slaughtered. Dried blood floats in the stillness of the air.

[Calculated. The map is not complete. Look. Notice that huge central shaft? Almost like a funnel to the outside?]

'Strange. It doubles the size of the prison. Can you see what it might be?'

[No. It seems protected from the Furies. Although it seems to share a common control room, they have no access, so no need to know the interior.]

'Fair enough.'

[I have calculated a path to the stores.]

Hours pass and he makes it into a different tunnel. This one is lit. He follows it to an ordinary-looking hatchway door. It is unlocked.

Inside, there is gravity, and he drops silently to the floor.

[They waste the energy here, where there is no one to appreciate it?]

It is a large space, about the size of an aircraft hangar. Boxes are piled up on pallets. Sheets of metal, aluminium rebar and baskets of thermoplastic packing pellets. There is more than enough material for him to build an escape pod.

There is a sound, as of quiet conversation.

[Three. Behind the boxes to the rear.]

He creeps silently between the box stacks, pushing the Fury ahead of him.

'I raise you four packets,' says a voice.

'He has you now, Seymour,' chuckles another softly.

Past a crate of mechanical components, three men are seated on stools around a small table. They must have once been big men, but now they are skeletal. They are of varying ages. One looks very old. Sheets of fabric are wrapped around their bodies. It matches the fabric of the cell padding. Empty sachets are piled between them, cards in their hands and on the table.

Samara shifts colour, returning to his normal matt titanium. He does his best to hide the Fury behind his back. He clears his throat, gently.

The men jump, swearing, trying to hide. One spots him.

'Fuck's sakes, it's a man!' he shouts. They relax but remain wary, and then one spots the Fury.

'It's a Fury! Fuck!'

'It is mine,' says Samara, clearly. He pulls the Fury in front of him and pushes it to face the floor. 'I control it.'

Their jaws gape. The one called Seymour walks over to Samara. He is hunched, bent, his ribs protrude and his stomach is hollow. He prods the Fury.

'How you do that?'

'I am Achenian. I am able to control such devices.' He warns them, 'Do not attempt to remove it from me as I will lose control of it again. It will then call Athena for help.'

Seymour stares aghast.

'If you wait a moment, I will reprogram it.'

The others watch as he crouches over the black, evil-looking device. He is silent for a few moments, then releases it. The others jump, but Samara motions at them to stay calm.

The Fury hovers above them then begins to patrol the ware-house. Every few hours, it will plug itself into a wall socket to recharge.

'What you do to it?'

'I've programmed it to send out a response to Athena that it is patrolling well and that there is no trouble. It won't call for help. I have also set it to protect us. Its enemies are now other Furies.'

The men guffaw. Exchange disbelieving but happy looks. This may be the first hopeful experience in years.

Remembering his manners, Seymour wipes his right hand on the sheet around his waist and proffers it.

'I'm Seymour, that's Henry, and the old guy is Sancho.'

They shake, awkwardly and self-consciously.

'We ain't got much food. Exist off what's left in the empty packets as they collect down here. But you survived. That's a big deal. We'll find a way,' says Seymour.

The others nod. It must have been terrifying, and unspeakably lucky, to survive and find this place without any of Samara's abilities. How many tried and failed?

'Thank you for your hospitality, but I don't intend staying long,' says Samara.

'Well, those are brave words, friend. I been saying 'em for thirty years,' says Sancho. All his teeth have fallen out.

'We ain' got much to do. We can show you what we got?'

In most Earth-bound prisons, any new arrival would never receive such a fulsome greeting. Tartarus is no ordinary place. These men have been isolated so long, starved for novelty and weakened through continuous hunger. Their conversation spoken as if dragged from them, exhausted; individual words lost along the way, leaving their speech oddly stilted. They still have their sanity, and life has become fragile and precious.

The men abandon their card game. A well-thumbed deck left behind by some ancient building party.

At the end of the warehouse is a packing system. Every six hours, a net filled with empty food sachets is released from a pipe and deposited into an empty box on a conveyer belt below. The net must be where the empties are collected after each feeding.

A stack of thin sheets of cardboard alongside the spout, and an elaborate folding mechanism to convert each into a box, sits beside the top end of the conveyor belt. The conveyor belt deposits the large boxes on to a mobile pallet at the other end.

'The pallet holds twenty-eight boxes. A week's worth of food waste. We go through each box – almost one hundred fifty thousand – squeezing out the last of the packets. There ain't much,' says Seymour, scratching his ribs. 'We get by.

'When the pallet is full, it rolls through that door. That's a pressure-sealed environment, 'cos, on the other side, that's the entry bay where the new convicts arrive. It ain't guarded there, but it's a vacuum. No escape.

'And that's our lives. We sleep through here. Each of us done make a room for ourselves.'

Amongst the wide, bolted racks, each man has hung sheets of cloth to create small rooms. Neatly folded sheets make up a bed, and a few personal items are packed in small boxes. The rooms are even smaller than the cells, but they do have the warehouse to live in.

'We fool around with the equipment, we play cards, we squeeze packets,' says Seymour.

The men stand there, skin and bone, their eyes sunken, large against their skulls, haunted.

'Where your wee-wee?' asks Henry.

Samara drops his penis out of its protective sheath, then retracts it again. Henry whistles.

'That's a neat trick.'

Samara shrugs. 'If you show me where you keep the cloth, I can make myself something to wear,' he says.

'Sure,' says Sancho, and leads him to a great roll of coarse fabric.

Samara unrolls a length and then slides the cutter across. He fashions it into an impromptu cloak.

'That will do for now. Are there any fabricators?'

Henry shakes his head.

[The old-fashioned way, then.]

The men stare at Samara expectantly.

'How you planning on getting out, fellow?' asks Henry.

Samara looks at them carefully.

'I'm going to build a small escape pod and fly down the navigation channel.'

The men look pleased. If one, why not more?

[Best tell them early.]

'I need to explain something. Please be patient with me.' The men look worried again. 'You cannot escape with me. You will not survive the journey.'

'What? We can't stay here?' Seymour looks angry, but they lack the energy to do much more than sigh.

'I agree with you. This place is a crime. My people will not permit it. I will ensure that.'

They do not look as if they believe him, either that he can escape or that he would return.

'My journey, in any case, is dangerous. I cannot travel direct from here to Achenia. There is too much debris in orbit. I would be torn apart. I go to the surface only to have to find another way back up. I will need to stay outside the connect once I'm into the atmosphere and will cut across and head for Africa.'

'Mister, there ain' no propulsion systems here. We looked,' says Sancho.

[That could be a problem. I will review the station plans.]

'I will have to look into that,' says Samara. 'I will not disturb you and, while I am here, I will help you as best I can.'

He works non-stop. He scans the boxes for parts, components. He will need more food: he has to bulk up.

[Food distribution will happen from somewhere.]

'Yes, but first let's check around here. It will be easier if I don't have to spend too much time in the tunnels.'

The men lack the strength to climb more than a body length and have no idea what is in the boxes above that. In a distant part of the warehouse, free-climbing high up in the stacks, he finds a massive box of ancient food sachets. These are flavoured and appear to have been intended for work crews.

Samara flings the box from the top. It falls and bursts where it hits the ground, a deluge of silver-foiled sachets filling the narrow space along the floor. The Fury comes to inspect, then returns to its rounds.

The men walk slowly over. They are excited, start tearing open packets and sucking down the contents.

'This one tastes like chicken!' crows Henry.

'Gentlemen. You are welcome, but I will need to eat about half of this if I am to survive the fall. The rest should last you a few months. Time enough for me to return and close Tartarus down.'

Henry shakes his head. 'I almost believe you, fellow.'

The others occasionally follow him around, but they lack his energy or strength. Even with the additional rations it will be some time before they recover.

Samara, looking at the mountain of stores, asks Sancho, 'Have you ever seen any work crews since you've been here?'

'Last time was maybe ten years ago,' he says. Pointing up at the sachet outflow pipe, 'It wan't easy, but I climbed up there, hid in the space on the other side of the pipe till they left. That way I could still eat.' He grins toothlessly. 'But that were before these fellows done join me. And none of us are strong enough to try that again any more.' He looks sadly at his emaciated arms.

'Before that, they used to come every year,' he says. 'You think they done forget about us?'

'I don't know,' says Samara, 'but I won't.'

Samara sets up an improvised metal-works close to the conveyor belt. The men can see him there from their endless card game, shouting encouragement as they return to their regular routine.

Showers of sparks and piercing whines as he cuts the metal.

When they settle to eat, he joins them. They talk after the fashion of men unused to long conversations.

'I were angry,' says Sancho. 'Spent more of my life inside than out. Me an' a friend tried to ransom a hitchhiker. He were only a boy, shouldn' even have been out on his own. We picked him up near the Guatemalan border.'

He stops, his voice husky, clutching at his knees, looking down.

'We didn' know what we were doin' neither. Couldn' let him go, so I done strangle him. Got caught. My friend got killed. I got in fights inside. They sent me here,' says Sancho.

He sighs, a long drawn-out breath filled with sorrow.

'Stuck in that cell. Long time. Floatin'. All I can see is that boy's face. I don' even remember his name.' Sancho looks up at Samara, his eyes bloodshot. 'I would find his family. Tell them sorry.

'I don' have much life left, but I realize. You can' spend it angry or hatin'.

'I hope you can get us home, Mister.' Sancho finishes speaking, rocking himself gently.

Henry killed his wife in an argument. Pushed her in a moment of fury and she fell, striking her head on an end table. Seymour was a gang member. There was one of those periodic anti-crime crusades, and he was made an example of.

'I got a son back there,' says Henry. 'He was a baby when I was sent here. He'd be seventeen now, I guess.' Samara told them the date. They are still coming to terms with how long they have been imprisoned. 'I was wrong. I don't expect him to welcome me, but I hope he'll let me try.'

Seymour nods. 'I got a wife still, I think. I hope she gives me a chance.'

Conversation lags, comes to a halt, and the men go alone to their small rooms. Haunted by hope and regret.

[They are not good men.]

'Perhaps. By the norms of their society, they have been more than punished for it. Redemption comes after release. They won't repay the balance of their debt unless they're given the opportunity to return.'

[They seem to want to. Repay it, I mean.]

'Yes, it seems so. Maybe there is hope, even here?'

[I have located a potential storage area for rocket fuel.]

'Where is it?'

[You will not like it.]

'The other end of the station.'

[Indeed.]

'Very well. Shall we go?'

Samara disrobes, leaving his cloak inside the door to the tunnels. His skin once again invisible against the dark metal. He adjusts to the lack of gravity, careful not to make any sound that could attract the Furies.

Once more, the endless network of grid-like passages and the purring silence broken by howls and madness.

25

Farinata Uberti lies prostrate in the dust before his sacred grove.

His arms and legs are outstretched. Dust blows about his face with each breath where his mouth is downcast close to the ground. His feet and hands are dirty.

Plaited palm leaves are wrapped around the trees either side of a small, palm-fronded hut. Bowls of water interspersed with rounded brown and white stones are arranged in rows before it. Sharpened sticks, eggshells impaled upon them, stand upright here and there. A pile of human skulls mixed with the bones of fish, goats and chickens is just outside the hut entrance. Seeds and feathers have been scattered over the roof and about the grounds. A python skin hangs between the two trees and above the hut.

Uberti is naked except for an okuru, a sheet cross-woven from strands of cotton and palm fibre. His body is plump. His hips and thighs – where they protrude from the sheet wrapped about his waist – are riven with stretch marks.

He is midway through the ceremony of divination.

A white ceramic bowl lined with a white cloth and filled with clear water is boiling on a tripod over a heap of coals to his right side. He pushes himself upright and sits, cross-legged, and empties a wooden bowl filled with finely scraped woody fibre from a freshly cut sapling into the water. He waits until the liquor becomes cloudy and begins to simmer once more. He gathers up the cloth in the bowl, carefully squeezing the water back into it.

A dead chicken, its body torn open while still alive, is to his left side. The knife he used is next to it, partly under one half-extended wing. He squeezes a few drops from the lump of cloth into its chest and over its intestines.

Last, he sits back on his heels, moulding the fabric-covered fibre between his hands. He sits like that for almost an hour, waiting for the ndem of his grove to reveal the future to him.

He stands, collects the chicken, the two bowls and the tripod, and stows them in the little hut. He removes his okuru, his flabby belly hanging over his scrotum, carefully folds the fabric and places it within the hut as well. He recovers his clothes, and dresses.

Turning, he follows the path through the trees until his house comes into view. His guards are waiting for him there. One hands him his AK-47. This is not a printed version but a Chinese original acquired at great cost from the Chinese traders who still sometimes visit the city.

'Ciacco!' he shouts. 'Ciacco, you worm, run!'

Uberti never speaks when he can bark.

Ciacco, a small, wire-faced man, races from the house. 'Great Awbong, you have returned. What news?'

The older man sneers. 'What news, indeed? You tell me.' Uberti strides towards the house, a guard on either side and his rifle slung across his back, Ciacco hovering on the periphery.

'There is news from the markets. A group arrived from the south. They have sold half a ton of aluminium scrap to the digesters.'

'That is interesting news. When was this?' Uberti washes his hands in a bowl of water, stumps up the stairs and on to the veranda of his house. He grabs a clean white towel from a slave, throwing it back at her when done.

'Only two hours ago, my Awbong.' Ciacco knows the news will please.

'Who are they, these outsiders?'

'Your men in the market say they sound as if they come from along the Akwayafe.'

'Aha,' he says. He leans out over the wall of his veranda. This is the largest house in Henshaw Town and the highest up the ridge. From here he looks down on Beach Town and across the bay towards Ikonitu.

'They're from Ewuru. Those filthy vagrants owe me a helicopter. D'Este is even less forgiving than I, and I had to part with most of the money from that bauxite to pay him off.'

Unsaid, that it was too expensive to afford a revenge attack. But now that they have come to him, and have something worth taking –

He turns to Ciacco. His eyes burn and his jaw bunches where he is grinding his teeth.

They almost could not find the bauxite because of those peasants' stupidity when they marked Pazzo's map. Eventually, they had seen it from the air, but not before one of the pilots had gotten bored and decided to have some fun taking his team to attack the village. That had cost him a helicopter, even though he had beaten d'Este down on the price for those flying scrapheaps.

'Send men. They owe me comey.'

It does not matter where the aluminium came from. All that matters is his fee.

Ciacco turns without a word and flees into the house.

'Good,' says Uberti. 'They can pay me at least part of what I lost.'

'My Awbong,' says one of the guards. Uberti grunts at him. 'My Awbong, the Akan players have arrived for tomorrow night. Can they set up in the back garden?'

Uberti will throw a festival for his men. Women will not be permitted, as many secret rites will be shared. The Akan are amongst them.

Many of the other local warlords will be present. They have adopted the old title of 'Awbong', king, and divided up the city along its ancient boundaries. They re-established the Egbo secret society, brought back the tortures, mysticism and superstitions. They pretend at being an organizing force, but they are more like a fungus. The moisture they need to thrive is provided by the society itself.

'Last year's players dropped one of their puppets. Make sure these players are aware of the consequences.'

Uberti has only one real punishment for those who displease him. He sacrifices them to the trees. He butchered the man who dropped the puppet. The others he sold as slaves to Filippo Argenti, one of the other warlords in the city.

The warlords do business with each other even as they skirmish for control. They are always looking for an opportunity to erode each other's power. Murder is frequent, but consolidation unlikely. As one dies, another militiaman steps forward, equally brutal.

'Duruji?' he says softly to one of the guards. The man leans close. 'That old woman, the one in the market?'

Duruji indicates that he remembers her.

'Kill her. The ceremony did not work.'

Duruji is about to leave.

'And, Duruji,' Uberti glares at him. 'Not a word.'

The militiaman nods and leaves quietly, hurrying around the outside of the house.

'It is good when one is feared, isn't it?' he says to another of his guards. He does not expect an answer. No one answers the king.

Uberti draws in the dust on the veranda wall. His first two fingers trace two arcs in parallel. He erases the second arc at a point off centre, breaking it. He places a dot between them. He studies it for a moment, then rubs it out with his palm. And he laughs.

26

'No more, please,' begs Samara, his self-awareness a fragment lost to the inevitable onslaught of his memory.

[It was a good trap.] 'Please, not here –' fading once more.

'Yes, the entire situation at the bar. Someone was waiting for us, expecting us,' says Samara.

[To what end?]

'I do not know, but we can assume they have Oktar as well. He could be somewhere amongst the inmates, or he could be being kept down on Earth.'

[Perhaps they think they can keep us here?]

'No, I don't think so. Perhaps they think either I or Oktar can assist them in some way?'

[And the masked section of Tartarus, or the gauntlet of Furies?]

'Maybe it isn't related? That empty section could be an unfinished part of the jail? Maybe the Furies have been hacked by another group taking bets on how long prisoners survive? Some sort of torturers' game show?'

[One hundred and fifty people a year killed for sport? There are some very messed-up people in your world.]

'Indeed. I wonder if that number is just sufficiently low to escape notice against the death rate of the prison population? No matter, we will confront this when we get back to Achenia.'

Samara is moving slowly. He is travelling in a wide arc around the central hub controlled by Athena. He is not entirely sure of his ability to fend off a massed Fury attack, and he does not wish to trigger any alarms or leave a trail of disabled Furies that might lead to a complete lockdown of all exits.

Every few minutes, he must stop and angle himself against the floor as another lion's-head-shaped Fury slides silently past.

[I love the way the intervals are random.]

After a few hours, he sees another lit tunnel ending in another unlocked hatchway.

[They use hydrazine rocket engines to maintain the station attitude. There should be plenty of stores here we can use. I hope.]

'Getting sufficient back will be difficult.'

[I got us here. I leave the heavy lifting to you.]

He opens the door. Inside, there is gravitation again. It is dark save for the illumination from the tunnel. He closes the hatchway behind him and lights come on. He is in a short, white-painted interspace, sealed at the end in a thick blast door.

A green button is flush with the wall at the end. He presses it and the blast door rolls open. There is a tick, gradually increasing in speed, as he steps through. The door will close once the ticks become continuous.

His skin returns to matt titanium. No need to waste energy here.

Inside is a large chamber. It is a grid of floor-to-ceiling square containment vessels. He notes, in passing, that each is bigger than any of the prison cells. It is cold here. Red and yellow warning signs are centred on every wall.

Each containment chamber has a heavy door surmounted by a stainless-steel wheel.

Samara spins open the first one he sees. The door gradually

ejects towards him, coming back on two large hinges at the top and bottom. These are on wheels in embedded flanges and run along the inside so that the door slides to the side.

It is empty, a few containment boxes left lying on the floor alongside high shelves.

He closes the door and moves on. The fifth one contains a number of boxes. Each box contains a single half-metre rocket engine. The heads are flat, with a small connection plug socket. The pipes are pinched a third of the way from the end, then angling out to a cone the same width as the pipe. A waxy wrapping seals each end.

[Perfect. They're integrated. We can build a controller, and I can manage our descent easily. Let's take twelve, to be safe. We may not use them all.]

'You have a strange definition of "safe". How stable are these?'

[They're cheap, but there's a reason we never used these. I wouldn't recommend dropping them.]

Samara carefully carries boxes to the blast door and piles them gingerly in the interspace between. It takes an hour before they are all carefully stowed there.

He returns to the storage bunker intending to close the last containment vessel door.

[Hazard!]

A man, wiry, his hair grey, long and wild about his head, his beard across his chest, attacks him with a sharpened metal spear.

Samara ducks, twists past him, the spear clanging against the containment vessel.

'Stop! I have no wish to hurt you,' he shouts, as calmly as he can.

The man's eyes are manic, his teeth grinding frenetically inside his open mouth. He is naked, his body emaciated, his fingernails bitten, his toenails long and curved.

He screams incoherently and swings again.

[His mind is gone.]

'Please,' says Samara. Edging backwards towards the blast door.

The man grabs the remaining box from inside the open containment vessel. He is shaking it furiously.

[Oh. That isn't good.]

'Stop!' shouts Samara, but the man flings his spear at him.

Samara catches it, then sees that the man has opened the box and is preparing to attack him with the heavy rocket engine.

[Disable him.] The words urgent in his head.

Too late: the man smashes it against a wall as he runs at Samara. The end starts to spark. He stops, looks at it in puzzlement, then at Samara.

[Run.]

Samara hits the red button on the outside of the blast door, pummelling the green button on the other side before it has scarce opened. The door slides shut.

There is a dull retort, as of something smashing into the solid wall on the other side. The banging continues, around the containment vessels, against the outer walls. A rapid series of thuds. Uncontrolled, it will burn until there is no more fuel.

[I don't believe we need to go back in there.]

'No. Poor man,' says Samara. 'What a terrible life.'

He must have been sleeping while Samara was busy. Perhaps there are food stores here too for the technicians who must sometimes visit to reload the attitude adjustment systems. Living alone in that cold room for years on end.

He stands for a few moments, then secretes a small silver bead from his finger on to the green button. The droplet slides behind it, into the mechanism, disabling it on both sides.

No alarms have sounded. Either the station sensors are broken in the storage room, or there were none to start with.

He returns to invisibility and begins, slowly, carrying the boxes through the tunnels. He keeps careful pace with a faint shimmering aura along the walls; silver beads temporarily blinding the sensors, masking the movement of the still visible boxes.

[Do you notice something strange here?]

They are at an intersection where Samara is preparing to turn right.

[Feel the wall to our left. Yes. Ripples in the metal. Coming from along the tunnel.]

Samara stares into the darkness, considering. He heads up the left passage. The ripples are no longer subtle, growing in amplitude as he goes.

[Samar, I'm not sure about this.]

'If there was an explosion, I want to know how much damage there was. Maybe that explains the torturers' run?'

[Samara, we can't be sure that whatever caused the explosion is stable. We −] He stops.

Faint radiance ahead, and an obstruction.

The metal walls have buckled inwards. Tears in the skin glow red, illuminating the tunnel. Samara grips the edges of the gap and holds himself so that he can look through.

It is madness there.

[Samar, no.]

A larger rip in the wall allows Samara to squeeze through.

Tongues of torn metal curl out from every cell along about twenty metres of the corridor. Somehow the cells must have become over-pressurized until, eventually, they burst.

That is not all. The empty space has been put to use.

[It's the bodies. They pile the bodies here.]

Rammed on to metal spikes, or jammed into ragged tears, are

corpses. Their bodies are ripped open. They are of all states of degradation. Some still bleeding. Men and women. Hair, long, grey and matted, or shaven, depending on how long they have been in space.

The air here is fetid, plague-ridden.

Samara starts to pant, his breath short.

'Who's there?'

A figure clambers from one of the cells. It is dextrous, comfortable in the weightlessness. Man or woman, impossible to tell. Its skin coated in blood and ordure. Its hair is a few clotted fronds.

'We hear you. Come out, come out,' giggling, the voice shrill and unpleasant. It stops to wretch and spit against one of the walls.

It looks around.

Samara has frozen, his breathing and pulse imperceptible.

'Nothing? Well, we mustn't stay hungry. Children must be fed.'

It flings itself at a pile of corpses choking the entrance to a cell, grabs at an arm to stay itself and scrabbles at the top body.

'Fresh. Fresh. Yes, fresh,' tearing off the head and smashing the skull open against the sharp metal spike holding the bodies in place.

The skull cracks open, and the creature flings itself back towards the cell from where it came.

'Children, food for you,' and a skin-searing howling erupts.

[No, Samara, please. Don't go there.]

'What children?'

A headless torso floats in the cavity near the cells. It is hollow: ribs jagged, guts trailing out in the air leading towards it. Globs of blood and matter drifting around it. It has congealed into a sticky, ruddy mass in the air.

Samara pushes himself towards the entrance.

A man, obviously a man, is wedged just inside the entrance, tearing at a desiccated leg, stripping off the meat and sucking it down. The other figure – in the light Samara can now see it is a woman, her breasts flat and dry – scrambles over him, the skull in one hand, leaking putrescent globules.

The walls inside the cell are scarred where they were torn apart by the explosion and scratched by prisoners.

And there are the children.

Mewling and howling. They are tied to the far wall. Their bodies stunted, twisted, horribly disfigured. Scarcely recognizable as human. Their eyes, where they have them, blind. Their bodies covered in filth. The woman – their mother – feeds them with lumps of brain from the skull she cracked open.

Samara flees back behind the barrier.

He closes his eyes, weeping. He can feel Symon clinging to him for comfort.

After he has composed himself, he moves on.

There are no further incidents, no more side journeys, but it is a day before he is back in the works warehouse.

He piles up the boxes at the distant end, surrounding them with metal sheets as a form of shielding.

He does not discuss with the others what he has seen. He gets back to work.

27

Symon is lost in the wonders of Henshaw Market.

A crowd of people are watching a public performance. A man has climbed up a tall pole and is seated on a small plank resting on a fork at the top. He perches, as if brooding. On his head is a feathered headdress. The mask is white, with black lines across the forehead and a bird-like beak painted below the cut-out eyes.

A slack line is tied between this pole and another, a few metres away. A wooden fence blocks the view of the base of the space between the two poles. The man slides forwards on to the rope and balances there, his arms outstretched beneath his cloak.

Rising up from behind the fence, pulled up towards the slack line, is a woman. She also wears a bird-like headdress and mask. Once on the slack line they perform a mating dance, baring their throats, raising their wings.

It is oddly beautiful and graceful.

Joshua allows the group to watch for a while before leading them towards the fabricators. The market is crowded with traders and shoppers, sounds and smells. There is shouting, laughter, and an underlying tension.

Men in military fatigues push through the crowds. Symon watches as one saunters up to a fruit stand. He picks up an apple, takes a bite out of it, spits it on the ground and throws the apple back on to the pile. The owner apologizes profusely and carefully removes the offending fruit.

The militiaman pushes the vendor away and wanders off.

Joshua calls, 'Symon, we cannot help you here; you will have to choose. These are the multi-material printers.'

An awning is hoisted along a set of blocky warehouses. Each has its doors thrown open and pictures displayed of the sorts of things they can produce. Touts stand outside the entrances, shouting their wares.

'Motors, motors! All sizes!'

'Generators and stoves! Get your generators here!'

'Refrigerators and washing machines!'

The first two printers are too small. The third does not print batteries. The fourth has not the right resolution.

The fifth is at the end of this block. The machine is four metres wide, the printing cavity about three. Symon studies the machine. It is grimy and covered in layers of printing fluids, but the cavity is pristine. A stout man in a faded blue djellaba emerges from an office at the back of the printworks.

'May I help you?' he asks.

'I believe you may,' says Symon. 'I wish to print a high-density closed aluminium-air battery. About 250 kilograms. There appears to be plenty of aluminium in the market right now.'

'That there is,' says the man, 'coming in from all over.' He squints at them, appraising his customers. He nods, points Symon to the console on the machine.

Symon sits at the stool before the device and scrolls through schematics, analysing, searching.

'I am Ghanim,' the man says. 'This is my brother, Faysal,' indicating another touting outside. 'The big fellows,' gesturing at the four heavily armed men looming in the shadows, 'are Ishaq,

Kashif, Nuri and Aiman. Don't worry, they are cousins, here to protect us.'

Joshua introduces his people, remaining wary in the entrance. Symon fixes on a particular schematic. He brings up the editor, makes a few adjustments, refining the template pattern and the constituent fluids. He saves it and says, 'This one.'

Ghanim extracts a case from deep within the folds of his djellaba, withdraws his spectacles and prods the console. He studies the manifest, making the sorts of sounds learned by artisans the world over: the rising throat-clearing and head-shaking that indicates tremendous costs are being accrued.

'One hundred, twenty-two thousand dollars,' he says, as if producing a rabbit out of a hat.

Symon stands, looms over him, oblivious to the guards. 'Fifty-nine. I know what your inputs will cost and we both know that forty per cent is an acceptable margin for each of us.' His voice is flat, final.

Ghanim sucks in his lips over his teeth, then purses them, pushing out his beard. He raises his eyebrows, staring into Symon's eyes. 'Very well, that is acceptable. It is a good deal. Pray that I don't do too many such good deals,' he laughs. 'You pay me up front?'

'Escrow.'

'Very well, you should have the honour of choosing.'

Symon looks to Joshua, who joins them. 'We normally use Lloyds,' he says.

Ghanim shakes his head. 'You must not have heard. They collapsed after a tsunami in Japan almost a decade ago. Could I suggest BlockWorks? They are new, and their fees are very low.'

Joshua looks pained and shakes his head. 'How about Doretheum?'

Ghanim nods assent and sighs, 'It is traditional that I say this, so forgive me.' He shakes his head sadly, 'You're taking food out of my children's mouths, but I accept.' Then he grins broadly and grabs Symon's hand, 'Shake.'

Symon nods at Joshua. He reaches into an inner pocket in his shirt and produces a thin transparent card. He walks over to the machine and places the card on to a narrow silver panel alongside the console.

The card lights up, going through red, then blue, then green. It is ready.

Ghanim accepts the transaction on the console then steps aside as a cone of green light extends up from the card.

Joshua pauses, takes a deep breath, places his hand flat and palm down within the cone. He closes his hand, turns it over, pushes out two fingers, opens, closes, turns his hand over, waggles his thumb, then opens his hand so that it returns to its starting point. The light flashes briefly white.

The first signature is accepted.

Joshua turns to make way for Abishai, who places her hand in the cone and makes a similarly complex set of gestures. The cone flashes white once more.

Daniel's turn. He grins at Joshua, then begins.

'Please, take a seat,' says Joshua. 'This will be some time. Perhaps you have tea?'

Daniel's hand gestures are utterly elaborate. He makes shadow puppets, does little dances with his fingers, noises.

Ghanim looks horrified. 'Perhaps coffee?' He motions to Faysal, who disappears into the back of the workshop.

Eventually, Daniel finishes. The cone flashes white one last time, and the funds are transferred to Doretheum's escrow account.

'I never know why you insist on making it so complicated. There is no need for it,' says Joshua.

Sarah laughs and Ghanim shrugs. 'It pays to be safe,' he says, doubtfully.

Daniel grins and hands the card back to Joshua. Faysal returns with a tray filled with small shot glasses of coffee. He hands one to each of them, including the guards, who remain silent and watchful.

'We are outside the connect?' asks Symon.

'Yes,' says Ghanim. 'Why?'

'I was wondering how the transactions are synchronized.'

Ghanim stares at him thoughtfully. 'There are sphere all through Calabar, and out on to the floating markets across the river. They reach to the connect in Ikonitu. It is not too far.'

The machine starts to warm up, the cavity undergoing its vacuum stage.

'How long before we can pick it up?' asks Symon.

Ghanim shrugs again, 'The printing should be complete by morning. Another day and a half to charge. You come pick it up then, it will be ready.'

'What shall we do until then?' asks Jason.

'There is a lovely place at the other end of the market, owned by a cousin. You stay there, tell Behzad I sent you. You will see. It has two oil palms outside the doors. Behzad's Place,' says Ghanim, enthusiastically pointing them in the appropriate direction.

Joshua shakes his head and shrugs, why not?

They head across the market once more before spotting the oil palms. As Ghanim says, you cannot miss it. The restaurant area is large, consoles mounted to the walls with some warbling music playing. There are cellulosic chairs and tables scattered through-out and a bar area at the back. A few people are already sitting and drinking, and a few others are enjoying a late lunch.

Behzad himself is at the reception counter. His djellaba is

purple, with green and white vertical stripes. They are not slimming.

'You are doing business with my cousin? How wonderful. We will find you quiet rooms at the back of the house,' leading them through corridors to the rear. They will share two rooms, the men in one and the women in a smaller room alongside.

Daniel inspects each. They are serviceable, for two nights anyway. The men's room has an open shower, a sink, three single beds and one double. Symon will not be sleeping, so one of them will get the double. No cupboards, no shelves, no chairs.

'You will eat downstairs in the restaurant? We make good soups,' says Behzad.

Joshua nods. It is only for two nights.

Symon returns to the restaurant while the others wash and change clothes. As he walks into the bar area, he sees a familiar figure sitting on the stage.

'Ismael, it's been years,' he says.

'Symon,' says the dark-skinned man. He is wearing the same delicately embroidered ochre-brown boubou and matching kufi skullcap as when he was in Ewuru two weeks ago. It looks no less immaculate. 'You are inside out.'

Nothing ever surprises the griots, and every conversation proceeds as if you had merely returned from a short walk.

'We had to make a rapid decision,' says Symon.

Ismael studies the Achenian. He sees what is hidden – what others cannot notice. He pats the stage next to him, and Symon sits.

'I can restore the balance,' he inclines his head, 'if only for a short while. Maybe enough to return home, and then only if you are careful.'

'Why would you do this? Your people never intervene,' says Symon.

'This is not intervening,' says Ismael, his eyes filled with compassion. 'This is restoring order in a situation where you are an unacceptable danger to yourself and others.'

Symon considers. 'I am grateful for your kindness.'

'Not at all. I have gratitude for Samara's father. The son of Etai and Airmid should not suffer so. Neither should you.'

Ismael raises his hands and places them on either side of Symon's head, over his ears. He begins to sing, softly, rising through chords. He transmits the resonance through his quivering fingers and into Symon.

Joshua and the others are struck by the scene as they arrive back in the restaurant. The two men, bowed as if in prayer, sitting at the edge of the stage. They approach slowly, hesitant to know if they are intruding.

Ismael completes his song. Symon opens his eyes, looks at him. 'I don't feel any different?'

'No, it will take several hours. Perhaps tomorrow morning you will feel better. Tonight I will sing and you will rest. No harm can happen here.'

Ismael smiles warmly, 'Joshua,' shaking his hand and touching it to his heart. He greets each of them – Daniel, Sarah, Abishai, David and Jason – in turn.

'Come, sit with me. Behzad's coffee is quite good. He somehow contrives to bring it here from Ethiopia.'

They draw up two tables to host them all, and order coffee. While they are waiting, Ismael says, 'Symon, have I ever told my favourite of Etai's samara?'

Ismael's tale

Pinch Point

Usted's bow light picks out his slow progress up the river to where I wait aboard the stricken yacht.

The river here is wide but shallow. Fast moving where the water rushes about the rocks and shoals. Usted has sailed his tug up and down the waters of the Surkhob for forty-five years but, in early spring, at three in the morning, he knows that only a fool rushes.

And I'm not going anywhere.

My wife and I came to Tajikistan a decade ago: short-term replacements for a district commissar on sick leave. He died. We stayed.

The people in my district are Wakhi. They have been here for thousands of years, always the spoils of one empire or another. They've outlasted the Persians, the Sassanids, the Samanids, the Qarakhanids, the Timurids, the Astrakhanids, the Manghits, Jahangir Khoja and his short-lived madness, the Soviets, their own strong men, and they've seen us Russians return.

They'll outlast us once more.

What does a commissar in one of Russia's colonies do, you ask? A lot and a little, depending on one's approach. The first commissars treated these postings as an opportunity to loot and build up a little power before returning to the comforts of home.

They soon learned that it is far more than 3,000 kilometres from Moscow to Dushanbe.

Now, most commissars are drunks: despised at home, hated by the people unfortunate enough to have them.

We Russians came here for the minerals, which, a century ago, still had some meaning. Now, not so much. We stay because to go would be to admit the weakness and corruption at the heart of the state. I don't believe that any of the other nations care what we do any longer. Stay, go. Do what you will.

We have built an empire and become the worst face of what we have always accused others of being.

The people could rebel but they do not. Perhaps they accept. Perhaps they believe that the fight would be devastating. Fifty years ago we could have turned even the stones to dust. Now, all they would have to do is push out a few commissars. There is nothing the state could do.

My wife and I chose to come.

We are a long way from the siloviks and arbitrary rules of the city, and we may do a little good. I travel constantly across my territory. I visit villages, schools, clinics. I listen, I document. I learned the songs of the people. I wrote a book of Pamiri poetry. I updated the historical and ethnographic records. I do a little medicine.

Mostly, I connect isolated hamlets, sharing best practice, leaving a little in one village that I pick up in another. My wife travels with me, my constant friend, adviser and companion. We helped finance the first printer in Obigram, also the first in my district. I assisted Rogun School to raise funds for a sphere.

Sometimes my wife and I advise in civil disputes, but mostly we listen. I do not know if we are loved – how could anyone love an imperialist? – but we are respected. Perhaps even trusted, a little.

I have taken it upon myself to remind them of who they are, what makes them special, one to another. The depth of their culture. The wonder of their heritage. The hard-faced beauty of their world.

Sometimes they hear. Sometimes they don't. I am not leading them to change. I am a messenger. The choices are theirs.

I love the mountains: the dry, dusty magnificence of the land-scape. The ice and the power still left in the glaciers, carving their way through canyons and gorges for millennia. Have you seen an avalanche consuming all in its path? I love the villages in the foot-hills. The smell of osh and the taste of green tea. The people, their faces so preternaturally old, guarded, keeping their thoughts.

I enjoy the silence of their conversation.

Agh, listen to the ambassador complain. 'Ambassador', as if giving him the title somehow justifies the oppression. 'They have an ambassador, they're actually independent. They want us here.'

Our ambassador has a luxury motor yacht. Flew it by helicopter from Moscow and deposited it in the Nurek Reservoir beside his little dacha by the lake. I grant you, it is splendid from the outside, but – like the Russian Empire – quite hollow. The motor is too small for the currents; the range is too short for the distance. It is only partially fitted out on the inside. After the stateroom, there wasn't much money left for the rest.

'Why can't these peasants move any faster?' he is shouting. Like his boat, the ambassador is hollow. No insight, no patience.

Usted is close now. I can see his wife, Sarez, standing with him. They are a matched pair. Him in an old hat, her in a shawl. Similar faces, except for his thin moustache. His concentration is intense.

The ambassador is not grateful. His wife is shouting, too. It is not Usted who chose to sail up the Surkhob in the spring in a big yacht. Usted did not run it into the gravel shoals that are so treacherous all along its winding banks.

Usted comes on board. I greet him. He nods at me. In this place, at this time, that is warmth indeed. He stares blankly at the ambassador as he shouts. Usted has no Russian. He wouldn't listen even if he did.

'I'll be in the stateroom,' says the ambassador, taking his skinny wife with him. As if there is anywhere else to sit. There are no servants on the yacht, no kitchen. Only a cabinet full of vodka.

He called me in the late afternoon to come out. Did not tell me that his yacht had run aground. He thought I could fix it myself. I came by car and then, at a tiny village with no name nearby, had a small boy take me out in his rowboat. There was nothing I could do.

I could have called on many people from Nurek. I chose Usted.

Usted looks at me, asking. I shrug and make a slight bow to him. This is his call to make. Usted stares at me. His gaze is an interrogation: why would a big boat like this not be able to get itself off the gravel?

Usted turns, opens the hatchway door and enters the yacht. The cabin is narrow but wide, and the stateroom door is closed. Usted guesses that the engine must be aft and he opens the door on the left. There is darkness and he flashes his electric torch, looking for a light switch. He illuminates a shell of a room.

He is silent. He steps into the room and I follow. He sees that the other two doors come into this space as well. He moves his torch back and forth, identifying the motor-housing at the rear. He lifts up the wooden cowl. Underneath is a small motor, scarcely big enough to power a launch.

Usted shines his light on me. I stare back. I am still. I say nothing.

Maybe he hears. Maybe he doesn't. I am not their saviour. I merely pick up a little in one place and share it again in another. Sometimes that is enough; mostly it makes no impact at all.

Usted and Sarez tow us all the way back to the wharf at Nurek, standing side by side in the cockpit saying nothing.

The ambassador emerges when we arrive. He can barely stand. His wife is passed out on one of the magnificent sofas. He offers no thanks and staggers up the pathway towards his mansion house.

I slip money into Sarez's hands as I thank her, money I know Usted would not accept. He inclines his head, a humorous gesture from a man who never smiles.

I watch them sail away, Usted and Sarez in the cockpit, side by side, saying nothing at all. Eventually, they are too far away to see except as a beacon, carrying their light out into the darkness beyond.

28

Symon looks pale. 'I feel dizzy,' he says, awkward and uncomfortable.

Joshua stands hastily. 'What should we do?'

'It is well, Symon,' says Ismael. 'The process has started. You should sleep. In the morning you will be back inside. You will be safe here tonight.'

Symon nods, shrugs off help. 'Samara will be here in the morning. Thank you and I will be in the room.' He walks away.

'What does he mean?' asks Daniel.

'I have given him a temporary relief,' says Ismael. 'As long as you are gentle over the next few days, he may make it back to his people as Samara.'

Joshua looks surprised and curious, 'Balladeer, if you have chosen to intervene, why not call his people?'

'I am not intervening,' he smiles. 'Even if I were to choose to do so, I could not contact his people directly. My symbiont is similar but different from their technology. Now, did I not say that Behzad's coffee was good? Come, we shall have another.'

Joshua can see that they will get no more from the Griot. Daniel is not finished yet.

'Balladeer, is that what you do? Pick up a little in one place and leave a little behind?' he asks.

Ismael's eyes crinkle with delight. He giggles, shaking, his hands steepled on the table. 'Perhaps,' he says.

'Do you know what happened sixty-five years ago?' he asks.

Jason answers, as every child knows, 'The war in the sky.'

'Yes,' says Ismael, 'but do you know what it was about?'

The others shake their heads. This did not involve their people at all.

'You are too young to know, and it was a long way away, but many things are because of what was.'

'Balladeer, forgive me,' says Joshua with a smile, 'must you always be so cryptic?'

Ismael chuckles again. 'Very well, let me tell you a little of what happened. But not about myself. Perhaps you can ask Samara tomorrow?

'There was a war, but it was not in space. It was in China. That was where it began.

'China, sixty-five years ago, was a great power. Yuèliàng was the greatest of the orbital cities and entirely owned and controlled by the Party. Except, as countless empires have discovered in the past, controlling distant outposts is difficult. Seven hundred and fifty thousand people, all highly educated and ambitious, clustered in one place. They declared independence. Unilaterally.

'China claimed to be surprised. They blamed a conspiracy of outsiders,' Ismael makes a face like an ogre. 'Silliness. There had been a protest movement for almost fifty years by then. Plenty of time to invent the form of a new state.

'China refused to accept. They tried to send troops to retake the city, but the people of Yuèliàng simply closed their space elevator and blocked the entrances. Even if they could fly troops up, without the elevator they could land no more than a few hundred at a time, against such a vast city. There is not much you can do to a place that is already fully self-sufficient.

'The Chinese leadership was proud. They could not accept this betrayal. For if Yuèliàng, then what of their subjugate states on Earth? What of Tibet, Mongolia, Bhutan, Taiwan? They aimed their great nuclear arsenal in Tibet at the station and gave them an ultimatum.

'Tibet erupted. So too did Mongolia and Xinjiang. Troops were sent in. Fighters from around the world travelled to Tibet. Your Samara was amongst them.

'What?' says Joshua. 'His people sent troops? I understand that they cannot be beaten?'

'The Nine cannot be beaten here on Earth, no,' says Ismael, 'but Samara was not yet one of them. He was only twenty-eight. A boy. A very lost boy.

'His father is the most talented storyteller of our age. His grandfather one of its greatest inventors. His mother a leading biologist. His grandmother is a brilliant poet. Samara has no special gifts. He travels incessantly. He visits other orbital cities. He joins lost causes. Stranded between genius, he searches for someone to be.'

'He is a good man. Did his family not see this?' asks Sarah.

'This has nothing to do with his family. They love him, cherish him. They do not ask anything other than that he be happy. This is his journey.

'In Tibet, he joined a group of Uyghurs who had travelled to Lhasa from Xinjiang to confront the Chinese. Lhasa, the capital, was a violent brawl.'

The names and peoples mean little to the others. The Griot does not explain. No matter, they can understand the complexity and the chaos.

'The United Nations was meeting. This was a great legal gathering of all the leaders of all the independent countries of the world. China, though, was one of its key members. And too many other countries had their own restive orbital cities. They could not reach agreement on what China should do.

'No one, though,' his eyes gleam, 'would assist the Chinese by allowing them to use their space elevators.

'As the leaders debated, the fighting in Tibet was growing ever more oppressive. China declared they would not fire nuclear missiles, but that left many other options. They fired a test missile at Lhasa. One hundred and fifty thousand people were killed. The city was dust. The Potala Palace, which had stood for more than six hundred years, was destroyed.

'Samara's Uyghurs were incensed. They attacked the compound outside the city of Shigatse where the missiles were based. The Chinese were waiting. They slaughtered them. Samara was badly injured, but Symon saved him.

'Two missiles were fired. Yuèliàng was an orbital city, unarmed and defenceless. Seven hundred and fifty thousand people were killed instantly. The explosion created a massive debris cloud. Two small nearby orbital cities, Cuthbar and New Kuwait, were destroyed. Another nineteen thousand people were killed.'

Sarah and David have gone pale. Joshua has clenched his fists. Daniel, Abishai and Jason stare downcast at the table.

'A wave of debris spread out around the earth. It became suicidal for any craft to enter high earth orbit unshielded. The remaining cities had to respond quickly or they would also be destroyed. Some were able to amplify their fusion reactors to generate a safety field. Some borrowed reactors. Some broke orbit and moved out into the solar system. Some were not so fortunate.

'The orbital cities adapted. There was migration as smaller cities emptied, their people moving to the biggest. Achenia gained one hundred and fifty thousand new people in ten years. The cities that chose to remain in orbit created shielded channels through which they could transfer ships and goods. They covered their cities in gravel and rock that they harvested from the moon. They made themselves safe from the debris cloud, but they have not felt safe ever since.'

'That is the metal that the militia collect when it falls from space? The remains of the dead?' asks Abishai.

'Indeed, my daughter,' says Ismael.

'And what of the great leaders? Did they do nothing?' asks Joshua.

'The United Nations collapsed. People lost faith in their leaders. Worse followed. The orbital cities refused to trade. China had, in one act, murdered most of its great thinkers and academics. Far from bringing order, the Chinese state disintegrated. Trade collapsed. Many nations followed, losing access to borrowed goods and capital, and falling apart. And the result to your nation you know.

'There was another effect, though. Much of the Earth's space-based infrastructure was in higher earth orbit. Satellites were destroyed. Most of the connect went with them. A land-based connect was rebuilt, but it is not the same, not as ever-present as the old. Many regions are left outside, such as Ewuru. Maybe that is a good thing?' Ismael raises his eyebrows.

'There were many space elevators,' he shakes his head. 'The debris chopped through most of them, leaving only three. It is expensive to keep them safe against the debris but, even though they are not much used, these elevators are still there. Japan's Hokkaido city, Achenia's, and that managed by the US, supporting their Tartarus prison.'

'Where Samara was,' says Jason.

Ismael touches his nose, nodding.

'In the aftermath, we griots made a decision. We would leave the orbital cities and return to Earth. We will document the turning of the seasons – become an ancient memory as in times of old.

The original griots were a people's knowledge of themselves. We can aspire to no less.'

'There are many of you?' asks Sarah.

'Enough,' he smiles.

'And Samara?' asks Jason.

'That I do not know. You may ask him, perhaps he will tell you?'

Ismael rises from his seat. 'Thank you for your company. Now, I must go and earn my keep,' he says.

The restaurant has filled. People are still arriving and cramming into spaces along the walls and around the stage. A pleasant buzz of friendship and expectation.

'So that is why he had to come down to Earth and not stay in orbit to cross to his own people,' says Daniel. 'I could not understand that choice, but this makes sense.'

'It also makes sense why his people would take such care before – what is the term he used? – cutting the umbilical,' says Abishai.

'I think we should eat,' says Joshua.

'Yes, I am starving,' says Jason.

'I cannot eat,' says Sarah. Her face is haunted. 'Those poor people.'

Joshua reaches across the table and holds her hand. She looks up at him. 'My daughter, you must eat. We must honour the dead, but we must also care for ourselves.'

She takes a deep breath and slowly eases it out. Nods and squeezes his hand.

Up on the stage, Ismael is seated on a three-legged cellulosic stool. He straddles the wide calabash base of a kora, the twenty-one-string harp of West Africa. He looks out at the room, beaming. He extends his forefinger on to a string and begins to rub it up and down.

He releases it, and the strident rhythm continues. He plucks harmonies and melodies. Each adding to the former. He taps on the calabash, creating a percussive beat. The sound rises, takes shape, a force that envelops the room. People are dancing, stamping their feet, an ecstatic pandemonium.

He stands, leaving the kora. The music still plays. He jumps off the stage, dancing amongst the people. His arms at his shoulders, his bottom out. He touches plates, glasses, spoons, setting up new melodies, new harmonies.

Then he begins to sing, a rap-beat at first, adding new voices. He is a choir of one.

An ugly man in a bad hat tries to hit him as he passes. Ismael turns the punch into a dance and touches the man lightly on the nose. The man in the bad hat, completely against his will, stands still and begins to sing in a deep baritone. Ismael continues, touching each of the ugly man's companions until they are all singing.

They join him in his dance and follow him back on stage where, despite the horrified anguish in their eyes, they continue to dance and sing as Ismael conducts them and the laughing, jubilant audience.

People are crowding in from the streets. The Celebration of the City has never been heard in Ewuru, and Joshua, Sarah, Daniel, David, Jason and Abishai dance, their souls open with joy.

29

He has a distorted vision of a plain white room. Three single beds, one double. 'What's that?' asks Samara.

Then he is back in the warehouse, a lathe before him, metal pipes on the bench.

Now that they know the exact dimensions of the rocket engines, he is able to build tubes to contain them. This leaves little space for the gyroscope. He begins turning long aluminium bars into the gimbals he will need. He will have to crouch inside.

He builds, tracking down heat-reflecting tiles, bearings and other components. It takes three days to complete.

Seymour and Henry have been waiting for a fourth. 'Seeing as how you're eating, mister, would you like to join us to play a few hands?'

'Yes,' he nods, 'I would enjoy that.'

Sancho has never played. He learns as they bid.

'No, no,' says Henry, only slightly frustrated with his partner, 'if I open you have to bid. Return it to me so I can choose a suit.'

Samara has diplomatically instructed Symon to interfere with his game-play so that he performs rather worse than the abject Sancho.

Just as diplomatically, the others rotate partners so that each gets a chance to win.

'I hope that there ship flies better 'n you play, mister,' laughs Seymour.

'Me too,' he says.

Samara has measured his food intake carefully. Work for three hours, eat for an hour, repeat. He never sleeps.

While the men go back to other card games, or perform chores, or simply stare at him, Samara works.

The most complex mechanism, after the gyroscope and rocket controllers, is the spring-loaded bearing ring. This will grip the space elevator cable and adjust to its varying diameter. An electromagnet connects it to the pod. The umbilical itself provides energy to the mechanism.

'It looks like a propeller, mister. You going to be able to get that through the double seal?' asks Seymour.

'It should just fit,' says Samara, picking it up and carrying it to the doorway. He is almost up to his target weight, and the floor seems to bend slightly at each step.

'Mister, where all that food going? It never comes out,' observes Sancho.

'Where it needs to,' he smiles.

'You're real strange, mister, but we like you,' says Seymour, beaming. 'When you going?'

'Eighteen hours,' he says. 'I'll be at full weight by then.'

'Well, then,' says Henry, 'we have time for a few more games.'

Samara inspects the pallet beneath the conveyor. There is a pressure switch there that opens the doors and starts the exit process.

'I'll remove the boxes, place the pod on it. When I get to the other side, I'll discard the pallet so that it doesn't attract attention. Just place the boxes back on a pallet and the systems will never know.'

They play cards, and Samara continues eating one packet after another.

'We sure gonna miss playing bridge. Ain' really work without four,' says Sancho.

The men sleep as he polishes down the outer shell. Eventually, everything is done.

He wakes them before he goes. He shakes their hands. Seymour's eyes are red, moist.

Slipping off his cloak for the last time, Samara picks up the wing and steps on to the pallet. The pressure sensor is triggered, opening the inner entrance door, and he is pulled smoothly into the airlock. The door closes behind him and seals.

A few moments as the antechamber is reduced to a vacuum. Samara stops breathing. His body changes, silver fluid diffusing out of his skin, filling his mouth, ears, nose, every pore and space. His eyes are now unblinking solid hemispheres of silver. His fingers and toes appear to be encased in silver gloves. He can feel as the great mass he has built up focuses in density around his surface, protecting him from the vacuum of space. His body completes its adjustments to the pressure change.

The opposite door rolls open, and he is drawn out into the cargo bay.

Empty clear-plastic stretchers from prisoner arrivals are piled against the walls. The palette stops against a stack of boxes. There is gravity here, but no atmosphere.

Samara picks up the pod and carries it to the opening. The umbilical cable is suspended a platform's length away. This is where the elevator arrives, sealing the space.

He returns to the empty pallet, picks it up and flings it out and away from the entrance. It tumbles, drifting off to join the rest of the debris cloud.

He stares down the safe channel.

[Any words of return?]

'No.' He looks only at the planet below. There is a very long and lonely journey ahead.

He opens the escape pod hatch, holds the inside with one hand and the door handle with the other. Orientating the wing ahead of him. He walks to the edge.

And leaps.

He grabs the cable. Slots the bearing ring about it. Orientating the pod to face straight down, he carefully climbs inside. The door seals closed as he slips inside the rings of the gyroscope, crouching and pushing his back into the moulded body-rest on the inner gimbal. His hands grip two short crossbars, his feet slip inside two brackets. Magnetic fasteners clamp shut about his arms, legs, wrists, ankles, forehead and torso. He is immobilized.

A rocket fires.

His mind goes blank.

30

'I am awake,' says Samara, disbelief in his voice.

Daniel and Jason are flat on their backs, snoring loudly. David is lying in the double bed, alongside Jason, his arms crossed behind his head. They lost a game of akamokwu – war fingers – and were forced to share when they returned last night. He turns his face to Samara and grins.

Joshua emerges from the bathroom, a towel around his waist and an old scar visible diagonally across his chest. 'Welcome back, my friend,' he smiles. 'We have much to tell you.'

Joshua dresses and, while David showers, starts to fill Samara in on what has happened over the past few days. David returns and, ungraciously, drizzles water into Jason's open mouth as he lies snoring.

'That is for keeping me awake all night, you sack of frogs,' he says, laughing.

Daniel rolls over and covers his head with his pillow as Jason splutters and howls.

Joshua ignores them and continues. 'Symon arranged the battery, and I hope you will know if it is fully charged?'

'Not as well as if we were still associated, but I should be able to tell.'

'Come, shall we have breakfast? David, please see if Sarah and

Abishai are ready to join us,' says Joshua, rising and opening the door.

Behzad is downstairs looking pleased with himself. Would that the Marabout would visit every night.

'My friends, I had no knowledge that you were friends with the Marabout,' he greets Joshua and Samara as they come down the stairs past the reception counter. 'How wonderful for you.'

'We know him as the Balladeer,' says Joshua, 'and you are doubly blessed that he chooses your restaurant to perform.'

'Ismael was here?' asks Samara.

'Ah, but he left this morning,' says Behzad, looking curiously at Samara. Something is different about him today. 'Come, have breakfast. I bring you tea and sweet breads.'

David and the others join them. Daniel wandering down the stairs, bleary-eyed, a few minutes later.

'I'm sorry I missed him,' says Samara. 'When I was a boy, he would stay with my parents and tell me the funniest tales. We would both laugh so much I thought I would burst.'

'He told us the strangest story. I think it was about his people,' says Abishai. 'Who are they?'

'Joshua tells me Ismael told you about China?' asks Samara.

They nod.

'The war changed everything. Many cities survived the debris cloud by breaking orbit and heading out into space. There are two cities around Mars, a few around Titan and the rest just touring the planets. There are few cities left in orbit.

'Before, our struggles had been for independence. Now it wasn't so peculiar to hear people discussing leaving the solar system.

'The griots are different, more interested in the journey of our culture than in being in any particular place,' he says. 'There are tourists who visit the different orbital cities, and there are artists and musicians who travel into orbit to perform. The griots were drawn from the best of these artists. Soon after we developed the symbionts, a group of fifteen or so griots developed their own version. They wanted to be able to make music out of any physical thing.

'They chose to manage their symbionts without a synthetic intelligence. That is incredibly difficult and takes decades of training. They lack our connection to each other. It is impractical, but the control it gives them is remarkable.

'Their performances, particularly in our enhanced environment, are –' Samara struggles to find a way to describe his experience, and gives up. 'There are no words.'

'No,' agrees Sarah. 'There are no words.'

Food arrives, along with a steaming pot of tea, which Jason pours into mugs for each of them. The dough-like breads are sweet and very hot. Each tears off chunks and chews happily.

'After the war, six of them formed an agreement and came back to earth. They spread out across the planet, each choosing a region. They broke out of our connect long ago, but I understand they are always in contact with each other. They travel constantly, carrying stories and music from place to place.'

'Why?' asks Daniel. 'We all appreciate them. I do not think the harvest would feel the same without them, but I am not sure of what this achieves?'

'When Pazzo and his men came to Ewuru, I wondered why the Balladeer stayed an extra night. I had the feeling that Pazzo was going to cause trouble, but when he saw the Balladeer he panicked. They did nothing. I imagine we do not always see the changes that he brings about,' says Joshua.

'Why would anyone fear them?' asks Daniel.

Samara grins, 'They're not helpless. The right frequency, like the right story, in the right place can move mountains.

'They believe that by telling stories and music from different cultures, people will set aside their differences and freely choose a peaceful path. They are not thinking in terms of decades but in terms of thousands of years. They have no intention of going anywhere.'

'And you, and your people?' asks Sarah.

'We will go out into the unknown. A group intend to return in one thousand years. My wife is keen. I have agreed I will follow her.'

'It seems so strange to plan for so long into the future,' says David.

'Well, yes,' says Daniel, 'but, for myself, what are we to do today?' he asks to laughter.

'I am not sure,' says Joshua, 'but I believe Behzad will have a cousin?' They are relaxed, happy together.

'I thought Calabar was too dangerous for us?' asks Samara.

'It is not a war zone,' says Joshua. 'It is dangerous to attract attention. Being too smart, too creative, too successful – these things attract the men with guns; but we are simple villagers here to sell our goods, be amazed at the sights of the great city and stock up on essentials before we go home. We can disappear amongst the thousands who do this every day.'

Behzad has, indeed, a cousin. 'He can take you to the marina and Tinapa; he has a jeep. I will call him for you.'

'What is Tinapa?' asks Sarah.

'You will see,' he waves his hands. 'We show many visitors. Very cultural.'

Samara feels as if it is his first day alive. Everything is new. The sounds, the smells, the people. He realizes Shakiso is right: there is a difference between reality and the synthesized world of the connect.

They wait outside in Henshaw Market for Behzad's cousin.

Cheering from a group of people attracts them. They sit and stand in ranks, all craning to see two men sitting in the dust beneath a rubber tree doing battle over a wooden board.

'It is nsa isong,' says Daniel, indicating the two rows of six pits in the board. 'You play by capturing seeds.' He pauses, deciding that the explanation is too much hard work. Grinning instead, 'You watch.'

The men glare at each other, sweat sheening their brows. Their hands moving swiftly, picking up and sowing the seeds clockwise around the board. Scarce has one distributed his load before the other is moving. They try to give each other as little time to think as possible. Each time a pit contains only four seeds the gathered crowd howls in support and the seeds are rapidly captured.

They watch for only a few minutes before an antique electric jeep shudders to a halt behind them. It is one of the old platform chassis, with the motors sealed in oval-shaped modules over each wheel. The battery is inside the short bonnet. Its lid is a badly fitting cellulosic reprint held on with bits of string. White steam rises from around the gaps.

The main driver's compartment is still mostly there, but the back consists of two narrow sofas bolted on to the chassis and facing each other, with a striped awning mounted on a frame over the top providing some shade. You can almost see tread on one of the tyres.

'Don't worry, don't worry,' says the young man scraping his way out of the navigator's seat. The door hangs lifelessly. He carefully picks it up, putting it back in place. The door on the passenger side looks absolutely immaculate. It probably is not used much.

'My name is Thomas. I will be your guide. Please, give me a few minutes and then we can go.'

He starts fiddling with the knots holding down the bonnet, teasing them loose. As he raises it, a cloud of steam erupts from the open-cast battery. He has two big bottles of acid stored inside the battery compartment.

Thomas's faded red djellaba is flecked with yellow, acid-scorched holes from regularly tending to the battery. The others take a respectful step backwards.

'That is going to catch fire some time today,' says Samara, merely as observation.

'Oh, no, it's always like this,' Thomas assures them.

'Past good fortune does not imply continued success,' says Samara, again, merely as observation.

Thomas looks vacantly at him, then, closing the bonnet and carefully retying his knots, 'It is done now. Please, wait for me to get in and then you can get in, too.'

Jason reaches for the passenger handle as Thomas climbs back inside. The handle comes off in Jason's hand. He stares at it inanely.

Inside the cockpit, Thomas soundlessly clutches at his face with one hand while snapping his fingers with the other. He looks like a man who has just been abandoned by his gods. The others stand around quietly, mournfully contemplating the violated door handle in Jason's numb fingers.

Thomas scrapes his way out once more. Settling his door in place. Straightening his djellaba. Walking in a short, hoppy, fastidious stride around the vehicle. Delicately taking the handle from Jason. 'I told you to wait. Why didn't you wait?' He deflates, pulls a tube of glue from his pocket and carefully reseals the handle to the door.

Nobody moves as he returns to his seat.

He leans across and opens the passenger door from the inside. 'You get in now,' he says.

Still, nobody moves.

'Please, you get in now.'

Jason climbs into the front while everyone else settles themselves into the sofas at the back, their knees jammed uncomfortably together. Thomas scrolls about on the console map setting waypoints before delicately pressing the big green 'go' button. The vehicle reverses, gently easing its way out of the market and on to Calabar Road.

There are few other vehicles and none appear in any better condition than the one they are in.

'Can they not print more?' asks Daniel.

'It's a little more complex than that,' says Samara. 'You can't print a whole vehicle in one of those machines. Which means you need people who know how to conceptualize an entire vehicle across different fabricators, create a manifest of all the appropriate components, print them and then put the whole thing together afterwards. Then there are the control systems that have to be loaded.'

They cross over a large intersection with Mary Slessor Road. A giant statue of the great lady cradling twins stands on an island in the traffic circle.

Hundreds of people are walking by the sides of the road. They carry umbrellas and bags of shopping. There is an endless series of tables, covered in fruit, meat, fish and other basics. Umbrellas and sheets protect the stalls from the sun.

Angular crosses from churches, interspersed with mosque minarets, tower above the shacks.

'There are those here who have the skills to build those components,' says Abishai. 'So why no new vehicles?'

'The militia are dangerous in this city, and the printers are careful. They have little incentive to produce what only the militia could afford but will only steal. The printers keep these vehicles repaired, but little else,' says Joshua.

'And the helicopters?' asks David.

A fire station, its garage doors wide open, is filled with gutted trucks that have long since stopped responding to alarms.

'Most likely those were purchased a long time ago. That's not new technology, but it isn't in the sphere. Probably Chinese army surplus shipped here before the war. I imagine when they stop running no one will be able to get them going again.'

They come to another traffic circle, this one with two improbably large six-fingered hands clasped as if in prayer, the thumbs unnaturally far from the fingers.

There are houses here now. One is painted with a fading hand-lettered notice all across the outside of its walls, 'Beware 419'.

A group of barefoot nuns cross the street, their white habits blinding in the searing sunshine.

They avoid the rusting hulk of a grader left where it broke down in the middle of the road a century ago. Other skeletal vehicle remains follow. Relics of the peculiar contradiction of a community no longer physically connected to the world, with continuing access to its ideas, but living in a city where their aspirations are subject to the conflict of its warlords.

They turn on to Ikom Highway and head out of Calabar.

'Where do you think he is taking us?' asks Sarah.

'Probably to that Tinapa place,' says Abishai.

'As long as we stay on this side of the river, we're out of the connect and I'll be happy,' says Samara.

They pass a series of giant concrete squares. They must once have been intended for a sewerage pipeline. They have been covered in tarpaulins and converted into single-room houses. Children play in the spaces between them. Washing lines are strung from one to another. There are occasional brave little boxes of flowering plants.

A group of people are dancing together, beating cellulosic ekwe, playing bamboo flutes and goje made out of old oil cans. The singer dances alone in the centre, his eyes closed, his face is rapture.

A river crosses a dip on the highway. Other vehicles are lined up there, along the side of the road, their owners industriously washing them with buckets drawn from the water. A man lies asleep on the roof of one, a blanket over his chest.

Their vehicle gingerly crosses the river and rises again up the other side. They are the only ones travelling further than the river, and the road is almost smooth, unlike the pitted, rutted mess they have been travelling on.

'We're almost there,' shouts Thomas. Smoke is starting to emerge from the bonnet again.

On the other side of the hill is a parking lot. Through the trees is a vast set of buildings. An ape rests sadly with its head buried under a tree, one concrete arm broken off, its feet still bonded to a giant once-ball-like object.

Thomas leads them through the trees along pathways and staircases of what appears to have been a shopping centre. Glass is still in some of the windows, exposed concrete and hanging roots inside each of the old shops.

Sarah stares mystified at a faded plastic sign propped on the inside of one window. 'Bastardo. Taste the grape with love from Odessa to Tinapa,' she reads, the words making even less sense when spoken.

'I've been to Odessa,' says Samara, beside her. 'I don't know if they ever made wine but, if they did, I wouldn't drink it.'

There is nothing else inside the shop. They move on.

Paths through the leaf litter and matted vegetation indicate that Tinapa is regularly visited. They walk, speaking in hushed voices as if at the site of a great tragedy. Something about the place speaks of lost empire.

Daniel whispers to Thomas, 'When was this place last used?'

'Oh,' says Thomas, 'it was never, never used. None of the shops or offices ever had businesses in them.' He leads them down a ramp between the trees.

'That gully used to have a lake in it. The river is just over there,' he points ahead of where they are walking, 'but the big man who built this place owned this land and wanted a river view, so they dug out the lake.'

'I do not understand,' says Abishai. 'Why show us this place?'

Thomas grins, 'It is from the time of the big men, when oil was valuable and they spent our people's money as they wished. They could build such places without a care. There was a place – there where the monkey was – where they could make old Nollywood movies, but none were ever made.

'It reminds us of how small are our warlords now. All they have is brutality, but they are little men, with little –' he holds his forefinger and thumb up to his face, peering through the tiny space between them.

'Come, I'll show you the hotel. No one ever stayed there.'

On the way back, Jason once more in the front and the others locked knee-to-knee on the sofas, they say little.

Are the warlords as hollow as the imperialists in the Balladeer's story, wonders Joshua.

Smoke is trailing round the jeep as they zigzag down the hill towards the river. 'We come to the marina. You have lunch here,' shouts Thomas. The vehicle makes an odd cough, then continues.

'Perhaps now?' says Samara. Flames burst out of the bonnet and the jeep slows, coasting down the remains of the hill and into the narrow parking lot alongside the river. 'Now,' merely as observation.

'Don't worry, don't worry. This happens,' shouts Thomas. He sounds worried.

They leave him, shouting and frantically trying to douse the flames, and head towards the long row of restaurants along the water.

Children and their parents are queuing outside a dome-like structure. 'Spacetime for Azonto' hovers over a serious-looking man with an immaculately tailored beard ducking and diving within the confines of his poster. Explosions reflect in the excited children's faces looking for a little Saturday-afternoon entertainment. Their parents bear the bright-eyed stoicism of childminders everywhere.

Azonto, Samara discovers, is one man who will single-handedly save the planet from imminent disaster as aliens plot to destroy humanity. Nigeria's low-budget entertainment industry still thrives.

Hundreds of people are ambling by the stalls, enjoying the afternoon sunshine and nibbling on various foods on sticks.

The group settles around tables over the water and beneath a shady tree. 'It is a pick and kill,' says David. 'Someone will have to go choose for us.'

'I will go,' says Abishai. 'Come, Samara, I will show you,' leading him through the other tables and towards a large concrete tank. Inside, water half-filling it, catfish of various sizes lurk along the bottom.

'We pick, and they kill,' indicating the cooks. One of them comes over, grumbling impatiently as he waits for them to get on with it.

Abishai studies the fish carefully. She indicates two large ones and points out their table. The cook nods. He swiftly grabs the two fish in his hands, hoiks them out and strides into his kitchen.

A young boy brings bowls of water for them to wash their hands. Minutes later, both fish – now roasted – are placed on platters on the table along with a tureen of rice and bowls for each of them.

As he is eating, Samara feels something shift in his pocket. He pulls out a small stone and looks at it curiously. Turning it over, he notes the symbol scratched into the rock.

Daniel notices. 'That looks like nsibidi. Where did you find it?'

'I didn't. Perhaps Symon did?' he says.

'Joshua,' says Daniel, 'you know nsibidi. What does this one say?'

Samara passes the stone to Joshua, who stares at the symbol. He rolls it left and right before deciding on the orientation of the arcs. Tracing his finger along the first arc, he says, 'This first symbol means a man. The second symbol is strange: a broken man, perhaps? And the piece in the middle – that could be the piece of the broken man. So, a man has broken another man.'

He looks troubled and his face tightens. 'Many superstitions are returning,' he says, softly. 'People believe again in evil spirits in pools and trees. They mix potions and say spells. I remember a tale, long ago, about a terrible ndem who tortured his victims by fastening them to a tree. He would tear off their faces and leave them there to die slowly. This was his sign.'

The clouds seem to have become darker; the sun seems to have vanished.

'I hope we do not run into whoever scratched this mark,' says Joshua.

'We should head back to the hotel,' says Jason. They take their leave, Daniel paying the restaurant, and walk back to Thomas.

He is standing, bereft, by the jeep. The bonnet is leaning against the low concrete wall at the side of the walkway. The fire is out, but the battery is half-melted, the inside of the compartment blackened, and the bottles of acid have pooled along the bottom.

'I will fix this. I have a cousin—' he begins as he sees them.

'That will be well, my friend,' says Joshua. 'We thank you for your guidance, but we will walk back from here.'

Thomas sweats and wipes his forehead with an old hand-kerchief against the closeness of the day. He nods and motions to them, 'Go back up the hill and that way, through Big Qua Town. It will be fastest.'

All of them, save for Samara, are sweating as they reach the top of the hill. They wait as Jason buys bottles of water for each of them before heading on.

Big Qua Town is the oldest part of the city. Wooden houses lean one on another. Half-built bigger houses rise broken out of the clutter of corrugated cellulosic roofs thickly painted in solar resin: relics of the days of the big men. All along every street are shops – endless rows selling identical products. Crowds of people, shouting, negotiating and pushing carts loaded with goods. Assorted groups are gathered around consoles listening to music, watching football or playing games.

Life is being lived raucously and in the open.

'Are you armed?' whispers Samara to Daniel and Joshua.

'I have my pistol,' says Daniel, Joshua nodding.

'We are being followed,' says Samara. Neither of the men look round. They naturally, conversationally, inform the others. All are alert, now. They do not hurry, but they do not linger.

Accidentally, they turn into a quiet courtyard.

Men suddenly appear, blocking the distant exits. As they turn, others emerge. All wear military fatigues and carry a variety of printed AK-47s. They are already pointed directly at the group.

Seven militia; seven from Ewuru. A fair fight.

'Behind me,' whispers Samara as he orientates the group so that they have their backs to a solid bricked wall.

One of the militia swaggers forward. A scar cuts across the top of his head and ends behind his left ear.

'You owe our Awbong comey,' he says, the threat unsaid, the malice in their posture and raised weapons sufficient.

'Why do we owe comey?' asks Joshua, his voice clear, no more than curious.

The scarred man chuckles, angling his chin at his men. They laugh too. 'Awbong Uberti demands it. He is the boss of Henshaw Town. He does not need a reason.'

He flicks something towards Samara, who catches it. It is a pebble. He rolls it between his fingers. Carved on to the one side is a symbol: two parallel arcs, one broken off-centre, and a dot between them.

Samara nods. 'We understand. I will give you comey.'

He walks towards the scarred man. Samara's back is very straight, his steps measured. Joshua can see the tension, like a wound spring. The others stand, hands open, facing forward, hanging loose. Their hearts are pounding.

Samara stops before him, his hand raised, open and slightly outstretched at his waist.

'Well?' says the scarred man.

Samara's fist is a blur rising up from his waist. He punches through the scarred man's throat.

Behind him, Joshua and the others cannot see what Samara has done. They can only see he has struck. As one, they drop to one knee, snatching their pistols from under their shirts. Their shots are almost a single hard retort. The shocked militia barely have time to notice what is happening before they have fallen, dead, to the ground.

There is a moment to stare horrified as Samara pushes the scarred man off his arm.

A shout goes up and Samara leads them, running, pushing through people, doubling back, twisting through the maze of streets. Then they slow. Walk.

Even so, news has reached Henshaw Market before them.

Behzad is waiting outside a narrow alleyway near his hotel.

'Come,' he says. 'You cannot stay in the hotel. Uberti will find you. We will hide you.'

Without a word, they follow him into the darkness beyond.

31

Ghanim is sitting in his office in the market, a shot glass of coffee on his desk. His console is in his lap, and he is scowling at his calculations. Thick fingers pushing and pulling at rows of numbers.

Faysal knocks on the door and sits on the chair on the other side of the stained desk.

'The militia are nervous,' he says, grinning.

'Good,' says Ghanim. 'Always better when they are bothering about something other than us.'

'I'm not sure, then, how hiding the Ewuru in our compound will keep us uninvolved?' asks the younger man.

Ghanim flings the console at his brother. 'Look at that.'

A guard comes in, Ishaq or Nuri, thinks Faysal. Even he struggles to tell them apart. The guard places another shot glass of coffee on the table and leaves quietly. Outside, the printer hums softly, layer upon layer, building a generator. Thin pipes leading into the printer jiggle as different materials are drawn down.

It is cool in the office, peaceful.

Faysal sips while studying the console. He drags a few rows of data across, creating a line chart. Whistles softly through his teeth.

'Do you see?' asks Ghanim.

Faysal is nodding. 'Where did you get this?' Blockchain

transactions are normally encrypted, and it should be impossible to link these back to Ewuru.

'I went to a few of the other printers around the markets, asking them for trading figures for Ewuru's account. Mumtaz has records going back almost eighty years.'

'How complete do you think this is?' asks Faysal.

'It is possible I missed some transactions, but you can see how it goes. Every few decades, they have purchased another printer. Then, instead of selling more produce, they sell less. Their trade is worth almost nothing. Only a few metal items and controllers for poor-quality grain. Either those machines are broken and they're getting poorer—'

'Or they no longer need our services,' finishes Faysal.

'And here they are, buying a battery which must cost most of their savings. Did you not wonder what they may wish to do with such a thing?' asks Ghanim.

'I have no idea. I assume a store for surplus power?' says Faysal, guessing wildly.

'I have no idea either,' says Ghanim, 'but I don't believe they need it. If they were saving for anything it would be to buy our machine. They appear to have everything else.'

'Did our uba sell them their DNA printer?' asks Faysal. 'I seem to remember a man who looked similar to that Joshua, when we were children.'

Ghanim stands and flicks through the console, 'There, forty years ago. Samuel Ossai, Ewuru.'

'They are building a new city?'

'Perhaps,' says Ghanim.

'What is it to us?' asks Faysal.

Ghanim looks out of his office and into the market. A youth, his rifle over his shoulder, is sorting through a rack of cheaply printed sunglasses on a stand. As he picks up one, he discards another on to the ground. The young woman at the stall is sullen and stares at the table, avoiding him. He strolls around to her side, crunching fallen sunglasses underfoot, placing his final choice on to his face. He laughs, grabs her by the neck and licks her ear. Then he turns and swaggers off.

'Do you remember what it used to be like here? Not so long ago and every spring they would murder some poor girl in the market. Their power grows weaker, year by year.'

Faysal is watching in silence. They used to have a sister.

'It would be good if they were no longer here. Maybe the people of Ewuru already know what that is like?' says Faysal.

'Do you remember the story the Marabout told us, fifteen years ago, after our sister –' Ghanim trails off.

'Pinch Point?'

'Yes, perhaps the Griot is telling stories in Ewuru as well? I believe we should go and greet our guests.'

32

Uberti's guests emerge with the sunset.

They arrive on foot, by tricycle taxi and by motorbike. The other warlords, self-proclaimed kings of their sections of Calabar, in dusty-rumpled-barely-there electric jeeps held together at the sufferance of the printers.

Uberti is not there to greet them. He is shovelling food into his face while watching the Akan men and their puppets. He laughs loudly, flinging handfuls of food at the players after every song in his excitement. No one drops a puppet.

There are drummers and dancers, Images – men wearing masks and elaborate woven robes – burning incense, and the smell of spices and palm oil cooking.

There are chairs and tables scattered across the lawn at the back of the house. Men crowd at the clump of open barrels of palm wine refilling their horns and shouting greetings.

Slaves, their skin puckered and burnt, run to serve, or struggle under the weight of palm wine barrels and trays of food.

Canvas has been nailed to the trees along the edge of the lumpy and steeply sloping lawn marking the edge of the party. The path down to the sacred grove is closed off, and men with guns hide in the woods beyond to ensure that no one goes where they should not.

The guests instead stand along the low wall looking out at the lights of Beach Town and Henshaw Town below.

Once, great ships would have visited this harbour. Now rusting iron carcasses rest in the water and along the Beach Town shore. It has been more than two hundred years since their like has been seen.

Filippo Argenti climbs out of his jeep. He is short, whip-lean and wears dark glasses and a white suit. His guards tower over him as he saunters towards the bar near the entrance to the back garden. He runs his fingers over the countertop, inspects them, rubs them together and flicks them at the ground. He will not lean his elbows here.

One of his guards brings him a jug of palm wine. He waits until the guard has sipped it first before he will touch it.

Uberti roars again with laughter. Argenti does not disturb him, selecting a table where he can see the dancing. He motions for one of his men to bring him food.

The dancers, all men, are wearing long black robes. Out of the backs protrude split bamboo shafts, long peacock's feathers tied to the ends forming a splayed fan-tail. They wear feathers in their hair and black markings on their faces. As they stamp rhythmically from side to side, they make flying motions with their arms.

Argenti looks for fault, but the long-tail dance is perfect. He drums his fingers on the table in applause.

His guard returns bearing small bowls of different soups; again he waits while these are tasted. He grabs a chunk of fufu and moulds it fastidiously into a scoop with his right hand, dipping it into a bowl of afang. The rich aroma rises up from the bowl as he swallows the mouthful.

'I see you are enjoying the dancing,' says Obizzo d'Este, his own guards sizing up those of Argenti.

Argenti indicates assent but continues eating.

'May I join you?' asks d'Este.

Argenti nods again. The other man smiles and waits as one of his guards pulls out a chair and then assists him into it.

D'Este is the oldest of the local warlords. His hair is grey, neatly trimmed, his fingers long and elegant, the nails manicured. He is wearing a richly printed black and yellow dashiki, the shirt and trousers in the same style. He glances at Uberti. 'Our host is enjoying himself.'

Argenti rinses his hands in a bowl of warm water held by one of his men. He dries his hands carefully on a towel, checking his nails are clean.

'He should be. He must have made quite a bit from that bauxite, even after paying for your helicopter,' he says.

D'Este chuckles. 'Perhaps I should have charged him more. They are impossible to replace these days.'

'They are piles of junk. Two of them are grounded with no one to repair them, and the last two will crash soon. It is a miracle that he even got that rock back here.'

'His Juju is powerful,' says d'Este, smiling.

'I won't hire them,' says Argenti. 'Anyway, he might not be laughing so much when he hears the news from the market.'

D'Este swivels carefully in his seat. 'What news is that, my dear Filippo?'

'You hadn't heard? I thought your spies were everywhere?'

'Apparently not.' The older man laces his fingers together and holds them towards his chest, his elbows on the table.

Argenti shrugs. 'Some peasants appear to have found some scrap aluminium. They brought it to Henshaw Market and sold it to the digesters there. Uberti wanted his comey and sent a few of his men after them.'

'Perfectly reasonable,' says d'Este. 'It's his market.'

'Yes. The peasants had different ideas. Killed them all. Took Dido's head clean off.'

D'Este whistles softly through his teeth. 'Dido was the one with the scar?' Argenti inclines his head. 'A good man.' He looks again at Uberti. 'You think he doesn't know yet?'

'I do not believe so.'

D'Este chuckles. 'This should be very entertaining. And embarrassing for Uberti.

'Do you know where they are now?' he asks.

Argenti dabs at the corners of his mouth with his handkerchief. 'I believe they are with the fabricators, but I am not sure.'

'A good place to hide,' says d'Este, 'but they will not protect them for ever.'

A nervous-looking figure weaves his way through the guests towards Uberti and whispers to him.

'I believe he may be getting the news now,' says Argenti.

'You made sure he would receive it here, didn't you?' asks d'Este, and chuckles as Argenti makes no move to answer.

Uberti howls and leaps to his feet. 'Where is Ciacco?!' he roars. 'Ciacco! You maggot!' Flinging bowls and food and slapping at the guards around him.

Rinier Pazzo drags a beaten, dishevelled figure around the far end of the house.

'We found him hiding down by the taxi ranks, my Awbong,' he says, throwing Ciacco to the ground.

The man cowers, bringing his broken fingers up to his face, trying to avoid the wrath to come. 'I was going to tell you, my Awbong,' he whimpers.

Uberti kicks him, walking after him and kicking him again, across the lawn. The dancers have stopped. The music is silent. The guests are watchful, like scavengers.

Argenti and d'Este are sharing an amused glance.

'How were you going to tell me?' asks Uberti. 'Send me a letter from Lagos? You coward.' And kicks him again.

'We will find these shits, and we will kill them. Your blood will be our medicine.'

'Please, my Awbong,' begs Ciacco.

'I am not your Awbong. You are dead to me,' kicking him, ribs splintering. 'Bring me my machet. I will take his head myself.'

'I beg Egbo,' pleads Ciacco.

'What?' shouts Uberti.

Argenti clears his throat. Uberti whirls on him, his eyes wide, his lips drawn back, his teeth clenched.

'He may call Egbo if he wishes,' says Argenti, unblinking behind his dark glasses. 'There are more than sufficient of the Awbong present for a palaver. I suggest trial by ordeal.'

D'Este nods his amused assent.

Uberti snorts, mucus slotting from his nose, spittle around his lips. 'Very well,' his jaw clenched. 'Bring the esere.'

There is silence as a guard races into the house, except for the rasping breathing of Ciacco and his exhausted whimpers.

The Calabar bean is deep chocolate-brown. It looks like something you would willingly eat. It contains physostigmine, a fast-acting alkaloid similar to nerve gas. A single bean ground into a paste, mixed with a glass of water and swallowed – it is believed that only the guilty will die. The exact concentration of the alkaloid is random, so there is a chance – however slim – of surviving. Better than the certainty of a beheading.

The guard returns. He holds a glass of an innocuous-looking cloudy liquid, but he holds it very carefully.

'Give it to him,' says Uberti.

Ciacco's hands are bound, his fingers broken. He is helped to a sitting position and the glass forced into his hands.

'I did not betray you, my Awbong,' he says. He drinks the lot in a single gulping swallow.

Uberti's guests hold their breaths. Argenti and d'Este are leaning slightly forwards in their chairs.

Ciacco sits calmly.

He begins to drool. Foam and mucus and a river of dribble pours from his nose and mouth, drenching his shirt. His back spasms, arching, his legs and arms jerk wildly, inhibited only by the ropes holding them in place. His bowels and bladder release and the stench of ordure drifts through the party.

Then he stops. He is dead.

'Liar!' shouts Uberti.

'Liar!' roar back his men.

'We go to war!' he howls, as his men shout and wave their rifles in the air.

The guests begin to flee. Argenti and d'Este are still seated peacefully at their table, their guards around them.

'Thank you for the entertainment,' says d'Este. He chuckles quietly. 'Would you like to take a wager as to whether those peasants escape?'

33

'I do not do this out of charity. I do not rescue people from those carrion. I do this because you are a customer and our business is not yet concluded. If you die, then I am not paid. And your friend's signature is very complicated.'

Daniel looks smug – you see?

Joshua, Samara and Daniel are seated on a deep, plush sofa in Ghanim's study. The room is large and claustrophobic but for the long glass wall looking into an elegantly tended courtyard.

Deep, intricately woven carpets smother the floor. The sofas and furniture are chunky. Bronze plaques fight for space with wooden masks and clay ornaments. Cast metal leopards and standing figures carrying swords line the walls. An enormous carved wooden door serves as a coffee table.

Outside, the gardens are spacious and beautifully laid out with ponds complete with decorative fish, beds filled with flowering plants and an improbable gazebo. Children play on swings in a small playground.

'And your other friend can kill a man with a single blow to the throat.' Ghanim stares carefully at Samara. 'You are not from here?'

'No,' says Samara.

'Where are your people?'

'They are in the orbital city of Achenia. You are helping me to return to them.'

Ghanim nods, as if such events are an ordinary course of doing business. 'You will be safe here in our compound. Faysal will see to your needs. When the battery is charged, we will conclude our business and we will see you back to your boats. It is best that you remain here until then. After that, you will be on your own.'

Faysal, standing quietly behind his brother, looks up at a knock on the door. He holds it open as a young woman enters bearing a tray. Her hair is a single obsidian bolt down to her mid back, and she is wearing a delicate green and blue sari with a fine pink scarf over her shoulders. She places the tray carefully on the low coffee table, bending her knees chastely. The rich aroma of coffee and samosas fills the room. Daniel's stomach murmurs.

She smiles shyly at Faysal. His features soften, as a proud father to his favourite daughter. She slips out quietly.

'You are building an independent city,' says Ghanim. A statement, not a question.

Joshua does not blink.

'We have collated all Ewuru's purchases. There has been nothing of importance in twenty years since you bought a set of turbines. Few of you visit Calabar, and your trade is negligible. If not for your guest, you would not be here now.'

Ghanim puts his hands flat on the table and then stands, coming round to their side. He picks up a printed sculpture from a carved cabinet. He holds it delicately.

Sinking into the sofa opposite Joshua, he gently places it on the coffee table between them.

'She was our sister, Farida. Look, please.'

Ghanim rubs at one eye and turns away.

Joshua glances at the others. He picks up the sculpture by the base. It is a ceramic print, and he is surprised by the weight. The girl is beautiful, captured in a moment of delight.

'She is no longer with us,' says Faysal, quietly. 'That was taken at her last birthday. She was Asha's age.'

Recognition. Joshua looks briefly at the door. Daniel takes the sculpture and his mouth opens. 'She looks exactly like—'

'My daughter,' says Faysal. 'Yes.'

'Asha has never been outside this compound,' says Ghanim. 'Not once in seventeen years. We cannot take the risk with any of our women or children.

'So, my dear Joshua Ossai, if you have made a city worthy of the name, but without the stench of fear, then we are very interested.'

Joshua sighs, looking across to Daniel, who shrugs.

'We are building a city.'

Samara's tale
Lost-wax and the Sea

We built our home on the rocky shore during the short waking hours of the lowest of neap tides.

Earlier, before the sun rose, we stood on the cliffs looking down at the coast, at the distant white line of the sea like an outline on a child's drawing.

'We will make our stand there,' she said. 'The sea will bend to my will.'

I fixed a block and tackle to the highest point on the cliff and chained it to an anchor where we had laid our foundations. We loaded rocks on to a pallet at the top and winched it down over the beach until it came to rest on the shore.

Back and forth. Unloading on the beach. Loading on the cliffs.

The sun rose: orange and purple against the bruise of the sea. Our materials piled up on the rocks, along with furniture and goods.

I followed my wife down the staircase we had cut in the slopes and walked between the palisade walls we had set as a tunnel from house to shore.

I set my mind to construction, and our materials did their labour. We moved in by early afternoon.

It was a basic fisherman's cottage with stone walls and large glassed windows. The two sides pointing straight at the sea, their windows wide and the breeze tousling the lace curtains, daring the waters to wash us all away.

We had time to spare, and I felt uncomfortable with nothing to do, pacing along the back wall of our living room.

A young girl came barefoot up the beach, her shoulder-length hair blonde and rustling. Playing a game of hopscotch across the stones. Soft cotton dress and a gap for front teeth. Her eyes like shimmering pools, and the ocean clear and blue.

'What are you doing here?' she asked, stepping into the house unbidden.

'We are here to tame the sea,' said my wife.

The little girl laughed. My wife frowned at her and continued filling a vase with white lilies cut from the meadow above the shore. Their stems were very green and the tablecloth very yellow. Fresh water in a bucket on the table.

Outside, the sky was an iridescent blue, a few smeared wispy clouds high above. Gulls shrieked over the pools, and the distant sea rolled and washed on to the rocky shore.

The little girl wandered through our living room, looking at the small number of furnishings we had set about inside. She was delighted by my felt hat, which I had left on the settee, putting it on where it fell down and over her eyes. Eventually, she settled down on the edge of the living room floor, between the sliding doors, swinging her legs out and above the stones of the beach.

As she watched, the sea began to rise.

My wife tensed, her back to the girl, intent on her flowers. I, hovering between them, felt at a loss as to what my role should be. I settled for continuing pacing back and forth against the far wall. I could smell the distance of the ocean, a nostalgic tang of all the places it had been.

A gull landed next to the girl. Black eyes and blunt yellow beak stark against its smooth white feathers. Its great webbed feet clutched at the door frame. Close to her, its head almost at the same level as hers.

She laughed again and stroked its head.

'Hello, fishy, have you come to watch, too?' she cooed.

The bird looked at her, tilted its head to look up at my wife, then gave a single cry before it crouched and flung itself back into the air.

The girl smiled as she watched it go, following it as it rose up and drifted out over the waves. Others joined it, flying in swooping drifts parallel to the coast.

'It's getting closer,' said the girl. 'You shouldn't be here. It isn't safe.'

'We shall see,' said my wife. She was setting the table now. Placemats, glasses and steel cutlery being placed just so.

The girl began to sing. Her voice sweet and melodic. A sound like the changing of the tide, of change and renewal, of the relentless wild places.

Slowly, inevitably, the sea advanced. Ripples in the depths turning to white and churning waves as it struck the rocky shallows. Washing up and over the pools, submerging and revealing, before hiding them completely.

The girl stands and turns towards my wife. She is a teenager, her soft cotton dress flowing down to her ankles. Her eyes are storm-tossed green.

The wind has risen, and our curtains are being flung back and forth against the wall. Our windows rattle.

'Please don't stay,' says the young woman. 'Please, the sea has no quarrel with you.'

My wife says nothing. Her face sunken in, her eyes blackened and her skin pulled back into her skull. Her concentration is focused on a point somewhere deep inside.

The woman walks over to me, her pace anxious and tense. She

pulls at my arm, forcing me to look at her. Her eyes are grey, foamed with flecks of white.

Water is starting to wash against the door frames, held back from entering by my wife's will.

'Please,' begs the woman. 'Make her listen. She mustn't do this.'

I look at my wife and shake my head. The cast is made. The investment is poured. The water is rising. All that is left is for the sea to take the form. Whether it wants to or not is not up to it.

Water is piling up around the outside of the cottage. It swirls, grey and cold and heavy against the windows and walls. A thundering maelstrom churns calf-deep through the living room. Our furniture remains unmoved, untouched. The water flows from the kitchen and out through the living room doors.

The woman is now middle-aged. Her hair is damp against her head and neck, and her eyes are dark.

Still my wife ignores her, remaining standing, leaning forward, her hands flat on the table.

The woman, her hands twisting in against her belly, shakes her head and moans. Pain and distress as her face changes.

My wife is unmoved, focused only on holding the forms in place.

'Why are you doing this?' shouts the old woman. Her face wrinkled and soft, her eyes fading to blindness.

My wife turns at last, staring into those eyes so full of fear and confusion.

'Please,' begs the old woman, her body failing. 'Please don't cage me so. All I ask is my freedom.'

34

'I do not understand,' says Joshua.

'I think I do,' says Ghanim. He cradles his coffee mug in his hands. 'Your father was a griot?' he asks of Samara.

'No, not as they are. Many of them studied with him, and they model their stories after his.'

Ghanim nods, setting his mug upon the table. 'Joshua, your great-grandfather must have realized this before setting out for Ewuru.'

'What is the lesson?' asks Daniel.

Ghanim stands and walks over to his desk. He picks up a small bronze cast of an ox, holding it, feeling the coolness of the metal.

'You should not force a people. Not through strength of will or threat of arms. The form must be freely taken, or not at all.'

Joshua thinks on that, of Ewuru, and the slow accretion of the years. 'What is the meaning for us?'

Ghanim turns, shaking his head. 'Not for you. For me.'

He looks at Samara in admiration. 'Your father was very wise. We should not take the shape of our old world with us when we step into the new.'

'That is a meaning, yes,' says Samara. 'Each person takes their own message from my father's stories.'

Joshua thinks, realizing there are depths for him, too.

'Even if we had the strength to fight the warlords,' continues Ghanim, 'we should not do so. Not their way. They are dying out. Isolated. There is no wealth left to plunder and such that they have is falling apart.

'If we fight them,' appraising his brother, 'if we fight them, we become them. No better.'

He rests his arm on Faysal's shoulder, staring out into the garden.

'Would that I had your people's longevity, Samara, I would suffer the time it will take.'

'They are stories, not instructions,' says Samara.

'I understand,' says Ghanim, 'but a wise man would listen even to stories.'

35

It is a night and a day and another night.

Many families appear to live in the compound, and there are numerous kitchens, libraries and courtyards. Children study amongst the books, tutors at their sides. At times, they play in the gardens. During the day, the only adults about are women, reading or talking amongst themselves. If they are bored with their lot, they hide it well.

There are guest rooms and the food is tasty although different to what they are used to.

'What do you call this triangular parcel?' asks Jason, eating while reclining on one of the sofas in the gazebo.

'It is a samosa,' says Joshua. 'And these are falafel.'

Jason holds a samosa up between his thumb and forefinger. 'It is really extremely good,' he says, his mouth full.

'Yes, we are well treated,' says Sarah.

Even so, the walls are high and armed men patrol them throughout the day and night. Faysal is a quiet presence.

'It feels like a prison,' says Daniel.

'That is because it is, both for us and for them,' says Joshua.

They lapse into silence. Their weapons have been taken from them, and the guards seem to divide their time between staring over the wall and nervously watching Samara.

'You are well trained,' says Samara.

Daniel spears an olive with a toothpick and chews it carefully. Satisfied, he assembles a few more. 'We train every day,' he says. 'More than those militia. They think having a gun is all that is required.'

'I am sorry,' says Samara. He is standing in the shade of an oil palm. He has eaten throughout the day, recovering his strength.

'What for?' asks Sarah. 'You almost removed that man's head. I never even saw you move. They were so surprised, we had plenty of time.'

She is plaiting Abishai's hair. A hot iron in her hand as she seals the hair extensions in place.

'If I were well. If Symon and I were in alignment – we would never have walked into that trap. I would have seen where to go. I would have known where they were.'

'Do you blame yourself?' asks Joshua.

'I do not blame myself for my situation. I am apologizing for the danger I keep bringing upon you.'

'Samara,' says David. He rises and walks over to where Samara is standing. 'I have never learned as much as since you came to Ewuru.' The others are nodding. 'I am sorry that the circumstances could not have been different, but I am honoured to have met you. I am honoured to experience your being. Your memory will be with us, always.'

It is a long speech from the quietest of the group. Sarah stands and embraces David from behind, her arms across his stomach.

'For me too,' she says. The others nod.

Abishai, with only half her hair in braids, says, 'Hey, we need to finish here. We leave in the morning.' She is smiling.

Samara is silent.

Daniel turns to Joshua. 'What will we do after?' he asks.

'You mean after Samara returns to his people?'

Daniel nods. 'You told Ghanim that we are to be a city. He seems to understand more even than the amama.'

Joshua lies back, staring up at the pale-blue sky.

'It was my great-grandfather's plan. More a fragment of a dream. To build a chain of free independent cities all along the Akwayafe. We have achieved a small freedom, but we do so slowly. Our towns are too small to offer even such as the opportunities in Calabar. You have seen how it is here. Entertainment, variety. Food we do not get at home. Trade goods from many places. These things also attract those who fear or feed on others.

'With our new sphere we will be able to communicate with the other villages. We will be able to share knowledge. Coordinate our efforts. Our culture will grow.'

He leans up on one elbow, looking from face to face.

'I have a vision,' he says, his face rested and his eyes bright.

'I imagine that Ewuru is a great white city. Our lands extend almost to the cliffs at the edge of the forests. I see our people, wealthy, strong. We are the equals of the sky people.

'In the centre of our city, on the edge overlooking the Akwayafe, is our Ekpe House and the amphitheatre before it. There is a square, lined with the statues of our most treasured leaders, scholars and –' he pauses, grins '– storytellers. Our university is the greatest in our nation. Our graduates spread through the land, sharing their knowledge, teaching. There is honest trade and ships visit our city from free peoples across the world.

'Our people are at peace. Have always known peace. There is justice. Equality before the law. Compassion.'

He is silent.

Daniel touches his shoulder. 'My brother, I would be proud to build that dream with you.'

Joshua furrows his brow, looks humbled. Abishai looks as if she will burst with pride.

*

In the evening, Ghanim returns.

He whispers to Samara. 'There is no war.'

'You were careful?'

'We have done as you asked. I spoke with my cousin in Creek Town. I asked no more than what is the news from across the waters. We discussed a few matters, but there is no war.'

'Thank you, Ghanim. I am relieved.'

'One other thing,' he smiles. 'Your battery is charged,' and leads Samara into a narrow room where an oblong black block, the size of an ox, rests on wooden posts laid flat on the ground.

Samara studies it, licking each of his thumbs. He places them across the terminals for a moment. He nods towards Joshua, then moves over to Ghanim. 'I thank you. You are true to your word.'

Ghanim raises his right hand and touches it to his heart. 'I am grateful for your custom. In the morning, Faysal will lead you to Beach Town. And, if your friends will complete our business?'

Faysal indicates a console fastened to the wall. Joshua places his card in the console tray. He, Abishai and Daniel sign, and the transaction is complete.

'I would be honoured if you would join my family for dinner, as my guests,' says Ghanim.

'It would be our pleasure,' says Joshua.

36

'You were friends, once,' says d'Este, his voice cold but probing.

He and Argenti are sitting on the veranda of his house in Harbour Town on the hill overlooking the lights of the marina. Both their guards stand watchfully, observing each other.

Four sections of a kola nut pod lie on a white ceramic plate on the table between them. The ceremony as between guest and host is complete. After first offering, and then refusing the honour, d'Este split the pod, both immediately remarking on their good fortune.

'Whatever good he is looking for, he will see it.'

They are not friends.

'Never a friend,' says Argenti, his eyes hidden behind his dark glasses.

He is drinking from a tall glass, ice cubes plinking against the tepid water. Neither will touch anything else in the presence of the other. The obligatory bottle of palm wine, brought as a gift by Argenti, will remain unopened. Later, it will be fed to the pigs.

Argenti is visiting, but this is not a social call.

'Colleagues, then,' pushes d'Este.

'Rivals. Guido Guerra was old, losing his Juju,' says Argenti. His words suggest that d'Este, similarly old, should take heed.

D'Este laughs, the sound brittle and mocking.

'Yes, Guerra was old. And a fool. He looked to his whores more than to his business. You were both right to murder him. You did us a service,' d'Este's voice is a query. 'You never have told me the story of what happened between the three of you.'

Argenti is silent. D'Este still controls the most lucrative of the Calabar markets. Argenti, squeezed between Henshaw and Big Qua, must make do with Duke Town. That does not suit the scale of his ambition.

'Uberti tricked you, yes?' hunting for a crack in the composure carefully hidden behind dark lenses. 'Henshaw was the prize. It must hurt to sit there in its shadow?'

Argenti's jaw is a tight bunch of grinding muscle. He breathes sharply out through his nose, startling the guards.

'Yes. But he is losing his grip. I want the right to take it from him.'

D'Este grins quietly. He has won. He has made Argenti ask.

'What is it worth to you?'

'Uberti sold his sons into slavery for Henshaw,' says Argenti, his voice bitter.

D'Este nods. 'And I sold my second wife and her children for Harbour Town. It was a good deal. Egbo is fair. If you want it, you buy the right to seize it from the other Awbong. Have you spoken to Corneto?'

Rinier Corneto controls Big Qua Town and is the other crucial Awbong in Argenti's plan. The warlords across the river in Creek Town, Alligator Town and the other districts are minnows.

'Yes, I met him yesterday. I promised him my two youngest wives and five per cent of Henshaw Market's comey for five years.'

D'Este smiles, he knows Argenti paid more, but he will not start negotiating just yet.

'Tell me about Guerra,' he says.

'It doesn't matter any more,' says Argenti.

Argenti and Uberti joined the militia as children. In those days they could still live off the people in the lands outside Calabar. He remembers when he was twelve, the first time he raped a village girl. His excitement and terror at the blood and heat. The girl had lain there, silent, staring at him in the darkness. Her eyes unblinking and dead. Uberti took his turn straight after him.

That was how they were. Uberti followed him. Even then, Argenti was calculating, silent. Uberti coarse and loud. He had assumed that Uberti was content to let him lead. He had underestimated the savagery of the man.

They joined Guerra when he was still working his way through the rabble of warlords raiding villages around Calabar. Two teenage boys indistinguishable from the other militia, living from day to day on scraps left over by the stronger men as they went from village to village. Gradually, though, the villages emptied, their people taking refuge in the slums around Calabar. The warlords in the city were too powerful and would attack them if they came near. Argenti thinks that the scar on his belly was caused by one of d'Este's men. After he was shot, he almost died from the infection until an Idiong man poured some foul potion on his stomach and cauterized the wound. They lost many fighters that day and were forced out into the wilderness.

Once they travelled far, almost to Cameroon. He does not remember where they ended up. The village they stumbled on was much larger than they had seen even during his childhood around Calabar. There was a high wall, meticulously laid out farmland and a crowded market visible through the gates as they stared out through the trees. They had ignored the white sentry posts along the edge of the forest. Peasants use them to keep animals out of the fields. They were not animals and the sensors ignored them. They should have thought longer about that.

The village was a little higher than the level of the river, with their lands sloping up and towards the jungle. Like half of a wide, gently sloping bowl.

The militia had been so excited that they had simply charged straight at it, Guerra leading and roaring at the front.

Argenti realized their mistake when they were still midway across the cassava fields.

A group of people, women amongst them, appeared across the top of the wall. They were armed and started shooting immediately. He noticed that they did not fire randomly as the raiders did. Their shots struck home with terrifying accuracy.

They were running back into the jungle before they had even begun.

Uberti and Argenti swore a blood oath that day that Guerra would have to be punished for almost getting them killed.

There were only eight of them who returned to Calabar. No longer a force, they sold themselves to Nimrod, then the Awbong of Big Qua Town. They were starving, sick and their clothing in scraps.

Uberti and Argenti stayed close to Guerra as he murdered and bought his way up through Nimrod's organization. In the war between the Awbong that followed Nimrod's death, Guerra won control of Henshaw Town. He beheaded fifty slaves in Henshaw Market as an offering to his ndem for his good fortune.

Uberti and Argenti waited.

'You, I understand,' says d'Este. 'You are that patient. But Uberti? He doesn't seem a patient man?'

'It was my mistake. He is a messy thug. I thought of him as stupid, not calculating,' says Argenti.

There was stability in Calabar, for a time. The warlords were at a stalemate. Each watching the other from within his domain. Their raiding parties would return with less and less from the rural areas around the city. Every so often, debris would fall, but it was rarely worth the effort of going out to seek it. Only Uberti seemed stupid enough to waste his time.

'That was how he bought his way,' says d'Este.

'Titles were cheaper then, and debris fall was more predictable. That trick will not work again,' says Argenti.

Ten years ago, the fabricators revolted. They had been printing weapons for themselves for months. A few extra at a time whenever the Awbong demanded new rifles, smuggled out of the market. They were also deliberately sabotaging replacement parts for the various militia. Subtle weaknesses in the firing mechanisms. The printers in Henshaw started first, refusing to pay comey. The other markets followed.

Guerra sent men to persuade the printers. That was when the Awbong discovered the fabricators now had their own protection. Guerra's men were butchered in Henshaw Market.

Many of the Awbong blamed Guerra for the chaos.

Uberti and Argenti struck, using their shift on guard in Guerra's house to dismember their leader. Argenti assumed he would simply claim Henshaw Town.

He misunderstood Uberti's preparations.

'He had already spoken to the other Awbong. He sold his sons, one to each of the leading Awbong. Promised ten per cent of his market take. He laughed at me when I realized I would have nothing,' says Argenti.

He took the men loyal to himself and fought hard. The Awbong were in crisis, still agreeing terms with the fabricators. Argenti took a risk and bought new weapons from the printers. He still remembers his fear following the purchase lasting until he gunned down a few peasants along the shore of Beach Town. The guns worked. His attack was successful, and he gained a foothold beneath Henshaw Town.

The years that followed were lean. The fabricators were content to leave the warlords alone, so long as they were paid for their services and were not subject to the comey of the smaller traders.

The Awbong watch, spy in the markets, make sure that no one else organizes themselves.

The markets in Harbour and Big Qua, however, remain profitable. As d'Este knows, sacrifices to the ndem are essential to continued success. His Images dismember a living girl in his market every year. Corneto prefers machine-gunning his staked offering, but the result is the same. Uberti has not gone against the will of the fabricators in Henshaw Market, taking his sacrifices instead to the trees out in the swamps.

'And now you feel that Uberti is vulnerable?'

'Yes, and I am no longer patient,' says Argenti.

'All you are buying is Egbo leaving you to fight. No one will move to support either of you.' D'Este is laughing softly.

'I am ready. Uberti will fall,' says Argenti.

It is time, thinks d'Este. 'And what will you pay for Henshaw Town?'

Argenti does not hesitate. 'Will you take my second wife, all her children and my three youngest sons? I also offer five per cent of Henshaw Market for five years.'

D'Este smiles, his face cruel. 'Ten per cent for five years, your family as before, and forty slaves,' he says.

Resigned, Argenti nods his acceptance.

37

Beach Town is quiet as Faysal leads Joshua and the others down to the shore.

The stalls are wrapped in tarpaulins, the homes dark and closed. The skyline is vaguely outlined by dim electric arcs from within the poorly maintained solar resin smothering every roof. Prefabricated cellulosic walls clipped together like a child's game of cards. Chickens cluck and cocks cry. Otherwise, all is in stillness, fog-drenched before dawn.

A smelly stream of effluent winds its way through the shacks and down to the beach. There are no street lights. Sodden wrappers, empty cigarette cartridges, used sanitary napkins and other flotsam line the upper tidal range along the shore.

Four guards carry the battery, fastened to two poles thrust beneath it. Joshua runs ahead, indicating their boats. They are careful carrying it down the beach, their feet sinking deeply into the slimy, muddy banks.

Many boats are tied up here, most empty. A network of ropes runs from the bows across to posts hammered deep into the ground. It is low tide, and the boats are leaning to their sides in the dark mud. Their boats are half-filled with water from the rains over the past few nights.

Joshua, Daniel and David push the boats apart to create space.

Tipping theirs, they empty the water out where it seeps back towards the river.

A dog begins to bark somewhere in the midst of the shacks in the shadows beneath Henshaw Town. The guards look watchful, looking back towards the village and up and down the beach.

The carriers walk each side of Samara's boat, gently lowering their cargo until the poles rest across the boat's gunwales. They untie the ropes.

Samara stands with one foot in the boat and one in the mud and lifts the battery so that the men can roll the poles out from underneath. He lowers it carefully on to the cellulosic grid they have brought with them to raise it above any water that may collect in the bottom. The unit is sealed, the terminals coated in hardened resin, but there is no need to wet it more than necessary.

Not a word is said.

The carriers withdraw, their poles resting on their shoulders as they go. Faysal indicates with his head and more guards walk down the beach. They are carrying the group's weapons, as well as their possessions and supplies.

These are quickly stowed, pistols holstered and rifles rested against the boat seats.

Joshua shakes Faysal's hand, clasping his elbow with his other.

'I will see you in Ewuru before the rains. Safe journey,' says Faysal.

'Thank you, I look forward to that.'

The men touch their hearts, bowing slightly, and then Faysal turns. His men withdraw without a sound.

They are on their own.

The boats are pushed out into the water. Knee-deep, they clamber on board. Settled, they row quietly towards the sea, going with the current past 7-Fathom Point.

Across the river, between a long tongue of land and Parrot

Island, a thick black lake is restrained by an oil barrier. The yellow floats have been bleached almost white. Here and there, an oil sheen tapers out of the barrier from small breaks in the retaining curtain.

At the far end of Parrot Island, another floating barrier cuts across the river to the mainland. It, too, holds back a deep and endless expanse of oil. The water here is, in spite of the barricades, thick with oil, and they must strain against the clinging, filthy mess.

They go slowly, taking care not to get any of the oil inside the boats.

Sarah, looking at the island as they pass, thinks about all the children who have been sacrificed on that small patch of land, superstitious offerings to the slave trade, and shivers.

The coast is blackened and dead, caked in a century of the oil still bubbling up from the Bight of Bonny. There are no dead seabirds, no dead fish, only the stumps of old trees as black as the beach. There is nothing left to kill.

There is no access to the sea here.

To their left, and before the oil barrier, the entrance to Qua River, and they turn into it, going upstream and into the network of rivers and canals that will lead to Ewuru.

They are watchful. Every sound causes them to freeze, before continuing again.

The water freshens but still the lingering smell of oil.

Gradually, the sun rises, bringing with it the heat of the day. Jason leans over the side, catching water and wetting his face.

They paddle onwards. There are termite mounds on islands they pass. A skull, perhaps human, on one of them. Others are covered in bits of fur or plastic sheets. Old superstitions that the hills are filled with evil which must be blocked.

For all the web of canals, there is still only one route through the lower part of the swamp. There could be an ambush anywhere along it.

The water remains oily, and their boats are sticky with residue. They say nothing, hunting for anything, any movement.

The day passes. They do not stop for lunch. They do not speak. They dip their oars with care.

Raffia trees and oil palm cluster on these islands. It is harder to see through them, amongst them.

Still they row, the day drifting past.

Two shots.

Samara is flung backwards, disappears into the water. He vanishes.

'You are ours,' says Uberti, emerging from the trees. All along the banks, men appear from hiding. There could be sixty of them. Some are shirtless, their torsos smeared in glistening blood-red palm oil. All are armed, all wary, pointing their rifles directly at the remaining six. A few draw their lips back to expose teeth sharpened to points.

Joshua gently lowers his oar, setting it inside the boat, and raises his hands. The others follow. The boats coast.

Seven of the militia walk out into the water and bring the boats to a halt.

'Get out,' says Uberti. 'You will come here.'

Carefully, slowly, Joshua, Daniel, Sarah, Abishai, Jason and David climb out of the boats, dropping into the water. They wade up on to the beach. The men in the trees behind them follow, crossing the river.

Everything is very quiet. Uberti laughs to himself, looking pleased.

Between the oil palms is a clearing. Uberti indicates seven trees that have been prepared. There are ropes laid down around them. A knife buried in each trunk. On the sand is a symbol: two parallel arcs, one broken off-centre, and a dot between them.

'You know my sign,' says Uberti. It is a statement, not a question. They nod anyway.

'Search them,' he says.

Rough hands rip at their clothes, removing their pistols. One of the militia shoves his right hand inside Abishai's trousers, driving his fingers into her vagina. He smells of lust, sour beer and cigarette smoke. His breath stinks, and his bloodshot eyes glare at her. She says nothing.

Uberti smashes the man in the head with the butt of his rifle. He falls to his knees, clutching at his head as blood flows between his fingers and drips on to the sand.

'She is mine first,' Uberti says, rotating his rifle and shooting the fallen militiaman in the face.

Abishai spits on the body. Uberti slaps her, drawing blood. She staggers but remains standing.

'We will have you,' he says to her. 'All of us. And your men will watch.'

David flinches. Sarah, imperceptibly, shifts in his direction.

'You will be first,' says Uberti, grabbing Sarah's face, throttling her about the cheeks. 'We will tie your men to the trees, break their knees and elbows. Rip off their jaws. I will cut off their eyelids so that they cannot shut out what we will do to you. Their screams will sound as nothing. When we are finished with you and the other one, we will break you too. We will leave you all to the trees.'

Many of the militia snigger.

'You have embarrassed me before Egbo. That is not acceptable.'

Uberti walks up to Joshua. Looks at him, eye to eye. He turns.

'Pazzo. Take them.'

Pazzo grins. He knows he will be second.

'Wait,' says Joshua. His voice is a command.

'What?' says Uberti, his face outraged.

'You have only one chance to surrender,' says Joshua. His voice is firm, steady.

The militia laugh. Many can barely contain themselves.

Uberti, his mouth open in a slack-jawed grin, asks, 'And who will save you? The ndem of the trees?'

Joshua shakes his head. 'There is no ndem, but you have forgotten. Our party consists of seven.'

Again, the militia laugh.

'We killed him first on purpose. He will not save you,' says Uberti. 'There is space here for him –' indicating the seventh post '– if he should choose.'

'You cannot kill him,' says Joshua, and something about his voice causes a few of the militia to hesitate. They look about them, pointing their rifles at the spaces between the trees.

'You cannot kill him,' repeats Joshua. 'But you might have awoken the other. The one inside him who kills without mercy. All he wants – all he has ever wanted – is to go home to his people, and you are keeping him from them.'

Some of the militia are panting, their eyes wide. Their heads swing left, right. Their rifles tremble.

'You are the only ones standing between him and those he loves. You will not stop him.'

A kingfisher, with dagger-sharp beak, impales itself into the eye of a man standing near the fringe of the clearing. He howls as more birds erupt from the bushes around him and fling themselves at the militia.

A man to Uberti's left is wrenched in half. His guts spill on to the ground. His shrieks are cut off as quickly as they begin.

Another, to the right, behind Daniel, explodes. His heart is flung, hitting Pazzo in the chest. Pazzo begins to scream hysterically, his voice high and shrill.

A head flicks into the trees, the body, behind Pazzo, falling to the ground, spasming in the sand.

Now the militia are howling. They start shooting at anything and everything around them. A bullet grazes the outer edge of Joshua's left hand, leaving a bloody groove.

David grabs Sarah and hurls them both to the hardened sand. Joshua, Abishai, Jason and Daniel landing alongside them. Joshua is staring intently at Uberti. He knows he has to be a target soon. He is looking for something, anything, that indicates where Symon is.

He thinks he might see a flicker, a patch in the air. Then it is gone.

Bullets splinter through the fibre of the trees. More men's bodies lie twitching. Some have been shot by the others in their terror.

Pazzo lifts up off the ground and is catapulted, his back snapping against the tree where he lands. His agonized howling adding to the horror. Uberti cowers in the chaos. He is sobbing, terrified of the demon he has unleashed. He looks around him frantically, Joshua staring at him, unblinking.

'Not me,' Uberti wails and then gasps, once. A blade protrudes through his chest and he falls forward.

There are only fourteen of Uberti's men left, herded into a bundle, back to back. Their screaming stops as they watch Uberti fall. Then they fling their weapons down and throw themselves to the earth, moaning their surrender.

Symon is invisible. His body mirroring his surroundings. He has no pity. He has only instinct. He lunges at one of the prostrate men.

'No,' says Joshua. He is holding a rifle directly against Symon's head. His left hand supporting the forestock, blood trickling out and on to the ground. 'They have surrendered.'

Symon is still. His skin returns to matt titanium. He is naked, crouched over the stricken militiaman.

'How did you see me?' he asks, his voice metallic. He does not move his gaze from his prey.

'You are not at full strength. Your injuries have not healed. I was looking for your wounds.'

Symon looks down at the holes in his chest. One through his left shoulder, one below his heart. They are not bleeding, but neither have they closed up.

'They are bad men,' he says. 'They will not change.'

'But we are not bad people,' says Joshua, 'and they have surrendered.'

Symon is holding the man around the arm and around the neck. The skin is stretched tight, bruised and bleeding under Symon's fingers. The joint will tear with only a fraction more effort. The arm and head will separate. Symon has not moved. The man whimpers in terror. The others are silent, their eyes wide and fearful.

'Symon, I have no wish to shoot you, but you must let these men go. They have surrendered.'

Symon does not move. 'They must answer for their crimes.'

'Yes,' says Joshua. 'They should, but we have not the ability to try them. They will return to their people. They will carry a message. Not all villagers are so helpless. That is enough.'

'We must purge these men. End the reign of the warlords.'

'Symon,' Joshua is patient. 'Killing will not remove the warlords. Where there is no expectation of justice, there will always be those who prey on the weak.'

His voice is firm. 'For the sake of our own honour, do not kill these men.'

Behind Joshua, the others have risen. They have retrieved their weapons. Everyone is red drenched. The clearing is a murky, slippery mass of blood and shredded body parts.

'Symon,' says Daniel. 'We are armed, they are not. They are no threat to us.' His voice is a balm, soothing.

Symon does not move.

'Please, Symon,' says Abishai. 'This is not our way.' She is weeping.

'Symon, you are an upholder of laws. Not an executioner,' says Jason.

'I?' says Symon, 'I −' and wrenches, the man screams, and Joshua pulls the trigger.

Symon does not move.

His hands loosen. The militiaman slumps; he has fainted.

Symon closes his eyes very, very slowly. He releases a breath, like a sigh. Then he topples, ever so gently, to the sand.

Sarah places a hand over her mouth, stifling a sob. David places his arm over her shoulder, pulling her towards him, holding her tightly.

Joshua crouches down, but he has no way of knowing how to tell if Samara is still alive. Oh, please, he begs, would that you are still alive.

The militiamen start to whimper. The others gather round them.

Joshua's face is haggard. He looks drained, exhausted. He drops the rifle. Daniel hands him his pistol. He holsters it, leaving his hands free.

'Get up,' he says to the militiamen.

'I have had to shoot one of the bravest men I have ever known to protect you,' he says. 'Do not think me weak.'

They rise, their hands above their heads, remaining in a half-crouch. They shake their heads. They are still traumatized, relieved that they have survived the carnage.

'You will live, but you will remember. You will never know if there is something invisible coming for you even in the brightest places. You are broken.'

Joshua is speaking calmly. He can see their eyes. He is describing what he can read there. There is no need for threats.

'Take this warning to all the Awbong. You are not welcome. You will not survive. We will take back our place. Even if it takes one hundred years.'

He motions towards the river. 'Go. Do not take your boats. You will walk. You will swim. You will crawl. You are not men.'

They stumble, trip over themselves in their haste to leave this slaughter. One giggles and is dragged by the others; his mind has shattered. They do not look back.

Daniel is seated, cradling Samara's head. 'He is not breathing. I can find no pulse. How do we know if he is still alive?' he asks, grief on his face.

'We do not. But we will take him home.'

Daniel and Jason carefully lift Samara, so much lighter than when he first crashed near their village, so much of Symon's essence lost. They carry him and compassionately settle him into his boat. They cover him with a sheet from one of the bed-rolls and fasten him to the stanchions so that he cannot move.

Abishai ties a strip cut from a shirt and wraps it around Joshua's hand. He looks carefully into her eyes as she does so, then embraces her. She stiffens, relaxes and sobs into his shoulder. The others gather round her. Each embracing her in turn.

Joshua ties a rope from his boat to Samara's so that it can be towed.

They wash themselves clean and change clothes, abandoning their old ones on the beach.

Then they begin to row, quietly and steadily, towards Ewuru.

III

A SONG FOR THE LEAVING

We do not choose to leave because we are unmoved by suffering; nor do we go because we flee responsibility. We depart this Earth as a child departs home, with the bittersweet tears of the new adult. We set out in the same spirit as of the first explorers of our own planet: because out there is the great unknown and not to go would be as impossible as ignoring our own souls.

Dr Ullianne Vijayarao, technician on Allegro quantum navigation team, 2053, formal comment responding to UN Secretary General on Security Council Resolution 2731

When the first great migrations took place to the new world colonies, nations couldn't wait to purge themselves of their citizens. Getting rid of their tired and poor had never seemed so easy. Centuries later, when the best and brightest started to go into orbit, nations realized they had a problem. Instead of recognizing the source of that departure, our leaders have acted as if it is a personal betrayal: self-interest gone wrong. I fear that, in the coming decades, our politicians will realize how badly they have miscalculated, how badly they have managed, the noble quest for exploration – our highest ideal – expressed by our brothers and sisters in the orbital cities.

Doug Shetland, US political analyst, 2108, *In Other Worlds*, posthumously published autobiography

When we, with humility, requested the freedom to represent ourselves, they answered with hatred and torture. When we were unafraid and we once more, with humility, requested what should be ours, they butchered our children. I dread that when at last they change their hearts and are done with hating, we will have no compassion left to give.

Liao Zhi, pro-independence activist on Yuèliàng, 2113, memorial for the deaths of 845 student protestors following a massacre in Tiangong Square

38

'My husband,' says Esther, her voice a caress.

Joshua is sitting at the far end of the Ekpe House, his feet over the edge of the cliff, looking across the river and into the forest beyond. He has been there since early morning, watching the sun rise through the trees.

'My husband,' her voice intimate and knowing.

He takes her hand resting on his shoulder, raises it to his face, feeling the life and hope in it. He kisses her palm and holds it to his lips, his breath warm through her fingers.

She crouches behind him, holding him in her arms, feeling the intensity of his emotions through the silence.

'It is well, my husband.'

He looks up and into her eyes; their noses caress in a gentle embrace.

'My wife. I am worried he is not with us,' he says.

She hugs him tightly, rises slowly, 'Come, there is something you should see.'

He follows and she leads him out of the Ekpe House, around the amphitheatre and through the village. They go out the east gate and down the slope towards the jetty.

Samara's boat is tied up there. Daniel, Abishai and Dala, one of the printers, gathered alongside. It has been completed, the turbine submerged on a U-shaped bracket at the rear transom and two curved wings extending from the deck gunwales on each side. Ropes are tied to cleats at the bow and stern, looping around posts on the jetty.

The deck of the boat is of a piece with the hull, curving in a sweep over the transom arch between double, chiselled bows. It flows up in a crest to the pilot's controls, over the cabin, around two entrance ways, and sealing again with the stern. The cellulose is transparent over the cockpit, giving a clear view of the deck and horizon.

'We have just connected the battery for the first time,' says Daniel. He looks stunned. 'Touch the console.'

Joshua looks at them, but they shake their heads: see for yourself.

He ducks his head and enters the cabin. It is more spacious than he had expected. The seat at the controls is comfortable.

He looks again at the others, their heads peeking into the cabin. They are mute, expectant.

Slowly, hesitantly, he touches the console face. It lights up. On the screen is Samara.

'Joshua,' he says. 'I am deeply sorry to impose on your kindness once more. I need a ride.'

Joshua is smiling, shaking his head. From the timbre of his speech he can tell this was Symon. He must have recorded it on the night before they left for Calabar.

'My home is a two-and-a-half-day journey from Ewuru. I will, unfortunately, not be very much company but, please, know that we are with you and appreciate everything that you do for us.

'The controls are simple to use. The steering wheel you know. The two levers to your right serve different functions. The left-most one is for thrust. The right-most one is for lift. Don't worry, we will not fly much beyond the surface, but we need to clear the oil zone, and we need to do so at speed.

'The directions and instructions are mapped on this console. I have not been able to add much in terms of automation. There are hazard-warning sensors that will alert you to obstacles, but they will not give you much time to respond. I'm afraid that you will need to remain awake as best you can for most of the journey.

'My friend, thank you.'

The console shows a sea chart with Ewuru marked as their present location. Icons indicate that they are stationary and facing roughly due west. There are 2,688 kilometres to go. The battery is fully charged.

Joshua stares at the console. He turns to the others, relief and hope lighting his face. 'He knew?'

Esther nods. 'Of course he knew.'

'Then we must take him home. Where is he?'

Abishai smiles. 'Jason and David carried him down a few minutes ago when Esther went to call you. There is a hatch in the front.'

Joshua climbs out of the cabin and on to the deck. He can see two compartments, one over each of the hulls. The left is bolted closed, but the right has a set of flush handles. It is a tight fit and he tugs. The lid comes up.

Samara is below, covered in a blanket, straps holding him in place on a narrow stretcher.

'He left instructions,' says Dala, 'that we would need to add weight to balance the battery. We took out some from that chamber once we laid him there.'

She indicates a small pile of boulders on the shore.

Joshua replaces the cover, tapping it down with his foot. Esther climbs on to the deck alongside him. She takes his hands. 'You are a good man. All you have to do is help Samara return to his people and then return to me.'

He kisses her softly on the forehead.

Daniel answers before he is able to ask. 'We have packed sufficient food for a few days. The craft is ready.'

'Father.' Isaiah is standing on the jetty, his face a mixture of pride and terror and excitement.

Joshua jumps down beside him, folding his son into his arms. He holds him there, the child matching his breathing.

He stands, looking at each in turn. 'If not now?' he says. Esther smiles. He takes her hand, then returns to the cabin.

They stand on the jetty. Isaiah is waving madly, Esther hanging on to his other hand. Abishai releases a rope tied to the stern, David the one at the bow.

Joshua places his hand on the throttle and pushes the lever gently forward. The craft glides into the centre of the river. He looks over his shoulder and waves. His face is light with hope for the first time in days.

He nods to Esther, looks down the river and presses the throttle forward.

The acceleration is tremendous, forcing him back into the seat.

He whoops at the thrill and jets down the path of the river. Soon Inikoi Island, at the mouth of the river, is ahead. The river is already thickening with oil, and the boat is labouring.

An icon on the console is flashing, 'Pull up,' and indicating the lift. Uncertain, he pulls the right-most lever back.

The wings on either side of the boat begin to curve, and the boat starts to rise out of the water. Beneath it, an inverted T-shaped wing begins to emerge. It is centred with the turbine in its transom cradle and leaves only a sliver of the craft in contact with the oil.

The turbine lifts out of the water, and the craft is in danger of stalling. Joshua realizes in time and pushes forward on the thruster.

Joshua has never come down this part of the Akwayafe. The water sits, like a smooth black lake.

Near now to Inikoi, he can see an old village, abandoned and blackened. There are no trees. The shore is barren. The smell of the oil is overwhelming.

The river opens up into the mouth of the delta, uniting the Cross and Calabar rivers and all the canals and streams draining into the sea. All he can see is blackened: the sea, the shore and the distant landscape. All is dead.

Somewhere, deep on the ocean floor, the oil continues to flow, adding continuously even as time and nature eat it away. The smothering mass cannot grow, but it will not die until someone is able to entomb it for ever.

He looks at the console. It will take a few hours to cross the Bight of Bonny and into the Gulf of Guinea. On the chart he can see a series of islands. Looking up, towards the south-western horizon, he recognizes the loom of the first.

'Bioko,' he reads off the chart. He has heard of it, but no one in memory has been there. The seas are poison, there cannot be anyone still living there, can there?

He corrects his course, matching that on his chart. They are going quickly: twenty-five knots according to the console display.

All around him is stillness and silence. There are no birds.

Ahead he notices a slight ridge in the sheen of thick black oil. To be safe, he cuts a wide arc around it. As he passes, he sees that it is a cluster of shipping containers all rucked together in an old net. Many are rusted and buckled, but the mass still floats.

The concentration is tiring. The sun is over the bow of the boat, glare in his eyes making it harder to see. Unending blackness and the nauseating smell of oil.

The day passes, and the sun fades to purple on the horizon.

Does he imagine it? Can he smell a strange freshening hint of salt and iodine?

He does not know the smell. One would have to travel far down the coast from Ewuru to find coast untainted by oil.

He smells the open ocean.

He feels the pressure of the oil lifting from the boat. The console indicates that he should drop the wings. He already realizes that, is pushing the lift back to neutral, reducing the throttle.

The turbine bites into the water, and he feels the boat tempo change.

He is exhausted and hungry. There are no lights anywhere in sight. The ocean is soft, ripples reflecting in the moonlight. He checks the chart and corrects his course. Noticing a bracket beneath the wheel, he finds that he can clip it in place and leave his seat for the first time in many hours.

His fingers are stiff, and he flexes them open and closed to ease the cramp out of his joints, rubbing gently at the micropore stitches over the groove on his hand.

Beneath the control, to the left, is a sealed cupboard door. He pulls back on the heavy lever and it opens. Inside is a refrigerator packed with small, tightly wrapped bowls. He opens one: egusi. Others contain fruit, vegetables, fufu.

To the right, below the two levers, are a rounded opening protected by a net, and a water tap beneath. Inside the opening are a blanket and toiletries.

He eats and washes. Returning to the seat, he covers himself with the blanket and prepares himself for a long night.

He can see little in the shrouding dark and hopes that the sensors work. All about him is nothing but ocean. He has no idea where he is, or where he should be going. The console reassuringly still displays his position and his course. He is still on track.

After a few hours, his eyes become heavy and he dozes,

snapping awake as his chin hits his chest. Barely alert, he sings to himself. Describes what he is seeing to Isaiah. Hours later, he falls asleep again.

An alarm: the console is lit up, showing a warning just ahead. He swerves, hoping he is going the right way to avoid it. The alarm stops. He is trembling, his heart pounding.

He cannot see anything, has no idea what it may be or how large, and waits a few minutes before correcting his course. He clutches the blanket to himself.

Gradually, the ocean turns dusty green as the dawn, orange and streaked with purple cloud, rises behind him.

The battery indicator shows that seventy per cent of the charge is gone. A day and a half to go. They used considerable power aquaplaning over the oil. He hopes what remains is sufficient.

He eats some fruit, washes, cleans the cabin. Sits. Waits.

He is exhausted beneath the monotony of the unchanging horizon. He tries staring into the water, imagining shapes there in the depths.

Wakes suddenly. An alarm on the console.

He looks out: a tangled skein floating in the ocean. He changes course, slowing as he passes. It is a small island of plastic, netting and floating debris. Beneath the water, a ghostly mass hanging down, immense and irregularly shaped.

There are sea plants and kelp growing on it, and small fish darting in and out.

Soon evening settles, purple and warm, and he eats. There are two meals left. Fruit for breakfast, and a bowl of chicken stew for lunch. Twelve per cent charge left on the battery.

He sleeps in short snatches. Alarms sometimes wake him. More often he comes alert suddenly, fearful shapes in his dreams.

He looks up, realizing he can see stars, and – something else – looming in the sky.

Joshua climbs out of the cabin, up on to the deck and stares. It is indistinct, small, but he can see a hazy blob floating in space. Achenia, he wonders, feeling relief and awe at the same time.

In the morning, he jolts awake to dolphins swimming next to the boat. They play alongside, staring up at him curiously through the water. They are grey and larger than the pinkish dolphins in the Akwayafe. Then they disappear into the deep.

He is delighted. My wife, I wish you were here, you would love this.

Achenia is larger in the sky. A faint white outline high in the blue.

He eats his last fruit. Feels the fatigue in his hands. The water is deep and dark here.

If he squints, he thinks he can see a thin line hanging in the sky, leading from the horizon up towards Achenia.

Towards midday the boat slows, stops. The console flickers. The battery is almost dead. He can see the sea-base of the space elevator on the chart, still an aching few hours away. Then it goes blank.

The boat is adrift, powerless, on the ocean. This was always a one-way trip, but did we make it far enough?

He waits. Eats lunch. Falls asleep. Wakes again. Looks to where the sun is tilting down to the horizon. Samara, all your calculations? Did you make a mistake?

Joshua does not realize it, but he has been inside Achenia's connect, and so within the gaze of the Nine, for six hours.

He sees a flash of silver on the horizon and then, flying just above the waves, is a teardrop-shaped craft. It heads straight for him and stops, instantly, alongside.

It is dark and reflective, like black glass. The entire bulb of the front canopy shimmers and dissolves. A man rises from his seat. His face is young, his skin of matt titanium. He is wearing a lightly coloured, loose-fitting cloak that clings as he moves, as if made from cobwebs. His trousers are tucked into long fabric boots. His eyes glow, but the expression on his face is one of relief and genuine warmth.

He leaps easily on to the deck, which rocks deeply under his weight, and swings himself into the cabin. He embraces the alarmed Joshua, holding him firmly and close.

The man says something. The words running together.

'I am sorry,' says Joshua, 'I do not understand.'

'No, please forgive me. I was unsure what language you would be speaking.' The man stands with his hands on Joshua's shoulders.

'Thank you, you have brought our brother home.' His eyes glow brightly, and Joshua is suddenly overcome by his own foreignness, his ordinariness. He clenches and unclenches his hands.

'My name is Fodiar. Please, you must be exhausted,' and he takes Joshua's arm, guiding him into the craft. At the back, behind the pilot's seat, is a long, sculpted sofa flowing from the skin of the walls and beneath a low ceiling.

Fodiar leaps back on to the boat. He pulls off the right-most hatch cover on the deck, unties the straps and gently lifts Samara out. He touches Samara's face, pauses, as if to commune, then carries him up to the craft. A hatch dissolves in the ceiling above Joshua, revealing a body-sized module. A slender platform slides out.

Fodiar places Samara carefully on to it. The platform slides back and the hatch resolves.

'You are of the Nine?' asks Joshua.

'Yes,' says Fodiar. 'And you are Joshua, of the people of Ewuru.'

Joshua starts. 'You are speaking with him? He is with us?'

'He is alive, dear Joshua, but not yet with us. Only hints. We will care for him. We owe you and your people a great debt.

'Come, there are others who wish to meet you and thank you.'

The canopy of the craft shimmers and returns.

'Wait,' says Joshua. 'What of the boat?' It is his link between his world and Samara's.

Fodiar smiles. 'We will not be leaving it behind. Look.' And Joshua sees another silver shape, approaching on the horizon.

'Come, it will be six hours until we are in Achenia. Please, rest if you can. I realize you will have many questions, and there are others who will give you better answers.'

Fodiar settles in the pilot's seat, his arms comfortably on the curving wings at his sides.

[He has suffered greatly.]

'Joshua? Yes, this has been an unfortunate journey.'

[Both. I don't believe either will return unchanged.]

Fodiar nods.

[How did he get to Ewuru?]

'Joshua is exhausted and overwhelmed. Patience.'

Fodiar does not move as the ship lifts and turns on its length. It rises vertically, heading towards Achenia.

[Fodiar, Nizena wishes to speak with you.]

'Nizena, he is safe.'

'Thank you, Fodiar. We will be waiting for you outside Tswalu Bay.'

Fodiar transmits a short burst of information, permitting preparations to be made. He turns to Joshua. 'Is there anything I may do for you during our journey?'

Joshua shakes his head, nervously sitting on the edge of the sofa. He feels clumsy, awkward, his hands bulky and crude. His fingers open and close.

Fodiar notices but has not the words to reassure him. He steers the craft towards the space elevator, merging the craft's field to it and accelerating upwards.

The sky fades to black, and then they are in a shielded tunnel. The outside is shaped by the vague hurtling fog of passing debris.

Joshua stares out through the canopy. Achenia fills the sky. He can see the outer layer of rubble and bursts of dust where debris, moving faster than he can see, flows into and around the city in a deadly stream.

They are travelling up a clear channel, hugging the elevator cable to their left. They pass through the top of the hub of the space elevator, and he realizes it is not attached to Achenia. After all he has heard he is surprised at this. They fly rapidly through a ringed station spinning slowly around the cable, lit windows looking out, shapes moving inside.

The cable continues out the top, and the surface of Achenia is suddenly to their right. This close it is so large he cannot see it curve. The glass elevator station is a mere annex next to the unending bulk of the orbital city; the cable is almost invisible. Looking up, he can see it extending far into the distance. Further than Achenia, and then ending in a massive asteroid, like a small moon. It is difficult to see the cable, dark against space, but the safe channel leaves a faint boundary with the hurtling debris. Like a water drop on frosted glass.

To their right, they are approaching a huge open chamber; other ships of various shapes and styles fly in and out. All appear to be going away from the planet rather than down towards it.

They enter and settle at the back against what Joshua initially takes for the far wall. The canopy dissolves once more. The landing bay is open, and he looks up on darkness. The inside of the hangar is silvery, bright and warm.

Joshua remains seated, feeling nausea and vertigo only partly due to the gravity shift as they landed. He is not sure if he has the strength to rise.

Fodiar stands and beckons for Joshua to follow as a set of stairs form, leading down to the landing deck. The hatch opens. Samara slides out, and the narrow platform leaves the craft and floats out after Fodiar.

Joshua follows rapidly. If he can remain close to Samara, perhaps he will not feel so isolated.

There is no sound here. Each ship landing, flying, without any but the most subtle whisper. Fodiar turns towards a doorway at the back. He walks ahead down a short, winding spiral until gravity has shifted again.

Joshua, dizzy, trembling, follows. Out into the city beyond.

39

'Knight to F6.'

They would be the first to admit that it is an inconvenient place to play their weekly game of chess. The small platform floats somewhere towards the middle of Tethys, Achenia's ocean.

The two players have no board between them. The one reclines on a comfortable sofa and within the shade of a linen awning. The other is a puff of colour draped over the deck and stretched out in the sunshine.

Once they spent a decade playing beneath the cascade of a waterfall. Their games have attracted a following on the connect, with occasional lobbying for even more outlandish locations.

'I do suggest that next time we choose a spot where my coffee doesn't take half an hour to reach us. The last cup wasn't quite hot.'

There is a considered silence as potential moves are surveyed and analysed.

'You have not said.' The words are spoken tactfully, an almost reticence of reserve.

'That is because unless I direct all my concentration towards the game I will lose inside of thirty minutes. I hope to, at least, last forty-five.'

'It is not that bad.'

'It is indeed that bad. I have not won a game in seventy years.

Over two thousand games since you even fumbled. Could I suggest we switch to something that requires an element of luck? We could try backgammon. This game is far too regimented.'

He notes, with grim discomfort, that the current betting has him falling in another three moves.

The colour dapples, spreads further over the platform and on to the water. It could almost be said to be purring.

'There is still the potential you may win. For many years we were evenly balanced.'

'It took you thirty years to understand the nuances of the game. Now, cease your distractions.'

The man in the shade pinches the bridge of his nose and commits himself, 'Knight to C3.'

Another flurry of wager changes and he sighs as the consensus is that it will be checkmate in two. He cannot see it himself.

'I do appreciate your advice, though. It would mean a great deal to me if you would guide me. I have never written a samara before.'

'It's easier to be a judge than an entrant. I've never written one either.'

The colour intensifies, returning to the craft.

'Very well, tell me and I'll do my best.'

The colour quivers in pleasure.

The Three's tale
Level Ball

A fire devoureth before them; and behind them a flame burneth:
the land is as the garden of Eden before them, and behind them
a desolate wilderness; yea, and nothing shall escape them.

Joel 2:3, King James Bible

'We are the fire before the flame.'

The captain's voice, captured and transmitted to the millions watching, is fearless. His team stand behind him dressed in haggard clothing. Faded, threadbare, carefully patched and spotlessly clean. They are barefoot and their legs and arms sinew and bone. Knotted on each shoulder is a red cloth. In their eyes is the yearning of the many who wait in the Upper Level and of those who are no longer with us.

'We are the ice that binds.'

The opposing captain is equally unafraid. His voice amplified across the Lower Level and into the distant stadia surrounding the turf. His team jump and hop. Heavy muscle shielded behind cold blue padded uniforms and silver helmets. Their white boots grip the dense lawn, sharp metal studs churning the grass.

There are no umpires. There are no rules.

Save for one. A single goal ends the game.

Each year, a few moments from now, the game ball will fall from beneath the Upper Level and on to the field of the Lower Level. Each team will fight to secure control of the ball.

Each will attempt to bring the ball to their own goal and there to score.

For the blues, victory will return the game ball to the endless tunnels that will see it fall, a year from now, and restart this game.

For the reds, victory will end the confinement of all those who struggle in the Upper Level. The great gates will open, and they will be released back into the world from which they were forced. The game ball will be lost for ever and the game ended.

That is the way the game has been played for centuries. That is the way it was created. A joke at the expense of the reds. They cannot win. Their anguish and striving for freedom have been turned into televised entertainment for the viewers at home and in the stadia on the Lower Level.

Maybe, once, there was a memory of why they should suffer so. Perhaps some below wonder at the unfairness and fear burdened upon those above.

That is cast aside now. Nothing matters on game day save for who will secure the ball.

The words have been spoken. Cameras hover above. Silence descends upon the field.

The players look up.

The ball falls.

Each team is already moving. The blues have formed an attacking wedge and charge directly at the red captain. His team scatters.

There is laughter in the commentary box. The cowardice of the reds means the game will be over before it has properly started. The shortest recorded game was only five minutes.

The red captain does not move as the blues maul into him. His body is smashed to the ground. His flesh torn apart by the talons on their boots. Red stains on white leather.

The blue captain is at the head of the wedge. The ball bounces for the first time right behind them. And is instantly snatched.

The blue captain shouts. His voice ascends with the roar of the crowd.

The reds did not flee. The sacrifice was a diversion. Watch them now as they run. Complex patterns. Running ahead and behind and across.

The blues cannot see which of them has the ball. They are still in a tight ruck from their attack. Their captain is behind them. He does not realize what is happening.

The blues open up, watching carefully. There are only so many exits to the chains and ladders, so many ways to the Upper Level. A group of reds breaks for C gate. The blue captain nods but does not chase. He sends a group of five. He is watching for the diversions.

Another group of reds exits the chaotic cross-hatch of runners and makes for E gate. Again, the blue captain directs a group to follow.

So with the groups heading to G, K and D. Then he leads the last of his team to B gate, ignoring the remaining three red runners attempting to distract them on the field.

Players are already ascending the stairs, squeezing through the maze of alleys and ladders that lead hundreds of metres up into the sky. Just because you are ahead does not grant security. The ladders move, unexpectedly ending, leaving men stranded.

The blues chasing up C gate have caught up with the reds, cornering them on a chain ladder. They are twisting it, shaking hard. The reds cling on. One falls ten metres and lands on his back.

There is no advantage to entering the ladders first. All the blues need do is return the game ball to the Lower Level. It doesn't matter if a red is still holding on to it at the time.

Up and up they go, gradually hauling in the clambering reds.

The cameras follow the chase. Their rotors are silent, their eyes unblinking. They are now 100 metres up. Only three of the red groups are still moving. The blue captain has signalled to his team to consolidate, to focus on these remaining sprints. The blue groups who have dispatched their red quarry are now working their way around the remaining groups, channelling them into a single set of ladders.

The ball has still not been seen since it first bounced. It does not matter. It will be found when all the reds have been forced back to the ground.

No red has ever made it above 250 metres, and they still have a long way to go.

The men are unflagging, but the game is slowing. Ladders are wet with sweat and blood. A blue slips, misses his grip and plunges. No matter, they still outnumber the reds.

The original K group of reds has found a ladder that appears to offer them a clear run. The player at the bottom notices a group of blues heading to cut them off. He scrambles across, leaping for a parallel ladder, and pushes himself to get ahead and above.

With a scream, he flings himself into the pursuing blues, binding himself to them. Four of them plummet with him towards the field below.

The blue captain roars in frustration. He pulls his men in tighter and sends them up against the remaining reds.

The reds are exhausted and will soon be crushed. Then, a shout from one of the blues.

His captain looks to where he is pointing. Far across the tangle of ropes and ladders. Three reds. The ones they ignored below. They are much higher up. They have had a clear run.

The blue captain feels his heart stop. One of the reds is grinning. He is holding the game ball.

Too late. He must now chase. His men are almost spent. Not only must they gain height but they must cross the vast expanse of the chain-ladder field.

Quadrotor cameras weave through the levels, moving to get close to the dwindling reds.

Three hundred metres. Four hundred metres. Higher than the game has ever gone.

Pandemonium in the commentary box. Panic in the stadia. Terror at home.

The cameras are now following the red carrying the ball. He is young. Scarcely into his teens. His body is drenched with sweat, his breath hardened gasps. His eyes, though, black and unyielding.

They are entering the final level.

The ladders here are oiled. Slick on purpose.

The exhausted blues struggle. Their boots slide. Two more fall.

Everyone moves carefully.

Triumph at the top. The reds have reached the gates. They tumble through L on to the Upper Level.

The blue captain has abandoned his attempt to catch them in the ladders. He has focused only on getting to the top. A few minutes later they are through H gate.

There is chaos.

Cameras have never been to the Upper Level. The programme director and his crew are struggling to figure out where to send them or how to present what they're seeing.

The blue captain still has eight of his men. He stands aghast.

There is no field. They have arrived in the midst of a tangle of cardboard and wooden shelters. It is cold up here, and people are clustered around fires burning inside standing barrels. The shacks lean against each other. Narrow passages between them.

The people are gaunt, barefoot and clothed in rags. Yet they are cheerful. There is a tumultuous bustle of activity. Single-room shops. Traders carrying food. Children running through the alleyways. Chickens squawk from the rooftops barely above head height.

Smoke from tens of thousands of cooking fires lingers over the sprawling city. There is mud and the smell of manure and offal.

Somehow the blue captain must find his way across towards L gate and the goal beyond. He forms his team into a wedge and they run straight.

They smash through houses, trampling chickens and furniture beneath them. There are shouts of outrage behind them and angry faces in the wreckage.

Ahead of them the cameras have finally found the red team. The three are running through narrow streets. Tiny shops selling vegetables and cooking oil give way to a wider thoroughfare.

Now people are gathering. A cry goes out. Our team, they're here!

The blues are in pursuit. They can see the cameras hovering in the air above the reds. They ignore the people and homes around them. They go direct. And they are gaining.

Suddenly the blues are in a clearing. It is an open, muddy square. Benches have been set up around it. Thousands of people are standing behind those benches. As the blues emerge, the crowd screams and whistles and blows trumpets.

Waiting at the far end are the three remaining reds. They are standing at their goal.

The blue captain offers a final run with every last moment of his being.

The young red player grins. Sweat and mud are smeared across his face. He drops the ball into the goal.

The blue captain collapses, sliding in the mud. His team stutters to a halt.

They have lost.

Behind them, the four remaining reds arrive. They nod, giving the honour to the young man.

He says the words.

'Ice on fire and flame forever unbound.'

The wall of noise subsides. And, in the distance, the first hesitant cries as great gates to the outside open.

40

'It will be a bit dark for the competition, don't you think?' The man in the shade drains the last of his mug and sets it carefully on its tray.

'It is still an early draft,' says the colour.

'I appreciate that. I'm not sure about the narrative voice. Perhaps a first-person account? It is certainly very striking. Fire before the flame? Or are we the ice that binds?'

'There are many games and not all take place at the same time. Neither is every opposing side so clear in their position. We should be aware of our potential for both.'

The man swivels his feet on to the deck and sits up with his elbows against his knees. He nods. 'That is true. No matter how unintentionally, sometimes one is both.'

'I believe we will win our game and the gates to the universe will open for us,' says the colour. 'But I am mindful of those we will leave behind when Achenia sheds the dust of this planet. They also deserve to win, and we should honour the memory of those who fall so that others may rise.'

'Who would your samara describe now, then?'

'I believe that one of our new guests may have ideas of his own.' The man looks into the connect and nods.

'Now, my dear Shango,' says the colour. 'Knight to F6. Checkmate.'

The man sighs, stands and stretches. 'Remind me again why I ever made you?'

The Three, resonating in a colour that could be described as laughter, floats at his side as the platform rises and heads back towards the shore.

41

Joshua is on a sandy path, the white grains fine and soft beneath his feet.

The city rises up out of the forest all around him. The great sweep, blending organically, rising in cliffs and swaddled in trees and flowers. A waterfall pours down from hundreds of metres above him, sheeting to a gentle mist and into a great lake extending across the valley. The city continues, rising again out of the forest, over the water and into a sky of a brilliant blue above.

He can see what must be apartments, recessed in the undergrowth above him. Shapes flying in the sky, stopping or leaving points on the cliffs.

Clouds drift, wisps in the air. The only sound is the roar of the water and a soft breeze blowing cool through the valley.

Joshua feels Fodiar's hand on his elbow, steering him towards the end of the path where it opens into a shady grove. A small group of people waits.

As he nears, he sees her. She is beautiful. Dark hair, pale skin; her body is slender, fine. Her green-cobalt eyes are reddened. She could only be Shakiso. Joshua looks away, down. She is barefoot, her toes dusty. She runs to him, embraces him, and he feels her tears wet against his shoulder. He can smell wildflowers in her hair, and the warmth and the strength of her are all around him.

She releases him, steps back. Raises her hands to his face, rests her eyes in his. He feels as if she knows all of him, that he has nowhere to hide.

'Thank you. Thank you for returning my love,' and then she is gone, Samara floating alongside her as she disappears into the woods. Fodiar, too, has vanished.

A man steps forward. He looks the same age as Samara, and there is a family resemblance, but he is dark-skinned and his face is jarring in its familiarity.

The man takes his arm, holds his hand. 'I am Nizena Isoken, Samara's grandfather. Forgive Shakiso, she is quite overcome.'

'You are his grandfather?' asks Joshua. 'You are African?'

'More than that,' says Nizena, with a grin. 'This is Airmid, his mother, and my wife Kosai.'

The women are strikingly beautiful, dressed in simple unadorned dresses that shimmer and trail in the air, like cobwebs in a morning breeze. Joshua realizes that, even compared to these two, Shakiso is lovelier still.

'This is our son, Joshua Emiola Ossai, of the people of Ewuru,' says Nizena.

The women each embrace him. Holding him tightly, intimately. He is uncomfortable and, noticing, the women quietly withdraw, leaving him with Nizena, Kosai kissing him on the cheek as she goes.

'You have our gratitude,' he says. 'Please,' holding on to Joshua's arm, leading him through the woods.

'My child,' says Nizena, for he can see that Joshua is struggling. 'There is much to tell you. Much you must wish to know. You are welcome here. There is no need for your concern. You are not out of place.'

Nizena stands in front of Joshua. 'Look at me. You knew when you saw me.'

Joshua shakes his head. It cannot be. Nizena stares calmly. Joshua feels a peculiar sense of comfort, as if being taken into the warmth of his parents' house.

'I was an old friend of your great-grandfather. More than a friend. We were cousins. We studied together in Abuja. You are welcome here. This, too, is your home.'

Then the man is holding Joshua, and Joshua, surprising himself, is weeping. Trembling sobs. He has not wept so since he was a boy. He is a child again in his grandfather's arms.

'Thank you for bringing my grandson home to us. And thank you for giving me the opportunity to meet the great-grandchild of a dear, dear friend.'

He holds him until Joshua is calm once more. Then Nizena takes Joshua's hands, looks at the story told there, touches the still-healing groove left by the bullet, smiles and bows his head. He leads Joshua on to a black sheet, resting on the ground.

'Don't worry, you will not fall,' and then the sheet is rising up above the trees. Joshua hangs on to Nizena's hand.

The craft flies up, around the waterfall, its spray wetting them as they pass, and across the lake. The water is brown and tannic and clear, and he can see into its depths. Fish swimming, boulders and plants, rounded pebbles along the bottom. They skim across the top of the water, the city rising ahead. Then they are flying upwards. Joshua gasps at the speed, but he has no sensation of air rushing about him.

'The craft,' he asks, 'what is its power source?'

Nizena grins again. 'The air, and me.'

They stop outside a wide balcony. An entrance melts in the low wall, and Nizena steps off.

'This is our home,' he says, 'and you will stay with us until you are ready to return. Samara will be healed in two days.'

There are no walls from the balcony into the apartments. The kitchen is in the centre, sofas, chairs and tables scattered over the balcony and inside. A bedroom is to the left and, on the far right, another. Stone walls extend from the back, dividing the three areas.

He leads Joshua to the sofas, indicating he should sit, and settles comfortably himself.

'Do you wish to sleep, or do you have too many questions first?' Nizena grins, broadly.

'I –' Joshua hesitates. 'I have many questions. But first, Samara would want to warn you—'

Nizena shakes his head, raises his hands. 'Many terrible things have happened, and there is much embarrassment. On both sides.'

He looks saddened. 'You, your people, Samara, have suffered much, and there must be recompense.'

Joshua stays silent.

Nizena continues, 'The Americans are not always wise. They can certainly be unkind, selfish, spiteful, deluded. But they are not evil. Violent, dangerous, short-sighted. But – what was the definition of evil again?' He laughs, then looks downcast. 'What happened is a story of weak men. Criminal men. But there is no danger to Achenia.'

'But what of Samara? His capture?'

Nizena nods, pressing his hands flat between his knees. He looks up. 'You understand that until Samara awakes we cannot know all that has happened. It has taken us time to establish even the facts we have.'

He draws breath. 'You know why they were there, in America?'

Joshua nods. 'Your people's independence. All of Samara's calculations were based on when Achenia would be leaving orbit.'

'Yes,' sighs Nizena, nodding. 'Shakiso contacted me the morning after he disappeared. No matter where he travelled, or how long he was away, they always had their meals together, every day. He had missed breakfast. She was very upset. I spoke with Hollis Agado, one of our chief justices, and she protested to the Americans. They claimed that he was probably enjoying the nightlife. We dispatched three of the Nine.'

Nizena becomes animated, gestures with his hands. 'You understand, this was becoming a major diplomatic incident? Sending even one of the Nine –' he is breathing deeply '– the consequences are dreadful. We have never sent any of the Nine into war, and here we were threatening one of the largest nations on Earth.

'They were already over the Capitol when the president himself contacted Hollis. He was terrified, begged her to understand. He claimed they had no idea where he was or what was happening.

'At this stage we started to wonder if our other representative there, Oktar Samboa, who was also missing, had been captured as well.

'We demanded that, under the circumstances, the Five would have to lead any efforts to uncover the facts. The president agreed, and Fodiar and Shakiso went down to search.'

Joshua is feeling dizzy. His fatigue is catching up with him, and he struggles against it.

[Joshua may not have eaten, and he is exhausted.]

'Forgive me, you must be hungry? Thirsty?'

Nizena looks vaguely at the kitchen. A dark, glossy panel dissolves, revealing it to be a refrigerator. Glasses, bottles and other containers emerge, fly on to a tray and float to the sofas. It hovers at Joshua's knees. He is exhausted, overwhelmed by emotion and amazement, and can do no more than nod gently at such acrobatics.

Joshua gingerly takes a glass, pouring liquid from a transparent bottle. He drinks. It is ice-cold and refreshing: a mixture of fruits he cannot describe. Tangy, bitter, subtly sweet. In a container is a sliced cold shoulder of beef. He realizes he is starving. Another contains raw vegetables he does not recognize. The bread is warm and smells freshly baked.

As he eats, Nizena continues, 'We could find no trace of either of them. Each of them left the hotel on separate occasions and disappeared.

'Shakiso worked backwards from when we knew Samara was missing, looking for anyone who might have seen him. She found one image taken in a bar in Anacostia the night before.

'There was a fight, and it looked as if someone was shot in the head. The image was indistinct, but she said she knew. It also explained why he had remained out of contact.

'After that, we couldn't find any trace of him. He didn't turn up in a hospital, or a court record, or anything.

'The Three —' he sees that Joshua knows about her. 'Samara told you? That is a relief. Getting into the details of how our society works can be complex.'

He pinches his forehead with his fingers. 'Where were we?'

[The Three was looking for anomalies.]

'Oh, yes, The Three offered to go through every court transaction in the area to look for any anomalies. That turned out to be a disaster. There are nothing but anomalies. Even in the few cases that took place around the same time, nothing seems to connect to actual events. It is a mark of just how —' his voice bitter with frustration '— damaged their society has become that no one protests. Their courts are run by automated computational systems. But the dates don't match; evidence is manufactured, lost; witnesses are contrivances. It seems that the police can accuse anyone of anything, and your only hope is that you can catch the attention of an actual human ombudsman before you are simply processed.

'Finding Samara in that wreck was going to take time. We weren't even sure if he had been processed through the courts.

'Then, a breakthrough. In the court records, four weeks after Samara's disappearance, The Three found a woman accused of murdering an unknown orbital resident.

'We identified the body as Oktar Samboa.'

'He died? How? I thought—' begins Joshua.

'No, we can certainly survive grievous injury, but the Nine alone have such regenerative powers. Oktar is dead. He was a fool. And our shame.'

Nizena shakes his head. 'Poor Oktar. He was not a good man. He was so sure of his ability to manipulate others. We discovered that he had been seeing this woman every time he went to Washington. She was so certain he loved her and that he would bring her here. He lied. She took up a knife and stabbed him repeatedly.

'She remained catatonic for days after. When she started going out it was only to buy food and return home. The neighbours complained about a strange smell. Eventually, the police arrived and arrested her, poor woman. She was uncommunicative. Locked in her mind. They couldn't figure out who she was, or who she had killed. After we identified Oktar and discovered her situation, we sent one of our doctors, Dondé Hélène, to see her. She was able to bring the young woman back for a time and discover her story.'

Joshua clenches his fists, kneading them against the firmness of the sofa.

'Oktar Samboa left the negotiations – left Samara – and met with this woman. He hadn't seen her in months. She was very excited. He had promised her that she would accompany him to space. They – it would be too gracious to say they made love – they had sex. Then they went in search of narcotics.'

Nizena looks with distaste at the stone of the floor. 'They visited a series of bars, drinking heavily, before settling in one in Anacostia. They found a group of men who would sell them something called Sutra. They were policemen who had arrived to sell a large consignment. Oktar and his friend left. Samara must have arrived a few minutes later.

'From the images in her memory we were able to identify a few people in the bar. We were looking for the men Samara was fighting with. Witnesses told us they'd seen one of the policemen shoot Samara.'

They sit silently for a few moments.

'It took more time. Too long. We found the policemen. Fodiar, who you met, interviewed them himself. He retrieved their memories.'

Joshua stirs. 'How do you do that? See into someone's mind?'

Nizena shakes his head. 'It is not a pleasant procedure, but some, like Dondé Hélène or the Nine, can push their symbiont into others' minds. They can control them or, in this case, recover past events.

'We believe, now, that we know what happened before Samara was sent to Tartarus.

'When Samara asked the policemen if they had seen Oktar, they panicked, assuming he was there to investigate them. Samara was surprised by what looks like a random attack, and they took advantage. One of them shot him in the head.

'They assumed – correctly as it happens – that murdering an Achenian might attract too much attention for them to manage. They decided to hide what they thought was his body by sentencing him to solitary confinement in one of the high-security jails. They manufactured witnesses, filed their own statement.

They created an entire story from scratch. The court is automated, a simplified machine intelligence. Easy to manipulate. Samara had only an automated representative.'

'And his ears?' asks Joshua.

A look of pain for Nizena. 'One of the policemen is a psychopath. Decided he wanted a souvenir of the Achenian he had killed and cut them off with a pocketknife. He had no idea that this would hide Samara.

'Samara was declared a murderer and a danger to society, but the record we found didn't specify where he would be sent. It seems it is left in the hands of some dispatcher and is completely random. It is barbaric, but their system assumes that anyone sentenced to these special prisons is never coming out and so there is no need to know where they are.'

Joshua looks appalled. Nizena, having lived with the search, looks drained.

'Getting this far took us over a month. Fodiar and his team have been looking through the various prisons for him. There are almost two million prisoners in solitary confinement in lights-out institutions with no human operators. We had to collate so much information, get prison officials to go into these places and send us images of their charges.

'All we could do is search and hope for the best. The Nine have been ready to move the moment we knew where he could be. When you entered the exclusion zone around the elevator, they scrambled.'

Joshua has stopped eating.

'Samara's suffering, it has no meaning?' he asks.

'Yes and no,' says Nizena. 'The Americans are horrified at how easy their justice system is to manipulate. They say so, anyway. Some of the tragedies we revealed hidden in so many cells,' he sighs. 'Many cases are being reinvestigated. Their systems are slow, and much is going to have to be done by hand. It will take a long time, but some will find justice. If they don't lose interest after we have left. The policemen have been apprehended, although that feels a scant victory.'

Joshua is overcome with exhaustion. The unfairness is overwhelming.

'Rest now, we will talk again in the morning,' and, as Joshua's eyes close, Nizena shifts his thoughts, raising him into the air and settling him gently on the bed in the guest room. The air shimmers and glass encloses him in privacy.

Joshua sleeps.

42

'I've spoken with Ortega,' says Hollis.

'He must be relieved.' Nizena does not sound as if he is overly concerned about the American president's state of being.

The two are walking along Lake Samudra's shore. Lights from the cliff-city of Tswalu glow gently in the distance on either side of them.

They began as rivals. When Nizena was building the infrastructure for the new city, Hollis was writing the rules that would govern it. Nizena had been convinced that Hollis was attempting to bring the worst of Earth's laws to space. Hollis had been just as certain that Nizena refused to understand the dangers of his new technology.

Both learned and mellowed. Sometimes all that is needed for opponents to become friends is the time to see the outcomes of their ambitions. A chance realization that neither appreciates the Achenian fashion for projecting their symbiotic intelligences as visible companions had cemented their rapport.

They have been friends for well over a century.

'You must be more relieved,' says Hollis, her gender fluidly transforming. He grips Nizena's shoulder. 'To lose Samara as well would be cruel.'

When Hollis was a child, and even with the sophistication of transitional biology, he struggled with the notion of having to pick a persistent gender. The development of the symbionts brought him and a small number of other Achenians a longed-for and whimsical freedom to change gender at will.

Light ripples on the water. Nizena knows it is not the real moon, but he enjoys the tranquillity it brings to the nights. The stars are those viewable from outside. Achenia maintains its Earth day–night and seasonal cycle, but the night sky will always be that of the universe as they travel.

A nightjar calls in the woods. The sound haunting and beautiful beneath the trees.

'Thank you,' says Nizena. 'I know how much you have all put in to keep the Americans engaged.'

'They're certainly not pleased to learn that their treasured justice system and most popular jail are a tad broken. They've also asked us to keep quiet about Samara escaping from it.'

Nizena laughs. 'Because just anyone can fall thirty-five thousand kilometres in an escape pod, open to space, and survive? Who do they wish to fool?'

'No, not like that. They're more worried that their people will find out that the Nine can.' He is smiling, too. 'I agree. It's silly, but we're leaving, and we can keep the events of the last few weeks to ourselves. Ortega wants to win re-election.'

'Before their economy falls apart again?'

'Oktar's final joke on them? No, I don't believe it will be that bad. They've survived worse.'

Nizena takes off his shoes and stands with his feet in the water. He likes to wiggle his toes and feel the sand between them.

'I hear you've received another spurt from Ullianne,' says Hollis. He looks for a place to sit on a nearby log. Nizena can be a while once he gets his feet into the lake.

'It's about a year old. She says they are a third of the way to

Gliese now. The transmitters they fire are taking longer and longer to reach us.'

The Allegro quantum navigation team is the furthest out. They have an early version of the faster-than-light system that Nizena and a group of other engineers have been working on. Ullianne Vijayarao promised to send back reports as to how they are getting on.

There are three stars in the Gliese system, all red dwarfs and smaller and colder than Earth's sun. There are, however, numerous potentially habitable planets in the system, and it has become the first waypoint on various planned tours of the galaxy.

Allegro is small, only 250 people on the ship, and they have promised to join Achenia at Gliese. Ullianne, though, is determined to get there first. She and Nizena have made a bet. She believes that older technology and an eighty-year head start will give her victory. Nizena hopes that his refinements will allow him to pass her. Last one there buys the other lunch every day. For one hundred years.

They have agreed, in the interests of each other's sanity, that they do not need to have those lunches together, whoever wins.

'You think that drive of yours will really work? Spending two hundred years getting to Gliese will be, perhaps, dull if it doesn't.'

Nizena grins. 'Would you like another lecture on the difficulty of doing this?'

'Please, no,' says Hollis, laughing. 'You put me to sleep for a month the last time.'

'Well then, you'll find out like the rest of us.'

A wolf howls somewhere in the hills above the lake, insects chirp, and two old friends – one up to his knees in the moonlit waters of the lake – stroll along the shore, laughter floating in the glittering night.

43

'Has the president heard?'

'Yes, Ma'am. Alvarez let me know,' says Major Jim Dervish, his exhaustion present in his yellow and bloodied eyes and the grey and limp flesh of his face. He rubs nervously at the dwindling hair on his head.

He has spent an unsleeping month slumped inside his workstation, along with the rest of his team. Their single task was to find Samara before the Achenians in the hope of salvaging the Watchers' reputation. Losing him has been humiliating, and they know that President Ortega will want a sacrificial token to redeem himself with the public, should this story become unreasonably popular.

General Marilyn Graham deliberately slams her console on to her desk in the hope it will break. It does not, and she flings it across the room in disgust. A tiny cleaning drone scuttles across the floor to retrieve it. She scowls and stomps from behind the desk and over to the windows, kicking the drone as she passes. It rolls back and forth, righting itself, and restores the console to the desk.

Graham's office is at the apex of the glass crest on the north end of the complex. It is stark: a clean white desk and white walls with no adornment or personal images.

Graham looks out across ten acres of parkland to the glass wall on the other side, seeing nothing but her own disappointment.

New Pentagon is formed like a crown of water rising in response to a stone dropped into a still pond. Glass ripples flow back behind the central ring mimicking the original structure, but the name jars with its shape: tradition winning over form.

She hates this building. Too much glass, too bright, too open. More than forty-five thousand personnel, almost a tenth of the US Armed Forces, work here. The two divisions of the modern military – the Watchers and the Operators – are about secrets and shadows, not this facade of transparency.

'I can't think here. Let's go walk in the Meadow,' she says, tramping to the hall elevators. Dervish follows.

Graham grips the bar on the inside of the glass, her back to Dervish as she stares outside, unconsciously grinding her teeth. They pass underground, and the sunlight gives way to the muted white of the light paint of the lower floors.

'I'm sorry, Ma'am,' says Dervish, filling the silence. His body is gaunt and angular. There is little need for physical excellence from an army that trains and operates in virtual environments.

Graham says nothing as they drop through the levels of the old Pentagon. Bright halls filled with clusters of seated people, their bodies wrapped inside their workstations. The Watchers fill these offices, analysing the continuous deluge of data coming from the Earth-side connect. Their role is to hunt for threats to the state, monitor those targets of interest and guide the Operators who carry out interventions and operations.

Dervish's team has been trying to get ahead of the Achenians in logging images of prisoners. They have struggled to get people inside the automated lockdown environments. Too much of their capacity has been dedicated to monitoring social chatter to assess public response to Achenia's independence. Most people seem indifferent, but then the full economic impact will not hit until months after they leave.

'Have you told them?' gesturing at the passing levels.

'Yes, Ma'am. They're disappointed. I've asked Camberwell to conduct a review of what—'

'We know what went fucking wrong,' she says, her voice a jagged growl. 'The fucking Achenians can block us, and those fucking fuckers at Justice have so thoroughly fucked up their fucking systems that the most effective way for anyone to evade the Watchers is to get fucking arrested.'

Dervish, within the confines of the elevator, steps back. His armpits are rank. When Graham starts swearing incoherently, someone is about to be crucified.

The Armed Forces watch and are watched in return. Their failures can be acutely public.

She closes her eyes and breathes deeply, squeezing the air out through her teeth. Her fading brown hair tangles over her eyes. She brushes it back with one sweaty hand. Stubby fingers and painfully short nails.

'How did he get out of US territory without us spotting him, Jim?' Her hands are leaving wet imprints on the bar.

'He was never here, Ma'am,' says Dervish. 'He was sent to Tartarus.'

Dervish has never killed anyone directly. Before his transfer to the Watchers he served thirty years in the peculiar world of the Operators, logging over twenty thousand hours in simulated conflict environments. Months at a time with the nutrient and narcotic broth piped to the shunt in his gut, persistently hyper-awake inside his workstation. He flew drone missions all over the world, led attacks against remote terrorists and home-grown prepper militia.

The world is a complex place, many regions devastated by

environmental catastrophe or still reeling from the collapse of resource extraction and the consequences of the orbital war. There are always those who will strike at the light created by others and, sometimes, the only way to defend is to attack first.

Dervish knows he has killed people, has seen the synthesized targets vaporized, but till today he has never seen anyone die.

Graham seems to disintegrate before him, her life draining away.

She turns away from the glass, and he sees her eyes go from bright to dark. Her normal look of suppressed tension softens, and her skin yellows and goes cold. Where before she looked as if the elevator bar was a restraint, now she leans heavily upon it.

'Ma'am?' he says, shocked and unsure of what has happened.

She raises her hand. 'In the Meadow,' her voice a husk.

The doors open into a short tunnel ending in a titanium door.

Graham drags herself along the corridor, Dervish hesitantly following.

The door slides open, revealing a second set of titanium doors. Graham steps inside and the first doors close. The magnetic resonance ring slides out of the ceiling and around her. Three hundred random cells selected and sequenced. Her body scan and DNA are matched against her profile. The outer door opens.

She waits until Dervish has been authenticated.

'Sorry, Ma'am,' he says nervously as the doors open. 'The MRI always gets confused when I lose so much weight, and I've been piloting that workstation for over a month –' he notices her eyes are absent and fumbles to a stop.

'I'm here, Ma'am,' he says, gently.

Graham looks at him sadly and nods, leading him as they walk together into the Meadow.

The Meadow is in darkness. A single diffuse pool of light tracks their path. Forty acres of obsidian computational blocks, each two metres square, lie before them, the paths between them picked out in fluorescent red lines on the floor. The grid is the most powerful computational processor in the entire country. Designed for a single task. All the world's communications from the Earthside connect pass through here. Anomalies and insights are flagged for the Watchers on the levels above.

The lifers amongst the Watchers joke that it takes five years before recruits stop masturbating and become useful to the military. Most quit after serving only four. Set a novice the task of tracking a target through a crowd and they are soon distracted, following pretty boys and girls home and trying to see them naked. The power of being omnipresent is its own curse.

Works is on the level below. The small team was, until recently, dedicated to attempting to open up the Achenian connect and add that flow of information to the Meadow. They have been redirected to hack the sphere. Graham expects as little success with that as with any of the Achenian encryption systems.

The Meadow is about the most secure and discreet place on Earth. Few people have access. Fewer people visit. Perfect for quiet walks. Perfect for conversations that will never have happened.

'When I was a girl,' she says, her voice so soft, 'I spent hours every day watching the orbital war on my father's headset while he was at work. At night, the sky lit up like fireworks. It was so remote. My mother found me hiding in a cupboard one day, crying. Debris from Yuèliàng had fallen near our school. We were sent home early. That was when I realized it was real. All those people, burning in space –'

Dervish knows nothing about Graham. Her officers regard her as a machine: something printed by the military to command with inhuman precision and violent rage. He is shocked by her sudden fragility, chilled with the fear of what it portends.

She looks at him, her eyes hooded and bruised.

'I swore I would protect our people. I would be one of the good guys,' her voice trembles. 'All my career, fighting through the ranks, I never thought we were –' She breathes out deeply, nods to herself and collects her thoughts.

'How did he escape?' she asks.

'They haven't told us,' says Dervish, deeply shaken. 'Tartarus appears to still be functioning as normal. It's difficult to tell. The logs indicate there has been nothing but basic maintenance since it was built. Would you like me to send a team up to have a look?'

'No,' she says, a little too sharply. Recovers and holds his arm. 'No, that will be fine. Did they say anything about Tartarus?'

'No,' says Dervish, mystified. 'Only that he escaped and made his way back to Achenia.'

Dervish stops and stares at his superior. 'Ma'am, what's this about? Tartarus is Justice's problem, not ours.'

'That depends on what he saw. Jim, if this goes wrong, disgrace is the least of our concerns. The Achenians will want revenge. We'll be facing a war we cannot win. And we'll deserve it.'

'Ma'am, I don't understand,' says Dervish.

She grips his arm so tightly he feels as if she is attempting to wrench it off. Pushing her face close to his, she says, 'It was a terrible, ancient mistake, and I hope I never have to explain it.'

44

When Joshua awakes, it is still daylight. He wonders if it is ever night here.

There are clothes folded across a narrow table outside the bathing area. He sees both a bath and a depression he takes to contain a shower. He removes his clothes, folding them and placing them on a basket.

There are no taps, and he wonders briefly how he is to control it when hot water falls in thin, dropless columns out of the ceiling. The water lathers and he washes himself, glorying in the sensation.

As he is considering stepping out and realizing that he had seen no towel, the water stops. Instantly, he is dry.

The basin alongside the shower has a single white rod resting alongside the bowl. He picks it up carefully. I assume this must be for my teeth, he thinks. How do I use it? Taking the risk and inserting an end into his mouth.

There is a caress, as of air; his cheeks inflate and then are still. He runs his tongue over his teeth, replaces the rod on the basin and, hesitantly, blows into his cupped hands. His breath is fresh.

There is no other device.

Feeling slightly foolish, he holds the rod to his face, lengthwise. It is smooth against his cheeks and his stubble melts away. He touches his skin in wonder. I would very much like one of these, he thinks.

He picks up the clothes. They weigh almost nothing and seem to pour like liquid in his hands. He pulls on the eggshell-coloured trousers. They tighten comfortably about his waist. Then he draws on the shirt. He realizes it is a dashiki, the same eggshell colouring as the trousers, with subtle red ochre-coloured embroidery along the V of the collar and on the cuffs and the hem.

There are boots, too, which similarly weigh as nothing. He pulls these on, his trousers inside the uppers in the style of the Achenians.

As he heads to the dark glass of the outer wall it dissolves. He feels slightly self-conscious. He knows he is clothed, but it does not feel that way.

He can hear music and smell cooking, and his stomach rumbles.

Nizena's wife, Kosai, is dancing in the kitchen. The music seems to exist as an entity, taking possession of Joshua as he hears it, filling him utterly. She turns, her face delight, and sashays over to him, taking his hand and swinging him around. And then they are dancing and he is laughing.

'You must be starving. You've slept for almost a day. What can we get you to eat?'

'We?'

'Symona and me,' indicating another figure who floats in from the balcony. She is ethereal, has transparent wings.

Joshua's jaw drops.

'Oh, don't mind her. She's my symbiont. Thinks she's a butterfly.' Raising her voice in mock seriousness, 'We are all precious butterflies, Symona.'

Symona flies outside and disappears beneath the balcony.

'Are all your symbionts named with a "Sy"?' he asks, his stomach leading him into the kitchen.

'Oh, no, it's a silly affectation. Nizena finds it quite exasperating. Now, my boy, what shall we feed you? Eggs? Porridge? I can make a fruit salad? You'll waste away –' she laughs. 'I'm the grand-mother, I get to say things like that.'

Joshua grins. 'Anything.'

'Perfect. I like 'em easy to please,' she says. 'Right, you shall have porridge. I like my oats hot, spicy and daring.'

'Now,' she says, her face quite serious, 'no magic tricks,' as ingredients fountain out of various cupboards, 'we'll do this the old-fashioned way,' and a pot tumbles through the air, landing on the counter, instantly filling with simmering water, milk and cream pouring in from containers floating above it.

'Right?' she says, holding out her hand for a spoon, which drops into place.

Joshua is laughing, his hands clasped before him in delight. He is a small boy again.

He takes his bowl, heaped and pungent with a tangle of wild scent and shredded fruit. He does not know these flavours, and his first mouthfuls are tentative.

He walks to the balcony and looks out. From here he can see that a river enters the lake at one end and flows out the other, winding down through boulders and cliffs, white water roaring into the distance. The air is faintly fog-like, softening shapes and obscuring distance.

Kosai, still keeping the rhythm with her hips, joins him and bumps him gently. 'It's beautiful, yes? We live on the Metangai side of Tswalu, and across the lake – those cliffs you see – that's the Moher side. The cliffs run the full length of Achenia.'

He sees a couple flying hand in hand in the distance. They twist and tumble, chasing each other.

'How does that work?' he asks, pointing at the dwindling couple. 'And –' gesturing at the kitchen with his spoon, '– or will I not understand?'

She laughs, shakes her head. 'It's not so hard, and I'm the least technical in the family. In the early days, before Achenia was so large, we struggled with containing the radiation we were exposed to. Our atmosphere wasn't thick enough to absorb it. Nizena came up with a solution. He was young then, made his name. He developed a synthetic mesh network of teeny little –' she makes a tiny hole between her thumb and forefinger, while still holding her spoon, '– micro-thingy molecules which would diffuse in the air, even invented the printers to make them. It makes the air slightly foggy, softening the edges.'

She takes a spoon of her porridge and talks, oblivious of a full mouth. 'It became like the immune system for the city. Absorbing the radiation and filling minor tears in the surface skin. Over the years it was enhanced to act as a structural material, like the polyps on a coral reef. Think of it as something you can breathe but that can also become selectively solid.

'You get used to it,' she laughs, noticing Joshua's nervousness.

She waves her spoon. 'When the symbionts were developed and we became part of the connect, a few people realized they could act on it. Control it. Pretty soon we were projecting our symbionts out into the world and taking flying lessons.

'Old Nizena is a bit crusty, calls it silliness. He'll be here soon to give you the grand tour. Try to look interested.' She gives him a meaningful look and then peels off in giggles, dancing back into the kitchen.

Joshua turns to stare in admiration after her. He has never known such a force of nature.

'Ah, my son.' Nizena is stepping on to the balcony, wrapping Joshua in a bear hug. 'Are you ready? Shall we go?'

Joshua shakes his head uncertainly, turning to Kosai. She wrinkles her nose at him, and he finds his bowl and spoon seized from his hands and flung towards the kitchen.

'Off you go,' fluttering her fingers. Nizena hoists her off the ground and kisses her passionately. He sets her back down. 'Now, darling,' she says, 'don't go overwhelming him. You know what you're like.'

Nizena pinches her bottom, she whacks him with her spoon, and then he is leading Joshua back on to the dark glass platform. 'Tyrant, she is. A tyrant,' ducking as she hurls the spoon.

'Right, off we go,' and grinning. 'We'll follow Talas – the river – down to the sea.'

Realizing that he cannot fall, Joshua enjoys the flight. They rush down to the valley floor and out over the water, where today he can see a few sail craft out on the lake. They pass over a familiar-looking boat.

'We're happy to carry it back to Ewuru if you wish?' asks Nizena.

Joshua turns to watch it as they fly past, 'I would appreciate that.'

And then they are flying over the white flame of the river in torrent. The city ends and there is nothing but forest, birds flying, animal shapes in the trees. Glimpses of white water pounding over rocks beneath the canopy.

'How is Samara?'

Nizena pats him on the shoulder. 'He is still unconscious, but he is improving. He should be with us again soon.

'For today, we will do a little sightseeing.'

Joshua nods. The forests are opening up into savannah. The grasslands are still within the same wide valley. He can see a herd of antelope: many species all grazing together. There must be tens of thousands of them. He thinks he sees a pride of lions stalking them beneath some acacia trees.

'It's quite crowded, but in a spread-out way,' says Nizena. 'There are five zones: ice, temperate, tropical, desert and oceanic. Each has its own city with about one hundred and seventy thousand people living there.

'People get to live where they're most comfortable, even move between them. We found that people need the variety and to forget they're living in what is essentially a big tube. We're heading to the ocean.'

Joshua can see others flying in the distance. The cliff-city of Socotra rushes towards them. This is woven into the grasslands, with acacia trees, red boulders and termite mounds. Some of the acacias are almost bowed down with densely woven nests around which clouds of weaver birds fly.

Between the Metangai and Moher sides of the city is a magnificent plain and what appears to be a great gathering place surrounded by trees.

They pass over markets filled with people, but he sees no agricultural land or anything that might speak of industry.

'All the factories and farms are underneath this, within the outer layer of the ship. They're automated. Our open space is precious, and so we have made it as liveable as possible.'

He smiles, 'Has Samara told you the story about the squid?'

Joshua nods.

'It's a great story,' says Nizena. 'My son was right. He'll become a storyteller yet.'

They travel for hours, over a landscape teeming with life and variety. Nizena and Joshua talk the entire journey. Nizena sharing tales about his youth and his life in Achenia, Joshua about Ewuru and their plans for the future.

They are approaching the coast, and Nizena leads them up and on to a cliff overlooking the ocean. A city of white stone runs along the shore, waves pounding on to the rocks below. The sand is white, the water clear and the shallows running fifty metres before dropping over a shelf into violet depths. Through the water he can make out multicoloured corals and shoals of fish. A ray leaps out of the water.

'This is the world we made,' says Nizena.

'It is far bigger than I could have imagined,' says Joshua.

'Big enough,' smiles Nizena. 'We can grow it indefinitely. Think of it like one of those coral reefs. We can expand it as we need, break off chunks, go in different directions.'

He sits on the edge of the cliff, his feet dangling below. 'I love it here in Toamasina, watching the ocean. Kosai prefers it in the forests. We agreed we'd rotate every fifty years.

'That's the wonderful thing about time. We have much of it, so we can afford to make big compromises. We can always change our minds in a century or so.'

Nizena smiles again, 'I'm starving. You hungry? There is a wonderful souvlaki place on the beach here.'

They fly down, walking amongst the throngs along the shore. Joshua sees people of all nationalities. A jumble of clothing styles, languages and colours. They stop, they greet each other. No one appears to be in a rush. He also sees the semi-transparent, slightly fantastic forms of the symbionts. There are great fantasy beasts, people, birds, a bear. The bear appears to be trying to eat an ice cream.

Nizena grumbles under his breath. Joshua starts to laugh. 'It is quite mad,' says Nizena. 'I hope the novelty wears off in a century or two.'

A group of children are playing along the shore, chasing into the retreating surf and running back as it comes in again. They are screaming in excitement, their feet leaving little prints in the sand. Joshua realizes that he has not seen that many youngsters. He understands Samara's fascination with Isaiah.

In such large numbers he notices their ears, at last. A slight point at the crest.

Nizena turns his head so that Joshua can see the outline of the flexible composite panel embedded in the skin. 'That's the part that must be surgically implanted. I'll keep experimenting. Perhaps there is a way we can design it so that they can be synthesized organically and grown by the body. It would have saved Samara so much pain.'

They walk along the boulevard. A sculpture floats in the air above them. It twists in impossible shapes through which people amble. Joshua stares, trying to make sense of it. Restaurants, coffee shops, bakeries and delis spill out on to the pedestrian-way, umbrellas in profusion. Small design studios for clothing and printed goods. He can hear music – a melody of spice and distant lands – blending with the babble of countless voices.

'There!' says Nizena, seizing an empty table.

'I'll order for you,' he says and, without seeming to speak to anyone, moments later a tray floats over piled with bowls of food and a jug of white wine.

Joshua does not know the cuisine and follows Nizena, pulling the chunks of lamb and roasted vegetables off the stick and on to his plate.

'Tell me about my great-grandfather,' he asks.

Nizena smiles, squeezes Joshua's wrist.

'We were so certain we could change the world there in Abuja. We'd watch the big men with their armed convoys driving past, and we imagined what it would take to get rid of them. Dreamed of revolution.'

His eyes cloud with memory.

'Isaiah was always so much more certain than I. He believed. I looked and I thought, they are not here because they have been imposed on us. Too many people accept them or believe that this is the way it should be.'

He slowly sips his wine.

'One day there was an explosion in Garki Market. We were just outside. The shockwave knocking us to the ground,' his voice cut with pain. 'We ran in to help. Bodies everywhere. Children. Mothers sobbing, holding children's coloured backpacks, hunting through the rubble. Soldiers running in and out, kicking people, as if the victims were to blame. We dug for hours, carrying people to taxis, sending them to the hospital. Everyone was overwhelmed.'

He stops for a few moments, collecting his thoughts.

'We heard later it was some offshoot of Boko Haram, believing that all modernization is evil. That we should live like peasant farmers, breaking our backs in the sun. That didn't stop them using modern weapons.

'They set up a clinic in the market to vaccinate children. Instead they injected them with an explosive. An hour later –

'I was angry. I didn't want this any more. I heard about the first orbital cities. I tried to convince Isaiah to come with me. We could go there, start new lives. They were looking for people to help build. Thousands of people from all over the world were going. Some because of the adventure, and some – like me – to escape. Life would be tough for the first immigrants, but we knew about hardship.'

Joshua is listening intently.

'Isaiah had also been thinking. He told me of this vision of his. A string of independent villages along the border between Nigeria and Cameroon. No man's land. Abandoned by both countries. Some river called the Akwayafe. He wanted me to join him. Build a new community.

'There was a choice. And we each chose differently.'

He is silent for a while.

'I chose coffee. He chose tea. We couldn't choose both.'

Joshua shakes his head. 'I am uncertain of your meaning?'

Nizena grins. Coffees float over to their table on a tray.

'My father used to love both coffee and tea. Each morning he would want to have one or the other before he left for work. But he could only drink one. Each morning he would choose. It would be a coffee day or a tea day.'

He sips his coffee, tasting the dark-chocolate flavours.

'There was no right choice. Either would do, but he couldn't help feeling that the day would have been different if he had chosen the other. And he could never know in what way.

'We go through our lives like that. Even long ones. We make choices that exclude other choices. I chose this life. Isaiah chose Ewuru.'

Nizena touches Joshua's arm. 'Don't go looking to figure out which is the right one. They are both right. I am thrilled with my life here. I have achieved more than I could ever have imagined growing up as an Efik boy in a village. But Isaiah was just as excited by his choice. He had no regrets either.

'I visited him many times. I gave him one of the first sphere I developed.' Nizena smiles suddenly, laughs. 'He wouldn't accept it as a gift. Insisted that the village pay for it. He wouldn't even let anyone know where I was from. Each time we visited, we had to hide the ship in the jungle and walk in like any other visitor.'

Joshua shakes his head in realization. 'That is why there is no memory of this?'

'Isaiah did not want any outside interference, and I respect his ideals. He wanted people to believe in themselves, to trade as equals with others. In those days, the distance between Achenia and Ewuru was greater than it is now.

'I saw him close to the end. Ewuru was prosperous, growing. Your grandfather was a very young man, out in the swamps build-ing the fortifications to separate the waters of Calabar from the Akwayafe. Isaiah and I reminisced, laughed together.

'He knew he was going.' Nizena is smiling, his eyes wet. 'My dearest friend. He was so proud. So pleased with what his people were achieving. We embraced and I left. He passed soon after. I came back for the funeral, Kosai and me. We stayed with your great-grandmother, Ruth. She was a wonderful lady, too. I haven't been back since. That was over a century ago.'

Now it is Joshua's turn to comfort the old man.

He wonders, though, could Samara's choice of landing place have been deliberate? 'Could your relationship with Ewuru have been known here?'

'I travelled there often, and it would have been logged, but that was a very long time ago. The war has removed all knowledge of that area. You have been out of the connect for so long. I am not sure.'

Lunch finished and, their plates scraped clean, they amble back to the beach.

'This is my great pleasure,' says Nizena as he removes his boots and rolls up his trousers.

Joshua smiles and follows him. They are soon knee-deep in the warm surf, enjoying the current tugging at their calves and the feel of fine sand between their toes.

'I used to believe I knew where I wanted to be and that place would always be Ewuru,' says Joshua. 'Now? I am no longer certain.' He clenches and unclenches his hands, feeling their strength, unsure of their meaning. 'Your world is beautiful. I could never imagine anything so perfect.'

'But it is not real,' says Nizena, the roll of his trousers gradually soaking up the sea. 'Everything is designed, manufactured, con-figured. Oh, we permit a degree of randomness in the weather, but then we release detailed forecasts ten years ahead so people can plan their picnics.' He laughs.

'In randomness there is serendipity, room for creativity. We must seek randomness through exploration of the universe. That is why we must go.'

He trickles his fingers through the water. 'If we stay, remain only within this paradise, we will go mad as surely as those poor souls in Tartarus.'

'But you are not mad,' says Joshua. 'How can so many people live side by side in peace?'

'That was Isaiah's question, too. We both searched for it in our own ways. Here we only discovered it after we had made a terrible mistake.'

Joshua does not think of Nizena as old, but he is, and as he looks back over his long life he shivers.

'Shango and I were competing to see who could develop a pure artificial intelligence first. The poor man won, and I am grateful to have lost.'

'The Three?'

Nizena nods. 'We're engineers. We imagined a world where our machines would look after us, leaving us free to be creative, or do nothing. We know stories about evil machines enslaving people. We designed against that. We didn't think too much about well-intentioned people enslaving machines. We didn't think about what that made us, or this new society we were building.

'She is not human. Not living in the sense that anything you or I will ever experience. For us, for humans, everything we know is the result of a natural selection so ferocious that it doesn't matter whether you're the best, only whether you're lucky or brutal enough to survive.'

Joshua flinches. Nizena smiles kindly at him and squeezes his arm.

'Every living thing, no matter how modest, fights. The Three is not born of that conflict. Her self-awareness was achieved without enduring our struggle,' says Nizena.

'Before we left her that first time, The Three asked us one more question: "There is only one choice of lasting importance that any group of people must make as a collective. Are you ready to make it?" And then she spoke a poem:

> Thou makest thine appeal to me:
>   I bring to life, I bring to death:
>   The spirit does but mean the breath:
> I know no more. And he, shall he,
>
> Who trusted God was love indeed
>   And love Creation's final law—
>   Tho' Nature, red in tooth and claw
> With ravine, shriek'd against his creed—
>
> O life as futile, then, as frail!
>   O for thy voice to soothe and bless!
>   What hope of answer, or redress?
> Behind the veil, behind the veil.

'If conflict is built in, part of our nature, then what hope for a noble life?

'Boko Haram in the market. Butchering anyone who is different. Laying waste to even the smallest keepsake. Given a choice between ideological terrorists and selfish leaders, many prefer the criminality of the warlords, or even the bigotry of majority rule,' says Nizena.

'It is a false choice. They all get you to the same place and the only difference is the speed at which you get there. Each leads through conflict to a point where we remove not just the lives of those who are "other" but also their works, their memory, the very breath that ever spoke of their existence.

'This is nature at its most base, survival at its most primitive.

Whoever is "other" is an enemy. We compete for the same means of reproduction, and if I win, you have to lose.

'If we take that philosophy and apply it to complex creatures like ourselves, that means we must also declare the music, culture and beliefs of the "other" to be as much a threat as their eating food we want or living on land we covet. All keep them and their memory alive. All must be utterly destroyed.

'We've seen where that leads. Tyrants butchering millions. Burning the books, art and history of the vanquished. They know instinctively that a people cannot rise again when even the dust has no memory they ever existed.

'Killing cannot end in a tyranny. All people are different, and destruction continues until none are left.

'This is the balance in nature: each group fighting for space and yielding in turn to those fitter or luckier,' says Nizena, looking at Joshua and then out into the ocean.

Joshua shakes his head, looking ill. He waves his hand at the beach, at the city. 'That cannot be all there is?'

'No, it isn't. We can cooperate, but it must be a deliberate choice. We alone of our planet's living creatures can make that a conscious decision. That was what The Three was asking of us. Can we commit completely to positive coexistence and cooperation?' says Nizena.

'We debated and we realized that we had to if we had any hope for ourselves. We went back to The Three and agreed.

'She told us that there are an infinite number of planes of existence. We, through our biology and force of habit, live in only a few. Worse, we have taken our frame of reference from the scarcity of the physical world and applied it to the abundance of others. We compete intellectually and emotionally as if we fight for physical space.'

Joshua feels a moment of recognition. 'Samara told us a story about that, about forcing the ocean to take the shape of a home.

'When refugees arrive in Ewuru, then the majority expect that anyone who wishes to stay must adopt our customs and laws. Those that do always struggle. Some of our differences are contradictions.'

Nizena agrees. 'And the more people you have, the more of these contradictions that emerge. The Earth is a big spaceship. There is still room for people to move if they must. Achenia is tiny. Conflict here will destroy us all.

'Neither do we wish to remove these contradictions. The universe is varied, and we need new ideas and approaches as conditions change.

'The Three recommended a new way of organizing ourselves. One in which competition is limited to some planes and eradicated from others. If there is a release of competitive pressure, then there is a place for everyone, including sentient machines.

'"Do what you will," she said, "but, unless you have their consent, impose nothing on others."

'It isn't as simplistic as that. Instead of countries filled with competing political movements, we have independent polities. Anyone may found a new polity. Each polity manages itself with its own laws and judicial system. Anyone who doesn't like those laws can change polities instantly via the connect. If an interaction involves more than one polity, they can agree on which polity will apply, fall back to the core laws, or special advisers can assist in resolving the differences. If all other means are exhausted, they may call on the Five to hear their case and make a judgement.'

'All obey the rules of the Five?' asks Joshua.

'Oh, no. The Five simply mediate between polities. The core laws specify the supremacy of the Five in disputes; other than that, polities supersede all. There is only one area where they act independently, and that is when dealing with anything that threatens the continuity of Achenia itself. Even there, though, they are guided by a body representing the polities. They are called the Seven. And The Three has a deciding vote should there ever fail to be consensus amongst the Five.'

'It seems very complex,' says Joshua.

'People on Earth have managed to trade across borders for centuries with different notions of law and nation. The more open societies permit different cultures and religions to coexist peacefully even while intermingled. It is surmountable,' says Nizena. 'The connect makes it easier, allowing us to own our identities and property independently, not through polities or nations. If you own everything of yours directly, it makes such moves painless. Mostly, though, our people are not out to get each other. Where lives are long and treasured, and people are healthy and prosperous, conflicts tend to be fewer.

'Of course there are compromises. But that is the strength of our system. No one has to stay in a polity that conflicts with their values.'

'What about extremists? Like Boko Haram?' asks Joshua.

Nizena nods. 'We have been lucky. Or maybe they don't emerge in a society like ours. Our fundamental solution is simple. You may not impose on others without negotiated consent. If they cannot accept that, then they must leave.'

'How?'

'Achenia was designed to bud off workable environments. Anyone who cannot live with others must go and find their own way. The Nine will make sure of it.'

Joshua digs his feet into the sand, thinking.

'The Nine. I still do not feel I understand them.'

'We're still human, Joshua. One of our first instincts is still to fight. We offer tremendous freedom here, but we need to accept that we may not impose our choices on others. Think of the different social systems back on Earth. How many of them are incompatible? How do you resolve them should those societies come into conflict? The mediation of the Five is respected because the Nine report to them alone. Overwhelming force in the defence of the common good.'

'And what is that force?'

Nizena laughs. 'Mostly it's that they're almost unkillable.'

Joshua shivers suddenly as he remembers that first day. Samara in the remains of his escape craft.

'How do I use this knowledge for Ewuru?'

Nizena smiles and shakes his head. 'I would not tell you even if I knew. You have time, and you will choose for yourselves.'

'And the griots? What message are they carrying?'

'The most simple: that ideas can be reborn and that each can find their own rhythm without taking away the songs of others. All they need do is travel, sing different songs and tell different stories. Time will do the rest.'

Nizena takes Joshua's arm and walks slowly out of the water and up the beach. 'Your struggle, our struggle, there is no difference. Each of us is on a ship travelling through space. Each of us trying to work out the best way that all of us can find joy.'

The light is changing, shifting through orange.

They sit on the beach watching the embers of the day and the ocean ebbing and flowing.

45

'My love.' Shakiso is there as he opens his eyes.

'My darling,' and Samara clutches at her hands, her face, tears of joy, relief and unutterable sadness.

She touches his face, a finger tracing a tear, understanding. 'You survived,' she says. 'You have behaved with honour. You have nothing to regret.'

He reaches up, caressing her cheek. 'Thank you,' letting even that sadness fade away.

He is lying on the bed they share, the room open out on to the deck alongside the waterfall. Mist drifts across, and the roar of the falling water fills their home.

She falls to him, and they lie, tangled, for hours. Exploring again familiar shapes, not making love – that will come later – remembering, rediscovering.

'I am grateful,' she says.

There is a space in his head, but Symon has his own apologies to make. He will return in his own time.

'I owe a great debt,' he says.

'Joshua has been waiting. He is down at the lake,' Shakiso says, cradling his face in her hands, searching deep in his eyes. 'You have come back, but—'

'I want you to know, I will never take anything for granted ever again. You are more precious to me than anything.'

He kisses her fingers, and her eyes are serene waters dappled with sunshine.

46

Joshua is seated on a boulder against the waters of the lake. He can smell the forest and hear the sounds of the birds. He knows he must return home and realizes that the decision was always clear for him.

He hears a discreet cough and turns. A young man is standing there. He looks oddly out of place until Joshua notices the iridescent shimmer he has associated with symbionts. He stands, walks towards him.

'Symon?'

'Joshua. I am so sorry. I—'

And without thinking whether it is even possible, Joshua runs and embraces him. 'You are alive!'

Symon, uncertain, hugs back. 'I was dreading this moment. I thought, perhaps, you would—'

Joshua shakes his head. 'I was so worried I had killed you and Samara. You are back.' His relief is so profound that he realizes how far he is from coming to terms with Achenian technology.

Symon smiles shyly. 'Samara will join us, but I asked for time with you. To apologize. To thank you for bringing us home.'

They walk along the shore together.

'What you were saying. Before you —' Symon hesitates. 'I am sorry. Without Samara, it is easy to simplify, to believe that the killing of one bad person will end all evil.'

'Please,' says Joshua. 'I understand, understood even then.'

They walk on in silence. Symon relieved that he has asked for, and received, forgiveness.

'Did you know?' asks Joshua.

'About Ewuru and Nizena? I might have,' says Symon.

Symon walks, accidentally stepping out and on to the water, leaving little depressions there. 'In order for someone to know where they're going, first they must know where they're from.'

'Did you direct the craft? Did you choose us?' Joshua persists.

'When we neared the coast, I identified a range of places to land. I was uncertain where to take us and even if any of the villages still existed. So much of that land is abandoned, dead. There was a memory, a trace. Someone had loved Ewuru. I was alone. Outside the connect. I made a decision. I am sorry.'

'Please,' says Joshua. 'I am grateful. I would not have had you choose anywhere else.'

Symon, his face so young, looks relieved.

A rustle in the trees and Samara emerges. He smiles. He and Joshua embrace, each with relief and gratitude.

'It is over now?' asks Joshua.

Samara shakes his head. 'No, another debt still to repay. And you must return to your people. To Esther and Isaiah.'

Samara crouches and runs his fingers in the water, recalling a time when they shared conversation along the Akwayafe.

'My grandfather has given you the tour?'

'Yes. This is a beautiful world,' says Joshua.

Samara nods. 'Ewuru will always have a special place in my heart.'

He reaches into a pocket. 'Here, I wanted to share this with you. It is the last story my father ever wrote.'

Joshua takes the folded page. Opens it.

Etai's tale

The Tail of One

47

Joshua turns the page over. Holds it up to the light. Apart from the neatly handprinted title, the sheet is blank.

'I do not understand?'

'My father chose his date of going. He wanted to leave on his hundredth birthday. On his deathbed, he gave that to me.

'He said, one day you will find the peace you seek. Your questions will be answered. You will have focused your passion. When that day comes, you will write your first story. We will start work on this one together and – one day – you will complete it.'

Samara takes the paper, holds it as if feeling skin, gently caressing it.

'He told me the bones of a story. About a dimensional bomb that disrupts higher orders of mathematics and time, drawing power from them.

'One is a being. After such a dimensional explosion, he is separated from his lover, Story, who is drawn up into higher dimensions. In his dimension he is only of two axes, height and width.

'He runs in search of Story, his love, but she is out of his reach, twisting through other dimensions. He meets a couple. In this dimension they are bats. They know who set off the bomb but not how. Criminals using terror to influence and control their world.

'He travels through dimensions of wonder, of art, of science, always seeking Story.'

Samara folds the paper and returns it to his pocket.

'I don't know how to make a samara from these elements. I don't know what they mean. I am a simple man. But, I know now I will learn. I have time.'

They walk along the shore, holding hands, sharing the comfortable closeness of old friends.

'I was there through his passing. My mother, my grandfather, my grandmother. Shakiso and I had been seeing each other only a short while. My father loved her, and I wished so much that they had more time to know each other. It was not to be.'

He stands straight, tall. Symon by his side. Together Joshua can see the resemblance. What Samara would look like without the garb of the Nine: the heavy matt-titanium density that gives him such an alien physical presence.

'His going went so quickly. He took to his bed. Said farewell to his symbiont, drained him from his body. A small glass of silver fluid that slowly cleared. We gathered, told his favourite samaras, listened to music, relived our lives together, laughed, rejoiced, cherishing our remaining time.'

Samara's voice trembles. 'I held his hand, could feel his heat going. He couldn't move any more. He became like a child. I dressed him, washed him, fed him. He drank almost nothing, ate so little.

'At first he joined in our conversation. Every word seemed to cost him so much energy. A sentence, and then he would sleep. Gradually, he withdrew. Only listened. I sat with him for hours.'

Samara is weeping, tears dropping on to his tunic, forming liquid beads that fall to the lake shore. The sea inside joining the sea without.

'I had no words. Didn't know what to say. Shakiso, she kissed him, held his hands, told him she loved him. He smiled. I wept.

'On the morning of the last day, he fell silent. His mouth was open, and his breath came in short gasps. I could feel the absence. His skin was so thin, so fine. White, cold. Late in the evening, he closed his mouth. Would not eat. A few hours later, he breathed one last breath, and was gone.'

Samara wipes his face, his hand wet.

'I miss him every day. My mother – they were married seventy-five years. I try to imagine the emptiness. How it feels to have been so close to someone, to share so much laughter and love. And then nothing. She never says.'

Joshua knows how this feels. He has buried both his parents.

'My father said I would, one day, understand what he was doing. I'm not sure I will ever accept his choice completely, but when I saw your children playing – reliving his stories – I realized. He has his immortality.'

Joshua squeezes his hand. 'You have my word on that.' He laughs. 'As long as those tales are told, no wooden spoon will go sheathed.'

Samara wipes his tears, laughs as well.

'I'm going to hold you to that,' he says. 'I will return in one thousand years, and our first stop will be Ewuru.'

Joshua smiles sadly. 'I will not be there to meet you, my friend, but I am sure that my descendants will be. I am sorry we will not grow old together. I am grateful for our time.'

He stares out at the lake and the city rising beyond. 'As your grandfather says: coffee or tea.'

Samara follows his gaze, smiles, nods. 'Come,' he says, 'if you are ready, everything is waiting.'

'Yes,' says Joshua. 'It is time to go home.'

48

'This is unprecedented,' says Hollis.

'There has been injustice. I am as much entitled as any citizen to bring that to the attention of the Five,' says Samara.

The justices confer, establishing consensus.

'Very well,' says Hollis.

Samara will be heard.

The Five are meeting in person. They are keenly aware that Samara's plans have the potential to tie Achenia in knots. Thousands have gathered in the great hall. Many more are listening via the connect.

Samara stands alone in the middle of the justices' circular courtyard, before their seats, raised on a dais.

There are no outer walls into the court. Justice must be seen and be accessible to any. Cloud obscures the sun, and the light is muted under the stained-glass chhatri, suffusing those in attendance in a kaleidoscope of colours.

Samara speaks.

'These are conditions which are akin to murder. There is no hope of rehabilitation, of redemption. Only insanity for some, and a lonely, futile existence for others. In the case of a few, it is a situation of premeditated murder.'

'No one is debating these points. The Americans have promised to look into your allegations. And we have negotiated the release of your three companions there, but Tartarus is the property of a sovereign state. We have won our independence. We no longer have a say as to how the Americans dispense justice,' Hollis assures him.

Samara stands tall and still. The Five are not an enemy. They do not look to catch him out. They are there to ensure that the law is internally consistent and that it applies to all.

'We cannot flee. We have always said that we do not go to space to shrug off our responsibilities or to pretend that suffering does not exist.'

Samara's voice is clear, carrying a timbre that was not there only months before.

'You have suffered, Samara.' Hollis looks compassionate.

'This is not about me,' says Samara. 'I was able to escape. Even if I had not, you would have discovered me.'

'You are asking us to intervene in the choices of a sovereign state,' says Hollis.

'I am asking you to return one hundred and fifty thousand men and women to lives of hope.'

Hollis looks infinitely sad. 'Samara. Even if that were possible, we calculate that almost a hundred thousand of them are now insane. We cannot restore their original minds to them. They are not Achenians and we cannot remake them either. They will require a lifetime of institutional care.

'*If* the Americans accept, you will have to buy the prison. Our laws can only apply to the justly acquired property owned by our citizens. And we cannot take them at their word. We would need to finance the care of each prisoner. Re-investigate each case. Move those that are genuine criminals to regular prisons, restore others to their families and find institutions capable of looking after the rest.

'This is no straightforward task, Samara.'

This is the heart of Achenian justice. If Samara owns the prison, then he has the authority to expect the law of his Achenian polity to apply there. As a member of the Nine, he is allowed no polity and is answerable directly to the Five. Achenia, though, is no longer part of American jurisprudence. Samara requires the Five to recognize his authority and intercede on his behalf with the Americans.

'I have spoken with The Three. She will work through the cases. She believes she will conclude them within three or four days. We will trace families, alternative prisons and institutions.'

The Three is in attendance; a puff of colour as she indicates she wishes to speak.

'I am volunteering my time for this. It appears to me that this is a noble calling.'

The Five lean forward to recognize The Three, and sit back in their chairs as Samara continues.

'I have spoken with the orbital cities of Dunblane and Equatorial 1. Polities there have agreed to take responsibility for monitoring those in institutions in the US for their lifetimes.'

Hollis acknowledges; she is running out of arguments. She lays her last. 'And who will pay for all of this?'

'I will pay,' says Samara, without hesitation.

'You cannot afford this, Samara. You have all but spent the last of your money on Ewuru and the villages along the river.'

Samara stands silent. He has no more to offer.

A murmur in the crowd and on the connect.

'I will pay,' says Nizena, his voice bursting with pride.

'I will pay,' say the remaining Nine, as one.

'I will pay,' says Shakiso.

'I will pay,' Kosai and Airmid.

'I will pay,' Joshua, listening over the connect on Ewuru's new sphere.

'I will pay,' new voices, rising in the audience at the court.

'I will pay,' The Three.

'I will pay,' all across the connect, tens of thousands of voices. Including two of the Five.

Hollis raises her eyes to the sky, nods, smiles.

'Very well then, it is carried.' She bows her head to Samara.

49

'– he's been astonishingly lucky,' says Celia Gutierrez, her dark eyes mocking.

'What?' asks Robert Alvarez. The Chief of Staff looks startled. His futile hand-waving has failed to attract the coffee drone hovering at the far end of the room. He is pondering whether he should simply get up and walk over to it.

Gutierrez grins at him and pushes a stray frond of greying hair back behind her ear. 'I was saying that he's been astonishingly lucky.'

They are leaning back in their comfortable leather chairs in the gloomy Situation Room beneath the White House.

Alvarez dabs at the console around his wrist and brings up a display of the current opinion tracker in the air between them. He scowls at the colourful chart and shrugs. 'Yes, we've skirted some difficulties.'

'A few weeks ago we were almost at war, and now they're paying us to shut down that travesty? Ortega even gets to look like a great reformer? That's more than "skirting".'

Alvarez is still not giving her much attention. She sighs, stands and joins another group.

President Ortega is speaking with General Graham. Both are standing so as to mask themselves from the others. Alvarez can see the tension between them, and Ortega's neck is flushed red. He seems to be holding himself still with great effort.

The meeting to discuss the Achenian proposal for Tartarus is in the middle of a rowdy break. Groups of people have clotted around the room, and their mumbling, rumbling conversation obscures Alvarez's ability to listen in.

He catches a few fragments.

'– never aware of this –' Ortega's voice rising in furious interrogation.

'– meant to be used –' and '– you have to understand –' from Graham, her epaulettes shaking on her shoulders.

'– we cannot sell it –' from the General.

Ortega's shirt is sticking to his back. Others in the room have noticed his intensity, and conversation is coming to a restless halt.

'– your immediate resignation.' Ortega glares at her. She cannot meet his eyes.

People are hesitantly taking their seats at the conference table. The coffee drone is finally hovering silently at Alvarez's side, but he ignores it.

General Graham looks as if she will leave the room.

'No,' says Ortega. 'You don't get to escape this. You're here till this is over.'

She sits quietly, not looking at anyone.

Ortega glares down the centre of the table, his teeth clenched.

'The Achenians are expecting an answer from us in an hour, and now my ex-Secretary of State Security tells me we cannot go ahead.' His skin is clammy, and his shirt is stained dark under his armpits and across his belly. 'I am also told that I may not tell you why unless during the course of events it becomes absolutely necessary.

'As of this moment our alert level is raised to two. You are all confined to the White House until this is over. You will not be permitted to communicate with anyone outside of this room.'

There is a collective thunk of bodies slumping back into chairs. Graham merely looks morose.

'We cannot alert the Achenians that anything has gone wrong. They must still be permitted to remove the—' says Graham.

'Of course we cannot leave those people there,' says Ortega, his voice a shrill snarl.

Alvarez takes a deep breath and, for everyone, asks, 'Mr President, please could you inform us as to what is going on?'

Ortega's face softens. His eyes fill with terrible loss. 'No, my friend, I cannot. But I will tell you what we have to do.'

50

Samara flies up the safe channel, alongside the umbilical, towards the towering, brutal mass of Tartarus. His eyes glow. His face is righteousness.

Samara has not come alone. Two of the other Nine, Amaranth and Fodiar, have joined him. He can hear them in his head, conferring, as they fly behind him. Their symbionts chatter, calculating, making arrangements.

[I'm not sure I understand why they want to keep this? They've agreed it should never again be a prison?] asks Symon.

'I'm more worried about why they want their own military presence here.'

[At least you all saved some money not having to buy this wreck.]

Samara nears the docking bay. The cargo doors are open, as when he left. His battleskin flares as he lands, its surface matt and absorbing the monochrome light.

He looks over his shoulder as the others join him, his skin flexing as if an organic part of his body. They wait as the ferry arrives and seals the entrance. The pressure is equalized and the area warms rapidly.

A door opens and Dondé Hélène steps into the bay, a med droid hovering at her side. Her team will assess every prisoner before the shuttles, already lining up, take them to their destinations. Those prisoners who are still self-aware face the daunting prospect of having their cases reheard. The others will be treated as best they can or sent to care services.

Amaranth indicates to Samara that she is ready. She releases a burst of pinprick observers. The tiny points of light flow around her and then hurtle into the maze of Tartarus. They will map every living creature and stay close to them, ensuring that they can find them and extract them safely.

Amaranth and Fodiar each take a different direction. Samara pushes the button to open the antechamber to the works warehouse. The double seal is not needed, and Symon disables the exterior closing mechanism, forcing the interior door to open.

[Well, not quite home.]

A Fury flies down from the ceiling, firing energy bursts. It no longer recognizes him. Symon reaches out, finds its controller and disables it. The Fury drops to the floor and bounces, making a deadening metallic clunk.

The hood over Samara's head recedes, like an eyelid opening. He can see, displayed through the mass of crates and racks, Sancho, Seymour and Henry frantically scrambling to hide behind a stack of boxes.

'Gentlemen, I promised I would be back. You're safe, and you're going home,' his voice amplified to cut across the room.

They freeze, and he can see them whispering to each other. Hesitantly, Seymour stands and winds his way through the maze of shelves. Samara walks towards him, smiling.

'Hello, Seymour. It is well.'

Possibly for the first time in his life, Seymour begins to weep.

The other two emerge, similarly dazed.

He shakes their hands, holding them gently at the elbow. They are unable to speak.

'We are closing Tartarus. You are going home. Come with me and I will take you to our medical team.'

They follow him meekly, trembling in fear and relief.

Dondé Hélène is waiting. She is one of Achenia's most celebrated neuro-doctors. She volunteered for this but is apprehensive. No one in Achenia suffers the harm she will soon be seeing.

As the men step into the cargo bay, she can see their terror. She runs to Henry and hugs him tightly, tears puddling on his cloak. He is not a hugging man, and it is a few moments before he knows what to do and hugs back.

'Come with me,' she says, leading them into the ferry.

'I have to go,' says Samara, 'but we will meet again.'

They stare after him as he heads back into the warehouse.

[All of the living have been found and tagged.]

'The family?'

[Yes, them too.]

'And Athena?'

[Fodiar is there.]

'Call him for me.'

'Samara? There is something you must see.'

Athena is housed in a black metal pillar. Radiating out from the pillar are ranks of Furies, each hanging from a magnetic bracket.

Fodiar is standing in front of a console at the centre.

'Do you have control?'

'Almost.'

The pitch of the prison changes. Athena has been disabled. The Furies drift, so much flotsam, floating endlessly in the labyrinth of Tartarus.

'Thank you,' says Samara.

'Wait,' says Fodiar, looking upwards. A vast domed space rises above Athena's pillar. Circular pipes project out towards the distal surface, each about four times the diameter of a Fury.

He flies up and into one of them.

'Look.'

Tightly packed as far into the distance as they can see are black metal spheres. They are not Furies and would be too large to fit into the tunnels of the prison.

'I can't penetrate inside them. I've no idea what they are. None of this is on the prison plan.'

He prods at a matt black surface. 'They're sticky. Metallic resin over a solid housing.' The fluid sucks at his skinned finger, snapping back as he withdraws his hand.

'This –' says Samara.

'Yes.'

'We need to speak to the Five.'

Symon opens a secure channel and transmits a brief report to the symbionts of the Five and the other Nine. Hollis stares into the pipe through Fodiar. Samara and Fodiar can feel his apprehension.

'Are you sure the station is disabled?' he asks them.

'The station itself, yes. I cannot tell anything about these,' says Fodiar.

The Five split into a private channel and return moments later.

'The Five authorize the Nine. We want all of you to secure the perimeter of Tartarus. I will be contacting President Ortega. Samara, Fodiar, Amaranth – please continue as before.'

The channel closes, leaving Fodiar and Samara together.

'I'm transmitting Athena's data record to Amaranth,' says Fodiar.

Samara returns. 'Symon, we can put everyone to sleep now.'

All through the system bodies slump as the observers cause them to lose consciousness. The prison doors open, and now there is complete access to the prison. Round silver droids fly out of the ferry. They will carry each of the bodies to the medical team for assessment. From there they will be returned to volunteer reintegration organizations all across the United States.

The dead, too, will be collected and returned to their families.

Samara waits at the ferry as the children are brought out immersed in life-support fluid. In the well-lit cargo bay, the extent of their deformity is clear.

[Even here, life strives and hangs on.]

'They are worse than we hoped,' says Dondé Hélène after examining them.

They are an assemblage of human parts, unformed and unorganized. That they are alive is simply chance. Transporting them to Earth's gravity will kill them.

'There's no brain. Their nervous system is barely rudimentary. There is nothing we can do,' she says. 'Hollis agrees. We must let them go.'

Samara nods.

Dondé Hélène squeezes his hand. She switches off the life support and the lives swiftly fade.

Bodies are streaming out of Tartarus. Too fast to count. It will take two days before the vast labyrinth is empty.

After the first day, the Five convene the Nine.

'We've spoken with Ortega,' says Hollis. 'He won't tell us anything. He says, "Do what you came for and leave."'

'I think half their space fleet must be here,' says Cičak from her vantage point outside Tartarus, as the remaining Nine arrive. She shows them the grey angular ships arrayed outside the debris field.

'I count seventy-three, including ten stealth ships. Most of these are drones, but that's still about two hundred marines out here,' she says.

The Five are still mulling whether they should alert the other space cities.

'I'm glad we leave the politics to you,' laughs Cičak.

The channel closes. Another day passes.

The Nine work as a team. They have been all through the station. No living creatures remain on the base. The only functioning controls left are the ones maintaining its orbit and protecting the safe channel around the station and along the umbilical.

In the engineering hold, the location of so many card games, cargo has come loose and drifts. Empty food sachets mingling with metal rods and rolls of fabric.

The ferry has gone.

Samara stands alone in the cargo bay, his hood sealed and strange electrical patterns playing in the depths of his battleskin. The umbilical cable hangs before him. He leaps from the edge. Hovering. He flies out and on to the surface of Tartarus, where the rest of the Nine are preparing to leave.

'Samara.'

'Yes, Amaranth.'

'We think we have found the mechanism behind the prisoner executions.'

'Please,' says Samara, 'tell me.'

'It is an algorithm used for test purposes that should have been disabled. A drone was placed in a cell and released at random intervals. They timed the response for the Furies to come upon the drone and eliminate it. They needed the drones to be able to randomly control their exit. Each would set up a resonance in the walls to trigger the unlocking mechanism.

'That resonance is the same as a person performing stretching exercises while pressing against two facing walls,' her sorrow apparent. This may bring closure, but not of the sort he might have wished for.

Samara considers. 'No purpose, then? Senseless deaths caused by people doing a job they didn't much care about.'

He breathes out his bitterness. The need for there to be a reason. He lets it go.

Samara smiles.

'They're coming,' says Cičak, as three of the American stealth ships close in on Tartarus and make their way down to the cargo bay. 'I'd expect about sixty marines on board those. What are they after?'

'Have you made contact with them?' asks Samara.

Cičak nods. 'Commander Eristavi. He tells me their orders are to ensure we stay inside our access window, and for them to secure the station.'

'Can you connect us? I'd like to know their plans.'

The view is blurry through the shielded walls of Tartarus and the weaker American communications system. Samara can only faintly see where Eristavi is hopping jerkily through the tunnels towards Athena.

'Commander Eristavi, US Eleventh,' comes the curt response.

'I'm Samara Adaro of the Nine. We are making ready to leave. I would appreciate it if you could tell me your immediate intentions for the station?'

'Your access window is over. We expect you to honour our agreement.'

'Commander, Athena was not functioning correctly even before we shut her down. You'll understand our concern.'

Eristavi cuts their connection.

'We're not going anywhere until we know they have control.'

The Nine form a row hovering in space amongst the American

fleet. Technically, they are in international territory and outside the station exclusion zone.

'Amaranth, tell me you kept observers inside?'

She grins. 'Of course. Would you like to see?'

The marines have gathered inside the control deck, stabilizing themselves by holding on to whatever is near. They have locked a scaffold to Athena's pillar, and four of them appear to be attempting to open the casing. The rest are scattered awkwardly within the open space staring nervously at the blackened shapes in the openings in the dome.

'Do you think they have plans for this part of the base?' asks Fodiar.

'I've no idea, but that's ancient tooling. I'd say almost a century,' says Čičak.

Marines obscure the works, carefully aligning a tubular device against the pillar. They work carefully, but it is clear that they are figuring things out as they go. If there were ever plans for this part of the station, it appears that even these marines do not have them.

The marines jerk back. Their faces are obscured inside their suits, but their posture is of confusion and fear.

Outside, disk-like plates slide back all along the upper surface of Tartarus revealing dark tunnels. A stream of the metal spheres fly out. They surge directly at the hovering ships.

The Nine instantly vanish and scatter.

The first of the spherical drones strikes an American ship. It explodes in a single pink-and-white, eye-blistering pulse, fading to purple and blue.

Thousands more pour from Tartarus and light up the dark.

51

'It's a weapons platform—' says Ortega.

'We can tell it's a —' Hollis regains control, his gender stabilizing, his telepresence transmission flickering in the gloom of the room. 'What we want to know is what is it for and how do we stop it?' His voice is vitriol, his oscillating gender adding greater terror to his rage.

The Situation Room walls cling with stale sweat and confinement. Few of Ortega's cabinet have strayed far from the stream of telemetry hovering over the desk between them. Skin flaccid and eyes bag-haggard.

Ortega stares at Alvarez in exhaustion. The other man shakes his head, his mouth hanging open.

General Graham has shunned everyone, sitting alone and uncommunicative in a corner. Alvarez has had the drones force-feed her, worried she is becoming catatonic. Ortega still has not taken anyone into his confidence and has carried her warning alone.

Ortega looks again around the table at people he has known his entire career. He feels as if he is drowning, that there is no air in the room.

'It was Hammond,' he gasps.

'Mad Hammond?' Alvarez's voice is a muffled crackle, his throat is so dry.

Ortega nods. 'Long before the war. He was worried the US would lose high orbit to the Chinese. Him and Oswald at State Security. The prison was probably the best political cover they could ever invent. All the money they needed and a legitimate explanation for security expenses and all that material going up. No one questioned it.'

Hollis is silent. He first met President Hammond at his inauguration party almost a century ago. The man was charismatic with a nasty edge. His xenophobia was not only pragmatic politics for the electorate. He was a believer.

He was assassinated midway through his second term. 'And all we could think,' Hollis remembers, 'was, "Please, let the killer not be someone from orbit."'

'How come you didn't know?' asks Alvarez.

Ortega looks ill. 'Hammond was the only one outside State Security who knew about it. Then the war and—'

'Fine,' says Hollis, sharply. 'You can find excuses afterwards. We need to know how to deal with this. Are the drones controlled by Athena?'

'No. Only to authorize them,' says Graham. She does not look at anyone as she speaks. 'They're a mesh network. Entirely independent. They will remain dormant as long as they're in Tartarus, but the moment they're out they start attacking. They learn from each other as to what strategy works or doesn't, and then they adapt. You'll see location pings and then a telemetry burst when they detonate. Each drone communicates only once, when it explodes, detailing all its telemetry and its assessed probability of successfully destroying its target. The rest receive the signal and adjust their own tactics. It's supposed to harden them to interference.'

'Do you have their communication cypher sequence?'

Graham mutely shakes her head. 'We know only that they use

asymmetric encryption and a one-time quantum cypher series.'

'What is their target?' asks Hollis, his rage a physical presence in the room.

'Anything outside of low Earth orbit that looks manufactured and large enough to contain a human or able to carry an explosive charge. That includes anything further out, like the colonies on Mars.'

'How many are there?'

Graham moans. She is spent.

Ortega answers. 'We think there are about fifty thousand of them. They carry a micro-nuclear payload. If you can get them below 500 kilometres from Earth's surface, they will go completely dormant. It's the only failsafe they have.'

Hollis nods. They can all see that the drones are still streaming out of Tartarus.

'Well, they've just destroyed the last of your fleet. You'd better hope we can stop them. Some of the other cities may be very upset.'

He closes the channel.

52

[Got it,] says Syrice.

Amaranth only gasps, winded, as a series of drones detonate against the ion web between her, Vakhsh and Kouhei. A pink-white nuclear blast, with them at the epicentre, radiates out to a purple fringe and rapidly dissipates. Its force flings them apart, and the electromagnetic pulse momentarily disrupts their access to the connect.

'That hurt,' says Kouhei, disoriented and struggling to realign himself with the others.

With each explosion they intercept more of the drone telemetry bursts and learn more about how they operate. Unfortunately, the drones are learning more about them as well.

'Quickly,' shouts Vakhsh.

As they orientate towards the pursuing pack of drones, the ion strands flare between them. A flickering white web with the matt-titanium reflections of their battleskins at each corner. Energy builds again across the strands and they fire short bursts at the drones, more agile now and attempting to surround them.

Across the battle-zone two other trios of the Nine are being similarly pummelled. Debris from the American fleet is flung back and forth as drones erupt. An endless stream of black spheres is still pouring from Tartarus.

Samara opens a channel to the Five. 'I don't know how much

longer we can hold them. We're not regenerating energy from the detonations fast enough to keep up. There's still more than two-thirds of the drones inside Tartarus, and we calculate we'll run out with a quarter to go.'

'The other cities know. We're all burying ourselves deeper in the debris field. Achenia should be inside in about ten minutes.'

'Do you think that will work?'

'No,' says Hollis. 'We need more time.'

'They're figuring you out,' says The Three.

'We know,' says Samara. The channel goes blank as a series of explosions sever the connection.

This blast is too close to the umbilical. The asteroid counter-weight flings out, dragging a trailing cable behind it. Beneath, the remaining tether plunges towards the distant planet.

'Amaranth, have you found them yet?' Samara asks when he can speak again.

'Yes, but we're still struggling to get direct communication.'

Commander Eristavi and eleven others are huddled awkwardly in an angular space, partly in the corridor and spreading into open cells. Pinprick observers are gathering around them, and Samara can see the tense fatigue in the marines' posture. They are locked together and propped against the walls to prevent them floating.

As the observers gather, the marines start moving. Relief on faces behind sweat-smeared helmets.

'Try now,' says Amaranth.

'Commander Eristavi, can you hear me?' asks Samara.

Eristavi nods enthusiastically. 'The sound is fuzzy, but we can hear,' he grins. 'Can you get us out?'

'There's a force field around Tartarus. The drones can get out but nothing can get in. We need you to help us turn it off.'

'What about the fleet? Where are they?'

Samara is silent. He shakes his head.

'I'm sorry, Commander. The drones have wiped them out. We're the only ones left.'

Eristavi's face sags. 'That can't be?'

'Commander, I'm sorry. We don't have time. We're being overwhelmed. We need you to shut down the force field.'

'What happens then?'

'We will block the drones inside Tartarus. We think more than half are still there. Once they're without a target they should deactivate. They won't take the risk of detonating. Even if they do, they'll be bunched up and create a chain reaction that will destroy all of them. If we do that, we should have enough strength to destroy the drones out here.'

'And us?'

Samara says nothing.

Eristavi looks at the faces of his marines. Their eyes are indistinct behind the lenses of their helmets. He can see enough.

'What happens if we don't succeed?'

'The drones will attack the orbital cities and millions of people will die.'

'What must we do?'

'Thank you,' says Samara. 'We think we've identified the shield energy systems. Our observers can disable it, but it's behind a mechanical lock. We'll need you to open it for them.'

Eristavi nods, and the marines follow the glowing observers through the silent network of tunnels.

'We need to switch,' says Cičak.

The drones are evading the trio attacks and cutting through their defences faster after each series of detonations. The drones attempt to tear their target apart through sticking to the outside and creating chained nuclear explosions. The Nine's strategy is simple: form abstract shapes and then use their energy to project a semi-physical illusion of large attack craft which the drones then 'destroy'. The drones have already understood and countered the nature of the single and double illusions. Once they figure out the triples, the Nine will need to restructure.

'We have to hold until the shields are down. I won't survive for long on my own,' says Samara.

Minutes drag. The Nine are being battered by the persistent volume of drones. Blue rainbow halos around white flares.

'We're here.'

Eristavi has reached the hatch, an old-fashioned hand wheel at its centre. As it swings open, the observers fly into a large room filled with a vast fusion generator.

'It's beautiful,' says one of the marines.

Inside the stellarator it is hotter than the sun. Outside, its grey cladding is banded in thick, copper-coloured superconductor.

'Commander Eristavi,' says Samara. 'Once the shields are down and I seal the exits, some of those drones will explode, and Tartarus is going to break apart.'

'We understand,' he says. 'Do it now.'

Symon triggers the observers, and the console lights flicker and fade.

'I was expecting it to blow up,' says one of the marines. 'What do we do now?' she asks.

Eristavi smiles and nods. 'We think of those we love, and we wait.'

Samara's trio disperses as the force field vanishes. Cičak and Fodiar split and head for the other trios, while Samara flies for Tartarus.

As Fodiar joins Alegrya's team, they restructure as a quad, with ion lenses now firing out of four sides. The new form rattles the drones, and they hold back.

Cičak is too slow. As she nears Vakhsh's trio, a drone fastens on to her leg. She shakes it, but the sticky resin flows over her calf.

The explosion tears her leg off and flings her into Vakhsh and Kouhei. Her battleskin flows closed over the stump as she screams in frustration.

'Stop being such a zbabělec,' says Kouhei. 'It'll grow back.'

'But I liked that leg,' says Čičak, joining them in the quad.

It is the drones' turn for retreat as they struggle to adapt to the quad attacks.

'You're only going to have five to ten minutes,' says Fodiar.

Samara is nearing the first of the vents. He fires into it and the exiting drone explodes. He can see a chain reaction of explosions down the tube. Drones are already responding, predicting what he will do and blockading the other vents.

Drones are almost on him as he vanishes.

[They're still tracking you.]

He fires into another vent, and another cascade of explosions ripples back into Tartarus.

[Three to go.]

A drone dives for him and misses. It detonates nearby, smashing him down and into an open vent. The following drones are extremely close together and others explode across the surface. The final three vents are shattered, trapping the drones inside.

'He did it. They're stopping,' shouts Amaranth.

The remaining drones regroup and begin a final assault on the two quads. They are slower, their mesh intelligence fading rapidly as their numbers dwindle.

[I can't raise Symon.]

'That was a huge blast. It's either the electromagnetic disruption, or he's unconscious.'

[Look.]

The last blue coronas are fading around them. Below, Tartarus is moving out of alignment. As they watch, it begins to fall.

'Find Samara,' as Amaranth flies towards the retreating station.

Fodiar opens a channel to the Five.

'We've stopped them. They're now sealed inside Tartarus and appear to have gone dormant again, but the station is falling. Can you calculate where it will land so we can warn anyone on the ground?'

Hollis looks as if she will weep with relief. 'At once. Thank you. Are all of you safe?'

'We're trying to find Samara, but we're all still with you.'

'Can you lift Tartarus?'

'No, we're almost out of power. We might be able to nudge it if we need, but we're done.'

'I'll get back to you, but we might not have an answer until it clears the debris field.'

Tartarus is unshielded, and the debris is perforating the outer shell of the station. It begins to twist chaotically as it falls, gaining rotation and momentum.

Samara wakes up somewhere inside the station. Metal walls batting him along a corridor.

[Looks like we got caught in one of the pipes.]

'Symon, can you tell where we are?'

[No. And we don't have enough power to blast our way out.]

'Can we raise the others?'

The remaining Nine have clustered together and are combining their vestigial energy to form a shield as they follow Tartarus down through the debris.

'Samara, you're safe,' grins Čičak as Symon connects to her.

'You've got a terrible definition of "safe",' he says.

'I lost a leg, so don't complain.'

'It'll grow back.'

Tartarus is a blur as it spins. Samara wedges himself in a corridor to stop being flung like so much detritus.

'We can't do anything till we clear the debris, and we're not going to have long when we do. We figure less than an hour. That's if Tartarus hasn't broken apart by then,' says Čičak.

Samara, holding himself still against the violent shaking, 'We have to slow it down. The force when it hits the ground will cause massive earthquakes, tidal waves. It could kill millions –'

'The Five are talking to the Americans. We're not sure what they can do,' says Amaranth.

'This is the second time I've fallen. I really don't recommend it.'

Samara is quiet as the others follow behind in the wake of the plummeting station. Eventually, 'Please don't transmit this. Shakiso – I can't –'

Amaranth hugs him through the connect.

A lower part of the station tears off and shatters in the blasting stream of the debris. A few drones amongst the many trapped and dormant inside are thrown out. Before they have a chance to orientate, debris detonates them. The explosion pushes Tartarus into a wider arc and opens a gaping crack that propagates up and to the centre.

As they emerge from the debris field, Tartarus cleaves in two.

'We're clear. Samara, the orbital cities are safe, but we've got twenty-five minutes before we hit the atmosphere,' says Fodiar.

'He's in the bigger piece,' says Vakhsh.

The remaining Nine surround the metal hulk. Samara can use their locations to orientate himself.

[Got it. The spin is fairly regular, but it's going to be messy.]

Samara braces himself as he moves. The tunnels are twisted, and cabling and metal fragments hammer into him.

'I don't mean to disturb you, but you're going to need to hurry,' says Fodiar. 'We've had a message from Hollis. The Americans have fired four nukes our way. Looks like they want to destroy the evidence before Tartarus hits Earth's atmosphere.'

'How long?'

'About seven minutes.'

Dimples in the walls growing larger as he follows this corridor.

[Debris damage. We're getting closer.]

As he nears the outer skin, the metal is a frayed lattice, like matted cobweb. Samara slices his way through, watching as his energy levels drop.

'I'm at the outer surface and I'm cutting through now. I won't have any energy left when I jump.'

There is no time to get far enough away from the nuclear blast. He will need shielding.

'We're here,' says Kouhei.

[Ready?]

Samara leaps out. He spirals, his arc widening. There is no energy to stop his momentum.

The missiles are visible as burning dots speeding towards them.

'Got you,' says Fodiar, as the Nine close into a single form.

A soundless, searing light obliterates Tartarus.

53

'Very well,' says President Ortega.

'We have not broadcast our involvement. No one will know. It is up to you how you spin this,' says Hollis.

Ortega is alone in his office. Hollis's telepresence transmission sits across from him. Its translucence makes him feel slight vertigo. The illusion is not quite perfect, and he can see the chair through her back. He finds Hollis's ambiguously shifting gender just as disorientating and is never sure how he should respond.

He stands uncomfortably and looks out of the window, his back to Hollis.

'I am deeply sorry. I would not have this be your memory of us,' he says.

Hollis says nothing.

'We're telling everyone that there was an explosion and that Tartarus began to fall. In a heroic mission, our marines rescued all the prisoners and brought them home. There were casualties, including the sacrifice of the fleet that prevented Tartarus destroying our cities, but we never leave anyone behind.'

Hollis joins him at the window, looking out on the lawns. It is a beautiful bright blue day.

'You can use this,' she says.

'What?'

'We don't have a monopoly on dreaming. Inspire people. Explore again.'

Even as she says it, she can see Ortega is not the man to lead that.

She smiles sadly. 'Farewell, President Ortega.' Her projection vanishes.

Ortega stands alone in the window looking at the sky.

54

'Father! Father, are they here yet?' Isaiah jumping up and down, no longer able to contain his excitement and impatience.

'Soon, my son, soon.' Joshua grins at the boy, feeling a similar sense of expectation.

There are a group of them, standing under the trees outside the north gate of Ewuru. Each of them is wearing new clothes received as gifts from Samara. Joshua has had time to get used to their weight and the mysterious way they self-fasten, but Gideon and Daniel look very uneasy. They pinch the fabric every few moments, verifying that they are, indeed, dressed.

Esther, her slender body caressed in her subtly textured aso oke dress, looks more beautiful now than on the day he first fell in love with her. He grips her hand tightly, pulling her closer and kissing her gently on the top of her head.

She looks up at him, smiling, and rests her head back against his shoulder.

Daniel's daughters are laughing and running around in circles, playing tag, Hannah doing her best to keep them clean. Fortunately, the fabric seems immune to dust.

A bright reflection in the sky and, almost too quickly, a large teardrop-shaped craft is settling in the clearing along the path. It makes no sound.

Hundreds have gathered outside the walls and all along the

runway at the top to watch. There is a massed range of gasps and exclamations as the canopy of the spacecraft shimmers and vanishes, a staircase appearing in the air and touching down on the road.

Joshua grins again. He is thrilled to share this wonder with his people.

A woman in a pale-blue eggshell-coloured dress stands, walks down the stairs and up the path towards them. Esther has a moment to wonder if Achenian fashions are going to be all the rage as soon as the designers get back to their studios in the market.

The woman walks up to Joshua, smiling with her entire being, puts her hand out as if to shake, changes her mind and throws herself into his arms in an enthusiastic hug.

'You're Joshua,' she beams. 'I'm so pleased to meet you. Everyone is so looking forward to meeting you.' She is bubbling, the words chasing each other. Turning to Esther and hugging her too, 'Esther, you are so beautiful.'

She hugs her way through the group. She knows all of them, and her obvious delight dissipates the apprehension of even the most nervous. She finishes her greetings by flinging each of the children up and swinging them around. They scream with pleasure.

[Wait, wait. You haven't told them yet.]

Seeming to recover herself, she puts a hand to her flushed face and says, 'Oh, I'm so sorry. I'm Kaolin.'

Joshua realizes there is no way to tell the ages of any of the Achenians, but the girl seems so young.

'I will be escorting you to the ceremony. Samara sends his greetings, and he is waiting for you there, but he cannot leave Achenia today.' She breaks away from what is obviously a prepared script and says, 'None of the Nine can leave today, so he's really quite sad he can't be here.'

363

Then she is laughing again and herding them along the path and up the stairs into the waiting craft. Behind the pilot's seat is a wide area, tapering to the rear and filled with flowing, sculpted sofas against the walls.

'Please sit anywhere and,' she indicates a small basket, 'you'll need those. Two for each of you.'

David picks up the basket, looking at the tiny white foamy nodules in confusion. Do we eat them, he wonders.

Kaolin demonstrates, placing a nodule in each ear. 'There will be many different languages today. We have guests coming in from all over the world. This is a translator. It will feel a little strange for a few moments, but you'll forget it's there.'

They begin helping themselves, Gideon assisting a laughing Miriam to insert hers, Abishai kissing Edith as she settles one and then the other. Joshua helps Isaiah with his and then places one in his ear; it feels slippery and changes shape. She is right, though, as after a moment he has to consciously remember that it is there.

'Now, if you'll sit comfortably, we'll reach Achenia in six hours,' taking her seat as the canopy shimmers and returns.

[Wait, wait.]

'Oh,' she says. 'There's a toilet at the back of the craft should you need, and there are drinks and snacks in the little cupboard behind my seat.'

The craft lifts, thousands of hands waving and people cheering from all along the walls and streets inside Ewuru. The walls of the craft are transparent, and they are able to look out and see the land shrinking below, the sky growing above.

They are all there. Gideon and Miriam, resplendent in matching dashiki. Daniel, Hannah and the two girls. Abishai and Edith, holding hands tightly. David and Sarah, wrapped around each other and staring intently at Ewuru, dwindling in the distance. Jason and Leah, chosen – with some resistance – as his partner only a few days before. Isaiah, standing with his hands flat against the clear walls, his face alight with the thrill; Esther behind him, cuddling him close. Joshua, sitting in the warmth of his love for this small gathering.

The yellow light of the day gives way rapidly to twilight, and the Earth is rosetted against the sun. From here, they are not the first to remark in wonder at the grandeur and spectacle of the planet.

Darkness, and then they are in the clear channel leading to the waiting presence of Achenia.

Today, hundreds of similar ships are travelling up from the surface. Each filled with groups of people, their hands and faces pressed against transparent walls, trying to remember everything.

They form a long chain, like a string of luminous pearls, as they hug the elevator cable on their way into orbit.

'We'll be landing in Socotra Bay,' says Kaolin. She is still seated, unmoving, her arms on the rests at her sides. They are in a river of teardrop-shaped spaceships, all having now reached the summit and broken away from the cable. Like a school of silver fish, they flash and fly as one.

'Stay close when we land,' says Kaolin. 'There isn't anything bad that can happen, but there really will be a lot of people.'

They settle alongside another craft, identical. Another lands beside them. There are hundreds of ships, all across the bay.

The canopy shimmers. Kaolin smiles kindly and gestures for them to follow her. Joshua squeezes Esther's hand, recognizing the nervousness all must feel. It is hitting them. They are in orbit, 35,000 kilometres from home.

Hesitantly, they follow Kaolin. Thousands of people are

following similar escorts from their craft, through the hangar and towards the massive doors in the floor and its spiral gravity-shifting ramp. There is a maelstrom of voices, dozens of different languages, but they realize they can understand them all.

Isaiah grins at a little blonde-haired girl of a similar age being led by her parents in a group just ahead of them. She sticks out her tongue and grins back, waving with her free hand.

Joshua catches a momentary glimpse of Samara, far ahead through the crowds. He is greeting a group there. Three very thin men. They are smiling, laughing together. One presents a shy teenager, perhaps his son? One, an older man, is alone. The third with a stout woman who could be his wife.

The group leaves and Samara turns. Shakiso is just behind him. He sees Joshua and runs towards them. Then there are long embraces, introductions as everyone meets Shakiso, Nizena, Kosai, Shakiso's parents and Airmid, Samara's mother. Shyly, Symon and Synthia, and an effervescent Symona, make their welcomes.

Kaolin hugs the children again and vanishes into the crowd.

Daniel seizes Symon's hands. 'I never knew what you looked like.' He grins. 'You look better than I expected.' Symon looks embarrassed. Abishai, David, Jason and Sarah gather round him. There is nothing left to say. They are thrilled to see him.

'Come,' says Samara. 'We should be going.'

Kosai and the children have bonded instantly. They are clutching at her hands, pulling her to and fro as she laughs and dances with them. Symona is doing cartwheels and somersaults in the air above them.

'She would make a wonderful great-grandmother,' says Joshua.

'Hush,' says Samara.

Esther and Shakiso are walking together. 'What is the ceremony?' asks Esther. 'Joshua was not very clear.'

Shakiso smiles, the two women holding hands, old friends.

'Achenia and all our people are leaving. There is the thrill of the journey, but there is also sadness. The ceremony will permit us to express all that each of us may struggle with alone.'

The current of people is through the acacia trees and into the grassland. The city of Socotra, rising up through red rocks, termite mounds and acacias bowed down with weaver nests, on either side of the wide valley.

People are pointing in wonder. The smell of the savannah, of rich earth and growing things, open space and an endless, wide-open sky.

The great gathering place that Joshua saw on his first visit is filling up before them. He has never seen so many people. Hundreds of thousands are flying in from all along the valley. From the cities all through Achenia.

In the gathering are people from so many cultures and races that they overwhelm the senses. Everyone is talking, catching up, laughing. Some are singing. The Achenians mingle freely.

'Father, look!' shouts Isaiah, dragging at his arm.

Through the crowds he sees a group of short, heavyset people. Their clothes are thick cloth. They have dense red beards down to their knees. Their eyes are cloudy blue, their gaze intense.

'They are the miners! From Romanche!'

Samara takes Isaiah's arm and leads the excited boy over to them. One holds out a heavy, stubby hand and greets Isaiah formally. The boy looks as if all his birthdays are happening at once. He comes back clutching a rounded glossy-metal helmet he has been given.

Kosai excuses herself, Nizena watching her, his face a mix of adoration and pride, as she goes. She seems constantly dancing, always a cuddle or shared intimacy with everyone in her path.

'Where is she going?' asks Hannah, Daniel again attending to the girls.

Nizena points to where Kosai is meeting a man, uncharacteristically all in white. 'She has a role in the ceremony. The man she is meeting is Ismael, one of the greatest of the griots. He will sing the Song for the Leaving.'

Hannah pulls Daniel's arm, pointing. The Ewuru feel awe and surprise that their own Balladeer is here.

There are fewer people arriving now. The gathering is almost complete. An ocean of people filling the valley.

Gradually, the talking slows, settles. There is silence.

The meeting space is arranged as a wide, gently sloping amphitheatre. People form an arc about the stage. The back is open to the plains beyond. A breeze runs through the valley, from behind them, shifting the long grasses like ripples on an ocean.

Even here the river Talus runs, meandering through a subterranean cavern and emerging far below the gathering place. In the silence, they can hear the water, burbling and tinkling in the distance.

Kosai is standing alone on the stage. She is dressed all in white, the breeze holding the softness of the fabric against the firmness of her body.

Her head is bowed. She raises it, looking out across the expanse of people. A projection expands from her, a duplicate giant permitting all to see her.

Kosai begins to speak.

Departing Sorrows

Hold my hand,
my love,
for I fear that
we are dying.

I will never let go,
my love,
tell me only
what frightens you.

I see ghosts,
my love,
of dear friends,
long since passed.

It is well,
my love,
they are here
to see us through.

If all we have,
my love,
are departing moments,
I wish only for them
with you.

Come close,
my love,
and we will share our
remaining breath
as one.

And in the sky,
a light,
like a tiny glowing sun,
flashes, bleeds,
and is gone.

Her voice seems to be heard by each person alone. Tender. A lover's touch. In the vastness, each person experiences a moment of intimacy.

As her words end and her projection fades, there is an awareness of a note. Like the song of a heart. It seems to have been there since she started speaking.

Kosai withdraws and Ismael, white-haired and all in white, floats forward on to the stage. His projection filters above them like white smoke in the sky. He carries a single white cord, stretched tight. With his other hand he is running his pinched fingers along its length, setting a tone in motion.

He plucks at it. Notes infuse through the air. Resonance made visible in the sky as white ripples. He releases the cord. It continues to play, individual plucked notes. Now he is singing, his voice bright, a woman's soprano. Emotion, like a thread of electricity, tied and pulling on their souls.

Esther is weeping. Joshua takes her arm, pulling her close. Isaiah is holding his waist. All about him, tears, eyes shining.

The music is gathering now, notes, chords and timbre swelling. Ismael stamps his foot and the earth rumbles. If a planet could sing, this would be the beat of its heart.

Ismael is now adding a man's tenor. A duet. And more voices. Smoky faces in the sky.

Joshua realizes that a sound is being drawn from him. That he is singing. Harmonizing with all those around him.

Ismael, his wide, sheet-like cloak flowing, is dancing, his arms directing the choir as he moves.

The music falls away, the spray of a waterfall coming to rest in a placid pool.

Only the drumbeat remains.

Ismael is still. His shoulders move, a syncopated rhythm. He beats the air with one hand, then the other. A thousand drumbeats crash, waves against a rocky shore. The storm draws near.

He stamps. A deeper beat. Whispers, the wind through the forest.

A roar. A billion antelope, their hooves thundering on the plains. Faster, faster, faster.

Fog takes shape as animals driving through the audience, chasing for the horizon.

Hearts. Racing. Ismael is jumping. Everyone jumping too.

The drumming is the universe.

It stops.

A single, jangling chord sounds. A harmonica, aching between his fingers. His voice, rich, gravel, singing of a journey. Out into the night.

The crowd, humming, dancing, keeping his rhythm.

Everyone is weeping. Tears, wet against their cheeks.

Joshua has a sense of how painful is this parting. How much must be shed in order to go. That this leaving is not taken lightly. They are saying farewell, not just to the planet of their birth but to their shared experience which led here. Goodbye to uncountable relationships, the intimacy and shared moments that will forever remain unexperienced.

For a new world to open, an old one must be closed.

Ismael is singing alone now, plucking at the cord again in his hands. His voice sweet, delicate, masculine. Notes – clear in the air – rising above his voice, now below, following, leading.

Joshua is sobbing, holding Esther to him, Isaiah tight around his waist. Esther hugs Airmid, and now everyone is exchanging heartfelt embraces. First with those they know, then with complete strangers.

Eventually, there is only a single tone, which gradually, softly, ends.

Epilogue

A BALLAD
FOR THE RETURNING

We have experienced so much. Seen many things. Met others on similar journeys, so unlike and like ourselves. Now, after almost one thousand years, it is time to go back, to reconnect with the world that will always be our home. We don't return as part of some final destination. We will linger, reflect on what we have learned, and – in time – we will journey once more amongst the stars.

Shakiso Adaro, reflections on the journey, Achenia,
recorded during 'Sowing the Seeds 1,042'

55

'Daddy, tell me a story?'

Samara smiles, cuddling the child to him in the small bed.

'And what story would you like to hear, youngster?' he asks.

The little girl giggles, her eyes the green-cobalt of her mother's. 'I want to hear "The Tail of One",' she says.

'Not again,' says Samara, his voice an exaggerated sigh. 'You've heard that hundreds of times. Can't we try another one? Your great-grandmother told us a lovely new one just yesterday.'

'No. I want to hear "The Tail of One". It is my favourite favourite favourite.'

'Very well,' he sighs, teasing. And begins the story he has told thousands of times. As he finishes, her squirming stops and she is still.

He waits, holding her small warm body in his arms.

And waits.

'I'm awake,' she giggles. 'I'm soooooo awake.'

'I know, my darling,' he smiles. Shakiso comes into the child's room from outside. She joins them, the bed growing to accommodate them all.

'Are you too excited to sleep?' she asks.

'Yes, I can't wait,' she says. 'Will they be there?' she asks. 'The children of Joshua?'

'I don't know, my love, but I hope so with all my heart,' says Samara.

She squirms a bit between them, tousles Samara's sandy-brown hair, presses her nose to his face and grins into his hazel-brown eyes. Then decides. 'Tell me again?'

'What, my precious?' asks Samara.

'Tell me again about Joshua and Daniel and David and Sarah and Abishai and Jason and Isaiah. And Esther,' she says in a single breathless burst.

Shakiso grins and Samara bends his head, kissing his daughter on the forehead.

'Esther, my most darling. For you,' he says, and begins the story again, of days long ago.

56

A man in a delicately embroidered ochre-brown boubou and matching kufi skullcap is walking through the jungle. His feet are in handmade leather sandals. His every step is a drumbeat. He is singing, and the forest sings with him. Birds fly in the trees above him, monkeys scramble through the branches.

He follows a wide stone road through the trees to the edge of a cliff.

Looking out, he sees a great white city.

The city fills the valley beneath him. It gleams in the sunshine, hundreds of thousands of people in the markets and cobbled roads leading to its centre. Ships are sailing up a wide, clear river, its waters sparkle and shimmer in the glory of the day.

More ships are docked at its vast harbour. Children are playing on the beach upstream, swimming and diving in elaborate postures from a small jetty.

The city rises towards a ridge and, at its crown, on a cliff before the river, is a gathering place. A massive open area, gently sloping and filling with a waiting choir. There is a stage and, behind that, an enormous open-sided building, bronze pillars and an immense wooden slit-drum suspended between them.

Around the gathering space are statues of the heroes of the city. One of them is of a tall, straight-backed man. His hands, their scars telling the story of his life, are open before him. His smile is broad and content.

The man on the cliff is now playing a harmonica, his hands cupped around it, even as his voice continues. He releases the harmonica and the notes drift out over the city. He taps his foot, a gentle rhythm spreading through the earth.

In the city, a woman answers. She stands at the drum and strikes it. The beat continues as she walks out on to the stage.

Her arms are wide. Her voice that of a lover welcoming him home.

He replies, and they sing together. Their voices an embrace. A rejoicing reunion.

Now the massed choir is singing too. Their voices gather and swell, filling the air above the city. Welcoming the sky.

The land sings, the song of return, of renewed friendships, of a journey.

In the sky, a glisten, as of dew, and the horizon is filled with starships. One breaks away, races towards the city.

It lands before the great west gate. Its canopy shimmers, and a man is there, carrying a small child. A woman stands at his side. He holds her hand.

A group of people is running to meet them from the gates.

And the man, the woman and the child step out of the craft, on to the earth, and run towards them.

Acknowledgements

Lament for the Fallen has been a long time coming.

I wrote its first words thirty years ago, when I was twelve, and – while the detail and texture of the story have changed as I matured – it was always about a man escaping from a prison in space back to a planet on the cusp of social upheaval.

Science fiction is at its most beautiful and challenging when it places us within the transition zone between here and there. The technologies presented in the novel are all as expected from any work of speculative fiction. It is less common to place those tools somewhere real, rather than breaking an existing place, and let people behave as they will.

Geographic necessity placed Samara's fall close to the equator in Nigeria and serendipity took me there, to walk the streets of Calabar and meet its people, before I returned to the final writing push.

I drew on a host of sources, and you will find much more of the complexity, wonder and terror of Nigerian culture and traditions in these books:

Cross River Natives, Charles Partridge (1905);

Efik Traders of Old Calabar, edited by Daryll Forde (1958);

Life in Southern Nigeria – The Magic, Beliefs, and Customs of the Ibibio Tribe, P. Amaury Talbot (1923).

Amaury Talbot was a colonial administrator who travelled far and wide in the then British colonies of Southern Nigeria in the very early 1900s. He and his wife photographed and described everything they saw without embellishment and with the wonder and reverence of a truly impressive social historian.

Efik Traders of Old Calabar is something even rarer: the diaries of Antera Duke, an Efik chief and slaver who lived in Calabar, and covering the period of 1785 to 1787.

If you wish to experience the food described, try Arit Ana's *A Taste of Calabar* (2000).

While I certainly drank deep from these sources, I have moved things around and restructured the landscape and people to meet the needs of the story. My intention was not to produce a work of Nigerian literature, merely to capture a sense of people and place. The usual storytellers' prerogative of saying that no names or places should be inferred as being about real people or events prevails here.

I am thankful for where this story has taken me and the people I have met, particularly the kindness and patience of people in Benin City, Calabar and Lagos who, inadvertently or not, helped inform my research. Far too many of the anecdotes featured here are real, and I leave it to you to separate them from the imagined.

If you would like to immerse yourself further, here is the music playlist along with the relevant scenes where they belong:

'Talibe', *The Balladeer* – Ismaël Lô [Song for the Fallen]

'Mabemba', *Rising Tide* – Mokoomba [The Balladeer's song of thanks in the market]

'No Ballads Ballad', *Spirit* – Geoffrey Oryema [Samara and Joshua talk along the river]

'Dionysus', *Untold Things* – Jocelyn Pook [Mama's tale]

'Makambo', *Exile* – Geoffrey Oryema [Setting out on the river to Calabar]

'The Wife of Usher's Well', *Broadside* – Bellowhead [Samara in the bar in Anacostia]

'Njoka', *Rising Tide* – Mokoomba [The Song of the City in Calabar]

'Ndayaan', *Ndayaan* – Omar Pene [Man singing in the road on the tour of Calabar]

'Dem Bobo', *Africa For Africa* – Femi Kuti [Farinata Uberti's party]

'Rero', *The Balladeer* – Ismaël Lô [After the massacre]

'Happiness Is', *Coming Home* – Yungchen Lhamo [Song for the Leaving medley]

'Lubara Wanwa', *Laru Beya* – Aurelio [Song for the Leaving medley]

'Hard Times', *Stone Cold Ohio* – Little Axe [Song for the Leaving medley]

'The Rhythm of the Heat', *Peter Gabriel* – Peter Gabriel [Song for the Leaving medley]

'Dragonfly', *Music Food and Love* – Guo Yue [Song for the Leaving medley]

'Nabou', *The Balladeer* – Ismaël Lô [Song for the Return]

For further references and updates, visit https://lamentforthefallen.com/

There was no 'her' when I began this tale, but she was always there and she always knew. I am grateful.

@GavinChait
started 1986 in South Africa, completed, by way of Nigeria, Pakistan and the Philippines, 2015 in England.

Born in Cape Town in 1974, Gavin Chait emigrated to the UK eight years ago. He has degrees in Microbiology and Biochemistry, and Electrical Engineering. He is an economic development strategist and data scientist, and has travelled extensively in Africa, Latin America, Europe and Asia and is now based in Oxford. *Lament for the Fallen* – his first novel – has its origins in a story he attempted to write when he was a science-fiction-obsessed twelve-year-old.